Short Stories by Guy de Maupassant

Short Stories by
Guy de Maupassant

Translated by Gerard Hopkins

Drawings by Nigel Lambourne

THE FOLIO SOCIETY LONDON 1959

PRINTED IN GREAT BRITAIN

Set in 10 point Scotch Roman, 1 point leaded
Printed and bound by Richard Clay & Co Ltd, Bungay, Suffolk

Contents

Illustrations

Introduction

In the autumn of 1916 I was sent for a short period of rest and relaxation (officially known as a 'Course') to the small township of St Venant in the Pas de Calais. Of rest there was more than enough, but relaxation had to be contrived. If there was a café (there must have been), it was certainly no Maison Tellier, but I do gratefully remember a bookshop—very small, very dusty, and very dark—in which were displayed a few stray paper-bound volumes of Maupassant's *Contes et Nouvelles*. I had heard of them—at school they had been spoken of with hushed enthusiasm as being 'pretty hot stuff' —but had never read a single one. Now I had time and opportunity, and I spent the rest of that brief period 'out of the line' in working my way—with a good deal of difficulty, guesswork, and misunderstanding—through the Master's triumphs of concision, so many of which had as background just such a small community as the one in which I was temporarily living.

At that time Maupassant was highly and widely appreciated, but his reputation, especially among his own countrymen, has suffered a sharp decline. That is no unusual fate for a writer. Death is, with curious regularity, followed by depreciation, and not until some years have elapsed does a true posthumous value become established. Maupassant has had to wait longer than most writers of high quality for his resurrection. True, he did for some time enjoy notoriety rather than fame for the 'heat' of his 'stuff', though the increasing rise in temperature where fiction is concerned since 1893 has fortunately caused him to drop behind in the scatological race. Now that his subject-matter no longer startles and shocks, he can be more seriously appraised and admired for his outstanding qualities as an artist of high rank. Sixty years and more have passed since his death, but it would be a bold—and perverse—critic who could deny him his rightful place among the few great short-story writers of the world.

He has been found wanting for two main reasons: that his fictions are, for the most part, concerned only with anecdotes (his novels are barely considered at all), and that his attitude is marked by an excessive and uniform cynicism.

Now, all short stories are primarily concerned with an 'anecdote,' that is to say with a clearly defined event which can be handled and presented within a limited space. Even *The Turn of the Screw* is a developed anecdote. What matters is the writer's success in drawing from the *mere* anecdote the implications and significance contained in it. It would be foolish to deny that Maupassant, at his worst, is too prone to rely for his effect upon the objective incident of his narration. On this he is inclined to lay the full weight of his story, to leave it to sink or swim on the merit of a sharp and sometimes superficial impact. Like most creative writers of genius he was prolific, and capable of producing a great deal of work below the level of his best. Many of the stories included in the present volume are, admittedly, little more than anecdotes, though the quality of the writing and the sharpness with which the scene presented is envisaged make it impossible to ignore them (*The Hand*, for instance, *A Vendetta*, *The Drunkard*, *The Inn*, and *Marocca*). Others, however, entitle him to rank with the very greatest of those who, from limited material, drain subtleties and developments to which men of lesser talents would find it necessary to devote a full-length novel. He was never a loose writer, but he was often a hurried one, for he was a man who made his living in journalism and worked under the merciless pressure of financial stress. But he had learned, from his master, Flaubert, how to make every word tell, and, more than most writers of fiction, he kept his eyes firmly fixed upon the object. The power of his concentrated stare has never been surpassed, and seldom equalled. What it saw, what it set out to see, was human nature. As he himself said, his purpose was to 'catch it in the act', and, unlike Flaubert (who, except in *Madame Bovary*, and then against his will, ranked technique above an interest in his fellow-mortals), he was endlessly fascinated by the antics and potentialities of men and women. On their depths and on their heights he directed his exquisitely focused lens. In a curiously wry manner he loved what he saw, and even the spectacle of Original Sin fascinated, rather than disgusted, him. He had learned from his teacher how to extract and express the full value of what he saw and, by the greatest economy of means, could achieve triumphs of revelation and interpretation which the more long-winded of his colleagues would have needed many chapters to record. Who, for instance, has ever 'got' more from a given situation than he did in that shortest of short tales, *Two Friends*—that model of the brief but never arid fiction? He knew the truth and the value of sentiment, though he never lapsed into sentimentality, which is but the small change of feeling.

Introduction

This accuracy of vision itself disproves the further charge of cynicism, which, let it be said in passing, is not strictly a matter with which literary criticism is concerned. The *donnée* of an author's work, the subject of which he chooses to treat, is, as Henry James pointed out in his admirable, and somewhat unexpectedly enthusiastic, essay on Maupassant, not the critic's business. You may like or dislike it, and that is all that can be said. The critic is concerned only to examine and appraise the use made of it, the degree to which the writer has achieved, or failed to achieve, his self-appointed task. But since the charge of cynicism has been so often levelled at Maupassant, it is fair to consider whether or no it provides a true basis for condemnation. Cynicism is the weapon of fear. The cynic, frightened of what he may find in the human state, refuses to admit the existence, or validity, of certain values. He is the very type of the irresponsible man who lightly sets out to blow sky-high such values as do not fit his preconceived (and interested) pattern of human behaviour. No such attitude can be attributed to Maupassant. He not only observed the acts and the emotions of human beings: he reacted to them. The cynic is not given to compassion, but Maupassant could both feel and express it. In the hands of a lesser man *The Mask* might well have become an ugly tale of moral squalor deserving only to be mocked. He, however, saw the pity of it, and, so seeing, gave to it a curious beauty. How different *Madame Tellier's Establishment* would have been had it been written by a true cynic, by, let us say, Anatole France, how full of knowing sniggers and depreciatory winks. Maupassant's telling of the story never weights the scales. What might have been amusingly sordid moves in a strange, though entirely unstressed atmosphere of innocence. Even the priest's ecstatic acceptance of his little miracle is shown for what it is—genuine and touching. Deprived of the 'tone' it creates, the tale would lack something of depth and significance.

When I first read the stories I found at St Venant, I thought how easy they would be to translate. I have learned how abysmally wrong I was. The task of finding an even adequate English equivalent is more than usually difficult. I claim for this version no other merit than that it does (I hope) provide some dim reflection of the vitality of its original. I shall consider myself more than rewarded if it can move its readers to make, or renew, acquaintance with a very great writer of fiction.

GERARD HOPKINS

Biographical Note

HENRI RENÉ ALBERT GUY DE MAUPASSANT, the son of a profligate, though aristocratic father and an artistic, sensitive mother, was born at the Château de Miromesnil (Seine Inférieure) on 5 August, 1850. He was educated at the Collège d'Yvetot and the Lycée de Rouen, after which he served for a short time in the army during the Franco-Prussian War. He then became a civil servant in the Ministry of Marine, followed by a period in the Ministry of Public Instruction. This phase of his life came to an end in 1880 when the publication of *Boule de Suif* in Zola's anthology *Les Soirées de Medan* brought him instant recognition as a writer, and it was to writing that he devoted the rest of his life.

While he was still feeling his way towards his vocation he was fortunate enough to come under the influence of Flaubert; it was from him that Maupassant learnt the secrets of his art and it was he who prevented Maupassant from prematurely publishing anything that would be unworthy of him. Between 1880 and the year he died Maupassant produced six full-length novels, including *Bel-Ami* and the autobiographical *Une Vie*, a number of travel books, the fruit of his love for the sea and of the continual urge he felt to visit new places, and, of course, the large number of short stories on which his fame mainly rests.

But, despite his love of vigorous exercise and his continual search after health, Maupassant suffered all his life from illnesses—both physical and nervous. Aggravated by the hectic pace at which he lived, it was this that led to his mind becoming unhinged, to an abortive attempt at suicide and, finally, to his being confined in an asylum until he died on 6 August, 1893.

Boule de Suif

FOR several successive days, the scraps and tatters of a routed army had been moving through the city. It was no organized retreat, but a purposeless flow of men, without units or discipline, of stragglers without uniforms, dirty, bearded, slouching, with no flag to rally them, no formation to give them a sense of unity, utterly exhausted, overwhelmed and incapable of thought or determination, keeping on the move from sheer habit, and dropping in their tracks whenever they stopped. Most noticeable of all were the hastily mobilized reservists, men of peace and substance, staggering under the weight of their rifles, militiamen, as easily prone to panic as to enthusiasm, as ready to attack as to flee, with, here and there, a few red-trousered regulars, remnants of some division ground to powder on the battlefield, gunners showing as dark patches among the odds and ends of foot-sloggers, with, now and again, the flashing helmet of a dismounted dragoon trudging heavily in the wake of the nimbler soldiers of the line.

There were, too, the legions of the *francs-tireurs*, all with high-sounding and heroic titles: 'The Avengers of Defeat'—'The Citizens of the Tomb'—'The Companions of Death'—but looking like nothing so much as mobs of ruffianly bandits.

Their leaders—former shopkeepers and grain-merchants, dealers in soap or tallow, temporary warriors given the rank of officers by reason of their money or the length of their moustaches, and weighed down with weapons, flannel undervests, and gold lace—talked in loud voices, discussing plans of campaign, boastfully declaring that they alone could carry on their shoulders the body of France in her death-agony. But frequently they went in fear of their own men, thorough-paced scoundrels the lot of them, often fantastically courageous, but out for loot and rape.

The Prussians, it was being said, were on the point of entering Rouen.

The National Guard which, for the last two months, had been carrying out cautious scouting expeditions in the nearby woods, sometimes opening fire on their own sentries and standing to at the sound of a rabbit in the undergrowth, had now been disbanded and

1

gone home. Their arms and their uniforms, their whole murderous equipment, which, a while back, had made them the terror of every main road for miles around, had now, suddenly, disappeared.

The last of the French soldiers had, by this time, crossed the Seine in an attempt to reach Pont-Audemer, by way of Saint-Sever and Bourg-Achard. In their rear, walking between two of his staff officers, came the general, all hope gone, unable even to attempt a stand with the disorganized rabble still nominally under his command, himself bewildered and caught up in the vast collapse of a people long accustomed to victory, and now, in spite of its legendary daring, disastrously defeated.

The city lay under a pall of peace, silence, and terrified expectation. Several pot-bellied citizens, their spirits drained by long years of prosperous trade, were uneasily awaiting the coming of the victors, shaking in their shoes lest spits and kitchen-knives should be looked upon as weapons of war.

Life seemed to stand still. The shops were shut, the streets silent. Every now and again, some inhabitant, disquieted by the stillness, would hurry on his way, keeping close to the wall.

The very agony of waiting bred a longing for the enemy to come.

On the afternoon of the day following the departure of the French troops, a few Uhlans—where from no one knew—rode through the city at a quick trot. Shortly afterwards a black mass descended from Saint-Catherine's hill, while two other invading tides began to flow down the roads leading from Darnetal and Boisguillaume. These advance-guards of the three main bodies arrived on the Place de l'Hôtel-de-Ville at precisely the same moment. Then, along all the nearby streets, the German Army arrived, deploying its battalions and making the flagstones ring with the harsh and measured tread of marching men.

Orders shouted in a guttural and foreign tongue eddied round the walls of houses which seemed dead and deserted, though from behind closed shutters eyes watched the invaders, now, by the laws of war, the masters of the city, free to dispose as they liked of life and fortune. In their darkened rooms, men and women were in the grip of that panic which is the product of those cataclysms of earth and heaven against which neither wisdom nor strength is of any avail—when all sense of security vanishes, and what once the ordinances of man and the laws of nature protected, is seen to be at the mercy of the brainless and the brutal. Earthquakes that bury whole communities under the ruins of their homes; rivers in spate, sweeping before them the bodies of drowned peasants, helpless cattle, and the beams of demolished houses; the relentless advance of victorious armies, killing those who would defend themselves, taking prisoners, pillaging in the name of the Sword, and saluting the God of Battles through the brazen throats of cannon—such are the horrifying scourges which undermine all faith in the justice of Heaven, in the protection of a merciful God, and the efficacy of human reason.

At every door small detachments were knocking and entering. After invasion, occupation. The time had come for the vanquished to show politeness to the victors.

After the first terror had died down, peace once more descended on the city, but now it was peace with a different face. In many houses a Prussian officer took his meals with the family. Sometimes, he was a man of breeding and had the decency to express the pity that he felt for France, and to say how much he disliked having to take a part in this war: then his hosts showed their gratitude for such consideration. Besides, a day might come when they would stand in need of his protection. If they handled him in the right way he would, perhaps, see to it that they had fewer mouths to feed, and, in any case, what point was there in getting on the wrong side of a man at whose mercy they were? To do so would be merely to display, not so much courage as rashness, and rashness was no longer one of the defects of the burghers of Rouen as it had been in the days when the heroic defence of their city had covered them with glory. If any further excuse for their behaviour had been needed, it was to be found in the Frenchman's national predilection for courtesy. What harm could there be, they argued, in being polite in the privacy of their homes, provided they indulged in no public familiarities with the foreign soldiery?

By slow degrees, the city began to recover something of its day-to-day appearance. Not many Frenchmen, it is true, as yet went beyond their own front doors, but the streets were swarming with Prussian troops. What made matters easier was that the officers of the Blue Hussars, who arrogantly trailed their rattling sabres over the paving-stones, seemed to show no more contempt for plain civilians than had their own Chasseurs who but a year before had sat drinking in the same cafés.

There was, however, something in the air, a subtle and mysterious emanation, strange and intolerable, which hung about the streets like a smell—the smell of invasion. It filled the houses and the public places, gave to the very food an unfamiliar taste, and

3

made people feel as though they were in a distant land among dangerous and barbaric tribes.

The conquerors demanded money, a great deal of money. The inhabitants paid up unfailingly—they were rich enough. But the more wealth a businessman in Normandy amasses, the more he suffers at having to sacrifice any part of it, and seeing a portion pass into the hands of others.

In spite of the apparent tranquillity, however, there were places a few miles downstream from the city, towards Croisset, Dieppe-dalle, and Biessart, where watermen and fisher-folk not seldom brought to the surface swollen German corpses in uniform, victims of a knife-thrust or a kick from a heavy boot, with heads stove in by a blow from a stone, or just pushed over the railing of a bridge. The river mud closed over these evidences of obscure acts of vengeance, savage, perhaps, but legitimate, mute testimony of unknown deeds of heroism, of stealthy attacks more perilous than battles fought in daylight, and without the reward of public acclamation.

For hatred of a foreign invader will always prompt to action a few intrepid men who are prepared to risk their lives for an idea.

Nevertheless, the victors, though they had subjected the city to their own inflexible discipline, had not committed any of those atrocities with which rumour had credited them in the course of their triumphal progress from the frontiers. Consequently, folk began to pluck up courage, and some of the merchants to turn their minds to business. Several had large sums of money invested in Le Havre, which was still in French hands, and these were planning to reach that port, travelling overland to Dieppe, and there taking ship. They used such influence as they might have with German officers of their acquaintance, and an exit permit was at last obtained from the Military Governor.

A large, four-horse *diligence* was engaged for the journey, ten persons booked their places, and arrangements were made to set off on a certain Tuesday morning before daybreak, so as to avoid the risk of a crowd gathering.

For the past few days frost had hardened the surface of the roads, and at about three o'clock on the Monday afternoon, heavy black clouds, moving from the north, had brought the snow. It fell uninterruptedly all that evening and all that night.

At half-past four in the morning, the passengers assembled in the courtyard of the Hôtel de Normandie, where the conveyance was awaiting them.

They were still sleepy, and the cold made them shiver under their wraps. They found it difficult to make one another out in the darkness, and their accumulation of winter clothing made them all look like fat priests in long cassocks. Two men, however, recognized one another, a third joined them, and they began to talk. 'I'm taking my wife,' said one. 'So am I.' 'Me, too.' The first added: 'We're not coming back to Rouen, and if the Prussians show up at Le Havre, we shall cross to England.' The plans of all three were identical, their mental attitude being much the same.

No attempt, it seemed, was being made to put the horses in. A small lantern, carried by a stable-boy, emerged, now and again, from one dark doorway, only to vanish again in another. The sound of horses stamping was muffled by a layer of straw and manure, and the voice of a man talking to the animals and swearing, could be heard coming from one of the outbuildings. A faint jingle of bells announced that the harness was being adjusted. The sound grew, until it became a continuous rattle changing its rhythm with the movement of the horses, stopping at times and then starting again in a quick, jerky fashion accompanied by the muted sound of heavy, nailed boots on the ground.

Then, suddenly, a door was shut and all sound ceased. The frozen passengers lapsed into silence, and stood where they were, stiff and motionless.

A thick curtain of white flakes glittered and eddied as the snow fell ceaselessly. It blurred all outlines, powdered every object with an icy covering, and in the vast silence of the winter city, nothing could be heard but the faint, drifting, indescribable rustle of falling snow, a sensation rather than a sound, a swirl of light atoms which seemed to fill all space and to be covering the world.

The man reappeared with his lantern, pulling after him, at the end of a rope, a melancholy and reluctant horse. He backed it into position at one side of the pole, adjusted the traces, and took a leisurely walk round to see that all was ship-shape, for he could use only one hand, the other being occupied with the lantern. As he went back for the second horse, he noticed the motionless group of passengers, and said: 'Why not get in? You'd at least be under shelter.'

This seemed not to have occurred to them, and they hurriedly took his advice. The three men settled their wives at the far end of the vehicle, and then got in themselves. Other indistinct and muffled figures followed their example and took possession of the remaining seats without a word.

They all buried their feet in the straw with which the floor was covered. The ladies at the far end had brought with them small brass foot-warmers, heated by some patent fuel, and these they now lit, extolling in low voices the advantages of these contraptions, and telling one another what all had long known.

At last, when the horses had been put in—six instead of four, because of the extra effort needed in the snowy conditions—a voice from outside said: 'All present?' A single one from within answered, 'Yes,' and the journey began.

The heavy *diligence* moved with extreme slowness. The wheels sank deeply into the snow, and the great lumbering conveyance creaked and groaned. The horses slipped, panted, and steamed. The driver's enormous whip cracked unceasingly, flicking here, there, and everywhere, twisting and straightening like a sinuous snake, administering a smart cut to one or other of the rounded cruppers, which immediately tensed with redoubled effort.

Imperceptibly the darkness was thinning into day. The drifting flakes, which one of the company, a man of Rouen born and bred, had compared to a storm of cotton-wool, were no longer falling. A grubby light was filtering through the dark, heavy clouds, making, by contrast, the white countryside glitter the more, with, here and there, a line of tall and rimy trees, and an occasional thatched roof under a cowl of snow.

The passengers looked at one another with curiosity in the gloomy brightness of the dawn.

At the far end, in the best seats, Monsieur and Madame Loiseau, wholesale wine-merchants in the rue Grand-Pont, were comfortably dozing.

Once clerk to a man who had been ruined in business, Loiseau had bought up the bankrupt stock and made a fortune. He sold very bad wine at a very high price to retailers in country towns, and had the reputation among his friends and acquaintances of being a shrewd old ruffian, a typical Norman, chockful of trickery and joviality.

His character as a rogue was so well established that, one evening, at the Prefecture, Monsieur Tournel, the author of several songs and fables, a man with a sharp, biting wit, and a local celebrity, seeing that the ladies of the party were on the point of dropping off to sleep, had suggested a game of 'Loiseau vole'*. The witticism had itself taken wing through the Prefect's reception-rooms, had gained an entry into those of all the hostesses of the city, and had set people laughing through the length and breadth of the Province.

* *Birdie-steal-away. (Translator.)*

Loiseau was himself a noted wag, some of whose jokes were good and others not, and nobody could mention his name without immediately adding: 'Loiseau really is the limit!'

He was a small man with a prominent stomach and a red face framed in grizzled whiskers.

His wife, a tall woman, strong and determined, with a loud voice and the gift of making quick decisions, ran the business to which her husband contributed facetiousness and a bustling activity.

Next to them was Monsieur Carré-Lamadon, whose superior social position found expression in a dignified manner. He occupied a solid position in the cotton-market, was the owner of three mills, an Officer of the Legion of Honour, and a member of the City Council. Under the Empire he had headed a benevolent Opposition, with the sole end in view of getting a better price for his eventual adherence to a cause against which he had fought, with, to use his own expression, 'the weapons of a gentleman'. Madame Carré-Lamadon, who was a great deal younger than her husband, made it her business to console those officers of good family who happened to be on garrison duty in Rouen.

She was seated opposite her lord and master, very small, very dainty, very pretty, wrapped in furs and looking with obvious distaste at the squalid interior of the conveyance in which she found herself.

Her neighbours, the Comte and Comtesse Hubert de Bréville, bore one of the oldest and noblest names in all Normandy. The count, an elderly gentleman of fine appearance, did all he could to accentuate with every artifice of the dressing-table, a natural resemblance to the king, Henri Quatre, who, according to a story held in great honour by the family, had got with child one of the de Bréville laides. Her husband had been rewarded by being made a count and a Provincial Governor.

Count Hubert sat with Monsieur Carré-Lamadon on the City Council, where he represented the Orléanist Party of the Department. There had always been a certain amount of mystery attached to his marriage with the daughter of a small Nantes ship-owner. But, since the countess had the airs of a great lady, was a better hostess than anyone in the neighbourhood, and enjoyed the reputation of having been loved by one of the sons of Louis-Philippe, the noble families of the province made much of her. Her *salon* had long occupied a leading position in the city, where it was the only one in which the manners of an earlier age prevailed. Entry to it was difficult.

The de Bréville fortune—all in landed property—produced, so it was said, an annual revenue of five hundred thousand francs.

These six persons occupied the far end of the *diligence*. They stood for the moneyed element in local society, a strong, untroubled cross-section of its own small world, decent, upright folk, with high principles and a proper respect for religion, looked up to by all.

By a strange coincidence, the wives were all seated on the same side. The countess had next to her two Sisters of Mercy, who spent the time telling the beads on their long rosaries, and muttering *Paters* and *Aves*. One of them was old, and her face, disfigured by small-pox, looked as though it had received a charge of slugs at point-blank range. Her younger companion was frail and sickly looking, with a pretty face and the chest of a consumptive, in which there burned that devouring flame of faith which produces martyrs and fanatics.

Opposite the two Sisters were a man and a woman on whom all eyes were fixed.

The man, a well-known local figure, was Cornudet, the 'democrat', and the terror of the respectable. For the last twenty years he had been wetting his great red beard in the beer-mugs of all the cafés patronized by the champions of democracy. With the help of several friends and comrades, he had managed to get through a sizeable fortune left him by his father, a former confectioner, and he was now impatiently awaiting the coming of the Republic, and the official appointment which so long a period of revolutionary tippling had earned him. On the Fourth of September, possibly as the result of some practical joke, he had been given to understand that he had been made Prefect, but when he had endeavoured to take up his duties, the members of the office staff who had been left in charge at the Prefecture, had refused to recognize him as their new master, and he had been compelled to beat a hasty retreat. Fundamentally a decent, inoffensive, and obliging chap, he had displayed tremendous energy in organizing the defences of Rouen, having pits dug in the flat open country, all the young trees in the nearby forests felled, and booby-traps set up on all the roads. Satisfied with these preparations, he had withdrawn into the city on the approach of the enemy. He had now decided that he would be more useful at Le Havre, where new trenches would certainly be necessary.

The woman, who was one of those who are generally known as 'Lights o' Love', had achieved fame by reason of her precocious

plumpness which had earned her the nickname of *Boule de Suif*—
Suet Dumpling. She was small, completely round, a mass of fat,
with puffy fingers constricted at the joints so that they looked like
strings of miniature sausages. Her skin was tightly stretched and
shiny. Her enormous bust showed prominently beneath her dress.
Nevertheless, she was appetizing and much patronized, so fresh and
blooming did she look. Her face was like a ruddy apple, or a peony
bud about to burst into flower, and out of it looked two magnificent
black eyes shaded by thick lashes. Beneath them was a charming
mouth, small, moist, provocative of kisses, and furnished with two
rows of gleaming, microscopic nibblers.

In addition to all this, she had, so it was said, many admirable
qualities.

No sooner was she recognized, than a ripple of whispers began
between the respectable ladies, and such words as 'prostitute' and
'public scandal' were hissed loudly enough to make her raise her
eyes. The look she gave her neighbours was so challenging and so
brazen, that a deep silence fell upon the company, and everyone
looked down, with the exception of Loiseau who stared at her with
randy eyes.

But conversation was very soon resumed between the three
ladies, whom the presence of the 'street-walker' had suddenly made
friends, almost intimates. It was their duty, they felt, to face this
shameless, mercenary creature from behind the prickly hedge of
their concentrated marital dignity. Legalized love always takes a
high line with its free colleague.

The three men, drawn together, too, by an instinct of conservat-
ism at the sight of Cornudet, were talking money in a tone which
implied a certain contempt for those who were poorer than themselves. Count Hubert spoke of the damage he had suffered at the
hands of the Prussians, of his losses in stolen cattle and lost har-
vests, but with the assurance of a great landed proprietor, a million-
aire ten times over, for whom these things mattered no more than
the results of a single bad year. Monsieur Carré-Lamadon, who had
been badly hit on the cotton-market, had had the foresight to send
six hundred thousand francs to England—something for a rainy
day which he took every opportunity to augment. As to Loiseau,
he had made arrangements to sell to the French Commissariat Department all the lower-grade wines left in his cellars, with the result that the State owed him a large sum of money which he was
expecting to collect at Le Havre.

All three of them exchanged quick, friendly glances. Though

widely differing in social status, they were bound together in the fraternity of wealth and that free-masonry of the 'haves' who can be sure of always finding money to jingle in their trouser pockets.

Such slow progress was their conveyance making that, by ten o'clock, they had covered less than ten miles. On three occasions the men had got out to walk up the hills. A faint air of uneasiness was becoming noticeable, for they had planned to stop at Tôtes for luncheon, and there seemed to be little prospect now of reaching that place before dark. All eyes were on the look-out for a wayside eating-house, when the *diligence* foundered in a snowdrift, and two hours were occupied in digging it out.

Increasing hunger was casting a gloom. Not an inn, not a tavern was to be seen anywhere. The advancing Prussians and the retreating hordes of famished French troops had scared all trade away.

The gentlemen went hunting for provisions at wayside farms, but failed to find so much as a loaf of bread, for the mistrustful country-folk had hidden what reserves they had from fear of being pillaged by the soldiers, who, having nothing to eat, were taking by force everything they came upon.

About one o'clock Loiseau announced that, no doubt about it, he had got a damned great hole in his stomach. The others had been similarly suffering for a long time, and the violent craving for food, which kept on growing, had put a stop to all conversation.

From time to time, someone yawned, and almost at once, somebody else followed suit. Every member of the company, in turn, according to his character, his breeding, or his social background, opened his mouth, either noisily and openly, or disguising behind his hand the gaping orifice from which came a thin cloud of vapour.

More than once, Boule de Suif had bent down, as though looking for something concealed under her skirt. She paused for a moment, glanced round at her neighbours, and then, quite calmly, resumed her upright posture. The faces of the others were white and drawn. Loiseau declared that he would gladly give a thousand francs for a knuckle of ham. His wife made something resembling a gesture of protest, but then relapsed into a state of apathy. It was always pain and grief to her when she heard anyone talking of throwing money away, and she could not even understand jokes on the subject. 'I must confess I feel anything but well,' said the count. 'I cannot think why it never occurred to me to bring something with us.' Each and all were indulging in the same piece of self-criticism.

Boule de Suif

Cornudet, however, had a flask of rum which he offered round.
But the suggestion was coldly received. Only Loiseau accepted a
thimbleful. When he handed the flask back he expressed his thanks
—'Good stuff, that: warms one up and stills the pangs.' The spirit
had put him in a good humour, and he announced his intention of
doing what had been done on the boat in the song—eating the fat-
test member of the party. This indirect allusion to Boule de Suif
shocked his more refined companions. No one said a word, and
Cornudet was the only one who even smiled. The two Sisters of
Mercy had stopped muttering over their rosaries, and now sat
motionless, with downcast eyes, and their hands tucked into the
wide sleeves of their habits—no doubt making an offering to Heaven
of the sufferings it had inflicted upon them.

But at last, at three o'clock, by which time they were in the middle of an interminable plain with not a single village in sight, Boule
de Suif stooped quickly down again, and this time produced from
under the seat a large basket covered with a white napkin.

From it she took, first a small plate and a little silver drinking-
mug, followed by an enormous *terrine* in which two whole chickens,
carved and dismembered lay under a covering of their own congealed
juice. Other good things could be seen neatly wrapped within the
basket: patés, fruit, and other delicacies, for she had prepared
enough food for a journey of three days, so as not to have to
touch the fare provided in wayside inns. The necks of four bottles
projected from between the packets of eatables. She took the wing
of a chicken and, delicately, began to eat it, together with one of
those little rolls which, in Normandy, are called 'Régence'.

Every eye was turned on her. A lovely smell spread through the
diligence. Nostrils twitched, mouths watered, and jaws suffered a
painful contraction which made itself felt just under the ears. The
contempt felt by the ladies for this 'tart' grew still more savage, as
though they were longing to kill the creature and pitch her out into
the snow along with her mug, her basket, and her food.

But Loiseau was devouring the *terrine* and its contents with his
eyes. 'I applaud your foresight, Madame,' he said. 'Some people
think of everything.' She looked up: 'Would you like some, Monsieur? It is hard to have to go without food all day.' He bowed:
'Really, I cannot refuse such an invitation! To be honest with you,
I have had about as much as I can stand. The fortune of war, eh,
Madame?' And, glancing round him, he added: 'At times like these
it is pleasant to come upon a helping hand.' He proceeded to spread
a newspaper on his knees, so as not to dirty his trousers, and, with

11

the point of the knife he always carried in his pocket, took possession of a leg all gleaming with jelly, tore it apart with his teeth,
and munched away with such obvious satisfaction, that a deep sigh
of distress went up from his fellow-travellers.

But Boule de Suif, in a gentle, humble voice, asked the two
Sisters of Mercy to share her meal. They both accepted her invitation, and, without raising their eyes, began to eat very quickly,
after first muttering their thanks. Cornudet, too, did not refuse his
neighbour's offer, and the five of them made a sort of a table with
newspapers on their knees.

Mouths opened and shut without intermission, swallowed and
masticated and gulped with the ferocity of wild animals. Loiseau,
in his corner, worked hard, and, in a low voice, begged his wife to
follow his example. She put up a prolonged resistance, but at last,
after a pang which gripped her vitals, gave in. Then, Loiseau, in a
few well-chosen words, asked their 'charming companion' whether
he had her permission to offer a morsel to Madame Loiseau. 'Why,
of course, Monsieur,' she said with a friendly smile, and held out
the *terrine*.

There was some embarrassment when the first bottle of Bordeaux
was uncorked. There was only one mug. Each passed it on after
first taking care to wipe the rim. Cornudet, acting, no doubt, on an
impulse of gallantry, touched with his lips the spot which was still
moist from those of his fair neighbour.

Then it was that, surrounded by those engaged in eating, and
half choked by the smell of food, the Comte and Comtesse de
Bréville, as well as Monsieur and Madame Carré-Lamadon, suffered
the pangs of that hideous torment with which the name of Tantalus
is still associated. All of a sudden, the manufacturer's young wife
uttered a groan which caused all eyes to turn in her direction. She
was as white as the snow outside, her head had fallen forward, her
eyes were shut, she had lost consciousness. Her husband, in a panic,
begged everyone to help. All lost their heads except the elder of the
two Sisters of Mercy, who, supporting the sufferer's head, and forcing the rim of Boule de Suif's mug between her lips, made her swallow a few drops of wine. The pretty young woman stirred, opened
her eyes, smiled, and declared in a die-away voice that she felt
much better now.

But, so that what had just happened should not happen again,
the Sister forced her to drink a full mugful of Bordeaux, saying, as
she did so, 'It is nothing but hunger.'

Then, Boule de Suif, blushing and embarrassed, looking at the

four still fasting travellers, stammered out: 'If only I dared offer these ladies and gentlemen . . .', and then stopped, as though fearing to offend. It was Loiseau who helped her out: 'Why, damn it all, in circumstances like these, we are all brothers and should help each other! Come, ladies! No standing on ceremony! Accept! Accept! Can we even be sure of finding a house in which to spend the night? At the speed we are making, we shall be lucky if we reach Tôtes by noon tomorrow.' There was a moment's hesitation, no one daring to assume the responsibility of saying 'yes'.

But the count cut the knot. He turned to the fat, frightened woman, and, with the air of a great gentleman, said to her: 'Madame, we most gratefully accept your kindest of kind offers.'

The first step, only, had been difficult. The Rubicon once crossed, they fell to with a will. The basket was almost emptied. It still contained a *paté de foie gras*, a lark paté, a piece of smoked tongue, some Bergamot pears, a slab of Pont-l'Évêque cheese, some little biscuits, and a cupful of gherkins and onions in vinegar, for, like most women, Boule de Suif had a passion for pickles.

It was impossible to eat up the woman's food without talking to her. So, talk they did, at first with a certain amount of reserve, then, as her manners seemed good, with greater freedom. Madame de Bréville and Madame Carré-Lamadon, who had an extensive knowledge of the world, were well versed in the art of being gracious without being patronizing. The countess, in particular, displayed that easy condescension to be found in ladies of high rank whom no contact can smirch. She was charming. But the forceful Madame Loiseau, who had the soul of a gendarme, was, as usual, crabbed and cantankerous, saying little and eating a lot.

The talk naturally turned on the war. Horrible stories were told about the Prussians, and a great deal was said about the gallantry of the French. All these people had taken to their heels, and all were eloquent in praise of the courage shown by others. It was not long before personal anecdotes were introduced into the conversation, and Boule de Suif described with genuine emotion, and that warmth of language which those of her profession sometimes employ when expressing their feelings, how she had come to leave Rouen. 'I thought at first that I would stay on,' she said. 'My house was stocked with food, and I would rather have fed a few soldiers than become a refugee, Heaven knows where. But when I saw those Prussians, it was more than I could bear! The sight of them just made me want to vomit! I cried with shame all day long! Oh! If only I had been a man! I used to see them from my window, the fat pigs with their pointed helmets, and it was as much as my maid could do to keep me from dropping the furniture on their heads! Then some of them turned up to be billeted on me. Well, I just sprang at the throat of the first man who came through the door. They're no more difficult to strangle than anybody else, and I'd have finished him off if I hadn't been dragged away by the hair! I had to lie low after that, and, to make a long story short, I took the first opportunity to skedaddle—and here I am!'

She was warmly congratulated. She rose in the esteem of her companions, who had been a great deal less courageous, and Cornudet listened to her with the approving and benignant smile of an Apostle. Just so might a priest have listened to a pious member of his flock praising God, for bearded democrats hold a monopoly of patriotism, as the men of the cassock do of religion. Then he chimed in with violent doctrinaire eloquence learned from the proclamations which had been appearing, day after day, on the walls and hoardings, winding up with a peroration in which he flayed that 'damned Badinguet fellow'* with his tongue.

But Boule de Suif at once flew into a towering rage, for she was a bonapartist. She became as red as a turkey-cock, and sputtered with indignation. 'I'd like to see any of you in his shoes. You make me sick! It's folk like you as have betrayed him! If France had been governed by no-goods like you, there'd have been nothing for it but to clear out!' Unperturbed by this outburst, Cornudet still sat with a superior and disdainful smile. There was an uncomfortable feeling that high words would have followed, had not the count intervened. With some difficulty he succeeded in calming the exasperated little spitfire, and declared, with authority, that all opinions, if sincerely held, were worthy of respect. Nevertheless, the countess and the manufacturer's wife, who nourished in their hearts the irrational hatred felt by all upper-class folk for the Republic, and that instinctive weakness which all women have for flamboyant and despotic governments, could not help sympathizing with this streetwalker, who had so natural a dignity, and held views which bore so close a resemblance to their own.

The basket was empty. The combined attack had soon made hay of its contents, and there was a general feeling of regret that it had not been larger. Conversation continued for a while, but there had been a marked cooling off in the atmosphere since eating had ceased.

* *A pejorative nickname for Napoleon III. (Translator.)*

Night fell. Gradually the darkness grew more dense, and the cold, to which the process of digestion had made them more sensitive, caused even Boule de Suif to shiver, in spite of her fat. Madame de Bréville offered her the use of her foot-warmer, the fuel of which had been renewed more than once since the morning, and the other gladly accepted, for her feet felt frozen. Madame Carré-Lamadon and Madame Loiseau gave theirs to the two Sisters.

The driver had lit his lamps. They shone brightly on the cloud of steam rising from the sweating cruppers of the two wheelers, and on the snow which lay on both sides of the road, and seemed to unfold beneath the moving beams of light.

By this time it was impossible to see anything inside the *diligence*, but there came a sudden sound of movement from between Boule de Suif and Cornudet, and Loiseau, peering into the murk, thought he saw the man with the long beard start back sharply as though he had been the recipient of a noiseless blow.

Two small points of light appeared upon the road ahead. It was Tôtes. They had been driving for eleven hours. The halts made for resting and feeding the horses brought the grand total of travelling-hours to fourteen. They entered the town, and drew up in front of the Hôtel du Commerce.

The door of the vehicle was opened. The only too familiar sound of a scabbard clanking over cobbles made all the occupants start. It was followed immediately by something barked out by a German voice.

Though the *diligence* was now stationary, no one showed any anxiety to get out. It was as though they expected to be massacred as they emerged. Then, the driver appeared, carrying one of his lamps, which suddenly caught in its beam, as it reached the furthest corner of the interior, two rows of startled faces, with mouths hanging open, and eyes staring with an expression of surprise and terror.

Standing beside the driver, and blindingly illuminated, was a German officer, a tall young man, excessively slim and fair, as tightly laced into his uniform as a woman into her stays, and wearing, cocked over one eye, a flat, highly polished cap, which made him look like the hall-porter of an English hotel. His moustache, which was inordinately long, and thinned out to a point on either side of his face until it ended in two blond hairs, so delicate as to be almost invisible, seemed to weigh down the corners of his mouth, and, by exerting a drag upon his cheeks, to impart a drooping expression to his lips.

He invited the travellers, in Alsatian French, to alight, saying, in a harsh, staccato tone: 'You vill pleece descend, leddies ant chentlemens.'

The two Sisters of Mercy were the first to obey, with the docility of dedicated women trained to submit. The count and countess made their appearance side by side, followed by the manufacturer and his wife, with Loiseau behind them, pushing his better-half in front of him, and saying to the officer, as he set foot upon the ground, 'Good-day, Monsieur,' more from considerations of caution than of good manners. The German, like all who wield unlimited power, looked at him without replying.

Boule de Suif and Cornudet, though they had been sitting nearest to the door, were the last to get out. Face to face with the enemy, they assumed a grave and haughty demeanour. The fat young woman did her best to keep control of herself and remain calm. The democrat, with a hand that trembled slightly, tugged at his long red beard. There was something faintly tragic about him. They both tried, as best they could, to be dignified, realizing that in a meeting of this kind, the individual is, to some extent, the representative of his country. Both were equally disgusted by the cringing attitude of their companions. She attempted to show a greater degree of pride than the respectable women with whom she was herded, while he, conscious that it was his duty to be an example to others, continued in his every gesture and his every movement, to express that attitude of resistance which had, earlier, led him to have the roads round Rouen made impassable.

They were all shepherded into the huge kitchen of the inn, where the German demanded to see the permit signed by the General Commanding at Rouen, in which each of the travellers was mentioned by name, described, and his civic status entered. He spent some time carefully scrutinizing everybody, and comparing what he saw with the information contained in the document.

Then he barked out: 'Goot!' and disappeared.

They breathed again. They were still hungry, and supper was ordered. It was half an hour before it was ready, and while two of the inn servants bustled about, seemingly concerned with preparations for the meal, the arrivals trooped off to look at the bedrooms. These were all situated in a corridor, at the far end of which a glazed door bore a number which left no doubt of the purpose of the room within.

They were just about to take their places at the table, when the landlord appeared. He was a former horse-dealer, fat and asthmatic, who wheezed in a husky, phlegmy voice. The name which he had inherited from his father was Follenvie.

'Mademoiselle Elisabeth Rousset?' he asked.

Boule de Suif gave a start and turned to him.

'That's me.'

'Mademoiselle, the Prussian officer wishes to have a word with you, at once.'

'With me?'

'Yes, if you really are Mademoiselle Elisabeth Rousset.'

She seemed flustered, turned the statement over in her mind for a moment, and then, without any beating about the bush, replied:

'Maybe he does, and he can go on wanting, because I'm not going.'

There was a general movement round her, an outbreak of talk, a voluble guessing at what could be the meaning of this summons. The count went up to her.

'You are wrong to refuse, Madame. Such an attitude on your part may make matters very difficult, not only for yourself, but for your fellow-travellers as well. It is always foolish to resist those who are the masters. There can be no danger for you in obeying—no doubt this message has some reference to a small formality which has been overlooked.'

The others all backed him up. She was begged, urged, and lectured. Eventually, she gave way, for obviously everyone was dreading the complications which might ensue from her impulsive refusal.

'All right,' she said at last, 'I'll go; but only for your sakes.'

The countess took her hand: 'We are all most grateful to you.'

She left the room. They waited for her to come back before sitting down to supper.

Everyone of those present bitterly regretted not having been sent for instead of this violent and hot-tempered young woman, and silently thought up a number of commonplace remarks for use in the event of his, or her, presence being demanded.

At the end of ten minutes she reappeared, breathing heavily, red in the face, and fuming with rage. 'The swine!' she spluttered: 'the damned low-down swine!'

They were all longing to hear what had happened, but not a word would she say, and, when the count insisted, replied with great dignity: 'No, it is nothing to do with you: I can't talk about it!'

Then they took their seats round a large soup-tureen smelling

19

strongly of cabbage. In spite of the recent disturbance, there was an air of gaiety about the meal. The cider was good, and the Loiseau couple and the good Sisters drank it for the sake of economy. The others ordered wine, with the exception of Cornudet, who demanded beer. He had a peculiar way of opening the bottle, of making the liquid froth, of looking at it while he tilted the glass, which he then held up between the lamp and his eye, so as properly to judge the colour. When he drank, his great beard, which was stained with the particular shade of his favourite brew, seemed to quiver lovingly, and he squinted, so as not to lose sight of the mug for a moment. At such times he seemed to be fulfilling the sole purpose for which he had been born. It was almost as though he had established in his mind a connexion—one might even say an affinity—between the two great passions of his life—Pale Ale and Revolution. Very certain it was that he could not taste the one without thinking of the other.

Monsieur and Madame Follenvie occupied the end of the table. He, wheezing away like a broken-down locomotive, gave his lungs so much work to do, that he could not talk while eating. She, however, never stopped prattling, but gave a complete catalogue of her feelings when the Prussians arrived, recounting everything they had done, everything they had said, and expressing her detestation of them, in the first place because they cost her money, in the second, because she had two sons in the army. She addressed her remarks mainly to the countess, because it pleased her vanity to think that she was conversing with a lady of quality.

Then, having delicate matters to discuss, she lowered her voice. From time to time, her husband broke in on her: 'It would be a great deal better if you talked less, Madame Follenvie.' But she paid no attention to him, and continued with her monologue:

'Them folk, Madame, just do nothing but guzzle potatoes and pork, when it isn't pork and potatoes. And don't you go getting the idea into your head that they're clean! Oh, no! They does their business everywhere, saving your presence, Ma'am. And you should just see them a-drilling for hours and days together. Out they goes into a field, and it's all marching forwards and then marching backwards, and turning this way, and turning that way. It wouldn't be so bad if they did a bit of ploughing when they're at home, or worked on the roads. But don't you believe it, Ma'am. Them military isn't a scrap of good to nobody! It's the poor folk as have to find food for 'em, just so's they can learn all about killing! I knows I'm nobbut a poor old body without learning, but when I sees 'em a-wearing of theirselves out marking time from morning till night, I says to myself, I says—when there's so many folk a-working hard to be useful, what reason is there in others a-working so hard to be hurtful? 'Tis nothing short of abomination to go a-slaughtering people, whether they be Prussians, or English, or Poles, or even French! When a soul takes revenge on somebody wot's done 'em a wrong, that's wickedness, that is, and he's condemned for it, but when un slaughters our lads like so many game-birds, that's goodness, and those as slaughters the most gets medals. Say what you will, I'll never get the hang on it, that I shan't!'

Cornudet raised his voice:

'War is barbaric when one attacks a peaceful neighbour, but a sacred duty in defence of one's own country!'

The old woman dropped her eyes:

'That be true enough when 'tis a matter of defending oneself, that be different: but wouldn't it be better to kill all they kind as do such things for their pleasure?'

Cornudet's eyes flashed:

'Bravo! citoyenne,' he said.

Monsieur Carré-Lamadon was deep in thought. Fanatical admirer though he was of the great soldiers of history, this old peasant-woman's good sense set him thinking how much wealth might be created for a country by all those unoccupied—and therefore dangerous—hands, by all that potential strength kept unproductive, whereas they might be employed on great industrial enterprises which would take centuries to build up.

Loiseau had risen from his chair, and had embarked on a low-voiced conversation with the landlord. The fat man laughed, and coughed and spat. His vast belly shook with mirth at the funny things his guest was saying, and he gave him an order for six barrels of Bordeaux wine, to be delivered in the spring, when the Prussians should have gone.

Since everyone was completely done up, tracks were made for bed as soon as supper was over.

But Loiseau, tired though he was, had missed nothing of what was going on, and as soon as he had got his wife snugly tucked into bed, he stationed himself at the door, where, putting now an eye, now an ear, to the keyhole, he made a serious effort to get the hang of what he called 'the mysteries of the corridor'. After about an hour, he heard a rustling, took a quick look, and saw Boule de Suif, seeming fatter than ever in her blue cashmere wrap with its edging of white lace. She had a candle in her hand and was on her way to

the door with the large number on it, at the far end of the passage.
Then, one of the bedroom doors was pushed ajar, and, when she
came back a few minutes later, Cornudet, in shirtsleeves and
braces, slipped out and followed her. They talked in low voices for a
moment, and then came to a halt. Boule de Suif appeared to be
denying him entry to her room. Loiseau, unfortunately, could not
hear what they were saying until they suddenly raised their voices,
and he caught a few words. Cornudet was eager and insistent.

'Don't be a little fool,' he was saying. 'What possible difference
can it make to you?'

She replied in a tone of considerable indignation:

'No, there's a time and a place for all things: here and now it
would be a positive disgrace!'

He seemed not to understand what she meant, and asked why?
At that she flew into a temper, and raised her voice still more:

'Why? D'you mean to say you don't *know* why—with Prussians
in the house, perhaps even next door?'

He said no more. This patriotic modesty of a tart who wouldn't
let a man make love to her in the face of the enemy, must have restored something of his flagging sense of dignity, for, after just
touching her cheek with his lips, he stealthily returned to his own
room.

Loiseau, by this time in a condition of no little excitement, left
the keyhole, cut a few capers, put on his nightcap, crept between
the sheets beside the leathery body of his legitimate mate, woke her
with a kiss, and murmured, 'Do you love me, darling?'

Then silence fell upon the house. But soon, from some unidenti-
fiable spot—it might have been the cellar or it might have been
the attics—came the sound of powerful, monotonous, and regular
snoring, accompanied by a quivering undertone, as of a boiler at
high pressure. Monsieur Follenvie was sleeping.

It had been decided to start at eight o'clock next morning, and
the company duly assembled in the kitchen. But the *diligence*, with
a layer of snow on its canvas roof, stood solitary in the middle of
the yard, innocent of horses and of driver. A search was made for
the latter in the stables, the hay-loft and the coach-house, but un-
availingly. Then, the men of the party went out, determined to
beat the countryside. They found themselves in the Square, with
the church at one end, and, on either side, two rows of low houses,
where a number of Prussian soldiers were in evidence. The first one
they saw was peeling potatoes. A second, further on, was scrubbing
out the barber's shop. A third, with a thick growth of beard up to

his eyes, had a small child in his arms. It was crying, and he started to dandle it on his knee. Fat peasant women whose men were 'away at the war', were indicating by signs to their obedient conquerors what job they should do—chop wood, ladle soup on to crusts of bread, or grind the coffee. One of them was even doing his hostess's washing, she being old and helpless.

The count, much surprised by what he saw, questioned the verger who was just leaving the presbytery. 'They're good lads, on the whole,' replied the old church-familiar. 'Not Prussians they do say: come from some place further off, though I don't know where. They've all got wives and kids at home, and this 'ere war's not much fun for 'em. A lot of tears, I dare say, it's causing way back in their own country, and a mort of misery, same as here. Folk in these parts ain't too badly off for the moment. These chaps don't do no harm, and they're good workers. The poor 've got to help each other, you know, sir. . . . It's the men at the top as makes wars.'

Cornudet, indignant at the friendly relations established between victors and vanquished, turned back, preferring to shut himself away at the inn. Loiseau could not resist making a joke: 'Repopulation; that's what they're up to.' 'Reparation, I would rather say,' replied Monsieur Carré-Lamadon with pompous solemnity. But of their driver there was no sign. He was finally discovered in the village café, seated at a table in friendly proximity to the officer's soldier-servant. The count put a question to him.

'Were you not told to have the horses put in by eight o'clock?'

'Sure I was, but later on I was told different.'

'What were you told?'

'Not to put them horses in at all.'

'Who gave you that order?'

'Why, the Prussian commandant, o' course.'

'Why?'

'I don't know nothing about why. You'd better go'n ask *him*. I was told not to put the horses in, so I doesn't put the horses in, and that's all there is to it.'

'When was that?'

'Last night, just as I was going to bed.'

The three men returned to the inn, feeling very uneasy.

They asked to see Monsieur Follenvie, but the servant-girl explained that, because of his asthma, he never got up before ten. He had issued strict orders that he was never to be called earlier, except in case of fire.

They wished to see the officer, but that was quite impossible, even though he did have his quarters at the inn. Monsieur Follenvie was the only person authorized to have access to him about civilian matters. The ladies went back to their rooms, and passed the time doing meaningless odds and ends.

Cornudet settled down under the high chimney-piece in the kitchen, where a great fire was blazing. He sent for a small table from the café and a bottle of beer, and there he sat, puffing away at his pipe, which, among his democrat friends, enjoyed a prestige nearly equal to his own, as though by serving Cornudet it was serving the Country. It was a superb meerschaum, beautifully mellowed by years of use, as black as its owner's teeth, but sweet-smelling, curved, and shining, fitting comfortably into his hand from force of habit, and providing the final, necessary touch to his appearance. He sat motionless, his eyes fixed now on the flaming logs on the hearth, now on the froth which crowned his mug, and, each time he took a pull at it, he ran his fingers through his long, greasy hair, with a look of extreme satisfaction, and sniffed at the drops of beer clinging to his moustache.

Loiseau, under pretence of stretching his legs, set off to collect orders for wine from the local retailers. The count and the manufacturer talked politics. Between them they forecast the future of France. The one put his faith in the House of Orléans, the other in the coming of some unknown saviour, who would appear when all seemed lost, a du Guesclin, a Joan of Arc, perhaps, or some new Napoleon I. Ah! If only the Prince Imperial were not so young! Cornudet, listening to them, smiled like a man who knows the secrets of Destiny. His pipe perfumed the kitchen.

On the stroke of ten, Monsieur Follenvie appeared. He was quickly questioned, but gave the same answer several times over. 'The officer said to me, he said, Monsieur Follenvie, you will see to it that the conveyance of these travellers is left without horses tomorrow morning. I do not intend that they shall leave without orders from me. You understand? That is all . . .'

Then they made another attempt to see the officer. The count sent up his card, to which Monsieur Carré-Lamadon added his name and all his titles. The Prussian sent back word that he would receive the two gentlemen in audience as soon as he had had his lunch, that was to say, about one o'clock.

The ladies reappeared, and they all managed to eat a little something, in spite of the general uneasiness. Boule de Suif seemed to be far from well, and deeply troubled.

Just as they were finishing their coffee, the soldier-servant came to conduct the two emissaries to his master.

Loiseau attached himself to them, but when an attempt was made to enlist the services of Cornudet, so as to give a greater air of solemnity to the proceedings, he proudly declared that he would never have anything to do with Germans, after saying which, he returned to his seat by the fire, and sent for another bottle of beer.

The three men went upstairs, and were ushered into the best room the inn could boast, where the officer received them, stretched at full length in an arm-chair, with his feet on the mantelpiece, smoking a long pipe with a porcelain bowl, and wrapped in a gaudy dressing-gown, filched, no doubt, from the abandoned house of some middle-class woman with bad taste. He did not get up. He made no attempt to salute them, and did not look round when they came in. He was a fine object-lesson in the boorishness which comes naturally to soldiers in the hour of victory.

After a few moments, he roused himself sufficiently to utter a few words:

'Vat is it zat you vant?'

The count took it upon himself to act as spokesman.

'We wish to continue our journey.'

'No.'

'May I venture to ask why you refuse our request?'

'Because I do not vish it.'

'May I respectfully point out, sir, that your commanding officer issued us with a permit to proceed to Dieppe? I do not think that we have done anything to justify this unhelpful attitude on your part.'

'It is zat I do not vish . . . Zat is all . . . You can go now again down the stairs.'

The three bowed and withdrew. They spent a miserable afternoon. The German officer's whim seemed to have neither rhyme nor reason, and they hazarded a number of fantastic theories. The whole party stayed in the kitchen. The most unlikely suppositions were put forward. Perhaps they were to be held as hostages—but for what purpose? Or made prisoner? Or, more likely, held to ransom? At this thought they were overcome with panic. The richer were the most terrified, expecting that they would have to buy their lives and their freedom at the cost of handing over bags of gold to this insolent soldier. They racked their brains for plausible excuses, wondering how they could disguise the fact that they were wealthy, and convince their jailer that, in fact, they were very,

very poor. Loiseau took off his watch-chain and hid it in his pocket. The gathering darkness gave added weight to their apprehensions. The lamp was lit, and, since there were still two hours to go before supper, Madame Loiseau suggested a game of *trente-et-un*. It would serve to distract their minds. The proposal met with general support. Even Cornudet, who had knocked out his pipe as a tribute to good manners, took part.

The count shuffled the cards and dealt. Boule de Suif got thirty-one right away, and very soon the players were so deeply absorbed in their game that they almost forgot their haunting fears. Cornudet, however, noticed that the Loiseau pair were in league to do a bit of cheating.

Just as they were sitting down to supper, Monsieur Follenvie reappeared. In his phlegmy voice he said: 'The Prussian officer wishes to know whether Mademoiselle Elisabeth Rousset has changed her mind.'

Boule de Suif remained standing. She was very pale. Then, suddenly, the blood flooded into her face and she flew into so violent a temper that she could scarcely speak. At last, however, she burst into a torrent of words: 'You can tell that filthy beast, that dirty dog, that swine of a Prussian, that I will never do what he wants— get that clear—never . . . never . . . never . . . !'

The fat landlord left the room. At once, Boule de Suif was surrounded, questioned, implored to reveal the secret of the mysterious visit. At first she was stubborn, but very soon her fury got the upper hand. 'You're longing to know what he wanted; well, then'— and her voice rose to a shout—'he wanted me to sleep with him.' So intense was the general feeling of indignation, that no one was shocked by the baldness of her language. Cornudet slammed his mug with such violence on the table, that he broke it. There was a perfect uproar of horror at what the beastly ruffian had suggested. A storm of anger swept through the room. All were at one in support of her refusal. It was as though each had been asked to be a party to the sacrifice demanded of her. The count, in a tone of the most intense disgust, said that people like that were no better than the barbarians of old. The women, in particular, expressed to Boule de Suif their feelings of intense and affectionate commiseration. The good Sisters, who never put in an appearance except at mealtimes, kept their eyes lowered, and said nothing.

All the same, when the first wave of indignation had spent itself, the company proceeded to the business of supper. Nobody said much. They were all thinking.

Boule de Suif

The ladies retired early to bed, leaving the men to their tobacco. A game of *écarté* was organized, and Monsieur Follenvie was asked to join in, so anxious were the others to pick his brains about the best way in which the officer's resistance could be overcome. But he had thoughts only for the cards. He heard nothing, answered no questions, but was continually breaking in with, 'Play, gentlemen, play!' So hard was he concentrating on the game, that he even forgot to spit, a piece of absent-mindedness which produced an occasional organ-note in his chest. His wheezing lungs ranged over the whole gamut of the asthmatic, from a deep and solemn bass, to a shrill huskiness reminiscent of a young cock's attempts at crowing.

Even when his wife, who was dropping with fatigue, came to fetch him, he refused to go to bed. So, she went alone, being by nature an 'early bird' who rose with the sun, while her husband was a 'night-haunter' who was always ready to sit up late with friends. 'Put my egg-flip in front of the fire,' he said, and went back to his game. When it was clear that they would get nothing out of him, the others of the party decided that it was time for bed, and they all parted for the night.

Once again, they were up early next morning, hoping against hope that they might manage to get away at last, and terrified at the thought of having to spend another day in the horrible little inn.

But it went hard with their hopes, for the horses remained in the stable, the driver was nowhere to be seen, and, having nothing better to do, they hung round the stranded *diligence*.

Lunch was a melancholy affair. There was a noticeable coldness in the general attitude towards Boule de Suif, for night—which brings counsel—had considerably modified her companions' earlier views. They resented her failure to contrive a clandestine meeting with the officer, which might have resulted in good news for them on rising. It would have been such an easy way out, and, after all, no one need have known anything about it. She could so easily have found a way of saving her face by telling the Prussian that she had decided to take pity on their distress. The whole thing could have meant so little to her.

But no one, as yet, put these thoughts into words.

In the afternoon, the count suggested a walk to the outskirts of the town. It might do something to relieve the killing boredom of having nothing to do. So, they all wrapped up, and started off, the only absentees being Cornudet, who preferred his fireside, and the

27

two Sisters, who spent their days either in the church, or with the curé.

The cold, which was daily increasing, was intense, and ears and noses suffered cruelly. The walkers' feet became so painful that every step was torture, and, when, at last, they came in sight of the open country, the white blanket stretching endlessly in all directions was so gloomy and so ominous, that all, with one accord, turned back with numbed brains and sinking hearts.

The four women walked in front, with the three gentlemen close behind.

Loiseau, who perfectly understood the situation, suddenly grew vocal. How much longer, he asked, was that 'damned bitch' going to keep them hanging about in this God-awful place? The count, always a model of good breeding, said that no woman could be pressed to make so painful a sacrifice, and that if it *were* made, it must be of her own free will. Monsieur Carré-Lamadon pointed out that if, as it was being said they would, the French forces launched a counter-offensive, the clash would inevitably take place at Tôtes. This remark had a sobering effect upon the other two. 'How about making a dash for it, on foot?' said Loiseau. The count shrugged: 'In this snow, and with our wives? Besides, we should be followed at once, rounded up, and brought back as prisoners at the mercy of the soldiers.' This was so obviously true that there was nothing more to be said.

The ladies were talking clothes, but a certain degree of constraint seemed to have shattered their previous harmony.

All of a sudden, at the end of the street, they caught sight of the officer. His tall, wasp-waisted figure stood out sharply against the snow. He was in uniform, and walking with his legs slightly apart, in the way peculiar to military men when they want to avoid dirtying their carefully polished high-boots.

He bowed as he passed the ladies, and stared contemptuously at the men, who still had sufficient sense of dignity left to keep from uncovering, though Loiseau did make a sketchy gesture of the hand towards his hat.

Boule de Suif went scarlet to the tips of her ears, and the three married women felt deeply humiliated at being seen by the Prussian in the company of one whom he had treated with such scant respect.

The conversation turned on him, on his face and his general appearance. Madame Carré-Lamadon, who had known many officers, and judged them with the eye of an expert, thought that he wasn't at all bad. She went so far as to say that she was sorry he wasn't French, for he would have made a fine Hussar, and all the women would have been mad about him.

When they got back to the inn, they found themselves at a loose end. The most trivial remarks led to barbed exchanges. Supper was eaten rapidly and in silence, and everybody went early to bed, in the hope that sleep might help to kill the time.

The party reassembled next morning with heavy eyes and frayed tempers. The women exchanged scarcely a word with Boule de Suif.

The church-bell began to ring. There was to be a christening. The fat young woman had a child which she boarded out with a peasant family at Yvetot. She saw it less than once a year, and never bothered her head about it, but now, the thought of the baby to be baptized, set her heart suddenly overflowing with tenderness for her own offspring, and she was filled with a desire to be present at the ceremony.

No sooner had she left the room than glances were exchanged, and chairs drawn closer, for, by this time, everybody knew that, sooner or later, something would have to be decided. Loiseau had a flash of inspiration. Why shouldn't the officer be told that he could keep Boule de Suif if he would let the others go?

Monsieur Follenvie undertook to act as go-between. But he soon returned. The German, who had a pretty extensive knowledge of human nature, had shown him the door, saying that he was going to keep all of them there until he had got what he wanted.

Madame Loiseau's vulgarity of mind could no longer be restrained. 'I don't see why we should be left here to die of old age. Going with men is the creature's way of making a living, and she has no right to pick and choose. She spread her net pretty wide in Rouen, I can tell you, and didn't even stop at cab-drivers. Yes, Madame, the driver at the Préfecture was one of them! There's very little I don't know about *him*; he gets his wine from us. And now that it's a question of helping us out of a difficulty, the brazen hussy starts putting on airs. . . . Personally, I think this officer is behaving very well . . . He has probably been deprived of female society for a long while. No doubt he would have preferred one of us three, but he is decent enough to make do with a piece of public property! He has a praiseworthy respect for married women! Don't forget that he is the master here. He has only got to say "I want", and he could call in his men and take us by force!'

29

The other two women shuddered. Pretty little Madame Carré-Lamadon's eyes were shining, and she looked rather pale, as though she were already being assaulted by the officer.

The men, who had been talking apart, now rejoined them. Loiseau, who was in a blind fury, favoured the idea of handing over 'the wretched creature', bound hand and foot, to the enemy. But the count, with three generations of ambassadors behind him, and looking every inch a diplomat, suggested a more subtle approach. 'She must be persuaded,' he said.

The women huddled together, talking in low voices. The discussion became general, each stating his, or her, point of view. But it was all very respectable. The ladies, in particular, made the most indecent suggestions wrapped up in refined phrases, and put forward with the most charming indirectness. A stranger would have understood nothing of what they were saying, so circuitous was their approach. But the thin layer of modesty which is to be found in all women of the world, is rarely more than skin-deep, and they revelled in this more than doubtful escapade, enjoying every moment of it, feeling that they were in their element, and manipulating the succulent details of sexual intercourse with the sensuality of a greedy cook preparing a dinner for somebody else.

Gaiety was soon the order of the day, so amusing did the whole thing seem to them after they had been discussing it for some time. The count ventured on a number of jokes that were rather near the knuckle, but all so beautifully worded that they were greeted with smiles. Loiseau, in his turn, loosed off several cruder indecencies which, however, nobody seemed to mind. The thought, so coarsely expressed by his wife, was uppermost in all their minds: 'It's her profession, isn't it? Why should she turn up her nose at *him* and not at others?' The pretty Madame Carré-Lamadon seemed even to be thinking that, if she had been in Boule de Suif's shoes, she would have put up far less resistance to the officer's advances than she would have done to those of many men she could think of.

Elaborate plans were made for the blockade. They might have been undertaking the investment of a formidable stronghold. It was agreed what part each should play, the arguments each should use, the manoeuvres each should carry out. The method of attack was settled, the subterfuges to be employed, the surprise assaults to be delivered, and all for the sole purpose of forcing an entry into a citadel of flesh and blood, and leaving the way open for the enemy to take possession.

Cornudet, however, remained aloof, a complete stranger to the whole affair.

So absorbed were they in their scheming, that they did not hear Boule de Suif enter the room. But the count's whispered 'Ssh!' brought all heads round. There she was. A sudden silence fell, and, for a moment or two, a feeling of embarrassment kept all of them from saying anything to her. But at last, the countess, who was better trained than the others in the duplicities of the fashionable world, put a question: 'Did you enjoy the christening?'

The fat young woman, still in the throes of recent emotion, gave a full description of the ceremony, of how everybody had looked, of how everybody had behaved, and even what the inside of the church was like: 'It's so nice to pray now and then.'

Until it was time for lunch, the ladies confined their efforts to being friendly with her. They hoped, in this way, to increase her confidence in them, and to make sure that she would show a proper docility when the time came to advise her on her course of action.

As soon, however, as they were all seated at table, the opening moves were made. These took the form of vague allusions to recorded cases of self-sacrifice: instances were quoted from ancient history: Judith and Holofernes were mentioned, and then, somewhat inconsequently, Lucrece and Sextus, and Cleopatra, who had taken all the enemy generals into her bed, and so reduced them to the condition of slaves. These were followed by a fantastic story which had bloomed in the imagination of these ignorant millionaires, to the effect that all the women of Rome had gone to Capua with the intention of rocking Hannibal to sleep in their arms, and, with him, all his lieutenants, and whole hosts of mercenaries. Women were cited who had arrested the onward march of conquerors by turning their bodies into a battlefield, into an instrument of domination, into a weapon, and, with their heroic embraces, had overpowered hideous and detested foes, sacrificing their chastity on the altars of revenge and patriotism.

There was mention, too, in veiled terms, of a certain Englishwoman of good family who had had herself inoculated with a horrible and contagious disease in order to transmit it to Bonaparte, who had been miraculously saved by a sudden indisposition at the very moment of the fatal meeting.

These stories were told in a restrained and decorous manner, with, now and again, little bursts of enthusiasm, deliberately designed to excite a spirit of emulation.

By the time this programme was brought to an end, one might

have been forgiven for believing that the one and only rôle of women here below, is to make a perpetual offering of their persons, and to abandon themselves endlessly to the whims and fancies of the military.

The two good Sisters seemed to have heard nothing of all this, so deeply sunk were they in their own thoughts. Boule de Suif did not speak.

All through the afternoon she was left to her own reflections. But, instead of calling her 'madame', as they had done hitherto, she was now addressed as 'mademoiselle', without anybody quite knowing why, as though the intention had been to bring her down a step or two on the ladder of general esteem which she had succeeded in climbing, and to make her conscious of her own shameful position.

Just as the soup was being served, Monsieur Follenvie entered with the same old parrot-phrase: 'The Prussian officer wishes to know whether Mademoiselle Elisabeth Rousset has changed her mind.'

Boule de Suif's reply was short and sharp:

'No, Monsieur,' she said.

But, as supper proceeded, the coalition weakened. Loiseau made three unfortunate remarks. All those round the table had been flogging their brains in an attempt to find yet other examples, but without success, when the countess, perhaps without premeditation, and merely from a vague wish to pay tribute to religion, questioned the elder of the two Sisters about certain outstanding events in the lives of the Saints. Many had been guilty of actions which we should regard as crimes, but for which the Church finds no difficulty in granting absolution when they have been committed for the greater glory of God and the good of one's neighbour. This was a powerful argument, and the countess turned it to account, with the result that, whether by reason of one of those tacit agreements, those veiled complicities, in which all who wear the priestly habit are past masters, or, quite simply from a fortunate lack of intelligence and a helpful stupidity, the old nun brought to the conspiracy a tremendous weight of support. They had thought her timid, but she now showed herself to be bold, verbose, and violent. She was not troubled by the gropings of casuistry. Her doctrine, it now appeared, was firm as an iron bar. Her faith knew nothing of hesitations. Her conscience was devoid of scruples. She accepted Abraham's sacrifice without difficulty, for she would have killed her father and her mother without a qualm, had she been ordered to do so from on high. Nothing, in her view, could be displeasing to the Lord if the intention were praiseworthy. The countess, enlisting the sacred authority of this unexpected ally, led her on to pronounce, so to speak, an edifying gloss on the moral axiom which states that 'the end justifies the means'.

'So, you think, Sister, that God accepts and pardons no matter what action, so long as the motive is pure?'

'Who could doubt it, Madame? An act deserving of blame in itself, may often be meritorious by reason of the thought which inspires it.'

And so they continued, unravelling God's will, predicting His decisions, compelling Him to take an interest in matters with which, in point of fact, He is very little connected.

This interchange was carried on in discreet, reticent, and shrewd language. But every word uttered by the dedicated woman in the white coif made yet another breach in the indignant resistance of the courtesan. Then, the conversation having slightly shifted its ground, the woman of the dangling rosaries spoke of the Houses of her Order, of her Superior, of herself, and of her sweet companion, dear Sister Saint-Nicéphore. They had been sent for to Le Havre to nurse the hundreds of smallpox cases in the military hospitals. She painted a picture of these wretched men, and described in detail the disease from which they were suffering. While they were being held up on the road by the whim of this Prussian, many Frenchmen might be dying whom, perhaps, they could have saved. Her special vocation was caring for soldiers. She had been in the Crimea, in Italy, in Austria. When she told the story of her campaigns, she stood revealed as one of those religious women of trumpet and drum, who seem made to follow in the wake of armies, to pick up wounded in the backwash of battles, and, better than any senior officer, to silence with a word great hulking and undisciplined louts; in short, as one of those true Sister Rataplans, whose very faces, ravaged and pitted, call up a picture of the devastations of war.

When she had stopped speaking, no one said anything, so excellent did the effect of her words seem to have been.

As soon as supper was over, all went to their rooms, not to come down again until late next morning.

Lunch was a peaceful meal. The seed sown the night before was being given time in which to germinate and bring forth its fruit.

In the afternoon, the countess suggested a walk. The count, as

33

had been arranged, took Boule de Suif's arm, and lagged behind the others with her.

He adopted that familiar, paternal, and faintly contemptuous tone, which elderly men employ when speaking to women of her calling. He addressed her as 'my dear child', stressing his own high social position and indisputable respectability. Without beating about the bush, he came straight to the point.

'So, you would rather see us left here, exposed, as you are yourself, to possible acts of violence which might result from the Prussian troops being held up, than consent to one of those—ahem, acts of accommodation which have been not infrequent in the course of your life?'

Boule de Suif said nothing. He was breaking down her defences by gentleness, by sweet reason, by an appeal to her feelings. He knew so well how never to be less than 'monsieur le comte', while still showing himself to be a ladies' man, and, when occasion demanded, both flattering and kindly. He spoke highly of the service she would be doing them, of their feelings of gratitude; then, suddenly, becoming politely playful, he proceeded: 'If it is any comfort to you, m'dear, he may think himself lucky—he won't find many young women as pretty as you are, in his own country.'

Boule de Suif still said nothing, and rejoined the others.

As soon as they got back to the inn, she went up to her room, and did not appear again. The suspense was terrible. What was she going to do? How terribly awkward it was going to be if she stuck to her guns!

Supper was announced. They waited for her, but in vain. Then Monsieur Follenvie appeared with the news that Mademoiselle Rousset was not feeling well. Supper need not be delayed any longer. Every ear was cocked. The count went up to the landlord, and in a very low voice, said: 'All going well?'

'Yes.'

Good manners forbade him to say anything to the others, but he gave them a faint nod. At once there was a general sigh of relief, and an expression of joy showed on every face. 'Damme!' said Loiseau, 'I'll stand champagne all round, if there is any to be had!' Madame Loiseau had the shock of her life when the landlord returned with four bottles. Everyone had suddenly become noisy and communicative. A universal spirit of licence held sway. The count seemed to notice for the first time how charming Madame Carré-Lamadon was: the manufacturer complimented the countess on her appearance. Conversation was lively, unrestrained, and sparkling.

34

Boule de Suif

All of a sudden, Loiseau, with an expression of uneasiness, raised his hands and called for silence. Everyone, already fearful, and now taken by surprise, stopped talking. He listened attentively, motioning them to keep quiet, looked up at the ceiling, listened once again, and then, in his natural voice, said:

'No need to worry: all is well.'

At first they failed to understand. Then, a smile went round the table.

At the end of a further quarter of an hour, he went through the same pantomime, which he renewed several times in the course of the evening. He pretended to be asking questions of someone on the floor above, and giving advice in words with a double meaning which he fished up from the murky depths of his commercial-traveller's mind. Now and again he assumed a melancholy air, and sighed—'Poor girl!' or muttered between clenched teeth, as though in a furious temper: 'Get to hell out of there, you bloody Prussian!' Sometimes, when least expected, in a voice vibrating with emotion, he said: 'Enough! Enough!' adding, as though to himself: 'I only hope we see her again; the bastard's killing her!'

These sallies, though in deplorable taste, gave amusement and did no harm, for indignation, like everything else, is the product of circumstances, and the climate which had gradually taken possession of the room, was heavily charged with salacious thoughts.

By the time dessert was brought in, even the women were indulging in discreet but doubtful witticisms. Eyes were shining. Drinking had been heavy. The count, who even in his more unbuttoned moments never lost his appearance of noble gravity, made several somewhat overstressed references to the ending of winter in the arctic regions, and the joy felt by shipwrecked mariners when they see the route to the South opening before them.

Loiseau, by this time on the top of his form, rose to his feet with a glass of champagne in his hand, and cried:

'I drink to our deliverance!'

All stood up and applauded. Even the two good Sisters, under pressure from the ladies, consented to moisten their lips in the sparkling wine which they had never yet tasted. They declared that it was like fizzy lemonade, but with a more delicate flavour.

Loiseau gave expression to the general feeling, when he said:

'Pity there's no piano. We might have had a bit of a hop.'

Cornudet, all this while, had not uttered a word, nor made a movement. He seemed to be sunk in thoughts of the utmost gravity, and now and again tugged angrily at his great beard, as though he wanted to make it even longer than it was. At last, round about midnight, just as the party was on the point of breaking up, Loiseau, who was decidedly unsteady on his feet, gave him a tap on the stomach, and in a voice far from distinct, said: 'Not 'zactly cheerful, y'aren't, 's evening, citizen: 'v'n't opened lips!' But Cornudet, throwing back his head, and turning on the guests a blazing and terrible eye, exclaimed: 'What you, all of you, have done today is an abominable thing.' Then, he rose to his feet, went to the door, said, once again, 'Abominable!' and vanished.

The first effect of this was like a douche of cold water. Loiseau, momentarily abashed, soon recovered his self-confidence, and suddenly burst out laughing. 'Sour grapes, ol' man!' he said more than once. 'Sour grapes, tha's wha's matter wi' you.' Then, since they did not seem to understand what he meant, he told them about the 'mysteries of the corridor'. At that, joviality returned in full flood. The ladies rolled and rocked like mad creatures. The count and Monsieur Carré-Lamadon laughed so hard that they cried. They wouldn't believe him.

'Are you sure? He wanted . . .'

'Saw't wi' m'y own eyes, I tell you.'

'And she refused?'

''Cos Prussian was in next room!'

'Not possible!'

'G've you my word!'

The count was choking with laughter. The manufacturer had both hands pressed to his stomach. Loiseau went on:

'Nacherly, doesn't see joke of it, 'sevening—far from't.'

Then all three started off again, laughing themselves sick, until they had to stop for lack of breath.

The party broke up. But Madame Loiseau, who was not unlike a stinging-nettle, remarked to her husband, as they got into bed, that that sour-faced Carré-Lamadon puss hadn't had much to laugh about: when women like that fell for a uniform, they didn't much care whether there was a Frenchman or a Prussian inside it.

And all night long, the dark corridor was alive with rustlings, faint, scarcely audible noises which sounded like breathing, the patter of bare feet, and the creaking of boards. No one went to sleep until late, as was obvious from the strips of light showing under the doors. That is the effect champagne has: it keeps people awake.

Boule de Suif

Next morning, a bright winter's sun had turned the snow to a dazzle of white. The *diligence*, harnessed at last, was standing in front of the door, and white pigeons, their heads sunk in their thick plumage, a black speck in the middle of each red eye, were strutting solemnly between the legs of the six horses, pecking for food between the steaming droppings.

The driver, muffled in his sheepskin, sat smoking his pipe on the box-seat, and the beaming passengers were hurriedly collecting food enough to last them for the rest of the journey.

Only Boule de Suif was missing. At last she appeared.

She looked faintly worried and shamefaced. She moved shyly towards her travelling companions, all of whom, as one man, turned their backs as though they had not seen her. The count took his wife's arm with a dignified air, and drew her out of range of the contaminating contact.

The fat young woman stopped dead in utter bewilderment. Then, plucking up her courage, she approached the manufacturer's wife with a timid 'Good morning, Madame.' The woman gave her an impertinent nod, and a look of outraged virtue. They all seemed busy about their own affairs, and kept at a safe distance from her, as though she were carrying infection in the folds of her skirt. There was a concerted rush towards the *diligence*. She was the last to enter it, and settled into the seat which she had occupied during the first part of the journey.

They seemed not to have seen her, not to know who she was, though Madame Loiseau, studying her indignantly from a distance, said in a low voice to her husband: 'I'm very glad I am not sitting next her.'

The heavy vehicle jolted into motion, and the journey was resumed.

At first nobody said much. Boule de Suif dared not raise her eyes. She felt indignant at the way in which she was being treated, deeply ashamed at having yielded, and fouled by the kisses of the Prussian into whose arms they had so hypocritically thrown her.

But the countess, turning to Madame Carré-Lamadon, broke the painful silence.

'I believe you know Madame d'Étrelles?'

'Yes, indeed; she is a friend of mine.'

'What a delightful woman!'

'Quite charming! So truly refined, so cultivated, and an artist to the tips of her fingers. She sings deliciously, and draws to perfection.'

The manufacturer was deep in conversation with the count. Through the rattling of the windows it was possible to catch a few words: 'Dividend'—'bills'—'bonus'—'securities'.

Loiseau, who had pinched the old pack of cards from the inn, greasy from five years of contact with unwiped tables, embarked on a game of bezique with his wife.

The two Sisters grasped the long rosaries hanging from their belts, crossed themselves, and started to move their lips more and more rapidly in a low mutter, as though they were engaged in a prayer-race, now and again kissing a medal, before returning once again to their hurried and continuous murmurings.

Cornudet sat perfectly still, deep in thought.

At the end of three hours, Loiseau picked up the cards, and said, 'I'm peckish.'

His wife reached for a parcel tied with string, from which she produced a piece of cold veal. This she proceeded to cut into thin, firm slices, and they both began to eat.

'We might do the same,' said the countess.

The suggestion was welcomed, and she set about unpacking the provisions which had been put up in sufficient quantity to supply the two couples. There was a long-shaped casserole with a hare moulded on its lid just to make it clear that there was hare-paté within, a succulent cold dish with its rivulets of white bacon-fat streaking the creature's dark-brown flesh, and mincemeat chopped very fine. There was also an imposing piece of Gruyère, with the words 'News in Brief' printed on its greasy surface, for it had been wrapped in a newspaper.

The two Sisters produced a section of sausage, reeking of garlic, and Cornudet, plunging both hands into the voluminous pockets of his loose-fitting overcoat, brought from one four hard-boiled eggs, and from the other, a hunk of crusty bread.

Having removed the shell from one of the eggs (and thrown the pieces on to the straw which covered the floor) he bit into it, scattering fragments of yellow yoke all over his great beard, in the dense growth of which they showed like stars.

Boule de Suif, in the nervous hurry of getting up and packing, had forgotten all about food, and now, choking with rage, she watched her neighbours placidly munching. A wild fury at first caught her by the throat, and she opened her mouth to give vent to a torrent of abusive words. But so violent were her feelings that she could not utter a sound.

No one looked at her; no one gave her a thought. She felt over-

whelmed by the contempt of these respectable brutes who had first
sacrificed her, and then rejected her as something unclean and of no
further use. She thought of the great basket packed with good
things which they had so greedily devoured, of the two chickens
shining with jelly, of the patés and pears, of the four bottles of
Bordeaux wine. Her anger snapped suddenly like a string stretched
too tightly, and she felt herself on the brink of tears. She made a
violent effort not to show her feelings and sat stiff and upright,
choking back her sobs. But her misery would not be denied. It
mounted to her eyes, and glistened between her lids. The next
moment two great tears were rolling down her cheeks. Others followed more rapidly, falling like drops of water seeping through a
rock, one after the other, on to her bosom's ample curve. She sat
there, rigid and upright, with staring eyes and a dead-white face,
hoping that no one would notice.

But the countess saw, and nudged her husband, as though to
say: 'What did you expect? It's not *my* fault.'

Madame Loiseau indulged in a noiseless laugh, and whispered,
'She's crying because she's ashamed of herself.'

The two nuns had resumed their praying, after first wrapping
what remained of their sausage in its paper.

Then Cornudet, who was busy digesting his eggs, stretched his
long legs under the seat opposite, leaned back, smiled like a man
who has just thought of something funny, and began whistling the
Marseillaise under his breath.

A shadow fell across the other faces. The street-song did not, it
seemed, appeal to his neighbours. There were signs that they were
growing nervous and irritable. It almost looked as though they
were about to start howling like dogs when they hear a hurdy-
gurdy. All this he noticed, but did not stop. From time to time he
even hummed the words:

> *Amour sacré de la patrie,*
> *Conduis, soutiens, nos braves vengeurs,*
> *Liberté, liberté chérie,*
> *Combats avec tes défenseurs!*

They were moving more quickly now, for the snow was harder,
and until Dieppe was reached, through the long, bleak hours of
travel, through the jolting of the road, in the gathering dusk, and
when the inside of the *diligence* grew pitchy dark, he still went on,
fiercely determined, with his vengeful and monotonous whistling,

forcing their tired, exacerbated ears, again and again, to follow the whole song through to the end, fitting to each note its appropriate word.

Boule de Suif was still crying, and, now and again, a sob she could not check broke from her in the momentary pause between two verses.

(16 April 1880)

Paul's Mistress

OLD Grillon's restaurant, that meeting-place of boating men, was
slowly emptying. There was much noisy shouting and mutual hail-
ing outside the door, where strapping young fellows in white singlets
stood gesticulating, with oars on their shoulders.

Women in light spring dresses stepped carefully into the waiting
skiffs, sat down in the stern and arranged their skirts, while the
master of the establishment, a powerfully built man with a red
beard, whose strength was proverbial, was busily engaged in handing down the ladies with one hand and keeping the light craft
steady with the other.

Then the oarsmen took their places. There was much flexing of
bare arms and throwing out of chests for the benefit of the gallery,
composed for the most part of prosperous citizens in their Sunday
best, workmen and soldiers with their elbows on the railing of the
bridge, all paying close attention to the spectacle.

One by one the boats cast off, the rowers swinging backwards and
forward with a rhythmical movement, and the swiftly-moving
skiffs, responsive to the long oars with their curving blades, glided
over the surface of the river, drawing away, growing smaller to the
eye, and finally disappearing altogether under the distant railway
bridge, making their way downstream towards *La Grenouillère*.

Only one couple still remained. The young man, pale-faced and
slim, with scarcely a trace as yet of hair upon his cheeks, had his
arm round the waist of a dark, thin girl with the quick movements
of a grasshopper. Now and then they gazed into each other's eyes.

'Come along, Monsieur Paul, hurry!' cried the proprietor, as they
walked towards him. Of all the regular customers of the establishment, Monsieur Paul was the best liked and the most respected.
He paid promptly and well, whereas the others needed a deal of
prodding, and not seldom disappeared leaving their score un-
settled. But, more important still, this particular pair served, in
some sort, as a living advertisement of the place, since the youth's
father was a senator. Should a newcomer ask: 'Who's that young
chap who seems so keen on his little piece?' some constant patron,
with a pompous and a knowing look, would answer in a low voice:

43

'Why, that's Paul Baron, the senator's son,' to which the other usually replied, 'Poor devil! He's got it badly!'

Madame Grillon, a decent body with a shrewd eye for business, called the young man and his companion her 'two turtle-doves', and appeared to look with sentimental approval on a mutual passion which was so good for trade.

The couple walked slowly. Their skiff, the *Madeleine*, was ready. But, just as they were getting into it, they stopped to kiss, much to the amusement of the audience gathered on the bridge. Then, taking the oars, Monsieur Paul set off in his turn for *La Grenouillère*.

When they arrived it was three o'clock, and the great floating café was packed with customers.

The immense raft, roofed with a tarpaulin supported on wooden pillars, is joined to the charming island of Croissy by two gangways. One of these terminates in the very middle of that aquatic pleasure-haunt, while the other leads to a tiny islet which boasts a single tree, and is popularly known as '*Pot-à-Fleurs*'. From there it gives access to the river-bank close to the bathing-place.

Monsieur Paul laid his boat alongside the raft and tied up. Then he clambered over the balustrade of the café, took his mistress by both hands, and pulled her up, after which they sat down opposite one another at one end of a table.

Across the river, along the road which follows the line of the tow-path, moved a slow procession of wheeled vehicles. Cabs alternated with the smart turn-outs of the 'swells'; the former, pot-bellied contraptions with sagging springs, drawn by broken-kneed nags with drooping heads, the latter with graceful bodies mounted on elegant wheels, harnessed to high-spirited, slim-legged horses, with arched necks and bits flecked with white, in charge of coachmen tightly buttoned into livery coats with high collars on which their heads were perched, sitting motionless upon their hams with a whip held upright on one knee.

The bank was thick with people: family parties, small groups, couples, or single, lonely figures. They were killing time by pulling up handfuls of grass, going down to the water's edge and climbing up again to the road, all crowded together in the same spot, waiting for the ferry. The heavy punt moved ceaselessly from one side of the river to the other, discharging its living cargo on the island.

The arm of the river, known as 'the backwater', on which the floating café looked, seemed to be fast asleep, so sluggish was its current. Whole fleets of skiffs and wherries, of canoes and water-cycles, cockleshells and craft of every shape and size, moved on the unruffled surface, criss-crossing and mingling, colliding, suddenly stopping and jarring the oarsmen's arms, only to shoot forward again under the propulsion of tensed muscles, slithering and flickering like long red and yellow fishes.

New arrivals were constantly turning up, some from Chatou, upstream, others from Bougival, down. Laughter and the sound of voices floated across the water from boat to boat—hails and questions and abuse. The tanned and knotted play of male biceps gleamed and glistened under the hot sun, and silken parasols, like strange, aquatic flowers, red and green, blue and yellow, glowed in the sternsheets.

July was blazing in mid-heaven: the air was all a-crackle with gaiety, and not a breath of wind stirred the leaves of the willows and the poplars.

Opposite, the harsh light beat upon the turfed and terraced bastions of the ever-present Mont-Valérien, and, away to the right, the lovely slopes of Louveciennes, conforming to the river's curving course, stood in a rounded semi-circle, showing here and there, through the thrusting greenery of gardens, the white walls of dotted country houses.

All about *La Grenouillère* the crowds were idly sauntering under those gigantic trees which make of this corner of the island one of the most delicious expanses of parkland to be found anywhere in the world. Women (for sale) with yellow hair, prominent breasts, exaggerated backsides, faces plastered with make-up, pencilled eyes, and blood-red lips, laced and compressed into absurd confections, were dragging their bright bad taste over the fresh green of the lawns. The young men with them looked like tailors' dummies, with their light-coloured gloves, their varnished boots, their thread-thin canes, and the monocles which served to emphasize the witlessness of grinning faces.

The island narrows at *La Grenouillère*, and, on the further side, where another ferry brings an unceasing flow of visitors from Croissy, the swift-flowing arm of the river eddies and swirls like a torrent. Here, on the bank a bridge-building detachment was encamped, and the men in their artillery uniforms were seated in a row on a long balk of wood, watching the river running at their feet.

The restaurant was filled with a howling, raging mob. On the wooden tables spilled drinks had made thin, sticky trickles, and the half-empty glasses were surrounded by men and women at least partially drunk. Everybody was shouting, singing, and generally kicking up a shindy. The men, with red faces, eyes bright with the glitter of alcohol, and hats pushed back upon their heads, were banging and yelling in response to that need to make a noise felt by primitive natures. The women, all on the look-out for the evening's prey, were putting in time with drinks bought for them. Such free space as there was between the tables was filled with the press of ordinary customers, groups of boating youths larking with female companions in short flannel skirts.

Someone was rattling away at a piano, giving the impression that he was playing with his feet as well as his hands. Four couples were prancing about in a quadrille, and several elegant and correct young men, who would have looked sufficiently gentlemanly, had not the fatal flaw shown in spite of themselves, were looking on.

The place was reeking with the strong stench of social scum; of upper-crust debauchery, and the decaying mustiness of not-so-high society; of counter-jumpers and corner-boys; of third-rate journalists and moneyed minors; of shady speculators, degenerate pleasure-seekers, and pox-eaten rakes; of a whole dubious mob made up of every variety of the underworld, some on the way up, others on the way out, some hailed in passing, others already beyond the pale, rogues, sneak-thieves, bullies, and sharpers with an assumed air of respectability and a challenging eye which seemed to say, 'If anyone suggests that I'm no better than I should be, I'll knock his block off!'

The air stank of folly, the gutter, and back-room *amours*. All the men and women had their price. There was a diffused atmosphere of sex. On the least excuse a fight was liable to start in defence of some worm-eaten reputation which a sword-thrust or a pistol-shot could only degrade still further.

Every Sunday a few of the local inhabitants were drawn there by curiosity. A few young, very young men, made their first appearance every year. A few idlers came to idle; a few ingenuous youths to go ingenuously astray.

It was well named *La Grenouillère*. Next to the covered raft where drinks were served, and close to the '*Pot-à-Fleurs*', there was a bathing-place. Such of the women as were adequately rounded used it to display their charms and attract clients. Others, less favoured, and with a fatuous air of superiority, though they had amplified their curves with padding, buttressed their bodies with steel, stiffening them here, modifying them there, watched with self-conscious scorn their floundering sisters.

On a small platform a gathering of male bathers was preparing to dive. Tall as hop-poles, round as pumpkins, knobbly as olive-trees, leaning forward or bent backwards by the prominence of their paunches, all of them invariably ugly, they jumped into the water with a deal of splashing which reached the drinkers on the raft.

In spite of the immense and over-arching trees, in spite of the nearness of the water, the heat was suffocating. The reek of spilled liquor, mingled with the smell of human bodies and the fumes of the strong scents with which the pedlars of love were drenched, lay evaporating in the furnace of the sun. But beneath these various odours floated a faint aroma of rice-powder, now vanishing, now reappearing, but never wholly absent, as though some hidden hand had shaken a giant sprinkler in the air.

The real spectacle was on the river, where the incessant coming and going of the boats drew all the gathered eyes. The women lolling in the sterns, facing their strong-wristed male companions, directed contemptuous glances at the other members of their sex who hung about the island in the hope of picking up a free meal.

Now and again, a crew would row past at racing speed and, drawing into the raft, would disembark with noisy chattering. Then, the assembled idlers on the shore, caught up in a momentary fit of madness, would set up a shout.

From round the bend in the direction of Chatou, fresh craft were constantly appearing. They drew nearer, they grew larger, and as soon as those in them were recognized, there was a fresh outburst of cries and calls.

A dinghy with her awning spread, manned by four women, was drifting slowly with the current. The one at the oars was small, slim, and had a wilting look. She was dressed as a sailor and wore her hair done high on her head under a hard boater. Facing her was a plump, flaxen-haired woman wearing trousers and a jacket of white flannel, sprawled on her back upon the floor-boards, with her legs resting on either side of the rower's thwart. She was smoking a cigarette, and at each thrust of the oars her breasts and stomach wobbled. Under the awning, in the stern, two tall, slim, pretty girls, one fair, the other dark, sat with their arms round one another's waist, their eyes unwinkingly fixed upon their two companions.

A shout rose from *La Grenouillère*—'Here comes Lesbos!', and suddenly the cry was taken up in a wild clamour. A fearful pushing and shoving ensued. Glasses crashed to the ground; people clambered on the tables, shouting in the frenzied din: 'Lesbos! Lesbos! Lesbos!' The noise echoed and reverberated, grew indistinct, was soon no more than a hideous, formless din, then, on a sudden, shot up once again, rose in the air, covered the expanses of the plain, filled the dense foliage of the trees, spread to the distant hillsides, and seemed to mount until it reached the sun.

The girl at the oars seemed unperturbed by this ovation, and calmly stopped her rowing. The plump blonde stretched at the bottom of the boat, raised herself on her elbows and looked around her with a listless air. The two pretty girls in the stern began to giggle and waved their hands to the applauding crowd. At that, the noise redoubled, till the floating café rocked and trembled. Men waved their hats and women fluttered handkerchiefs. All the voices, shrill and deep alike, took up the cry of 'Lesbos!' It was as though the whole corrupt gang were greeting an acknowledged leader, like a naval squadron firing a salute of guns as the admiral steams by.

The numerous fleet of river-craft acclaimed in turn the female boatload, as it resumed its sleepy way and drew into the bank a little further on.

Unlike the others, Monsieur Paul had taken a key from his pocket, and into this he blew with the full force of his lungs, producing a shrill whistle. His mistress, whose face had gone dead-white and her body tense, clutched at his arm in an attempt to stop him, and this time there was a blaze of fury in the eyes she turned on him. He, for his part, seemed to be worked up to a high pitch of exasperation, inspired, perhaps, by an access of male jealousy, by a deep-seated, confused, instinctive fury. When he spoke, his lips were trembling:

'It's perfectly loathsome! They ought to be thrown into the water with stones round their necks, like bitch-pups!'

At that, Madeleine quite suddenly flew into a passion. Her voice was harsh and shrill, and words poured from her lips as though she were pleading in her own defence:

'What business is it of yours? They're free, aren't they, to do as they like, without having to give an account to anybody? Stop behaving like a young hooligan, and stop poking your nose in where it doesn't belong!'

But he broke in on her:

'That's for the police to decide! I'll jolly well see they're given a taste of Saint-Lazare!' *

She turned on him like a little spitfire:

'You!'

* *Saint-Lazare was, till 1932, a Reformatory for women. (Translator.)*

48

'Yes, I . . . Meanwhile, I forbid you to speak to them . . . D'you hear? . . . I won't have it!'

She shrugged, and in a quieter voice replied:

'My dear boy, I shall do exactly as I please. If you don't like it you can lump it, and clear off—the sooner the better! After all, I'm not your wife, so pipe down!'

He said no more, and they sat there glaring at one another, with set faces, and breathing hard.

At the far end of the huge wooden construction, the four women were making an almost theatrical entry. The two in men's clothes led the way. The thin one had the appearance of a wizened little boy. There were yellowish patches on her temples. The other, her flabby body packed tightly into her flannel suit, her great bottom distending the seat of her wide trousers, looked, for all the world, like a fat goose, as she waddled along with her enormous thighs and her turned-in knees. The other two followed behind, and a crowd of oarsmen pressed forward to shake them by the hand.

They had rented a small chalet at the water's edge, and there they lived like two married couples.

Their vice was openly flaunted, acknowledged, obvious. It was talked about as something perfectly natural, and this, somehow, gave them an endearing quality. There were whispered stories of strange dramas born of fierce feminine jealousies, and of secret visits paid to the little riverside house by a number of well-known women—actresses for the most part.

One of their neighbours, provoked by all this scandalous gossip, had informed the police, and a sergeant, accompanied by a constable, had gone round to investigate. Their mission was one of considerable delicacy, since no charge could be preferred against the tenants, who were certainly not prostitutes. The sergeant was at his wits' end, the more so since he did not even know the nature of their suspected misdemeanour. He questioned them in a haphazard fashion, and eventually turned in a monumental report establishing their innocence.

The laughter caused by this incident had spread as far as Saint-Germain.

They were now making a mincing perambulation of the restaurant, like visiting royalty. They seemed to take a pride in their notoriety, pleased to be so stared at, to feel their own superiority to this crowd, this rabble, this plebeian mob.

Madeleine and her lover watched their slow approach. There was a smouldering flame in the girl's eye.

When the leading couple reached the end of their table, she called out, 'Pauline!' The fat woman turned her head, and stopped, still holding the female ship's-boy by the arm.

'Why, Madeleine! . . . Come and talk to me, darling!'

Paul tightened his grip on his mistress's wrist, but the air with which she said, 'You'd better keep out of this!' had the effect of silencing him, and he stayed where he was, alone.

The three women were standing in a group, chatting gaily in low voices. From time to time, Madeleine shot a furtive glance at Paul, accompanied by a sly and spiteful laugh.

At last he could bear it no longer, but jumped to his feet, and in a moment was beside her, trembling violently. He gripped her shoulders 'You are to come with me! I have forbidden you to have anything to do with these—these horrors!'

But Pauline, raising her voice, let him have the benefit of her fishwife's vocabulary full in the face. There was an outburst of laughter round them. People pressed forward, standing on tip-toe to get a better view, and the young man stood rooted to the spot under the storm of filthy abuse. He felt as much dirtied by the words as though he were being pelted with garbage and, to avoid the mounting scandal, turned away and leaned for a while on the balustrade, looking at the river, with his back to his triumphant tormentors.

And there he stayed, occasionally, with a quick, snatching movement of the hand, flicking away a tear which had formed in the corner of his eye.

The truth of the matter was that he was madly in love, without knowing why, in spite of his refined instincts, in spite of reason, in spite, even, of his will. He had stumbled into this passion as a man might stumble into a muddy pot-hole. Tender-hearted and fastidious by nature, he had dreamed of an exquisite, ideal, and thrilling experience, and now he was bound, hand and foot, body and soul, to this grasshopper in woman's flesh, who was really like every other girl, exasperatingly stupid, waspish, skinny, and not really pretty. He was held prisoner by that mysterious, all-powerful, female enchantment, that prodigious, inexplicable domination of the flesh, born of none knows what, which can fling a man, no matter how intelligent, at the feet of any nondescript young woman with nothing in her to explain so fatal and so sovereign a power.

He could feel that, behind him, something unspeakably vile was going on. He could hear the laughter, and it tore at his heart. What should he do? He knew, but could not do it.

Paul's Mistress

He stood staring at a fisherman sitting motionless with his rod upon the further bank.

Suddenly, the man jerked at his line. There was a small silver fish flickering at the end of it. He tried to get the hook out, twisting it this way and that, but in vain. At last, worked into a frenzy of impatience, he began to tug, and finally tore out the whole of the creature's throat, with a bundle of guts attached. Paul was seized with a fit of trembling. It was as though he, too, had been ripped open to his very heart. That hook, he felt, was the true symbol of his love. If he must tear it out, then everything within his breast would come out with it, hooked to a deeply embedded, crooked piece of iron, tied to the end of a line. And that line was Madeleine.

He felt a hand upon his shoulder, and gave a start. Turning his head, he saw his mistress there beside him. They neither of them spoke a word, and she, like him, leaned on the balustrade and stared into the river.

He tried to think of something to say, but could find nothing. He could not straighten out the tangle in his mind, the confusion in his feelings. All he was aware of was the joy of having her there with him. He was conscious of a shamefaced cowardice, a longing to forgive her everything, to acquiesce in everything, if only she would never more abandon him.

After a few moments, he asked her, very softly, 'Shall we go? It will be nicer in the boat.'

'Yes, my sweet,' she said.

He helped her into the skiff, supporting her body, holding both her hands in his, all gentleness now, but with a few tears standing in his eyes. She looked at him with a smile, and they kissed again.

Then they moved away upstream, very quietly, skirting the willows on the bank basking in the heat of the afternoon.

It was barely six o'clock when they reached the Grillon restaurant. Leaving the boat, they set off on foot across the island, in the direction of Bezons, through the fields which lay behind the screen of poplars on the river-bank.

The tall grass, as yet unscythed, was thick with flowers. The sinking sun spread a carpet of russet light and, in the diminished heat of the day's end, the floating exhalations of the hay were mingled with the damp smell of the river. The air was impregnated with a gentle languor, with an ethereal happiness which lay upon the scene like a light mist of contentment.

A swooning weakness came upon their hearts. They felt at one with the calm splendour of the evening, with the vague, mysterious

51

quiver of expanding life, with the melancholy, searching poetry of growing things revealed to human hearts at this quiet and silent hour.

All this he could feel, but to her it meant nothing. They walked on side by side, and, suddenly, sick of saying nothing, she began to sing. In her thin little tuneless voice she sang a popular song of the streets, a tawdry thing remembered, and the sound cut sharply across the deep, harmonious stillness of the dusk.

He looked at her, and felt an unbridgeable abyss between them. She struck at the grasses with her parasol, her head a little drooping, her eyes on her feet, and continued with her singing, making a skein of sounds, attempting little flourishes and venturing on trills. That narrow little head of hers which he so much loved was empty, empty, with nothing in it but this meaningless tune, and such thoughts as happened to take shape in it, were like the music. She did not begin to understand him. They were further apart than if they had not lived together. Did her kisses never go further than her lips?

And then, she looked at him again and smiled. Stirred in his deepest being, he spread his arms in a renewed upsurge of passion, and held her tight.

Because he was crumpling her dress, she broke from his embrace, murmuring, to make amends: 'I really am very fond of you, my sweet.'

But he caught her round the waist and, in a frenzy of madness, broke into a run, dragging her behind him. He kissed her on the cheeks, the temples, and the neck, jumping up and down from sheer happiness. They flung themselves breathless at the foot of a bush ablaze with the beams of the setting sun, and, without pausing to take breath, they made love together there, though she completely failed to understand his state of exaltation.

They were on their way back, hand in hand, when suddenly, through the trees, they saw the dinghy with its load of women. The fat Pauline saw them too, for she sat up and blew kisses to Madeleine. Then, she called across the water: 'Till tonight!'

And Madeleine cried back, 'Till tonight!' Paul on a sudden felt as though his heart had turned to ice.

They went on their way to dinner. Under a leafy tunnel at the water's edge, they ate in silence. When darkness fell, the waiter brought them a candle enclosed in a glass globe, which gave a feeble, flickering light. From where they were sitting they could hear the explosive cries of boating parties in the big room overhead.

Towards the end of the meal, Paul, taking Madeleine's hand in his, said:

'Darling, I am feeling very tired; what would you say to going early to bed?'

But she saw through the trick, and gave him one of those enigmatic and perfidious looks which show so quickly in a woman's eyes. After a moment's pause, she answered: 'You must do as you please, but I have promised to be at the *Grenouillère* dance.'

The smile with which he answered her was heartbreaking, one of those smiles which hide a rending pain, and his voice was sad though loving: 'If you were really fond of me, we'd stay here, just the two of us.' Without opening her lips, she said 'no' with a movement of the head. He was insistent: 'Please, please, my pettikins.' At that she broke in roughly: 'You heard what I said. There's the door. Go to bed if you like; no one's stopping you! I have promised, and I mean to keep my promise!'

He put his two elbows on the table, framed his face in his hands, and sat there, miserably brooding.

The boating folk came down, still chattering loudly, and set off in their skiffs for the dance at *La Grenouillère*.

Madeleine said to Paul: 'You'd better make up your mind whether you are coming or not. If you aren't, I shall ask one of these gentlemen to be my escort.'

Paul got up. 'Let us go,' he said in a low voice.

And they went.

The night was dark and full of stars. The air was hot and heavy with suppressed sensuality and a sense of fermentation, of vegetable growth, which made the breeze feel stagnant. It touched their faces with a warm caress and made them breathe more quickly, almost pant, so dense and laden did it seem.

The skiffs got under way, each with a paper lantern at the prow. It was impossible to see the craft, only the coloured lights moving quickly, and dancing on the water, like frantic fireflies. Voices sounded in the darkness.

The boat with the two young people, moved smoothly on. Sometimes, when another passed by at speed, they could suddenly make out the white back of the oarsman, lit by his lantern.

As soon as they had rounded the bend, *La Grenouillère* appeared far off. It was dressed for festival, adorned with clusters of lights, with garlands of coloured lamps, bunches of brilliance. Several heavy punts were moving slowly on the Seine, with elaborate domes and pyramids, complicated erections outlined in lights of different colours. Flickering festoons drooped to the river, and, here and there, a lantern, red or blue, at the end of an immense, invisible fishing-rod, looked like a dangling star.

All this illumination spread a glow around the restaurant, lighting from top to bottom the great trees upon the banks, their trunks showing pale grey, their leaves a milky white, against the deep blackness of the over-arching sky.

The orchestra, consisting of five local musicians, cast far and wide its thin and jigging tunes. Madeleine began to sing again.

She wanted to go at once to the dance-floor. Paul wished to take a saunter through the island first, but had to yield to her insistence.

The crowd of onlookers was, by this time, much thinned out. Only the owners of the boats remained, with a sprinkling of solid citizens, and, here and there, a few young men with girls upon their arms. The director and organizer of this noisy entertainment was trying to look dignified in a shabby dress-coat. But his ravaged face betrayed the purveyor of cheap public pleasure.

The fat Pauline and her companions were nowhere to be seen, and Paul breathed freely once again.

Dancing began. The couples, face to face, cut extravagant capers, kicking their legs high in the air under the very noses of their partners.

The women, as though their limbs were double-jointed, flung themselves about, leaping in a swirl of skirts, revealing all their underclothing, kicking above their heads with most surprising ease, wriggling their stomachs, waggling their bottoms, shaking their breasts, and spreading all around a strong smell of sweating female flesh.

The men squatted like toads, making obscene gestures, writhing, grimacing, hideous, turning cartwheels on their hands, deliberately clowning, mincing with a sort of fantastic and farcical elegance.

A stout maid and two waiters were busy serving drinks.

Since this floating establishment had only a roof and no walls to screen it from outside, the wild, dishevelled dancing showed against a background of peaceful darkness, and a sky powdered with stars.

Suddenly, Mont-Valérien opposite stood out as bright as day, as though a great blazing fire had been lit behind it. The glow spread, grew more intense, and slowly took possession of the sky, describing a pale, white, luminous circle. Then a reddish object appeared, grew bigger, and glowed like red-hot iron upon an anvil. It became gradually rounder, seeming to emerge from the ground, and the

moon, breaking free of the horizon, rose gently into space. The higher it climbed the fainter grew its colour of hot red, turning first to yellow, warm to begin with, then lighter and more dazzling, and the planet, as its distance increased, seemed to diminish in size.

Paul's eyes were, for a long time, fixed on it, and, lost in contemplation, he forgot his mistress. When he turned round again, she had gone.

He searched, but could not find her. He raked the tables with an anxious eye, went here, there, and everywhere without a pause, questioning now one and now another. Nobody had seen her.

Thus was he wandering, a martyr to uneasiness, when one of the waiters said to him: 'If you're looking for Mademoiselle Madeleine, she has just left with Madame Pauline.' At that very moment he caught sight of the ship's-boy, and the two pretty girls, standing at the far end of the room, their arms round one another's waist, watching him and whispering.

He understood, and dashed off into the recesses of the island like a madman.

He ran at first towards Chatou, but, just as he was coming into the open, stopped and retraced his steps. He began to search the wooded secrecies, to wander here and there distractedly, pausing now and again to listen. All over the wide scene the toads were uttering their brief, metallic note.

Over by Bougival some bird he could not recognize was singing modulations on a scattering of notes. The sound reached him muted by distance. On the wide stretches of the grass the moon shed a soft radiance like powdered cotton-wool. It shone through the leaves and flowed like water over the silvered poplar-trunks, riddling with gleaming rain the quivering tops of the tall trees. The heady poetry of this summer night had its effect upon him in spite of himself; it struck deeply through his crazy agony, stirred his heart with a sense of ferocious irony, goading to madness in his gentle and contemplative spirit the need he felt for an ideal tenderness, the longing to pour out his passion of grief upon the breast of an adored and faithful mistress.

So strangled was he by rending, urgent sobs, that he had to stop.

Then, the crisis past, he once again set off.

Suddenly he felt as though a knife had been thrust into his heart. Behind a bush he saw two figures locked in an embrace. He ran towards the spot. But, at the sound of his approach the lovers quickly moved away, still clasped, still kissing as they walked.

He dared not call, knowing only too well that she would not reply. He was overcome by the dread of seeing who they were.

The recurrent measure of a far quadrille, the blaring solo of a cornet, the hollow laughter of a flute, the shrill frenzy of a violin, tore at his heart and set an edge upon his sufferings. The wild and limping music tripped here and there beneath the trees, now muted, now increased by a passing puff of wind.

On a sudden he told himself that perhaps she had come back. Yes, that was it: why should she not? He had lost his head for no reason, had been stupidly carried away by his fears, by the undisciplined suspicions which, for some time now, had had possession of him.

In one of those strange interludes of calmness which sometimes come to even the worst despair, he walked back towards the dance.

He took the room in at a single glance. She was not there. He made the round of the tables and, with a shock, found himself once more face to face with the three women. Despair must have given him a strange and comic look, for all at once they burst out laughing.

He ran for safety, plunged again into the tangle of the island, panting as he went. Then he paused to listen, and stood for a long while thus, for there was a humming in his ears. But, at last, he thought he heard ahead of him a little shrill of laughter with which he was familiar. Quietly he moved forward on his hands and knees, parting the branches with his hands. His heart was pounding so heavily that he could scarcely breathe.

There was a murmur of two voices, but he could not hear what they were saying. Then they fell silent.

He felt an urgent longing to run away, *not* to see, *not* to know, to escape for ever from the wild passion which had him in its grip. He would go back to Chatou, take the train, never to return, never to see her again. But the picture of her rose sharply before his eyes, of her as she looked on waking in their warm bed, snuggling up against him like a kitten, throwing her arms about his neck, her hair a wild disorder, her eyes still shut, her lips half parted for the first kiss of the day. And the sudden memory filled him with a frenzy of regret, a madness of desire.

Again the sound of voices reached him and, bent double, he went towards it. Then a faint cry came from underneath the branches close to him. A cry! One of those cries of love which he had come to know in the wild moments of their passion. He crawled still

further forward, as though drawn irresistibly, conscious of nothing
. . . and then, he saw them.

If only it had been a man with her! Not this! Not this! Their very
infamy was like a chain holding him prisoner. And there he stayed,
struck down, appalled. It was as though he had, unaware, stumbled
on the mutilated corpse of the woman he loved . . . a crime against
nature . . . a monstrous thing . . . profanation unspeakable.

And then, unsought, the memory came to him of the little fish
with its guts torn out . . . But Madeleine was murmuring 'Pauline!'
in the same tone of passion as she had used to murmur 'Paul!' And
so frightful was his pang of agony that he turned and ran as hard
as he could go.

He twice collided with a tree, tripped over a root, and then ran
on. Suddenly he found himself upon the river-bank, that arm of
the river where the current is swift. It showed clearly under the
moon. The seething water was lashed into eddies on which the
moonlight played. The high bank overhung the water like a cliff, at
the foot of which lay a broad band of darkness where the currents
swirled and joined.

On the further bank the country houses terracing the heights of
Croissy gleamed in the full bright light.

Paul saw it all as in a dream, as through the mists of memory.
He thought of nothing, understood nothing, and all things, even
his own existence, had a vague and insubstantial reality, seemed far
away, forgotten.

There was the river. Did he realize what he was doing? Did he
truly want to die? He was mad. Yet, he turned back towards the
island, back to her and, in the stillness of the night, broken only by
the far, the muted, the persistent music of the dance, he cried aloud
in a high-pitched, scarcely human voice, one single, terrible word:
'Madeleine!'

It drove through the wide silence of the night, and echoed back
from all the distant hills.

Then, with a tremendous leap, the leap of a beast at bay, he
plunged into the river. The water swirled where he had struck it,
and then closed over him. From the spot where he had vanished
wide circles spread until they reached the further bank, their
ripples shimmering in the moonlight.

The two women heard the cry. Madeleine sat up. 'That was Paul!'
A suspicion stirred in her. 'He has drowned himself,' she said. She
hurried to the river, followed by the fat Pauline.

A heavy boat with two men in it was circling the spot. One was rowing, the other apparently hunting for something in the water with a long pole. 'What are you doing?' cried Pauline. 'What has happened?' A strange voice answered: 'A man's just drowned himself.'

The two women pressed close to one another, their faces drawn and tense. They were following with their eyes the movements of the boat. The music from *La Grenouillère* sounded a soft and distant gaiety. Its cadences seemed to marry with the probing of the men. The river, which now concealed a corpse, swirled and eddied under the moon.

The search went on and on. The horrible time of waiting made Madeleine shiver. At last, after half an hour at least, one of the men called out 'Got him!' Very gently he raised his long gaff. Something bulky broke the surface of the water. The other shipped his oars, and together they hauled in the lifeless mass and tumbled it into the bottom of the boat.

Then they moved into the bank, seeking a well-lit and level landing-place. Just as they stepped ashore the women came up with them.

When she saw the object at her feet, Madeleine recoiled in horror. Under the light of the moon, his face had already a greenish look. His mouth, his eyes, his clothes were slimy with mud. His clenched and rigid fingers were horrible to see. A sort of blackish liquid covered all his body. His face was swollen, and from his mud-caked hair dirty water was oozing.

The two men examined him.

'Recognize him?' asked one.

The other, who was the Croissy ferryman, had a moment's hesitation. 'I think I seed that face afore but 'tis not easy to make out the features.' Then, suddenly, 'Why, o' course, 'tis Monsieur Paul!'

'Who's Monsieur Paul?' said his companion.

'Why, Monsieur Paul Baron, the senator's son, the young fellow as was so much in love!'

The other observed philosophically: 'Well, his fun's over now: a pity, all the same, when one is rich.'

Madeleine had fallen to the ground and lay there sobbing. Pauline walked over to the body, and said: 'Are you sure he's dead?'

The two men shrugged: 'Not much doubt about it after all that time.'

Then, one of them asked: 'Staying at Grillon's place, wasn't he?'

'Yes,' said the other. 'Better take him back there: they'll have a bit fire.'

Paul's Mistress

They returned to their boat and got it under way, moving slowly because of the strong current. Long after they had disappeared from sight, the regular sound of the oars could still be heard.

Then Pauline took the weeping Madeleine in her arms, fondled her, embraced her, and spoke words of consolation. 'It wasn't your fault, was it? No one can stop men from making fools of themselves. This is what he wanted, and so much the worse for him!' Then, pulling her to her feet: 'Come, darling,' she said. 'You can stay with us. You can't go back to the Grillons' place tonight.' Once more she kissed her: 'You see,' she said. 'We'll soon have you all right again.'

Madeleine scrambled to her feet, still crying. But her sobs were less violent now, and she laid her head on Pauline's shoulder. As though taking refuge in a tenderness closer, more intimate and more assured, she slowly walked away.

(1881, or earlier)

The Story of a Farm-Girl

As the weather was very fine, the farm-hands had finished their meal more quickly than usual, and had made off into the fields.

Rose, who did the work of the house, was left alone in the huge kitchen, where the last embers were slowly dying out under the cauldron of hot water. Every now and again she drew some off and slowly washed the crockery, occasionally pausing to look at the two square patches of light which the sun, shining through the window, imprinted on the long table, with all the faults in the glass plainly shown.

Three adventurous chickens were pecking about for crumbs under the chairs. Farmyard smells and waves of warm air from the cowsheds came in through the open door, and in the silence of the blazing noon, the crowing of the cocks was clearly audible.

When the girl had finished her task, wiped the table, cleaned up the hearth, and arranged the plates on the tall dresser at the far end of the room next to the loudly ticking clock in its wooden case, she paused for breath. She felt faintly dizzy as though a weight were pressing on her, though why she should have this sensation she did not know. She looked at the grimy plaster on the walls, at the smoke-blackened beams in the ceiling from which cobwebs, dried herrings, and strings of onions were hanging. Then she sat down, overcome by the accumulated smells which the heat drew from the earth floor: the varied smells of all the things which had been spilled on it over the years and left to dry. With them was mingled that of the milk creaming in the cool dairy next door. She had meant to do some sewing, as usual, but somehow she felt too weak, and went instead to get a breath of fresh air at the door.

There, stroked by the sunlight, she felt a soft warmth about her heart, and a sense of physical well-being coursing through her legs and arms.

Just opposite, a thin, shimmering haze was rising from the dung-heap. Hens were squatting on it, doing a little scrabbling for worms with one claw, and, in the middle of them, strutted a cock in all his pride. He kept picking out one or other of them, and moving round her with a little clucking call. The object of his choice got up with a bored air and submitted to his attentions without the slightest show of excitement, subsiding on the ground and taking his weight upon her outspread wings. Then, she shook the dust from her feathers, and resumed her former position on the dung-heap, while he crowed loudly, enumerating his triumphs, and all the cocks in all the yards crowed back, as though issuing their challenges, from farm to farm, to tournaments of love.

Rose looked at them without a thought in her head, then raised her eyes and was dazzled by the powdery splendour of the blossom on the apple-trees.

Suddenly, a young colt, bubbling over with the joy of life, galloped past her. Twice he made the round of the tree-lined ditches, then came to a sudden stop as though surprised to find himself alone.

She, too, felt a longing to run, to make some movement, but also a strong desire to stretch her legs out in the warm, still air, and rest. She took a few hesitating steps, shutting her eyes, filled with a sense of animal contentment, and then, quite calmly, went to look for eggs in the hen-roost. There were thirteen of them, and these she took and carried to the house. When they were ranged upon the dresser, the kitchen smells got the better of her again, and she went back into the open, to sit for a while upon the grass.

The farm-yard in its circle of trees seemed to be sleeping. The high grass, from which the yellow dandelions shone out like spots of light, was of a vivid green—the new, fresh green of spring. The shadows of the apple-trees lay in tight little circles at their feet, and the thatched roofs of the farm buildings, on which grew irises with sword-like leaves, were faintly smoking, as though the dampness of the barns and byres were seeping through the straw.

She reached the open shed where stood the carts and traps. There, in the ditch, was a deep green hole filled to the brink with violets, the scent of which spread all around. From the top of the bank a wide stretch of country was visible, a stretching plain of growing crops, with, here and there, a clump of trees, and scattered groups of distant workers like dolls, horses like toys, pulling a child's plough with a man behind it no bigger than a finger.

She fetched a bundle of straw from one of the barns, threw it into the hole, and sat herself down. Then, not feeling altogether comfortable, she undid the bundle, spread out a bed of straw, and lay there on her back, with her arms behind her head, and her legs stretched out before her.

Slowly her eyelids drooped, and she lay wrapped in a delicious lassitude. She was just about to drop off to sleep when two hands closed over her breasts, and she sat up sharply. It was Jacques, the farm-lad, a hulking great fellow from Picardy, who had been making up to her for some time past. He happened, that day, to have been working in the sheep-fold, and, seeing her lie down in the shade, had tip-toed over to her, holding his breath. His eyes were shining, and he had bits of straw in his hair.

He tried to kiss her, but she was as strong as he was, and smacked his face. Realizing that cunning, rather than brute strength, would best serve his purpose, he begged her pardon. They sat together, side by side, chatting in friendly fashion. They agreed that the harvest looked like being good, that the year had begun well, that the old man was not a bad sort. They talked about the neighbours and the place, about their native villages, their childhood, and the parents they had left so long ago and would, perhaps, not see again. Thinking of those days, she grew maudlin, and he, having only one idea in his head, crept closer, rubbed against her, trembling with, absorbed by, his desire. She said:

''Tis a long time since I saw my mum. To be so long apart is hard.'

And she gazed, unseeing, into the distance, across the many miles which lay between her and the village she had left, far away to the north.

All of a sudden, he flung his arm about her neck and snatched a kiss. With her clenched fist she struck him full in the face, so violently that his nose began to bleed. He got up to lean his head against a tree. Overcome with remorse, she went across to where he was standing, and said:

'Do it hurt much?'

He burst out laughing. It was nothing, really and truly. It was only that she had got him bang in the middle of the face. 'Little spitfire!' he muttered, and gave her an admiring glance. Quite suddenly he felt respect for her, and an affection different from what had gone before, the beginning of genuine love for this solid, powerful piece of womanhood. When the blood had stopped flowing, he suggested they should take a walk. He feared her fist if they should stay there side by side. Unprompted, she took his arm, and they walked together down the avenue like an engaged couple out for an evening stroll.

'You didn't ought to treat me so disrespectful like, really you didn't, Jacques,' she said.

The Story of a Farm-Girl

He protested that that wasn't what he had meant. It was just that he was in love with her.

'So, 'tis marriage you mean?' she asked.

He hesitated, then gave her a sidelong look, while she, for her part, stared before her, seeing nothing. She had plump, red cheeks, a full, protuberant bust under her loose cotton jacket. Her lips were thick and moist, and the upper part of her breast, which showed bare above her bodice, was beaded with small drops of sweat. His longing for her grew strong in him again, and he murmured in her ear:

'Yes, 'deed it is.'

At that she flung her arms about his neck, and held him tight so long that both of them could scarcely breathe.

From that moment, the tale of love, which never varies, began between them. They dallied in corners, they arranged moonlit meetings in the shelter of convenient hay-ricks, and, at meal-times, they kicked one another black and blue with their heavy clogs, beneath the table.

Then, gradually, Jacques began to show signs of getting bored with her. He went out of his way to avoid her, they spoke but little, and no longer planned and plotted the former lovers' meetings. She felt an uneasy doubt: she grew glum and melancholy, and it was not long before she realized that she was pregnant.

At first she was appalled, but soon dismay gave place to anger, and every day her anger grew because of the way in which he now avoided her.

At last, one night, when everyone was sleeping, she slipped out noiselessly. Bare-footed and in her petticoat, she crossed the yard and pushed open the door of the stable where Jacques slept in a large box, filled with straw, over his horses. When he heard her he pretended to be snoring. But she pulled herself up beside him, and, kneeling in the straw, shook him until he was forced to sit up.

Then, when he mumbled, 'What d'you want?' she said between clenched teeth and trembling with fury: ' 'Tis marriage I want: you promised, and you mun make an honest woman of me!'

At that he burst out laughing, and replied:

'If a man mun marry all the girls a's tumbled with, there'd be no end!'

She took him by the throat and flung him on his back so that he could not break free from her stranglehold, and shouted full in his face: 'I'm in t' family way, d'you hear? And you mun marry me.'

65

He gasped and spluttered, and there they stayed speechless and without moving in the dark silence broken only by the champing of a horse pulling hay from its manger, and munching it.

When Jacques realized that she had got the upper hand, he stammered out:

'If that's how 'tis then, I'll marry 'ee.'

But she no longer trusted to his promises:

'You mun have the banns put up at once,' she said.

'That I will.'

'Swear by God!'

For a few seconds he hesitated, then making the best of a bad job, answered her:

'I swear by God!'

Then she relaxed her grip, and left him, without another word.

It was some days before she had a chance to speak with him. He kept the door of the stables locked each night, and she dared not make a noise, for fear of scandal.

And then, one morning, she saw a stranger at the midday meal.

'Has Jacques gone away?' she asked him.

'Why yes, I've took his place.'

She was trembling so violently that she could not take the stewpot from the hook. But later on, when everyone was back again at work, she went to her room and cried into the pillow so as not to be heard.

She tried to find out what had happened, but in such a way as not to arouse suspicion: yet, so obsessed was she by the thought of her misfortune that she was convinced that those she questioned were sniggering behind her back. The only satisfaction she could get was to be told that he had left the district.

PART II

Life for her, now, was one unceasing torment. She worked like a machine, paying not the least attention to what she was doing. She had but one thought in her head: 'Supposing it gets known!'

This constant brooding made it impossible for her to concentrate. She could not even think out ways of avoiding the scandal which she felt was bound to come. With every day that passed, it crept nearer, as certain, as unavoidable as death.

Each morning she was up before the others, and, with a desperate doggedness, tried to see her shape in the tiny scrap of broken looking-glass she used for tidying her hair, so eager was she to know whether the moment had come when all those on the farm would tumble to the truth.

All day long she kept pausing in her work, looking herself over to make sure her swollen belly was not already visible beneath her smock.

In this way months went by. She scarcely spoke at all, and, if anybody put a question to her, failed to grasp its meaning. There was a dazed and frightened look in her eyes, and her hands were trembling so badly that her master said to her:

'How stupid you've been lately, girl!'

In church she hid behind a pillar and dared not go to confession, for she dreaded a meeting with the curé, to whom she attributed a superhuman power of reading consciences.

At meals, the glances of the others made her nearly faint with terror, and, in particular, she felt convinced that her secret would be discovered by the cowherd, a small, precocious boy with a glittering eye, who never left her side.

One morning, the postman brought her a letter. It was the first that she had ever had, and she had to sit down to get over the shock. Perhaps it was from him! But, since she could not read, she sat trembling with anxiety, looking at the sheet of paper covered with black marks. She put it in her pocket, not daring to confide in anyone. Frequently she stopped in her work to take a peep at the neatly spaced lines and the signature beneath them, vaguely hoping that their meaning might be suddenly revealed to her. At last, half-mad with anxiety and impatience, she went to see the village schoolmaster who told her to sit down, and read as follows:

'MY DEAR DAUGHTER: This is to tell you as I am very bad. Our neighbour, lawyer Dentu, has took his pen in hand for to tell you to come if you can.

For your loving mother,

(Sgd.) CÉSAIRE DENTU,
Deputy Mayor.'

She went away without a word, and, as soon as she was alone, collapsed beside the road. There she lay till nightfall.

When, at last, she reached the farm, she broke the bad news to her master, who told her she could be away as long as she liked. He would get a daily girl, he said, to do her work, and would take her back when she returned.

Her mother was at her last gasp, and died on the very day of her arrival. Next morning Rose was brought to bed of a seven-months' child, a hideous little skeleton of a creature, so thin that it gave one the shudders to look at him. From the way he clenched his poor little fleshless hands, like crab's claws, he appeared to be continually suffering.

All the same, he lived.

She explained that she was married, but could not take charge of the baby, and she left it with some neighbours who promised to look after it.

Then, she went back to the farm.

For a long time her heart had been bruised and battered, but now there was born in it, like the sun at dawn, a feeling of love for the sickly scrap of humanity she had left behind, which was unlike anything that she had ever known till then. But even this was a new cause of pain to her, for it nagged at her at every hour and minute of the day.

What most tormented her was a mad longing to fondle him, to take him in her arms, to feel against her flesh the warmth of his tiny body. She could not sleep at night, and all day long she thought of him. In the evening, when her work was done, she sat by the fire, staring into the flames, lost in a daydream.

She began to be talked about, and there were jokes soon flying round. Who was this unknown lover of hers? Was he handsome, she was asked? Was he rich? When was the marriage to be, and how soon would there be a christening? Then, she would run away and cry in secret, for the questions were like pins in her flesh.

She tried to find relief in work, and, thinking always of her child, sought out ways of making money for him.

She determined to work so hard that her master would be compelled to raise her wages.

Little by little, she took charge of everything, and even had one of the other girls turned off because there was now no need for her. She saved money on the candles, on the corn which she decided was being thrown too freely to the fowls, and on the fodder for the livestock. She came to be as miserly with her master's money as though it had been her own, and, by striking good bargains, managed to get a good price for the produce of the farm, and never allowed herself to be taken in by any peasants who had things to sell. In such matters her word was law. She oversaw the hired men, and had charge of the household accounts. In next to no time she had become indispensable. So careful an eye did she keep on everything, that the farm, under her direction, became more and more prosperous. 'Old Vallin's girl' was soon the talk of the neighbourhood, and her master never grew tired of saying: 'Worth her weight in gold to me, she is.'

Time passed, and her wages were unchanged. The tremendous amount of work she did was accepted by her employer as something to be expected of any loyal servant, and she began to realize, not without bitterness, that though the farmer, thanks to her, was putting by an extra fifty or hundred crowns a month, she was still getting only her 250 francs a year, not a penny more, not a penny less.

She decided to ask for a rise. Three times she sought an interview with her master, but, as soon as she found herself in his presence, talked of other things. She felt shy about raising the question of her wages, as though there were something shameful in doing so. But, at last, one day, when the farmer was eating alone in the kitchen, she said, with obvious embarrassment, that there was something rather special she wanted to ask him. He looked at her in some surprise, with his two hands on the table, one holding his knife, point upward, the other a piece of bread. She grew restive under his concentrated gaze and asked if she could have a week's holiday, seeing as she wasn't feeling quite herself.

He agreed at once, and then, embarrassed in his turn, added:

'And there be summat as *I* wants to talk about when you gets back.'

PART III

The child was close on eight months old and did not recognize her. He had become pink, chubby, and dimpled, a little lump of animated fat. His fingers had little rolls of flesh between them, and he wriggled them delightedly. In a sudden access of animal passion she flung herself upon him, as on a prey, and hugged him so hard that he began to howl with terror. Then she, too, began to cry because he did not know her, but reached out his hands to his foster-mother as soon as he caught sight of her.

But by next day he had grown accustomed to her face, and chortled when she came to him. She took him out into the fields, ran about like a mad creature, holding him in her outstretched hands, and sat with him in the shade of the trees. Then, for the first time in her life, and though he could not understand a word, she opened her heart to another, telling him about her sorrows and her work, her fears and hopes, and wore him out with the violent hunger of her kisses.

F   *69*

She found a never-ending pleasure in rubbing him down, washing him, and putting on his clothes. She even enjoyed wiping him when he made a mess, as though these intimate tasks confirmed her in her motherhood. She never tired of looking at him, nor could she get over the wonderful fact that he was hers. As she danced him in her arms, she would say in a low voice, over and over again: 'Thee's my own little man! My own little man!'

She cried all the way back to the farm. No sooner had she got there than her master sent for her. She obeyed the summons with no little surprise, and, in spite of herself, feeling very nervous, though she did not know why.

'Sit down,' he said.

She did as she was told. For several moments they stayed like that, side by side, both embarrassed, both uncomfortably conscious of their idle hands, not looking at one another, for all the world like a couple of yokels.

The farmer, a stout man of forty-five and twice a widower, was jovial and headstrong. He was quite obviously feeling awkward, an unusual thing with him. At last he seemed to have made up his mind, and began to talk in a rather vague sort of way, mumbling his words, and looking out of the window all the while.

'Rose,' he said, 'have thee ever thought o' settling down?'

She turned deathly pale, but said nothing, and he went on:

'Thee's a good girl, steady, active, and saving. A wife like you would be the making of any man.'

She still sat motionless, with a frightened look on her face, not even trying to understand his meaning, her head in a whirl, as though some great danger were hanging over her. He waited for a moment, and then spoke again:

'A farm without a mistress, mark'ee, can never be up to much, not even with a servant as good as 'ee be.'

Then he stopped, not knowing what more to say, and Rose sat staring at him with the terrified look of someone convinced he is in the room with a murderer, and ready to make a dash for it if he so much as lifts a finger.

Five minutes passed, and then he said:

'Well, what about it?'

There was a sad expression in her eyes as she replied:

'What about what, master?'

He snapped at her:

'Why, marrying I, damme!'

She straightened up suddenly, then slumped back in her chair as though exhausted, and did not move again. She looked like someone who has been stunned by the news of some great misfortune. The farmer grew impatient:

'What more do 'ee want I to say?'

She stared at him with panic in her face, and twice said, in a choking voice:

'I can't! I can't!'

'Why can't 'ee? Don't 'ee be a little fool! You shall have until tomorrow to think it over.'

He hurried away, much relieved at having got the business off his chest, and feeling sure that, next day, his servant would accept a proposal which was better than she could ever have hoped for. For him, too, it would be an excellent stroke of business, since he would be getting permanent possession of a woman who would certainly be worth more to him than the best marriage portion for miles around.

Nor was he troubled by any feeling that he was marrying beneath him. In a working countryside all are approximately equal. The farmer goes ploughing with his men, and they, as like as not, become masters in their turn. As for servant girls, they are constantly making a match of it with their employers without any change in their habits or their way of life.

That night, Rose did not take her clothes off, but sat down as she was upon her bed. She felt so dead-beat that she had not the strength even to cry. Her condition was one of complete inertia. She was no longer conscious of her body, and felt as scatter-brained as if she had been teased out like wool for mattresses.

Only now and again could she collect some odds and ends of thought, and they made matters worse, because they filled her with a fear of what might happen.

Her terrors increased, and whenever, in the sleeping silence of the night, she heard the clock downstairs slowly ticking off the hours, she broke into a cold sweat. Her brain grew muddled, nightmare followed nightmare in a half wakefulness, and her candle burned itself out. Unreasoning panic gripped her, the sort of panic which gets a hold on country-folk when they believe that an evil spell has been laid upon them and feel a mad longing to get away, to escape, to run before the wind of disaster like a ship in the teeth of a gale.

An owl hooted. In a moment she was wide awake. She passed her fingers over her face and through her hair, then, like someone walking in their sleep, went down the stairs. When she reached the yard, she crouched low so as not to be seen by any furtive haunter of the night, for the moon, on the point of setting, was casting a bright light upon the fields. Instead of opening the gate in the fence, she climbed the bank, and, as soon as she reached open country, set off in a straight line, at an easy, rapid trot. From time to time, unconsciously, she uttered a shrill cry. Her long shadow moved with her, and sometimes a night-bird fluttered round her head. Dogs in the farmyards barked as they heard her pass, and one of them jumped a ditch and pursued her, snapping at her heels. But she turned on it, shrieking so loudly, that it fled in silent terror to the shelter of its kennel.

Occasionally she came upon a family of young hares romping in the grass, but when she reached them in her headlong run, like a distraught Diana, the timid creatures scuttled off, the mother and her young going to ground in a furrow, while the father bolted, as hard as he could go, his long, pricked ears outlined against the orb of the sinking moon now dropping over the edge of the world, casting its level light across the plain like an enormous lantern standing on the ground.

The stars faded into the depths of the sky, a few birds twittered, day was breaking. By this time she was worn out and breathless, and when the sun rose in crimson splendour, she stopped dead.

Her swollen feet refused to go further. She caught sight of a pond, a large pond, in which the stagnant water looked like blood in the red glow of the coming day. She limped slowly towards it, with her hand pressed to her heart, meaning to bathe her legs.

She sat down on a tuft of grass, took off her heavy boots now filled with dust, slipped off her stockings, and plunged her blue legs into the water, to the surface of which an occasional air-bubble rose and burst.

A delicious coolness struck at her feet and moved upwards to her neck, and suddenly, as she stared at the deep expanse of standing water, a sense of giddiness came over her. She felt a mad longing to be swallowed up completely. Good-bye to suffering there, good-bye for ever. She did not think about her child. All she hungered for was peace and utter rest: all she wanted was to sleep and never wake. She stood up, arms lifted, and took two forward steps. She waded in until the water reached to her thighs, and was about to throw herself in, when a series of sharp, burning pricks in her ankles sent her scrambling back to land. She uttered a despairing cry. From knees to feet long black leeches were sucking at her life-blood, clinging to her flesh, and swelling visibly. She dared not touch them, and screamed in horror. The noise she made attracted the attention of a peasant who was passing some way off with a cart. He came to her and pulled the leeches off, one by one, dressed the wounds with leaves, and drove her back to her master's farm.

She kept her bed for a fortnight, and, on the morning when she left it for the first time, was sitting by the house-door, when suddenly the farmer came and stood before her.

'Well,' he said: 'everything fixed between us now?'

At first she said nothing, then, since he made no movement, but stood staring at her with unblinking eyes, she managed to find her tongue.

'No, master, no; I can't do it.'

At once he flew into a temper:

'Can't, my girl, can't? And why the devil not?'

She began to cry, and said again:

'I can't.'

He stared, and shouted in her face:

'Maybe you got a lover, eh?'

She stammered, trembling with shame:

'Maybe.'

His face was red as a poppy: he was spluttering with rage.

'So that's it, you slut! Tell me who the fellow is! A penniless, half-starved scallywag, I'll be bound. Who is it? Come on, tell me!'

And, since she uttered not a word, he said:

'So, you won't! Well, *I'll* tell you. 'Tis Jean Baudou, I'll bet!'

'Oh no! Not him!' she cried.

'Well, Pierre Martin, then?'

'No, master, no!'

In a fury he ran through the names of all the young men of the neighbourhood, but she said no to each in turn, powerless to do more, and dabbing at her eyes with the corner of her blue apron. But he fought with mulish obstinacy to get the truth out of her, scrabbling at her heart to find her secret, as a gun-dog will dig all day at an earth to get at the animal he can smell within. Then, suddenly, he shouted:

'Darn me, if it's not that Jacques, who was working on the farm last year. Everyone said as he was sticking to your heels and swearing as he'd marry you!'

She made a choking sound, and the blood rushed into her face. All of a sudden, her tears stopped flowing, drying upon her cheeks like water on a red-hot iron.

'It isn't him!' she cried. 'It isn't!'

'Be 'ee so sure o' that?' asked the sly peasant, thinking he had a partial hold upon the truth.

She answered with a rush of words:

'I swear 'tis not!'

She tried to think of something on which to make good her oath, but dared not call on God.

He broke in on her:

'He was allus getting you in corners, and goggling at you over meals. Did you give him your word, now, did you?'

This time she looked him in the face:

'No, never, never. An' I swear by the good God that if he came back now and asked me, I'd have nowt to do with 'un.'

She sounded so sincere that the farmer hesitated. When he spoke again it was as though to himself.

'Then what's all t'botheration 'bout? Come you'd got yourself in trouble, 'twould be known. And, seeing as there's been no con-sequences, what for should a girl refuse her master? There must be *some* reason.'

She said no more: she could not speak for pain.

He said once more, 'You won't?'

She heaved a sigh: 'I can't, master,' and he turned upon his heel.

She thought she had got rid of him, and, for the rest of the day, felt almost at peace, but as worn-out and drained of strength as though she, and not the old white horse, had been turning and turning, threshing the grain since early dawn.

She went to bed as soon as she could and fell asleep at once.

In the middle of the night, two hands, fumbling at the bed, awoke her. She started up in terror, but recognized at once her master's voice.

'Don' ee be afeared, Rose,' he said. ' 'Tis only me: I want a word wi'ee.'

At first she was amazed, then, as he tried to creep within the sheets, she guessed what he was after, and trembled violently, know-ing herself to be alone in the darkness, still heavy with sleep and naked, beside a man who wanted her. She did not, to be sure, con-sent, but her resistance was half-hearted, for she herself was strug-gling with an instinct which is always powerful in simple natures, and ill-protected by the flaccid will of those who, from their birth, are soft and sluggish. She turned her head this way and that to avoid the farmer's kisses, her body writhing and twisting under-neath the blanket, worn out by the unending struggle. Drunk with

74

desire, he soon grew rough, and tore the bedclothes off. She knew then she could fight no longer. Obedient to the tactics of the ostrich, she hid her face between her hands, resistance at an end.

He stayed with her all night, and next night came again, and every night thereafter.

They lived together.

One day he said to her: 'I've had the banns put up: us'll be spliced next month.'

She made no answer. What could she say? She could stand out no longer. What could she have done?

PART IV

They were married. She felt as though she were at the bottom of a well with walls impossible to climb, a pit from which she could never escape, with disaster ready to fall on her at the first opportunity. She saw her husband as a man whom she had robbed, and, sooner or later, he would know it too. Then she thought of her child, the source of all her woes, but also of the only happiness she had ever known.

Twice a year she went to see him, and, each time, came back home sadder than ever.

But, slowly, habit calmed her fears and stilled her heart, so that life became for her less perilous, though deep down a vague fear lingered still.

Time passed. Her child was now six years old, and she was almost happy. But suddenly the farmer's temper took a turn for the worse. He would sit long at table after dinner was over, with his head in his hands, a melancholy figure gnawed with grief. His speech became more edged and even brutal. It was as though he had some grudge against his wife, for there were times when he answered her harshly, almost angrily.

One day when a neighbour's child had come for eggs, and she, overburdened with work, was sharp with him, her husband suddenly came in and said ill-naturedly:

'If t'were yourn, you wouldn't talk to 'un like that.'

She was so distressed that she could say nothing in reply, but went back into the house with all her fears revived.

At dinner her husband neither looked at her nor spoke to her. He seemed to hate and distrust her, to have found something out.

She lost her head and dared not stay alone with him. She made her escape, and hurried to the church.

It was growing dark. The narrow nave was plunged in shadow, but she could hear a step in the direction of the choir, for the sacristan was preparing the sanctuary lamp for the night. The tiny, flickering point of light, drowned in the darkness of the church, seemed to Rose like a last despairing hope, and with her eyes firmly fixed on it, she fell to her knees.

The small lamp rose into the air to the sound of a rattling chain, and, soon after, she heard the regular clump of clogs on the stone floor followed by the swish of a dragging rope. Then the thin note of a bell sent the Angelus sounding through the gathering mist. When the man came back into the church, she joined him.

'Is monsieur le curé in his house now?'

And he replied:

'I 'spec so: always dines at Angelus time.'

With a trembling hand she pushed open the gate in the fence of the presbytery garden.

The priest was just sitting down to his meal. He offered her a chair.

'I know what you have come about. Your husband has already had a word with me.'

The poor woman very nearly fainted. The man of the church continued:

'What is it you want, my child?'

He rapidly swallowed several spoonfuls of soup, some part of which spilled over on to the front of his greasy cassock.

Rose dared not speak a word, dared not ask for help. She got up, and the curé said:

'Be of good cheer.'

She went away and returned to the farm, scarcely knowing what she did. The master was waiting for her. The hired hands had left during her absence. She dropped heavily at his feet, burst into tears, and said:

'What is it you have against me?'

He began to shout and swear:

'Just this: why, in God's name, have you given me no children? When a man takes a wife 'tis not to stay alone with her all 's life long. That's what I's got against you! A cow as has no calves is worthless, and that goes for a woman as can't produce no kids!'

She blubbered, she stammered, she said again and again:

''Tis not my fault! 'Tis not my fault!'

At that, he spoke more kindly:

'I han't said as how it is, but 'tis vexatious all the same.'

The Story of a Farm-Girl

PART V

She thought of nothing now but having a child, another one, and she confided her longing to all and sundry. One of the neighbours told her how to get what she wanted: she must give her husband a glass of water with a pinch of ashes in it to drink each evening. The farmer agreed to make a trial of this concoction, but it had no effect.

'Perhaps,' they said, 'there is some secret way,' and made inquiries. They were told of a shepherd, twenty-five miles off, and one morning Vallin harnessed the gig and started off to see him.

The shepherd gave him a loaf of bread on which he made certain signs. Herbs had been kneaded into the dough, and both husband and wife were told to eat some of it every night before having intercourse.

The whole loaf was consumed, but without any result.

Next, the schoolmaster revealed certain mysterious practices of love, unknown to country-folk. These he declared were infallible.

They failed.

The curé advised a pilgrimage to the Shrine of the Holy Blood at Fécamp. Rose went with the crowd, prostrated herself in the Abbey, and mingling her prayers with the crude outpourings of her companions, asked that she might be made once more fruitful. But this, too, was in vain. She became convinced that she was being punished for her first wandering from the path of virtue, and was filled with an overwhelming sense of grief.

She was rapidly pining away under the weight of her affliction. Her husband, too, was aging visibly. He was generally supposed to be eating his heart out with useless hopes.

Then, open war broke out between them. He abused and beat her. All day long they quarrelled, and at night, when they lay panting in their bed, filled with bitter hatred, he showered abuse and filthy insults on her.

A night came at last when, unable to invent any further way of making her suffer, he told her to get up and wait in the rain, outside the house, for day to break. Seeing that she did not obey him, he seized her by the throat and struck her in the face. She neither spoke nor moved. In a frenzy of exasperation, he knelt upon her stomach, and, with teeth clenched, and mad with rage, hit her again and again. In a moment of desperate revolt, she flung him

77

back against the wall. Then sitting up she hissed at him, in a voice he had never heard before:

'*I*, at least, have had a child . . . by Jacques . . . He was to have married me, but he ran away.'

He was utterly dumbfounded, no less beyond control than she. He stammered:

'What was that? What was that?'

Then, through her sobs and tears she said:

''Twas why I wouldn't marry 'ee. I couldn't say more then, for you'd 'ave driven me and my baby starving from your door. He as has never had a child, don't understand!'

With surprise mounting in him, he said, scarce knowing what he said:

'*Thee* wi' a child, *thee?* . . .'

Through her sobs she said:

'Took me by force, thee did: and never did I want to marry 'ee, as well 'ee know . . .'

He got up, lit a candle, and started to pace up and down the room, his hands behind his back. She lay all crumpled on the bed, crying still. All of a sudden, he came to a halt in front of her:

''Tis all my fault, then, that I gave you none?' he said.

She made no answer, and he resumed his pacing. Then, stopping again, he asked:

'How old's the brat?'

'Just rising six,' she muttered.

'Why b'aint 'ee said nowt of all this afore?'

'How could I?' she wailed.

He stood there motionless.

'Now get thee up,' he ordered her.

She did so, painfully, and seeing her upon her feet and leaning heavily against the wall, he suddenly began to laugh with the old raucous laughter of his happier days. Then, since she stared at him, uncomprehending, he said:

'Us'll fetch back that brat o' yourn since seemingly us can't have one of our own!'

She was so frightened that, had she had the strength to move, she would have run from him.

'I'd planned to 'dopt one, and now here be the very thing us want. I been to t'curé for to ask 'bout orphans!'

Then, laughing still, he kissed his tearful, half-dazed wife on both her cheeks, shouting as though she were deaf:

The Story of a Farm-Girl

'Come on down, mother, and see if there be any soup still left. Hee! but I could drink a jugful!'

She slipped on her petticoat and down the stairs they went. While she was on her knees blowing up the fire under the pot, he kept on marching up and down the kitchen with a beaming face, saying again and again:

' 'Tis the best news I've had! I dursn't tell no one, but eh! I'm glad, proper glad.'

(26 March 1881)

An Adventure in Paris

Is there any keener emotion than a woman's curiosity? What would she not do to know, to touch, to experience at first hand all that she has dreamed of? Once her restless curiosity has been aroused, a woman is capable of any folly, any act of rashness. Nothing will stop her. I am speaking here of women who are really women, who have the subdivided mind of the true female. It may seem, upon the surface, cool, rational, and of a piece: but, in fact, it is made of three compartments. The first contains all that is unquiet and restless in the sex; the second, its wiles and tricks, coloured with the seeming complexion of sincerity to be found in the devout sophistical and much to be dreaded. In the third is the strange charm of the gutter, a fond deceiving, a delicious perfidy, and all that pretty waywardness which drives credulous lovers to suicide, though others find it quite enchanting.

She, whose adventure I am about to relate, was a little provincial nobody, who, until it happened, had led a dull life of blameless respectability. To others it seemed calm and smooth. It was passed in the company of a busy husband and two children whom she brought up as an admirable mother should. But her heart throbbed with unsatisfied curiosity, with a devouring itch for the unknown. She was for ever dreaming of Paris, and read the fashionable journals with greedy eyes. The accounts of parties, dresses, and amusements set her brain on fire. But what most filled her with a sense of delicious mystery were the hints, the peeps into half-hidden privacies, conveyed in skilful and elusive references which set her dreaming of guilty and dangerous delights.

From her country fastness she saw Paris in a glow of wealth, magnificence, and fascinating corruption.

She spent the long nights lulled by her husband's snores as he lay beside her with a silk handkerchief tied round his head. And she thought about all the famous men and women whose names adorned the front pages of the papers, seeing them as great stars gleaming in a sombre sky. She tried to picture their lives—the ceaseless round of maddening debaucheries, the orgies, so terribly voluptuous and worthy of old Rome; refinements of sensuality so complex that she could not even imagine them.

The boulevards she fancied as a melting-pot of human passions, and the houses as most certainly concealing the mysteries of monstrous loves.

She felt age creeping on her. She was growing old without having learned anything of life except those routine occupations, so odiously monotonous and flat, which, so people told her, constitute domestic happiness. She was still pretty, for, though preyed upon, wasted, and convulsed by secret ardours, she was preserved in her tranquil existence like winter fruit in a closed cupboard. She was beginning to wonder whether she would die without ever having run the risk—or being given the chance—of incurring eternal damnation, or flinging herself, just once, into the full tide of Parisian vice.

Perseveringly she made her plans for a trip to Paris, found a pretext, got some relatives to invite her, and, since her husband was kept at home by his work, set off alone.

No sooner had she arrived than she managed to rake up an excuse for staying an extra two days, or rather, two nights, if necessary, and wrote to her husband that she had run into some old friends who lived in the suburbs.

Then, she started off on her voyage of discovery. She rambled up and down the boulevards without encountering anything more exciting than the representatives of loitering and licensed vice. She peered into the big cafés, and scrupulously read the personal column of the *Figaro* which, every morning, sounded in her ears like a tocsin summoning her to love. But nothing set her on the track of those orgies of actors and actresses in which she so longed to participate. Nothing revealed to her the whereabouts of those temples of debauchery, which she thought of as places where the doors would open only to some magic word, like Ali-Baba's cave, or as resembling the catacombs of ancient Rome where men had celebrated the mysteries of a persecuted religion.

The relatives with whom she was staying, being only middle-class folk, were in no position to introduce her into the company of those public figures whose names haunted her. In despair, she began to think of going home again, when chance came to her aid.

One day, when she was walking down the Rue de la Chaussée-d'Antin, she stopped to look into the window of a shop filled with those objects of Japanese bric-à-brac which are so highly coloured that they immediately attract the eye by the gaiety of their appearance. She was gazing at the delicately carved ivory grotesques, at the great glittering enamelled vases and the curious bronzes, when she heard, from inside the shop, the voice of the proprietor. With much bowing and scraping he was showing an enormous, pot-bellied china mandarin to a tubby little man with a bald head and a grey beard. It was, he was saying, a unique piece.

Every word he spoke, and the name, an illustrious name, of his client, sounded in her ears like a trumpet-call. The other customers —young women and elegant gentlemen, obviously much impressed —were casting quick, sidelong glances at the famous writer who was staring with such an air of passionate absorption at the china figure. Both were so ugly that it was impossible to choose between them. They might, indeed, have been brothers.

The shopman was saying: 'I will let *you* have it for a thousand francs, Monsieur Jean Varin, which is precisely what I paid for it. The price to anybody else would be fifteen hundred. But I value my literary and artistic patrons, and always allow them special rates. They all come to me, Monsieur Varin. Why, only yesterday, Monsieur Busnach bought a large antique goblet from me, and quite recently I sold two sconces—like the one over there (lovely thing, isn't it?)—to Monsieur Alexandre Dumas. If Monsieur Zola were to see what you have in your hands, he would snap it up at once!'

The man of letters could clearly not make up his mind. He was sorely tempted by the object, but no less concerned about the price. He took about as much notice of the staring bystanders as if he were alone in a desert.

She pushed open the door with a trembling hand, and a bold, unblushing look. It never occurred to her to wonder whether he was handsome, elegant, or young. He was Jean Varin, and that was enough for her: Jean Varin in person!

After a prolonged inner struggle, and much painful hesitation, Varin put the figure back on a table. 'I am afraid it is too dear for me,' he said.

The shopman redoubled his eloquence: 'Oh! Monsieur Varin, too dear? Why, it is worth every penny of two thousand!'

The famous author, still looking at the china figure with the enamelled eyes, said sadly: 'I dare say it is: but it is more than I can afford.'

Carried away by a sudden impulse, she came forward.

'How much would you let me have that figure for?'

Somewhat surprised, the man replied: 'Fifteen hundred francs, Madame.'

'I will take it.'

The eminent Monsieur Varin who, till that moment, had not so much as noticed her, turned sharply. He looked her up and down with half-closed eyes, taking in the general effect, then studied her more in detail, as a connoisseur.

Lit by the flame which had formerly only smouldered within her, she looked charming and animated. Besides, it is not every woman who will buy a curio costing fifteen hundred francs!

With enchanting delicacy she turned to him, and said in a voice trembling with emotion:

'I really must apologize, Monsieur, for being somewhat hasty. Perhaps you had not finally decided?'

'Indeed I had, Madame,' he said with a bow.

But she, strung up to a high pitch, continued: 'If, today or at any other time, you change it, you have only to say the word. I should not have bought it had I not seen that it attracted you.'

He smiled, visibly flattered. 'How do you know who I am?' he asked.

Then she spoke of the admiration she felt for him, mentioned his books, and waxed eloquent.

The better to converse at his ease, he had leaned one elbow on a piece of furniture, and now, looking fixedly at her with his sharp eyes, was clearly trying to make her out.

Now and again, the shopman, pleased at the thought of how much publicity this little incident would bring him, called from the other end of the shop: 'Take a look at this, Monsieur Varin, is it not a beautiful piece?' Then all eyes were raised, and she tingled with pleasure at being seen in intimate talk with a Famous Man.

Carried away by her feelings, and greatly daring, like a general about to order a charge, 'Monsieur,' she said, 'I want you to do me a great, a very great favour. I want you to accept this manikin as a small memento from a woman who admires you passionately and whom you have known for just ten minutes.'

He refused. She insisted. He still refused, but much amused and laughing heartily.

She stood her ground. 'Very well, then: I shall take it in person to your house, if you will tell me where you live.'

He would not give her his address, but she got it from the owner of the shop and, having paid for her purchase, hurried out in search of a cab. The writer ran after her, not wishing to run the risk of accepting a present from somebody he knew nothing about. He caught her up just as she was entering the cab and, jumping in after her, very nearly fell on top of her as the vehicle jolted into motion. Then he sat down beside her in a thoroughly irritable state of mind.

Say what he might, she was obdurate. Then, just as they reached his door, she stated her conditions. 'I will consent,' she said, 'not to leave this with you, if you, on your side, will give me your word to grant my every wish for the rest of the day.'

The whole thing seemed so fantastically odd to him, that he agreed.

'What do you usually do at this time?' she asked.

He hesitated for a moment, then:

'I go for a drive,' he said.

In a determined voice, she called to the coachman:

'To the Bois!'

They started off.

She made him point out to her all the well-known women whom they saw, especially the raffish ones, and give her intimate details about each of them, their lives, their habits, where they lived, and in what particular vices they indulged.

Darkness fell.

'What do you usually do about now?' she asked.

'I drink an absinthe,' he said with a laugh.

With perfect gravity she replied:

'In that case, Monsieur, let us drink an absinthe.'

They went into a large café on the boulevard which was his especial haunt, and where he met his colleagues of the pen. These he introduced to her. She was wildly happy, and kept thinking to herself: 'At last! At last!'

It grew late:

'Is this your dinner-time?' she inquired.

He answered: 'Yes, Madame.'

'In that case, Monsieur, let us dine.'

When they left Bignon's:

'What do you do in the evenings?' she said.

Looking at her fixedly, he answered:

'That depends: sometimes I go to the theatre.'

'In that case, Monsieur, let us go to the theatre.'

They went to the Vaudeville, on a free pass, thanks to him, and, glory of glories, the whole house saw her sitting with him in the balcony stalls!

An Adventure in Paris

When the performance was over, he kissed her hand with an air: 'It remains for me, Madame, to thank you for a delightful evening. . . .' But she would not let him finish:

'What do you do at this time every night?'

'Why . . . why . . . I go home.'

She broke into a little tremulous laugh: 'In that case, Monsieur, let us go home.'

They said no more. Now and again she shuddered all over, half wanting to take to her heels, half wanting to stay. But, deep down, she was determined to see the thing out to the very end.

As they walked upstairs, she felt so excited that she had to cling to the handrail. He went ahead, lighting the way with a wax-vesta, and breathing heavily.

As soon as they reached his room, she quickly undressed and slipped into bed without saying a word: and there she lay, pressed to the wall, waiting.

But she was as simple as only a provincial lawyer's wife can be, and he as demanding as a pasha with three tails. They did not begin to understand one another.

Then, he went to sleep. The night drew on, the silence broken only by the ticking of a clock, while she lay motionless, thinking of the nights with her husband while, heartbroken, she looked by the yellow light of a Chinese lantern at the little man beside her. He lay stretched on his back, with his stomach making a protuberance under the sheet and looking like a gas-filled balloon. His snores were like the sounds made by a wheezy organ-pipe, interspersed with snorts and comic bouts of choking. His twenty hairs took advantage of these hours of sleep to stand up in the oddest way, as though enjoying a respite from being for so long smarmed down on his denuded scalp. A trickle of saliva came from one corner of his mouth.

At last dawn showed a little light between the curtains. She got up, dressed without making any noise, and had already got one half of the door open, when the lock gave a sudden squeak and he woke up, rubbing his eyes.

It was some moments before he had completely recovered consciousness. When, however, the memory of all that had happened came back to him, he said:

'So, you're going, are you?'

She stood there in some confusion:

'Why, yes,' she said hesitatingly: 'it's morning.'

He sat up in bed:

'Now it's *my* turn to ask *you* something.'

She did not speak, and he continued:

'I've been devilishly puzzled about you since yesterday. Be honest with me, and explain why you did all you did do, because, you see, I just don't understand.'

Very quietly she moved close to the bed, blushing like a young girl.

'I wanted . . . to know . . . about vice . . . and . . . well, it isn't much fun.'

Then she ran out of the room, down the stairs, and into the street.

An army of street-sweepers was busy sweeping. They swept the pavements and the roadway, pushing all the filth into the gutter. With the same regular movement as hay-makers raking the fields, they pushed the mud before them in a semi-circle. She came upon them in every street, like mechanical dolls, moving as though all activated by the same spring.

And she felt as though something in herself had just been swept away and down into the sewers. Her own overheated dreams.

She returned home cold and exhausted, with nothing in her head but the sound of the sweepers cleansing Paris in the dawn light.

As soon as she was back in her own room, she broke down and sobbed.

(22 December 1881)

In the Spring

WHEN the first fine days arrive, when the earth wakes up and all is green again, when the warm and scented air feels soft upon the skin and sets the heart beating, then we are conscious of vague desires. A sudden sense of happiness, hard to define, makes us want to run about, to wander at random, to seek adventures and gulp down heady draughts of spring.

The winter just past had been hard, and this need to bloom and blossom worked in me like wine, like the bubbling of rising sap.

One morning, when I woke, I saw above the nearby roofs a wide expanse of sky ablaze with sunshine. The canaries in their cages were twittering, the servant-girls on every floor were singing, a gay sound rose from the street, and I left the house with a holiday heart, to go I knew not where.

The passers-by all smiled at me: a happy breeze stirred in the warm light of the returning spring. It was as though the wind of love were blowing through the town: in the eyes of the young women in their morning frocks there was a hidden softness, and in their walk a lighter grace. My heart was filled with a sweet agitation.

Without knowing how, without knowing why, I reached the bank of the Seine. Steam-boats were gliding downstream to Suresnes, and I felt an immense longing to go running through the woods.

The deck of *La Mouche* was thick with passengers, for the first sunshine of the year draws us irresistibly from home, and everyone seems on the move, coming and going, and chattering with chance neighbours.

My own was a girl—a little working-girl, no doubt—with that grace one finds only in Paris. She had a sweet little head of golden hair framing her face in a cluster of curls which had the look of frizzled light. It touched the tips of her two ears and crowded on her nape, dancing in the breeze, and, lower still, was turned into a down so fine as to be scarcely visible but which I felt a fierce desire to kiss.

I stared so hard that she turned her eyes to mine, then quickly lowered them, while a tiny pucker, like the beginning of a smile, dimpled one corner of her mouth, where there was that same fine down, silky and pale, which the sun just faintly touched to gold.

The unrippled surface of the river here grew wider. There was a sense of warm peacefulness in the air, and a living murmur seemed to fill the circumambient space. She raised her eyes, and this time, since I did not turn away my own, she really smiled. So charming did she look that I saw in her a thousand things I had not noticed until then: depths unsuspected, a charming tenderness, that poetry of which we dream, and a promise of the happiness we look for endlessly. I had a mad desire to open my arms and carry her away to some spot where I might speak to her of love.

I was about to start a conversation when someone touched me on the shoulder. I turned my head, surprised, and saw a very ordinary man, neither young nor old, who was looking at me with a mournful air.

'I should very much like to have a word with you,' he said.

I pulled a face. No doubt he noticed it, because he added:

'What I have to say is of the utmost importance.'

I got up and followed him to the far end of the deck.

'Monsieur,' he then continued, 'when winter comes with cold and rain and snow, the doctor tells us every day to beware of chills, bronchitis, pleurisy. We take a thousand and one precautions. We wear flannel next the skin, a heavy overcoat, and thick-soled shoes. For all that, we are lucky not to have to spend two months in bed. But when spring returns, with its leaves and flowers, its warm, relaxing breezes, with that scent of fields which is so disturbing to the heart, and feelings that have no rhyme nor reason—there is no one by to say: "Monsieur, beware of love!" It lies in waiting, prepared to pounce, round every corner. Its nets are spread, its weapons sharpened, its treacheries prepared. Oh, my dear sir, be on your guard against love! It is more dangerous than colds, bronchitis, pleurisy. It shows no mercy. It makes us all do foolish and irreparable things. The Government should paste large warnings on the walls: *Spring is here again: Frenchmen, beware of love!* just as we see *Wet Paint* scrawled on the house-doors. But, since the Government does no such thing, I act instead of it, and say "Beware of love!" It will get you, and I feel it my duty to put you on your guard, as in Russia men warn a passer-by that his nose is freezing.'

Dumbfounded by this strange original, I assumed a dignified air and said: 'It seems to me, Monsieur, that you are meddling with what does not concern you.'

He made an impatient gesture and replied: 'Oh! Monsieur, Monsieur, if I saw a man in danger of drowning, should I leave him to perish? Listen to my story, and then, perhaps, you will understand why I have ventured to address you in this way.

'It all happened at this season, a year ago. I should tell you first, Monsieur, that I work in the Ministry of Marine, where our seniors, the Heads of Departments, take advantage of their commissions as pen-pushing officers, to treat us as so many lower-deck ratings! But let that pass. From my office window I could see a patch of blue sky across which swallows were flying, and felt a prompting to dance among the black-jacketted files.

'So great did my longing for liberty become, that I decided, though it was most distasteful to me, to seek an interview with my chief. He was a churlish little creature and always in a bad temper. I told him I felt ill. He gave me a nasty look and exclaimed: "I don't believe a word of it! Still, I suppose you'd better clear off home. How d'you suppose an office can be run when it's staffed by fellows like you?"

'So I slipped away and reached the Seine. The weather was just as it is today, and I took an excursion ticket to Saint-Cloud on *La Mouche*.

'Ah! Monsieur, how much better it would have been if my chief had refused me his permission!

'The sunlight made me feel expansive. I was in love with everything; the boat, the river, the houses, my fellow-travellers—everything. I wanted to embrace something, no matter what. Love was making ready to trap me.

'Then, all of a sudden, at the Trocadéro, a young woman came on board, carrying a small bandbox, and sat down facing me.

'She was pretty, Monsieur; I don't deny it. But it is astonishing how much better women look on a fine day in early spring. They have an appeal, a charm, a something for which I can find no word. The effect they have on one is like the wine one drinks after the cheese.

'I looked at her, and she looked at me, but only now and again, like the girl next to whom you were sitting just now. This frequent exchange of glances made me feel I knew her well enough to start a conversation. So, I spoke to her, and she replied. She was as pretty as paint, no doubt about that. She went, Monsieur, straight to my head.

'She got off at Saint-Cloud: I followed her. She was on her way to deliver an order. When she reappeared, the boat had just left. I started to walk beside her, and the sweet softness of the air made us both sigh.

'It would be nice in the woods,' I said.

'She answered: "Yes, very nice!"

' "What would you say to our taking a stroll there, Mademoiselle?"

'She gave me a quick, sidelong look, as though to judge what I was worth; then, after a slight hesitation, agreed. So there we were, side by side among the trees. Under the still thin foliage, the thrusting grass, as vividly green as though it had been varnished, was flooded with sunlight and full of little animals, intent, like us, on love. Birds were singing everywhere. Then my companion started to run, to frisk, to caper, for the country smells had made her drunk. And I ran after her, jumping and gambolling as she was doing. How mad one can be at times, Monsieur!

'And she sang, too, Monsieur, with a wild abandon, many things, operatic airs, Musetta's song! How poetic did I find Musetta's song just then! . . . I was almost in tears! It's rubbish like that which turns our heads! Believe me when I say, never go walking in the country with a girl who sings, especially not if she sings Musetta's song!

'She soon got tired and sat down on a bank. I lay at her feet and took her hands in mine, small hands, all speckled with needle-pricks which woke a tenderness in me, and I thought: "They are the blessèd stigmata of labour!" Oh! Monsieur, Monsieur, do you know what they really mean, those blessèd stigmata of labour? They would tell you, if they could, of work-room gossiping, of whispered smut, of the mind fouled with filthy stories, of virtue lost, of the idiocies of tittle-tattle, of daily chores, of the limited intelligence of a lot of silly women herded together . . .

'Then we gazed for a long time into each other's eyes.

'Oh! what a power there is in women's eyes! How it troubles one's peace of mind! How deep it seems, how filled with promises, how haunted by the infinite. One calls such gazing—reading the heart! Oh! Monsieur, what humbug! If one could really read another's heart, how much wiser one would be!

'Well, I was swept off my feet, driven mad! I tried to take her in my arms. She said, "Hands off!" . . .

'Then, kneeling at her feet, I poured out my heart to her, poured out upon her knees all the tenderness with which, for so long, I had been choking. She seemed astonished at my change of manner. She looked at me from the corner of her eye, as though she were saying to herself: "So that's your little game, my lad! Well, we shall see!"

'In love, Monsieur, men are always the half-wits, women always the chafferers.

'No doubt, I could have had her there and then, but what I had been looking for, you see, was not a body but an ideal. I had wasted my time with a display of fine feelings, when I might have been better employed.

'When she had had enough of my high-flown sentiments, she got up and we walked back to Saint-Cloud. Not until we reached Paris did I leave her. She looked so sad on the way home that I asked her what the matter was. She said: "I was thinking that one does not have many such days in one's life." My heart beat so hard that I thought it would burst.

'I saw her again on the following Sunday, then on the next one, and on all the other Sundays. I took her to Bougival and Saint-Germain, to Maison-Laffitte and Maison-Poissy—those high-spots of suburban dalliance.

'In the game of passion the little hussy played her cards only too well.

'In the long run, I lost my head completely, and three months later I married her.

'What else would you expect, Monsieur, of a lonely wage-earner without relations or anyone to give him good advice? He tells himself that life with a woman would be very sweet, so off he goes and marries one.

'But that is not the end. My own case is typical of many. No sooner had she got me safely locked up in matrimony than she started to nag and abuse me from morning till night. She knows nothing, understands nothing, chatters without ceasing, sings Musetta's song at the top of her voice (oh! what a buzz-saw it has become!), quarrels with the coal merchant, tells the concierge all about her home-life, entertains the servant-girl with all our bed-room intimacies, blackguards me to the tradespeople, stuffs her head with so many stupid stories, with superstitions so idiotic, opinions so grotesque and prejudices so monstrous, that I cry from sheer discouragement, Monsieur, every time I try to talk to her.'

He stopped speaking, a little out of breath and deeply moved. I looked at him. I felt such pity for the poor, simple-minded devil that I tried to think of something to say. But, just at that moment, the steamer stopped. We had reached Saint-Cloud.

The girl who had done such damage to my heart, got to her feet and made ready to land. She passed close to me with a sidelong glance and a furtive smile, the sort of smile that drives a man mad. Then she jumped down on to the landing-stage.

I hastened in pursuit. But my neighbour seized me by the arm. I shook him off with an impatient gesture. He clung to the tails of my coat and dragged me back, saying: 'You shall not go! You shall not go!' in so loud a voice that every head was turned in our direction. There were chuckles and guffaws from the bystanders, and I stood there, motionless and raging, but too cowardly to face the ridicule and scandal.

Then the steamer started off again.

The girl was still upon the landing-stage, and watched me being carried into the distance. There was a look of disappointment on her face. My persecutor whispered in my ear:

'I have done you the best of services,' and rubbed his hands.

(1881)

Mademoiselle Fifi

MAJOR the Count von Farlsberg, the Prussian commandant, was just finishing the reading of his mail. He was stretched out at length in a tapestry-upholstered armchair, with his booted feet on the elegant marble mantelpiece, in which, during the three months that he and his officers had been using the Château d'Uville as part of the army of occupation, his spurs had made two deep grooves which had got deeper every day.

A cup of coffee stood smoking on a small marqueterie side-table which was stained with spilled liquor, burned by cigarette-ends, and gashed by the conqueror's pen-knife. Whenever he sharpened a pencil, he scratched upon the top of this graceful piece of furniture, figures or drawings as the fancy took him.

When he had finished with his letters and glanced at the German newspapers which the post-orderly had just brought him, he got to his feet and, after throwing on the fire three or four enormous pieces of green wood—for these gentlemen were gradually cutting down all the trees in the park to keep themselves warm—he went to the window.

The rain was coming down in torrents, a real Normandy rain which looked as though it were being discharged by the hand of someone in a fury, a slantwise rain, thick as a curtain, forming a sort of a wall painted in oblique strokes, a lashing rain, splashing and drowning everything, such rain as is to be seen only round Rouen, that chamber-pot of France.

He looked down for a while at the sodden lawns and, beyond them, at the flooded Andelle which had burst its banks. He was tapping out a Rhineland waltz with his fingers on the window-pane, when a sudden sound made him swing round. It was his second-in-command, the Baron von Kelweingstein, who held the rank equivalent to that of a French captain.

The major was a giant of a man, broad-shouldered and sporting a fan-shaped beard which covered his chest like a bib. His size and strutting solemnity produced the impression of a military peacock displaying a spread tail on its chin. There was something at once cold and mild in his blue eyes, and he had a scar on his cheek from a sabre-cut which he had received in the Austrian war. He enjoyed the reputation of being a good sort as well as a gallant officer.

The captain was a small, red-faced man with a prominent stomach, tightly belted. He was clean-shaven, and in certain lights his cheeks, so fiery was the stubble, looked as though they had been rubbed over with phosphorus. Two of his teeth had been knocked out one rowdy night, though he could not remember exactly how, with the result that his speech was thick and sometimes difficult to understand. The top of his head was completely bald, tonsured like a monk, with a fleece of small gold and glittering curls clustering round the bare patch.

The commandant shook him by the hand, and gulped down his cup of coffee (the sixth that morning) while listening to the daily duty-report read by his subordinate. Business over, both men went to the window. They agreed that the life they were living was a pretty dismal affair—not that it mattered much to the major, who was phlegmatic by nature and a married man. The Baron-captain, on the other hand, was a gay dog, a brothel haunter, and an insatiable womanizer, and for the last three months he had been suffering severely from the chastity enforced upon him in this god-forsaken hole.

There was a knock at the door, and, in response to the commandant's 'Come in', one of the automaton-like soldiers of the little garrison appeared on the threshold. There was no need for him to say anything, for his mere presence at that hour announced that luncheon was on the table.

In the dining-room three junior officers were waiting: a lieutenant, Otto von Grossling, and two second-lieutenants, Fritz Scheunaubourg and Marquis Wilhelm von Eyrik, a small, fair-haired creature who was arrogant and brutal with his men, harsh in his dealings with the conquered, and as explosive as a gun.

Since their coming into France, his friends had known him only as Mademoiselle Fifi. This nickname he owed to his dandified appearance, his small waist which made him look as though he were wearing stays, his pale face on which the budding moustache scarcely showed, and also from the habit he had acquired of constantly using the French phrase, *fi, fi donc*, when he wished to express his sovereign contempt for people and things. His speech was slightly sibilant.

The dining-room of the Château d'Uville was of regal proportions. The fine old mirrors, starred with pistol shots, and the towering panels of Flemish tapestry, slashed with sabre-strokes and, in many places, hanging in rags, were only too eloquent of the way in which Mademoiselle Fifi employed his leisure hours.

There were three family portraits on the walls—a knight in armour, a cardinal, and a judge—all smoking long porcelain pipes, while a noble lady, very tightly laced, in a faded gold frame, proudly displayed an enormous charcoal moustache.

The meal proceeded in almost complete silence. The battered and dilapidated room always had a gloomy appearance, but now, under the downpour, it looked darker and gloomier than ever. The old oak parquet of the floor had the appearance of being as resistant as the stone flags of an ale-house.

When the five officers, having finished eating, settled down to drink and smoke, the conversation turned, as it always did, to the subject of boredom. Bottles of cognac and liqueurs made the round of the table, and the drinkers lay back in their chairs, endlessly sipping and never taking from their mouths the long, curved pipe-stems which terminated in egg-shaped bowls painted in colours bright enough to delight the heart of a Hottentot.

When their glasses were empty, they refilled them with gestures of weary resignation. But Mademoiselle Fifi kept breaking his and having it replaced by one of the soldier-servants. A haze of acrid tobacco-smoke enveloped them, and they seemed sunk in that condition of morose and drowsy intoxication which comes over those who have nothing to do.

Suddenly the Baron sat up, jerked into a movement of revolt. 'God in Heaven!' he swore, 'we can't go on like this: we've got to *do* something!'

Lieutenant Otto and second-lieutenant Fritz, both of them Germans with the typically solemn and heavy faces of their race, chimed in:

'But what, sir?'

For a few seconds the Baron sat deep in thought. Then he said:

'What? Why shouldn't we have a party?—that is to say, of course, if the commandant will let us.'

The major took his pipe from his lips:

'What sort of a party, Captain?'

The Baron moved his chair close to his commanding officer. 'If you will give the necessary leave, sir, I will arrange the whole thing. I will send *Old Duty* into Rouen to round up some girls—I know where to find 'em. We'll put on a supper. There's everything we need here, and at least we shall be assured of a gay evening.'

Count von Farlsberg smiled and shrugged:

'You're quite mad, my dear fellow!'

By this time, all the officers were on their feet, crowding round their commander, begging him for his permission. 'Do let the captain fix it, sir! We're all so terribly bored!'

At length, the major gave way. 'All right, then,' he said, and the Baron at once sent for *Old Duty*, a veteran non-commissioned officer who had never been seen to smile, but carried out with anxious devotion every order given by his superiors, no matter what it was.

Standing to attention, with a completely expressionless face, he listened to the Baron's instructions and immediately left the room. Five minutes later, one of the transport-wagons, with a hooped canvas roof, set off at a gallop under the driving rain, drawn by four horses.

At once a flicker of life showed among the assembled officers. The loungers sat up in their chairs, faces brightened, and conversation became general.

The major asserted that it was getting lighter—though the rain was coming down as hard as ever—and Lieutenant Otto declared with conviction that the sky was going to clear. Mademoiselle Fifi seemed to be finding it impossible to keep still. He kept on getting to his feet and sitting down again. His bright, hard eye was looking round for something to break. Suddenly, staring aggressively at the moustachio'd lady, the fair-haired young oaf drew his revolver:

'Well, at any rate *you* won't see what goes on,' he said, and, without leaving his chair, took careful aim. With two successive shots he punched out both the portrait's eyes.

Then he shouted: 'I say, let's do a "mine".' At once, all talk broke off short, as though some new and powerful interest had got everyone in its grip.

The 'mine' was his own invention, his own particular form of wholesale destruction, his favourite amusement.

When Count Fernand d'Amoys d'Uville had left his château on the approach of the enemy, he had not had sufficient time to take anything away with him, or to hide much except the domestic silver which he had stuffed into a hole in one of the walls. He was a very rich man who lived in great state, and, before his hurried departure, the great saloon, opening into the dining-room, had presented the appearance of a combined picture-gallery and museum.

The walls were hung with canvases, drawings, and water-colours of great value, while, distributed over shelves and tables, and displayed in glass cabinets, were many *objets d'art*—porcelain, statu-ettes, Dresden figures, Chinese grotesques, and specimens of Venetian glass.

Very few of them were left now. Not that they had been looted: the Count von Farlsberg would never have approved of *that*. But, from time to time, Mademoiselle Fifi had arranged one of his 'mines', and whenever that happened, all the officers had spent a riotous five minutes.

The little marquis took what he wanted from the saloon, in-cluding a Chinese *Famille Rose* teapot. This he filled with gun-powder. Then he carefully inserted a long, thin piece of tinder down the spout, lit it, and ran with this improvised infernal-machine into the next room. Then he hurried back, shutting the door behind him. The Germans all stood waiting with child-like grins of anticipation on their faces, and, as soon as the ex-plosion had rocked the château, rushed in a crowd to see the result.

Mademoiselle Fifi, who was first through the door, clapped his hands with delight at the spectacle of a decapitated terra-cotta Venus. The others set about collecting fragments of china, express-ing surprise at the fantastic effects of the explosion, carefully examining the most recent damage, and loudly maintaining that some of the havoc had been caused by an earlier 'mine', while the major, like a fond father, looked on at the shattering results of this wholesale Neronic cataclysm. He was the first to leave the room, smiling indulgently, and saying: 'Very successful effort, very successful indeed.'

But such a stench of powder-fumes and tobacco filled the dining-room that it was impossible to breathe there. The Commandant threw open one of the windows, and the officers, who had come back for one last glass of cognac, crowded round it.

The damp air blew into the room, bringing with it a powdering of raindrops which sparkled on the officers' beards, and the smell of flood-water. They looked at the tall trees bending under the downpour, at the mist-filled valley and the distant church spire standing like a grey needle in the blanketing rain.

Since their arrival its bells had ceased to ring. This, if the truth be told, was the only form of resistance which the invaders had encountered in the neighbourhood. The church tower, and it alone, had made a stand against them. The curé, to be sure, had raised no difficulties in the matter of billeting and feeding the Prussian troops. He had even, on more than one occasion, consented to drink a bottle of beer or a glass of wine with the enemy Commandant, who occasionally made use of him as a friendly intermediary between the German troops and the population. But ring the bells he would not. He would rather have been shot. It was his manner of protesting against the invasion, a peaceful protest, a silent protest, to be sure, but the only one, he said, befitting a priest who was, by calling, a man of peace and not of blood. Everyone for ten miles round praised the firmness and heroism of the Abbé Chantavoine, who dared to recognize a state of public mourning, and to proclaim it through the medium of an obstinate silence.

The whole village, roused to enthusiasm by this resolute action, was prepared to back their good pastor to the end and to run any risks, since it regarded this silence as safeguarding the national honour. The peasants felt that they had deserved better of their country than either Belfort or Strasbourg, that they had given no less outstanding an example of loyalty. It would, they decided, redound for ever to the glory of their village. But in every other way they did what they were told to do by their Prussian conquerors.

The Commandant and his officers frequently enjoyed a good laugh over this inoffensive act of courage, and, since the whole district showed, in general, a spirit of compliance, they willingly put up with this patriotic taciturnity.

Only the little Marquis Wilhelm would have dearly liked to compel the priest to ring his bells. The tactful consideration shown by his commanding officer in this matter infuriated him. Every day he begged permission to produce one 'Ding-dong-dong', just one, if only to give them a good laugh. This he asked with a kittenish grace and the wheedling insistence of a mistress asking a favour. But the Commandant refused to listen to him, and Mademoiselle Fifi consoled himself by letting off another 'mine' in the Château d'Uville.

The five men stood grouped for a few minutes round the window, breathing in the damp air. Lieutenant Fritz said with a thick laugh: 'Zeeze laties vill not for zeir bromenade goot veather haf.'

Whereupon they separated, each having duties to attend to, and the captain being much occupied with preparations for the dinner.

When they met again as darkness was falling, they laughed a good deal at seeing their fellows all spruced up and shining, as for a full-dress review, pomaded and scented and fresh as daisies. The Commandant's hair looked less grey than it had done in the morning, and the captain had shaved with the utmost care, leaving only his moustache, which burned like a flame under his nose.

In spite of the rain, the window had been left open, and now and again one or other of them went to it to look and listen. At ten minutes to six the Baron declared that he could hear a distant rumble. They all rushed to the window, and soon the great wagon galloped up, the four horses spattered with mud to their bellies, steaming and panting.

Five women got out on to the steps, five buxom wenches chosen with care by one of the captain's friends to whom *Old Duty* had delivered a message from him, with his card.

They had not needed much persuading, feeling certain that they would be well paid, and having already, in the course of the past three months, had a good deal to do with Prussians. They were as much resigned to them as they were to the general situation. 'It's all in the day's work,' they had agreed on the drive out from Rouen, hoping, no doubt, by adopting this attitude, to still a last few prickings of conscience.

They were taken at once into the dining-room. Under the bright lights it looked gloomier and more dilapidated than ever, and the table, loaded with food, fine china, and silver brought from the hiding-place in which it had been stored by the owner, gave to the whole place the appearance of a thieves'-kitchen after a successful day.

The captain, with a beaming face, took possession of them as of familiar objects, sizing them up, kissing them, sniffing at them, appraising their value as 'ladies of pleasure'. When the three younger men showed signs of wanting to pair off with them, he used his authority to stop any such an attempt to jump the gun, reserving to himself the right to share them out properly with all due consideration for rank and the claims of seniority.

To avoid all argument, discussion, and any suspicion of favouritism, he lined them up according to size, and, turning to the tallest, barked out, as though on parade: 'Name?'

She answered in a loud voice:

'Pamela!'

'Number one,' he announced, 'name, Pamela, allocated to the Commandant.'

Then, having kissed the second in the row, Blondine, to establish ownership, he awarded the plump Amanda to Lieutenant Otto, Eva, *the Tomato*, to Second-lieutenant Fritz, and Rachel, a young, dark-haired girl with eyes as black as ink, a Jewess whose snub-nose showed as an exception to the rule that all her race are aquiline, to the junior officer present, the effeminate-looking Wilhelm von Eyrik.

All of them, as a matter of fact, were pretty and well-covered, though none were remarkable for any individuality. The daily practice of love, and the communal life of a bawdy-house, had had a levelling effect upon them, so that they looked much of a muchness.

The three younger men tried to whisk their partners away at once, on the pretext of showing them where they could brush their hair and generally clean up. But the captain wisely set his face against this, saying that they were quite clean enough as they were to sit down to dinner, and that if they went upstairs now they would most certainly want a change when they came down, and so would upset all his arrangements. His experience carried the day, and the three officers had to be content with frequent anticipatory embraces.

Rachel had a sudden choking fit. She coughed until the tears came into her eyes, and was blowing smoke out of her nose. The marquis, under cover of a kiss, had just puffed cigar-smoke into her mouth. She did not lose her temper, however, and did not say a word, but in the look she gave her partner out of her dark eyes, there was a smouldering fire of anger.

The company sat down. The Commandant seemed very pleased. He made Pamela sit on his right, Blondine on his left, saying, as he unfolded his napkin: 'This was a charming idea of yours, Captain.'

Otto and Fritz behaved with the same good manners they would have shown to ladies of fashion, thereby somewhat embarrassing their companions. But the Baron von Kelweingstein gave full vent to his vicious propensities, grinning from ear to ear, and talking smut. His crown of red hair made his head look as though it was on fire. He was familiar in Rhenish-French, and his bar-parlour compliments, which he spat out through the gap in his teeth, reached the girls in a shower of spittle.

Not that they understood a word. They showed no reaction until he began barking obscenities in a garbled accent. At that they broke into a concerted scream of merriment, laughing like lunatics, falling against their neighbours, repeating the words which the Baron had deliberately mispronounced for the pleasure of hearing them make filthy answers. They hiccupped all he wanted, for the first bottles of wine had already gone to their heads. Then, pulling themselves together, and letting habit have its way, they kissed

the moustaches to right and left of them, pinched arms, squeaked, drank from the glasses held out to them from all sides, sang snatches of French, and bits of German songs which they had learned from their daily commerce with the enemy.

Very soon, the men, excited by the heady draughts of female flesh offered to their eyes and hands, lost all control and started to shout and break up the china, while the soldier-servants behind them attended to their wants with expressionless faces.

Only the Commandant kept a hold on himself.

Mademoiselle Fifi had taken Rachel on his knee, and, cold-bloodedly working himself up into a state of excitement, began madly kissing the black curls at her neck, sniffing up the delicious warmth of her body and all the fragrance of her person through the narrow gap between her dress and her flesh, and sometimes pinching her so hard that he made her cry out. By this time he was worked into a frenzy by his craving to cause pain. Clasping her in his arms so tightly that he seemed to be trying to make their two bodies one, he pressed his lips to the Jewess's fresh mouth, and kissed the breath out of her. Then, suddenly, he bit her with such violence that the blood began to trickle down her chin and inside her bodice.

Once again she looked him straight in the eyes, and, dabbing at the hurt, said in a low voice: 'I'll make you pay for that!' And he, with a hard laugh, replied: 'Oh! I'll pay all right!'

With the dessert came the champagne. The Commandant rose to his feet, and in the same tone he would have used to propose the toast of the Empress Augusta, said, draining his glass:

'The Ladies!'

There followed a string of toasts, drunken toasts and bawdy barrack-room toasts, mingled with obscene jokes which sounded all the coarser because of the men's ignorance of the language.

One after the other, they staggered to their feet, attempting witticisms or making clowns of themselves. The women, who by this time were dead drunk with a vacant look in their eyes and a thick taste in their mouths, applauded wildly.

The captain, meaning, no doubt, to give an air of gallantry to an otherwise squalid orgy, raised his glass once more, and cried:

'I drink to our victories over these ladies' hearts!'

Whereupon, Lieutenant Otto—a sort of Black-Forest bear—rose in his turn. He was soused in liquor, and quite beyond knowing what he was doing or saying. In an access of patriotic alcoholism, he shouted:

'I drink to our vic'tries over these la'ies' country!'

Drunk though they were, the women said nothing. Rachel, however, trembling all over, turned to this master of repartee:

'You may not think it,' she exclaimed, 'but I know Frenchmen in whose presence you would not dare say a thing like that!'

The little marquis had still got her on his knee. The wine had made him gay. 'Then I've never seen 'em,' he spluttered. 'Soon as we turn up, can't see 'em for dust!'

The girl, driven to desperation, screamed in his face: 'That's a lie, you swine!'

For a second, he looked at her with his light-coloured eyes, as he had looked at the picture when he shot it to pieces with his revolver. Then he started to laugh again. 'Say wha' you like, my beauty, bu' if they're 's brave as all that d'you think we sh'ld be here?' Then, suddenly roused to frenzy, he shouted:

'We are the masters here! France belongs to us!'

She jumped off his knee and collapsed into her chair, while he, holding his glass over the table, said again:

'France belongs to us! The French belong to us! The woods, the fields, the houses of France belong to us!'

The others, by this time completely out of control and caught up in an access of military, brutish enthusiasm, seized their glasses and drained them, yelling 'Long live Prussia!'

There was no protest from the women, who were now thoroughly frightened. Even Rachel could make no reply.

Then the little marquis, holding his refilled glass over the Jewess's head, shouted:

'An' the women of France belong to us, too!'

She jumped to her feet so violently that she knocked the glass out of his hand. It crashed to the floor. The golden wine drenched her black hair, as though she were being baptized. With trembling lips she outfaced the officer, who was still laughing. In a voice choking with rage, she said:

'That at least is not true! The women of France will never belong to you.'

He sat down the better to enjoy the joke, and aping what he took to be the accent of Paris, mincingly remarked:

'Ah! zat is goot; vat then, may I ask, are you doing here?'

Shocked into silence, she at first said nothing. She was so shaken that she did not fully catch his meaning. Then, as it dawned on her, she flung back at him, in a voice of fierce indignation:

'I am not a woman! I am a whore! and that is all you Prussians want!'

Before she could say more, he slapped her full in the face, but just as he was raising his hand again, she snatched a little silver fruit-knife from the table, and, so quickly that no one could see what was happening, drove it into the base of his throat just where it met the breast-bone.

What he was about to say was never said. He stood with his mouth open, and a dreadful look in his eyes.

There was a general roar from drunken mouths, a noisy scrambling to drunken feet, but she, pushing Lieutenant Otto's legs so that he fell headlong, ran to the window, opened it before any-one could get within reach of her, and jumped out into the dark-ness and the streaming rain.

Within two minutes Mademoiselle Fifi was dead. Fritz and Otto drew their swords and made as though to slaughter the women who were grovelling on the ground and clinging to their knees. Not without difficulty, the major prevented the butchery, had the four remaining women locked into one of the bedrooms under the guard of two men, and then, as calmly as though he were draw-ing up his troops for battle, proceeded to organize the pursuit of the fugitive, not for a moment doubting that she would be caught.

Fifty men, goaded on by threats, were sent into the park, and two hundred more combed the woods and houses of the valley.

The table, cleared in a twinkling, was now made to serve the purpose of a mortuary slab, and the four officers, sobered by the recent happening, stood stiffly at the window staring into the night with the stern expressions of soldiers on duty.

The rain was still falling heavily. The darkness was filled with the sound of splashing and the aimless murmur of water flowing, of water falling, of water dripping and water gushing.

Suddenly a shot rang out, followed by a second very far away, and for four hours there was little to be heard but occasional detonations, close at hand or distant, rallying shouts and foreign words barked out by guttural voices.

At dawn all the men returned. Two soldiers had been killed and three others wounded by their comrades in the excitement of the chase, which had been conducted in unrelieved darkness.

Rachel had not been found.

The inhabitants were subjected to a reign of terror. Their houses were turned inside out, and the whole countryside was overrun, beaten, and thoroughly worked through. The Jewess, it seemed, had vanished without trace.

The General, informed of what had occurred, gave orders that the whole affair was to be hushed up in the interests of discipline. He severely censured the Commandant, who duly punished his officers. The General had said: 'We do not make war for fun nor for the purpose of enjoying the company of prostitutes.' The Count von Farlsberg, in a state of exasperation, was determined to get his own back on the district under his command.

But he needed a pretext for giving full rein to his fury. He therefore sent for the curé, and gave orders that the church bell was to be tolled on the occasion of the funeral of the Marquis von Eyrik.

Contrary to expectation, the priest was docile, submissive, and respectful. When the body of Mademoiselle Fifi, borne by soldiers, preceded, surrounded, and followed by soldiers with rifles loaded, left the Château d'Uville on its way to the cemetery, the bell sounded for the first time since the Prussians' arrival in the village. It rang a funeral knell, but in so lively a manner that a friendly hand might have been stroking it into life.

It rang again that night: it rang the following day and every day. No one could have asked more of it. Sometimes, after dark, it started ringing all by itself and sent a few quiet notes speeding through the night. They seemed to be inspired by a strange gaiety, and had been set going no one knew why. The country folk said the bell was bewitched, and only the curé and the sacristan would go near the tower.

The reason was that the poor girl was living there in an agony of mind and quite alone. The two men brought her food in secret.

And there she stayed until the German troops departed. Then, one evening, the curé having borrowed the baker's cart, she was driven to the gates of Rouen. She got out and hurried back to the bawdy-house. The Madame had thought that she was dead.

She was taken from it some time later by a patriot without prejudices, who loved her, first, for what she had done, after a while, for her own sake. Finally, he married her. In this way she became a lady—no worse than many others.

(1881)

Madame Tellier's Establishment

THEY were in the habit of going there every night, about eleven, quite simply, as though they had merely been dropping in at a café.

Six or eight of them, and always the same, not at all the gay-dog type, but decent citizens, shopkeepers, and specimens of the local youth. They would take a glass of Chartreuse, tease the girls a bit, or have a little solid conversation with Madame, whom everybody treated with respect.

Then they would go home to bed, before midnight. Sometimes, the young men would stay.

The house was quite small, cosily respectable in appearance, painted yellow and standing on a street corner behind the church of Saint-Etienne. The windows commanded a view of the harbour, with its clutter of ships unloading, and of the great salt-marsh known as 'La Retenue' with, beyond it, the 'Virgin's cliff' crowned with an old grey chapel.

Madame came of good peasant stock in the Eure Department. She had taken to her profession as another might have chosen to be a dressmaker or a linen-draper. The dishonourable taint which, in the big towns, hangs about prostitution, is unknown in the Normandy countryside. The peasant says 'It's a sound profession,' and sends his daughter to keep a harem as he might send her to run a girls' school.

As a matter of fact, the establishment had been left to her by an old uncle. She and her husband had formerly had an inn at Yvetot. They sold it on the spot, having decided that the business at Fécamp would pay them better. One fine morning they had taken it over, at a time when it was going downhill for lack of custom.

They were thoroughly good folk, and were soon popular with the neighbours and staff alike.

Two years later, Monsieur died of a stroke. His new way of life had made him flabby and sedentary. He had grown very fat, and good health had killed him.

Madame had settled down into a respectable widowhood, and, though all her 'regulars' had courted her, their efforts had been fruitless. She had a good reputation in the place, and even her girls could discover nothing to her discredit.

She was tall, well-covered, and comely. Living, as she did, in the dim light of shuttered rooms, she had become rather pale, and her face shone as though covered by a thick layer of varnish. Her forehead was framed in a thin trimming of wispy false curls, and these gave her a youthful look which was strongly at variance with the mature curves of her figure. She was invariably gay, and her honest face was always wreathed in smiles. She was fond of a joke, though there was a faint air of reserve about her which change of occupation had not yet dissipated. Coarse words always slightly shocked her, and when some unlicked young cub referred to her establishment by its proper title, she was angry and outraged. She had a sensitive nature and, though she treated her girls as friends, she was never tired of pointing out that they were not really 'her sort'.

Sometimes, on a week-day, she would set off with some of them, in a hired fly, to where a little river runs beyond Valmont, and let them romp upon the grassy banks. These expeditions were like nothing so much as the outings of schoolgirls enjoying a half-holiday, running madcap races and playing childish games, giving full vent to the high spirits of young creatures living a pent-up existence for whom a day in the open air provides a mild form of intoxication. They picnicked off cold meat, sat on the ground, drank cider, and went home when the light began to fail, deliciously tired and in a mildly sentimental mood. On the return journey they hugged Madame, treating her like a good, kind mother brimming with the milk of human kindness, and endlessly indulgent.

The 'establishment' had two entrances. On the corner it provided a slightly shady café which catered for sailors and the lower orders of the town. Two of the women dealt with the requirements of this section of Madame Tellier's *clientèle*. With the help of a youngster called Frédéric, who was fair, beardless, small, but as strong as an ox, they kept the rickety marble-topped tables supplied with jugs of wine and bottles of beer, and, perched on the customers' knees with their arms round their necks, encouraged them in their drinking.

The other three women (there were only five in all) formed the aristocratic element, and attended only on the upstairs company, except when they were needed below and the first-floor room happened to be empty.

This, known as the 'Jupiter', was where the more solid citizens spent their evenings. It had a blue wall-paper, was embellished with a picture of Leda lying beneath a swan, and could be reached only by way of a spiral staircase leading from a narrow, modest-looking door which gave on to the street. Above this door, behind a screen of wire-netting, there burned from dusk till dawn, a little lamp of the kind which, in small towns, are still lit before images of the Madonna set in niches in the walls.

The house was old, damp, and had a faintly musty smell. Now and again a whiff of eau-de-Cologne drifted down the passages. Sometimes when a door was suddenly opened downstairs, there came, like a clap of thunder, the gross babble of the café customers, which brought to the faces of the privileged an expression of uneasiness and disgust.

Madame, who was on familiar terms with those customers whom she regarded as her friends, never left the salon, but sat there listening with interest to the local gossip they brought with them. This serious conversation made a change from the inconsequential chatter of the three women. It was, as it were, an oasis in the desert of doubtful jokes which were the stock-in-trade of the paunchy gentlemen who found relaxation, every evening, in the harmless, if somewhat undistinguished, laxity of taking a glass of liqueur in the company of prostitutes.

The three ladies of the drawing-room floor were called Fernande, Raphaële, and Rosa la Rosse.

The staff being limited in numbers, the idea had been to make each member of it a sample, an abstract, of one particular type, so that all the patrons of the establishment might find within its walls the realization of their ideal type of womanhood, or, at least, something approximating to it. Fernande stood for the 'Golden Girl'. She was very tall, verging on the stout, flaccid, very much the country type, with a chronic display of freckles, and fair hair worn short. This last was somewhat colourless, and looked like combed hemp. There was very little of it, and it barely covered her head.

Raphaële, who was from Marseilles, and a typical water-front moll, was cast for the indispensable rôle of the *lovely Jewess*. She was thin, with prominent cheek-bones which she plastered with rouge. Her black, thickly greased hair hung over her ears in ringlets. Her eyes would have been fine, had not the right one been disfigured by a white speck. An aquiline nose jutted over a strongly-marked jaw and two false upper teeth contrasted strongly with the lower ones to which increasing age had given the dark colour to be seen in old wood.

Rosa la Rosse was a little bundle of fat, mostly stomach, with very short legs. She had a raucous voice and spent her time, from morning till night, singing songs which varied between the bawdy and the sentimental, and in telling interminable and pointless stories. She never stopped talking except to eat, and never stopped eating except to talk. She was perpetually restless and as nimble as a squirrel in spite of her fat body and diminutive feet. Her laughter was a cascade of shrill screams, endlessly audible here, there, and everywhere, in bedroom, attic, bar—all over the house. It never seemed to be about anything in particular.

The two downstairs women, Louise, nicknamed Cocote, and Flora, known as Balançoire, because she had a slight limp—the one always dressed like a figure of *Liberty*, with a tricolour sash, the other got-up like a comic-opera Spaniard, with copper sequins dancing in her carroty hair at every uneven step she took—looked like a couple of kitchen-maids dressed for a carnival. They were unremarkable lower-class females, neither worse- nor better-looking than many others, and perfect examples of the inn wench. They were known along the water-front as the Two Pumps.

An uneasy peace, the product of jealousy, held sway among these five, and, thanks to the wise, conciliatory attitude of Madame, and her inexhaustible good temper, it was rarely troubled.

The establishment had no competitor in the little town, and was much frequented. So superior a tone had Madame succeeded in giving to it, so agreeable and attentive was she to everybody, and so well known for her easy kindliness, that she had come to be widely respected. There was nothing the 'regulars' would not do for her. They were filled with elation when she was more than usually friendly, and, whenever they happened to meet during the day on their lawful occasions, would say: 'See you this evening, you know where,' as if they were saying: 'The café, as usual, after dinner, eh?'

In short, Madame Tellier's establishment was a convenient place of meeting, and few, if any, failed to turn up at the nightly gathering.

One evening, towards the end of May, the first arrival, Monsieur Poulin, the Timber Merchant and a former mayor, found the door shut. The little lamp in its wire cage was unlit. No sound came from the interior. The house seemed to be completely dead. He knocked, gently at first, then more noisily, but there was no answer. Then, he went slowly back up the street, and, on reaching the market-square, ran into Monsieur Duvert, the Ship-Owner, who was headed for the same port of call. They returned to the house together, but with no

success. There was a sudden outburst of noise close to them, and, as they turned the corner, they came upon a crowd of sailors, both French and English, who were banging on the shutters of the café with their fists.

The two honest citizens immediately took to their heels, so as not to get involved, but a faint 'pss't' brought them to a halt. It was Monsieur Tournevau, the Fish-Salter, who had recognized and hailed them. They explained matters to him, the hearing of which affected him the more since, as a married man and the father of a family, he was closely watched and could get away from home only on Saturday evenings, *securitatis causa*, as he put it, alluding to a certain measure of hygienic caution about the recurrent periods of which his friend, Doctor Borde, kept him regularly informed. This was one of his evenings, and he would, therefore, be in a state of privation for a whole additional week.

The three men took a roundabout way to the harbour, and, in the course of their walk, met young Monsieur Philippe, the Bank-Manager's son, one of the 'regulars', and Monsieur Pimpesse, the Tax-Collector. They all turned back, together, along the Rue 'aux Juifs', intending to try once more. But the sailors, by now in an angry mood, were laying siege to the house, throwing stones and shouting, with the result that the five first-floor customers beat as hasty a retreat as possible, and started to wander through the streets.

The next fellow-sufferers they met were Monsieur Dupuis, the Insurance Agent, and Monsieur Vasse, the Judge of the Commercial Court. A long walk began, which took them, first, to the jetty, where they sat in a row on the stone parapet and looked at the white-horses. The spume on the crests of the waves made livid patches of light in the darkness, which vanished as quickly as they came, while the monotonous sound of the sea breaking against the rocks filled the gathering dusk all the way along the cliffs.

When the melancholy wanderers had stayed there for a while, Monsieur Tournevau came out with: 'Not very cheerful, I must say!' To which Monsieur Pimpesse replied: 'It certainly is not!' After this exchange they all moved slowly off again.

After proceeding along the street, called 'Sous-le-Bois', which dominates all this section of the coast, they turned back across the wooden bridge over La Retenue, passed close to the railway line, and once again debouched into the market square. At this point a quarrel suddenly flared up between the Tax-Collector, Monsieur Pimpesse, and the Fish-Salter, Monsieur Tournevau, about an edible fungus which one of them declared that he had found in the neighbourhood.

Boredom had so frayed their tempers that they might have come to blows had not the others intervened. Monsieur Pimpesse made off in a fury, and, almost at once, a fresh altercation arose between the former mayor, Monsieur Poulin, and the Insurance Agent, Monsieur Dupuis, on the subject of the Tax-Collector's salary and probable perquisites. Angry words were falling thick and fast when a tempest of terrifying yells burst over their heads and the crowd of sailors, sick of waiting in vain in front of the locked and bolted house, swarmed into the square. The men were walking two by two, with linked arms, in a long procession, and shouting furiously.

The group of law-abiding citizens took refuge in a doorway, and the howling mob disappeared in the direction of the abbey. For a long while the noise could still be heard, growing fainter, like a storm moving away. Silence returned.

Monsieur Poulin and Monsieur Dupuis, still furious with one another, went off in different directions, without saying good night.

The other four resumed their walk, instinctively making their way downhill in the direction of Madame Tellier's establishment. It was still shut, silent, and impenetrable. A quiet but pig-headed drunkard kept tapping at the café window, then stopped and called in a loud voice to Frédéric, the waiter. Getting no reply, he decided to sit down on the doorstep and await developments.

The others were just about to turn away, when the noisy crowd of men from the harbour appeared again at the end of the street. The French sailors were bawling the *Marseillaise* and the English, *Rule Britannia*. There was a concerted rush towards the house, and then the tide of drunken brutes ebbed in the direction of the waterfront, where a battle ensued between the representatives of the two nations. In the general hurly-burly one Englishman sustained a fractured arm, and one Frenchman got a broken nose.

The drunkard who had stayed outside the door, was now crying as old soaks and thwarted children cry.

The citizenry then dispersed.

Peace gradually returned to the troubled town. Here and there, and now and then, the sound of a voice rose in the still night air, then faded away into the distance.

But one lone man was still wandering aimlessly. Monsieur Tournevau, the Fish-Salter, disconsolate at the thought of having to wait for a whole week, hoping for some stroke of luck, and not realizing what had happened, was furious with the police for sanctioning the closing down, in this way, of a public-utility which they had taken under their wing, and watched over with a fatherly eye.

He turned back to the house, sniffing at the walls like a dog, trying to find a reason for the extraordinary occurrence. It was then that he saw a notice stuck on the door. He quickly struck a waxvesta, and read the following words written in a large, uneven hand:

Shut on the occasion of a First Communion.

Then he walked away, knowing that now there was nothing left to hope for.

The drunkard had fallen asleep, stretched at full length across the inhospitable threshold.

Next morning, all the regulars, one after the other, found some excuse for walking down the street, with bundles of papers under their arms to provide some ostensible reason for being there; and, with a sidelong glance, each read the mysterious notice:

Shut on the occasion of a First Communion.

PART II

The fact of the matter was that Madame had a brother who had long been established as a carpenter in their native village of Virville in the Eure Department. At the time when she was still the innkeeper's wife at Yvetot, she had stood godmother to her brother's daughter, when the child had been christened Constance Rivet, she herself being a Rivet on her father's side. The carpenter, who knew that his sister was in a good position, had never lost sight of her, though they rarely met, each being fully occupied with his, or her, concerns, and because they lived at a considerable distance from one another. But now, since the girl was close on twelve years old, and was to make her First Communion that year, he had jumped at this opportunity to renew acquaintance with his sister, and had written to say that he relied upon her to be present at the ceremony. The old people were dead, and she could scarcely refuse to give the support of her presence to her god-daughter. Consequently, she had accepted her brother's invitation. His name was Joseph, and he hoped that, by showing her sufficient attention, he might get her to make a Will in his daughter's favour, Madame having no children of her own.

His sister's profession in no way troubled him, especially as no one in his native place knew anything about it. All that people said of her, when her name was mentioned, was: 'Madame Tellier has settled in Fécamp', the implication being that she was living on money of her own. Virville is at least fifty miles from Fécamp, and, for a peasant, fifty miles of road are as difficult to cross as is the ocean for one bred in a city. The inhabitants of Virville had never been further afield than Rouen, and there was nothing to draw those of Fécamp to a tiny village of five hundred households in a remote corner of the flat land and in a different Department. Nobody, therefore, knew anything.

But as the date of the ceremony drew near, Madame found herself in a state of considerable embarrassment. She had no assistant manageress, and could not dream of leaving her establishment to its own devices even for a day. The jealousies which existed between the ground-floor and the first, would be bound to burst out. She felt sure that Frédéric would have a drinking-bout, and when he was drunk he would punch anybody's head for no reason at all. So, she decided to take the whole of her staff with her, excepting only the waiter, to whom she gave a forty-eight-hour holiday.

Her brother, when consulted, raised no difficulty and undertook to put the whole party up for the night. The eight-o'clock express, therefore, carried away Madame and her companions in a second-class compartment.

As far as Beuzeville they were alone, and chattered like a lot of magpies, but at that station their carriage was invaded by a couple. The man, an old peasant, was wearing a blue smock with a pleated yoke and wide sleeves caught in at the wrist with white stitching. On his head he had an ancient top-hat, the brown nap of which had a shaggy look, and, in one hand, he was carrying an immense green umbrella, while in the other he had hold of a large basket from which projected the frightened faces of three ducks. His wife, who sat stiffly upright in her rustic finery, had the look of a hen, for her nose was as pointed as a beak. She sat opposite her husband, completely motionless and obviously embarrassed at finding herself in such smart company.

For the carriage was glowing with an assortment of dazzling colours. Madame was all in blue, blue silk from head to foot, with, over her dress, a red shawl of imitation French cashmere which was quite blinding in its intensity. Fernande was finding it difficult to breathe in a Scots plaid, the bodice of which, tightly laced by the efforts of her companions, forced up her sagging bosom into a heaving double-dome, which gave the impression of being in a state of liquescence under the stretched fabric.

Raphaële had on her head a feathered arrangement which looked like a nestful of birds. Her dress was of lilac, speckled with gold. It struck a faintly oriental note which went well with the Jewess's cast of feature. Rosa la Rosse was wearing a pink skirt with wide flounces which gave her the appearance of a podgy child or a dwarf run to fat. The Two Pumps looked as though they had contrived their get-up from old window-curtains of that flowered material which dates from the time of the French Restoration.

As soon as they were no longer alone in the carriage, the ladies assumed prim expressions and began to talk of serious matters in the hope of making a good impression. But at Bolbec, a gentleman with light-coloured whiskers, several rings, and a gold chain, joined the party and stowed away on the rack a number of parcels wrapped in American cloth. He appeared to be a good-natured fellow and a bit of a wag. He raised his hat, grinned, and asked in a free-and-easy way:

'You garrison-ladies been posted somewhere else?'

The reaction to this question was one of confused embarrassment. Madame was the first to say anything, and she did so sharply, as though to vindicate the honour of the regiment:

'I'd thank you to keep a civil tongue in your head, young man!'

'Sorry, I'm sure: perhaps I should have said *conventual!*'

Madame, finding nothing to say to this, or perhaps feeling that she had already sufficiently put him in his place, inclined her head with a thin-lipped acknowledgement.

The new-comer, who was seated between Rosa la Rosse and the old peasant, began to wink at the three ducks whose heads were sticking out of the big basket. Then, as soon as he felt that he had got the attention of his audience, he started to tickle the creatures under their beaks, making facetious remarks the while, just to lighten the atmosphere.

'So we've left our little pond, have we, quack-quack-quack, just to see what the little spit's like, quack-quack-quack!'

The wretched fowls kept turning their heads to avoid his fingers, and were struggling desperately to get out of their wicker prison. Then, suddenly, all three uttered a lamentable quack! quack! quack! There was an explosion of laughter from the women. They craned their heads forward, pushing and shoving to get a better view. They appeared to be madly interested in the ducks, and the whiskered gentleman redoubled his buffooneries.

Then Rosa took a hand in the game, and, leaning across her neighbour's legs, kissed the three creatures on the beak. At once,

119

all the others wanted to kiss them, too. The gentleman took the ladies on his knee, jumped them up and down, pinched them, and addressed them in the most familiar fashion.

The peasant couple, even more disconcerted than their fowls, rolled their eyes like lunatics. They did not dare make a movement, and their old wrinkled faces showed neither a smile nor a tremor.

The gentleman—who was a commercial traveller—thought it a good joke to offer the ladies braces, and then, taking one of his packages from the rack, opened it. This was by way of being a sly dodge, for it contained an assortment of garters.

There was every variety: blue silk, pink silk, red silk, violet silk, mauve silk, flame-coloured silk, all with metal clasps in the form of cupids embracing. The girls uttered little cries of delight, and scrutinized the samples with that seriousness which comes naturally to women as soon as they get their hands on articles of dress. They exchanged questioning glances, sometimes a whispered word or two, while Madame longingly handled a pair of orange garters broader and more imposing than the rest, and just the very thing for an employer of female labour.

The gentleman sat waiting. A brilliant idea had just come to him.

'You must try them on, my dears!'

There was a general cry of protest, and the ladies, one and all, tucked their skirts between their legs as though fearing that they were in imminent danger of being raped. He, meanwhile, was quietly biding his time.

'If you don't want 'em, I'll put 'em back,' he said. Then, slyly: 'Tell you what, those as try 'em on shall have a pair free, gratis, and for nothing!' But they sat stiffly, in dignified silence, refusing the proffered bait. The Two Pumps, however, looked so unhappy that he made another cast. Flora Balançoire, especially, was so torn with longing that she was visibly hesitating. He pressed her hard. 'Come along, my dear: only needs a bit of courage: the lilac pair would match your dress to perfection.' This was too much for her. Pulling up her skirt she displayed a great milkmaid's leg in a badly fitting coarse stocking. He bent down and adjusted the garter, first below her knee, then above it, tickling her gently to make her squeal and wriggle, after which he presented her with the lilac pair.

'Who's next?'

There was a chorus of 'Me! Me!' He began with Rosa la Rosse, who exhibited a shapeless object, solidly round and without the trace of an ankle, a regular 'sausage of a leg' as Raphaële was fond of saying. Fernande was complimented by the traveller, who waxed enthusias-

tic over her powerful columns. The skinny shanks of the handsome
Jewess met with less applause. Louise Cocote draped her petticoat
over his head as a joke, and Madame felt herself compelled to inter-
vene to put a stop to such unseemly behaviour. But, finally, she
herself extended her leg, a beautiful Normandy leg, plump and
muscular, and the traveller, surprised and entranced, gallantly, like
a true Frenchman, raised his hat as a tribute to so supreme a
masterpiece.

The two peasants, stiff with horrified amazement, were stealing
sidelong glances at these goings-on, and so exactly like a brace of
fowls did they look, that when the gentleman with the light-coloured
whiskers sat back, he made a clucking noise in their faces, which let
loose another storm of laughter.

The old people got out at Motteville, with their basket, their
ducks, and their umbrella. As they moved away, the wife could be
heard saying to her husband:

'Just a lot of riff-raff—they'm be off back to that ther sink o'
niquity, Paris.'

The agreeable pedlar left the train, in his turn, at Rouen, after
behaving so grossly that Madame had felt obliged to give him a
piece of her mind, which she did, winding up, as though with a
moral tag, 'And this will be a lesson to us not to speak to strangers!'

At Oisel they had to change, and, at the next station, found
Monsieur Joseph Rivet waiting for them with a large farm-cart furnished with chairs and drawn by a white horse.

The carpenter politely kissed all the ladies, and helped them into
the conveyance. Three of them sat on chairs at the back; Raphaële,
Madame, and her brother sat on chairs in front. Rosa, having
nothing to sit on, made herself as comfortable as she could on big
Fernande's lap. Then they started off.

But from the very first, the nag's jerky amble shook the cart so
terribly that the chairs began to dance about, throwing the passengers up into the air, to right and left, so that their arms and legs
moved like those of marionettes. Their faces were contorted with
terror, and they uttered shrill screams of alarm, now and then cut
short by a more than usually violent bump. They clung to the
sides of the cart, their hats fell forward over their noses, down their
backs or on to their shoulders, while the white horse kept moving,
with its neck extended, every so often, flicking his straight little
backside stump, which was completely devoid of hair and looked
like a rat's tail. Joseph Rivet, with one foot braced against a shaft,
the other leg doubled up under him, and his elbows very high, held

the reins, all the while making a clucking sound with his tongue which caused the nag to prick its ears and quicken its stride.

On either side of the road stretched the green countryside. Patches of flowering colza showed as undulating expanses of yellow. They gave off a strong but wholesome smell, sweet and penetrating, which the wind carried to a great distance. In the rye, which was already tall, the cornflowers showed their little azure heads, which the women wanted to pick, but Monsieur Rivet would not stop. Here and there a whole field seemed soaked in blood, so numerous were the poppies which had invaded it. Through this coloured plain, the cart, laden with a great cluster of even brighter blossoms, moved to the trot of the white horse, vanished behind the tall trees of a farm, then reappeared where the foliage ceased, and, under the blazing sun, continued on its way between the green and yellow crops, starred with red and blue, carrying its garish load of women.

One o'clock was striking when they stopped at the carpenter's door.

The bones of all the company ached, and they were pale from hunger, for they had had nothing to eat since they had started from Fécamp. Madame Rivet bustled out, made them get down one by one, and gave each a kiss as soon as her feet touched the ground. So eager was she to make much of her sister-in-law, that it looked as though her endearments would never cease.

A meal was laid in the workshop, which had been cleared of its benches in readiness for the morrow's dinner.

A good omelet followed by sausage cooked in cider, soon restored the high spirits of the travellers. Rivet raised his glass to the health of his guests. His wife did the cooking and the serving, handed the dishes, took away the empty plates, whispering in each person's ear as she did so: 'Sure you've had all you want?' The piles of planks leaning against the walls and the heaps of shavings swept into the corners gave out a fragrance of planed wood, that resinous smell of a carpenter's shop which penetrates right into the lungs.

There were calls for the little girl, but she was at church and would not be back till evening.

Then the company went for a stroll in the fields.

The village was small, and built on either side of a main road. Ten or so houses facing this single thoroughfare were occupied by shopkeepers—the butcher, the grocer, the carpenter, the cobbler, the baker, and the café. The church was at one end of this so-called street, standing in a small churchyard and shadowed by four enormous lime-trees which grew in front of the porch. It was built of chipped flints, had no pretensions to style, and was crowned by a slate-roofed belfry. Immediately beyond it stretched the open country, with here and there a clump of trees hiding a farmstead.

As an act of courtesy, Rivet, though in his working clothes, had taken his sister's arm, and walked beside her with a solemn and self-conscious air. His wife, quite overcome by Raphaële's gold-spangled dress, followed behind her and Fernande. Bunchy Rosa brought up the rear with Louise Cocote and Flora Balançoire, whose limp was more pronounced than usual because she was so tired.

The inhabitants came out on to their doorsteps, the children broke off their games, a lifted curtain afforded a glimpse of a head in a muslin cap, an old woman on crutches, and almost blind, crossed herself as though a religious procession were passing, and, for a long time, the eyes of everyone in the village followed the progress of the lovely city ladies who had come so far to attend the First Communion of Joseph Rivet's little girl. The carpenter was basking in a haze of glory.

As they passed the church they could hear the sound of children singing, of thin young voices chanting a song of praise to Heaven. But Madame would let nobody go in for fear of disturbing the little angels.

After a walk, in the course of which Joseph enumerated all the chief properties, and gave, in detail, their yield in crops and livestock, he took his party home and settled the ladies in.

There was not much room, and it had been arranged that they should sleep two to a bed.

For once, Rivet would sleep in the workshop on a pile of shavings, and his wife would share their bed with her sister-in-law. In the room next door would be Fernande and Raphaële. Louise and Flora were accommodated with a mattress on the kitchen floor, and Rosa was given a small dark cupboard to herself at the top of the stairs, next to the garret where, also for once, the young Communicant would have a shake-down.

When the little girl came home, kisses were rained on her. All the women wanted to fondle her, for they needed an emotional outlet, and had to find employment for the acquired habit of professional cajolery which had led them to kiss the ducks in the train. They took her on their knees in turn, stroked her soft fair hair, and pressed her in their arms with little outbursts of vehement and spontaneous affection. The child, who had been brought up to be docile and sensible, and was, just then, wrought up to a high pitch of religious exaltation, endured these effusions with silent resignation.

Guy de Maupassant

It had been a hard day for everybody, and very soon after the evening meal there was a general move bedwards. The village lay wrapped in that limitless country stillness which seems to have an almost religious quality, that silence and that sense of peace which closes round the heart, strikes deep into the human consciousness, and seems to spread upwards to the very stars. The girls, accustomed to the noisy night-hours of their trade, found a new emotional thrill in the tranquillity of the sleeping countryside. They shivered a little, not from cold, but from a feeling of solitude which comes to restless and uneasy hearts.

No sooner were they bedded, two by two, than they snuggled into one another's arms, as though seeking protection against the invading silence of the slumbering earth. But Rosa la Rosse, in her dark cupboard, alone and little used to sleeping with her arms unoccupied, was overcome by an emotion at once painful and indefinable. She lay turning and tossing, but sleep would not come, and then, all of a sudden, from behind the wood partition at her head, she caught the sound of muffled sobbing as of a crying child. She was frightened and called aloud uncertainly. A small voice, broken with sobs, replied. It was the little girl, who, used to sleeping in her parents' room, was feeling frightened in her narrow garret.

The delighted Rosa got up and, very quietly, so as to awaken nobody, fetched the child. She took her into her warm bed, clasped her, kissed her, fondled her, and treated her with exaggerated manifestations of tenderness, after which, feeling calmer, she fell asleep. The young Communicant lay till morning, with her head on the naked bosom of the prostitute.

At five o'clock, the hour of the *Angelus*, the church bell ringing at full pitch wakened all five women, who normally slept the morning through, that being the only time of rest they had from their exacting labours. In the village, the country-folk were already out and about, the women hurrying from door to door, talking with animation, carrying short muslin frocks starched stiff as cardboard, or outsize candles adorned half-way up with bows of gold-fringed silk, and marked with grooves cut in the wax to indicate where the bearers' fingers should go. The sun was already high, the sky of an unsullied blue except where, low on the horizon, a faint rosy flush still showed the vanishing trace of dawn. Whole families of hens were parading in front of their roosts, and, here and there, a black cock with gleaming neck lifted his red-combed head, flapped his wings, and flung a brazen challenge on the air, which was echoed by all his fellows.

Carts were arriving from the nearby parishes, and discharging at the different doors tall Norman women in dark dresses, with fichus crossed upon their breasts and secured with little silver brooches of great age. The men wore blue smocks over brand-new frock-coats, or over ancient party garments, the tails of which hung down below the bottom edge.

When the horses had been stabled, a double row of rustic conveyances were left standing beside the main road—traps, gigs, and wagonettes of every shape and every degree of age, some pitched forward on their noses, others sitting on their backsides with their shafts in the air.

The carpenter's house was as busy as a beehive. The visiting ladies, in petticoats and dressing-jackets, with their thin, short hair, faded and worn with use, hanging down their backs, were engaged in dressing the little girl.

She was standing upright and motionless on a table, while Madame Tellier directed the movements of her flying-column. They washed her, combed her, did her hair, put on her dress, and, with the help of a multitude of pins, arranged the folds of the skirt, took in the waist—which was a great deal too large—and generally tidied and embellished her. When all was finished to their satisfaction, the long-suffering little victim was told to sit down and not move, while the party of excited acolytes hurried away to titivate themselves.

The bells of the little church resumed their ringing. Their thin tinkle rose into the air, and was soon lost, like a feeble voice, in the blue immensity.

The young Communicants emerged from open doorways, and made their way towards the village hall which housed the two schools and the *mairie*, and stood at the other end of the street from the 'House of God'.

The parents, all in their Sunday best, with the self-conscious looks and awkward movements of those whose bodies are forever bent over their work in the fields, followed behind. The little girls disappeared in a snowy cloud of muslin which looked like whipped cream, while the little men, resembling nothing so much as waiters in embryo, with their hair smarmed down, walked with their legs astraddle so as not to dirty the bottoms of their black trousers.

It was a justifiable cause of pride in a family when its own small heroine was surrounded by a flock of relatives who had travelled from a distance to be present at the ceremony. Consequently the carpenter's triumph was complete. The Tellier regiment, with

Madame at its head, marched behind Constance, her father arm-in-arm with his sister, her mother walking with Raphaële, Fernande with Rosa, the Two Pumps side by side. The spectacle was truly impressive, and every whit as fine as a General Staff in full uniform.

The effect upon the village was overwhelming.

On reaching the school building, the girls fell in under the coif of the good Sister, the boys under the hat of the schoolmaster, a good-looking man who performed his office with an air. The whole body then moved off to the strains of a hymn.

The male youngsters walked in double file between the rows of unharnessed vehicles, followed by the girls, similarly disposed. Out of consideration for the visitors, the inhabitants had yielded pride of place to the ladies from the town, who came immediately behind the children, prolonging the double line of the procession still further, and looking, in their bright dresses, like the set-piece of a firework display.

Their entry into the church was sensational. The congregation pushed and jostled and turned their heads to look. Even the more pious of the ancients chattered almost in raised voices, so amazed were they by the sight of all these ladies more glitteringly garbed than the Cantors in their chasubles. The mayor offered them his pew—the first one to the right, close to the Choir—and Madame Tellier took her place there, with her sister-in-law, Fernande, and Raphaële. Rosa la Rosse and the Two Pumps, together with the carpenter, occupied the one behind.

The Choir was filled with kneeling children, girls on one side, boys on the other, and the tall candles in their hands looked like lances leaning in all directions.

In front of the lectern stood three men, all chanting at the tops of their voices, dragging out indefinitely the syllables of the sonorous Latin, prolonging the interminable *a-a* of the *Amen*, as though they would never leave off. They were supported by a single monotonous note brayed from the wide metallic gullet of the Serpent. The shrill voice of a choirboy gave the response, and, from time to time, a priest in one of the stalls, wearing a square biretta, got to his feet, jabbered something, and sat down again, while the three Cantors started off once more, their eyes glued to the great book of plain-song which lay open before them on the spread wings of a wooden eagle mounted on a pivot.

Then silence fell. The congregation knelt as one man, and the officiating priest appeared, old, venerable, and white-haired, bending his head above the chalice which he carried in his left hand.

Madame Tellier's Establishment

Before him walked the two servers, dressed in red, and behind him came a great crowd of choristers in clumsy great boots, who lined up on either side of the Choir.

A small bell tinkled in the great silence, and the Divine Office began. The priest moved slowly from side to side before the golden tabernacle, genuflecting, and intoning the preparatory prayers in a cracked voice, tremulous with age. As soon as he stopped, the Cantors and the Serpent struck up with one accord, and several men in the body of the church chimed in, though less loudly and more humbly, as befitted mere members of the congregation. Suddenly the *Kyrie Eleison* leapt heavenwards from every breast and every heart. Grains of dust and fragments of worm-eaten wood actually fell from the old vaulted ceiling, dislodged by this explosion of sound. The sun beating on the slate roof turned the little church into an oven and, as the ineffable mystery drew near, a surge of emotion, a moment of intolerable suspense gripped the children's hearts and made their mothers' throats contract.

The priest, who had sat down for a few moments, now rose and moved to the altar. With his silvered head uncovered and his hands trembling with age, he made ready to perform the supernatural act.

He turned towards the faithful, and, stretching out his hands, said: '*Orate, frates*, brethren, let us pray.' The old man stammered the mysterious and culminating words in a low voice. The bell tinkled several times in succession. The kneeling crowd called upon God. The children were almost fainting, so unendurable was the emotion which had hold of them.

It was then that Rosa, her face buried in her hands, suddenly remembered her mother, the village church of her childhood, her own First Communion. It was as though that long-past day had come again, when she, so tiny then, had been almost smothered in her white dress. She began to cry, at first quietly, the slow tears oozing from between her lids, then, as memories swarmed and her emotion grew, more loudly. She took out her handkerchief, dabbed at her eyes, covered her nose and mouth to stifle her cries, but all in vain. Something like a rattle rose in her throat, and two deep and rending sighs made answer; for Louise and Flora, kneeling beside her, their hearts wrung by similar memories from a distant past, were moaning, too, swept by a torrent of tears.

But, tears being contagious, Madame, in her turn, soon felt a moisture in her eyes, and, turning towards her sister-in-law, noticed that all those in the pew were also weeping.

Under the priest's hands, the body of God took on substance. The children, victims of a sort of pious dread, and now barely conscious, had fallen to their knees upon the flags. Here and there throughout the church, a woman, a mother, a sister caught up in that strange sympathy which strong emotions breed, and affected, too by seeing the fine ladies kneeling in their pews shaken and sobbing, was saturating her checked cotton handkerchief, and pressing her left hand to her throbbing heart.

As a spark will set alight a ripened cornfield, so did the tears of Rosa and her friends sweep, in a moment, through the congregation. Men and women, old and young, in brand-new smocks, were soon sobbing their hearts out, and above their heads there seemed to hover something superhuman, a spirit diffused, the miraculous breath of an invisible, All-Powerful Being.

Then, from the Choir, there came a short, sharp sound. The good Sister had rapped her service-book, as a sign that the Communicants should take their places, and the children, shaking in an access of divine fever, approached the sacred table.

One whole row kneeled down. The old priest, holding the silver-gilt paten in his hand, passed in front of them, extending to each, with two fingers, the Blessed Host, the Body of Christ, the World's Redeemer. They opened their mouths, their dead-white faces twitching convulsively, and the long napkin spread beneath their chins rippled like running water.

Suddenly, a sort of madness seemed to take possession of the church, the noise, as it were, of a crowd roused to frenzy, a storm of sobs and stifled cries. It passed like one of those gusts of wind that set the tree-tops swaying in a forest, and the priest stood motionless, a wafer in his hand, paralysed by emotion, and saying to himself: 'God is among us, and in this way manifests His presence. For I did call unto Him and He is come down upon His kneeling people.' In a rush of ecstasy he babbled prayers as one demented, unable to form the words, prayers of the spirit.

He finished administering Communion in such a state of exaltation that he could scarcely stand upright on his feet, and, when he drank the blood of his Lord, collapsed under the fervour of his thankfulness.

Behind him, the congregation gradually grew calmer. The Cantors, sustained by the dignity of their white surplices, resumed their chanting, though with unsteady voices still moist with tears. The very Serpent seemed to croak as if it, too, had been weeping.

Then the priest raised his hands and motioned for silence. Passing between the two rows of Comunicants lost in an ecstasy of joy, he approached the Screen.

The congregation had sat down again with much scraping of chairs and much noise of noses being blown. But, as soon as they saw the priest, they became silent. He began to speak in a very low, subdued, and hesitant voice.

'Dear brethren, sisters, and children, I thank you from the bottom of my heart. You have just made me happier than I have ever been in all my long life. For I have felt the presence of God descending upon you in answer to my prayer. He came: He was present here among you, filling your hearts and drawing tears from your eyes. I am the oldest priest in this diocese, and today I am also the happiest. A miracle has been wrought among you, a great miracle, a true miracle, a sublime manifestation. While Jesus Christ was entering, for the first time, into the bodies of these little ones, the Holy Spirit, the Heavenly Dove, the very Breath of God came upon you, possessed and ravished you, so that you were bent like reeds beneath the wind.'

Then, in a stronger voice, turning to the pews in which the carpenter's guests were sitting:

'First of all,' he said, 'my thanks go out to you, my dear sisters, who have come from so great a distance. Your presence among us, your visible faith, your lively piety, have been for all of us a salutary example. You have been for my parish a means of edification, and your emotion has warmed our hearts. Without you, this day, perhaps, would not have had so truly divine a character. Sometimes, the presence of but a single chosen lamb is enough to induce Our Lord to show His loving-kindness to the flock.'

His voice faltered, and he added:

'May the Grace of God be with you—Amen.'

Then he went back to the altar to bring the office to a close.

Everybody was in a great hurry to be gone. Even the children were restless, exhausted by so long a continuance of spiritual tension. Besides, they were hungry, and, one after the other, parents melted away to get dinner ready, without waiting for the final Gospel.

Outside the church there was a noisy crowd, a confusion of shrill voices among which the sing-song Normandy accent was predominant. The villagers formed up in rows, and, when the children appeared, each family pounced upon its own.

Constance found herself seized upon, surrounded, and embraced by the whole houseful of women. Rosa, in particular, seemed to be prepared to go on fondling her for ever. At last, however, with Rosa taking one hand and Madame Tellier the other, with Raphaële and Fernande acting as train-bearers so as to keep the long muslin train from trailing in the mud, and with Louise and Flora bringing up the rear with Madame Rivet, the child, rapt, and wholly possessed by the God she carried within her, set off for home surrounded by her guard of honour.

Dinner was served in the workshop on long trestle tables.

The noise of merrymaking came through the door which stood open to the street. Feasting was now the order of the day. Through every window of the village could be seen tables crowded with guests in their Sunday finery, and from every house came sounds of jollity. Peasants in their shirt-sleeves were busy drinking brimming mugs of unwatered cider, and in the middle of each party could be seen two children, here two girls, there two boys, being entertained by one or other of their respective families.

Occasionally, in the torrid heat of noon, a farm-cart would pass by, drawn at an ambling trot by its old nag, and the smock-clad driver looking with envious eyes at the scenes of revelry.

In the carpenter's house the gaiety was to some extent subdued, for the after-effects of the morning's emotion had not yet been wholly dissipated. Only Rivet himself was in really good form, with the result that he was drinking to excess. Madame Tellier was keeping a careful watch on the time for, if they were not to lose two successive working-days, they would have to take the 3.55 train which would land them back in Fécamp by the evening.

The carpenter was doing his level best to distract her attention from the clock, in the hope of keeping his guests until the following morning. But Madame adroitly countered all his efforts. Business, after all, was a serious matter.

As soon as coffee had been served, she told her girls to waste no time, but to get ready at once. Then, turning to her brother, she said: 'Please have the horse put in at once,' and went to make her own final preparations.

When she came back, her sister-in-law was waiting to have a word with her about the child. A long conversation ensued, in the course of which nothing definite was decided. The countrywoman played her cards shrewdly, and made a great display of affection, but Madame Tellier, who had got the little girl on her lap, refused to commit herself to anything more than vague promises. She

would think the matter over, she said: after all, there was plenty of time, and they would be seeing each other again.

But there was no sign of the cart, and the girls had not reappeared. From above came a confused noise of loud laughter, scuffling, screams, and hand-clapping. This went on until their host's wife went round to the stable to see whether the conveyance was ready. Madame took this opportunity to go upstairs.

Rivet, very drunk and half undressed, was making vain efforts to rape Rosa, who was helpless with laughter. The Two Pumps had got him by the arms, and were trying to calm him, profoundly shocked at such a scene after the morning's ceremony. Raphaële and Fernande, however, were urging him on, bent double with laughter and holding their sides. At every blundering attempt he made, they screamed the more. He, in a blind fury, and with all his buttons undone, was trying to shake himself free of the two women, and doing his best, at the same time, to tear Rosa's skirt off, spluttering and shouting at the same time: 'So you won't, won't you, you little bitch!' Madame, in a state of high indignation, flung herself upon her brother, gripped him by the shoulders, and pushed him so violently from the room, that he hit the wall.

A minute later, they heard him in the yard, sluicing water over his head; and when he showed up again with the cart, he was in a decidedly subdued state of mind.

They took the same road as on the previous evening, and the little white horse started off at his brisk, dancing trot.

Under the blazing sun, the high spirits which had been held in check during the meal, broke loose. This time, the girls thought it great fun to be jolted about. They jostled each other's chairs, and screamed with laughter, into such a state of excitement had they been worked by Rivet's unsuccessful assault.

There was a dazzling shimmer over the fields, and the wheels raised two long clouds of dust which remained suspended in the air above the road, long after the cart had passed.

Suddenly, Fernande, who had a passion for music, begged Rosa to sing. The girl needed no begging, and immediately obliged with a forceful rendering of *Le Gros Curé de Meudon*. But Madame cut her short, thinking that particular song scarcely suited to the day: 'Let us have something of Béranger's', she said. Then Rosa, after a brief hesitation, struck up *La Grand' Mère*, in a voice that had seen its best days:

> *Ma grand'mère, un soir à sa fête,*
> *De vin pur ayant bu deux doigts,*

Nous disait, en branlant la tête:
Que d'amoureux j'eus autrefois!
Combien je regrette
Mon bras si dodu,
Ma jambe bien faite,
Et le temps perdu!

The others, following Madame's lead, all joined in the chorus:

Combien je regrette
Mon bras si dodu,
Ma jambe bien faite,
Et le temps perdu!

'That's the stuff!' cried Rivet, roused by the tum-ti-tum of the tune, and Rosa went on:

Quoi, maman, vous n'étiez pas sage?
—Non, vraiment! et de mes appas,
Seule, à quinze ans, j'appris l'usage,
Car, la nuit, je ne dormais pas.

They all shouted the refrain; Rivet tapped with his foot on the shaft, and marked the rhythm with the reins on the back of the white nag, who, as though stimulated by the tune, broke into a gallop which flung the ladies in a heap, one on top of the other, at the back of the cart.

They scrambled to their feet, laughing like mad creatures, and the song continued, bawled at the tops of their voices over the countryside, under the blazing sun, between the ripening fields of corn, to the mad gallop of the little horse who worked himself into a positive fever whenever the chorus came round, and, each time, covered his hundred yards, to the great delight of the passengers.

Here and there a stonebreaker straightened up and watched, through his wire mask, the lunatic and noisy conveyance dash past him in a cloud of dust.

When they got down in the station yard, the carpenter grew sentimental:

''Tis a shame you be going,' he said: 'Us could've had a power of fun!'

Madame replied, with solid good sense: 'There's a time for everything: we can't have a holiday every day of the week.'

Rivet had a flash of inspiration: 'Tell you what I'll do,' he said.

'I'll look you up at Fécamp, next month!' And he gave Rosa a knowing look with his bright and roguish eye.

'Now don't you go getting ideas,' Madame concluded: 'come if you like, but, mind, no nonsense!'

To this he made no answer, and, hearing the whistle of the train, set about distributing kisses all round. When it came to Rosa's turn, he tried to get at her mouth, but she, laughing with her lips tight closed, kept it from him with a quick twist of the head. He held her in his arms, but could not get what he wanted, being impeded by the long whip which he had kept in his hand and waved despairingly behind her back.

'Passengers for Rouen, take your seats, please!' cried the guard, and they climbed into the train.

There was a short sharp blast from the guard's whistle, followed by a more powerful one from the engine, which noisily emitted a jet of steam, while the wheels began to turn very slowly and with an obvious effort.

Rivet left the platform and ran to the gates of the level-crossing, so as to get one last look at Rosa. As the compartment with its load of human merchandise passed him, he cracked his whip, and, hopping up and down, roared at the top of his voice:

Combien je regrette
Mon bras si dodu,
Ma jambe bien faite,
Et le temps perdu!

As the train vanished into the distance, he watched a white handkerchief which somebody was waving from a window.

PART III

They slept all the way to Fécamp, and when they reached the house, refreshed and rested for the night's work, Madame could not resist saying:

'It was very pleasant while it lasted, but it's nice to be home.'

They hurried over supper, and then, when they had changed into battle-order, waited for the usual customers. When the little Madonna lamp was lit again, all who passed that way knew that the sheep had returned to the fold.

The news spread with lightning speed, no one knew how, no one knew by whom. Monsieur Philippe, the Bank-Manager's son, carried his obligingness so far as to send an express-messenger to Monsieur Tournevau, pent in the prison of his family.

The Fish-Salter was in the habit of having several cousins to dine every Sunday evening, and they were all quietly drinking their coffee, when a man turned up with a note. Monsieur Tournevau, in great excitement, tore open the envelope. All it contained was the following message written in pencil:

Cargo of cod salved: boat just got in: good business for you: come at once.*

He fumbled in his pocket, gave a few coins to the bearer, suddenly went red to the tips of his ears, and said: 'I'm afraid I shall have to go out.' He handed the mysterious and laconic message to his wife, rang the bell, and, when the maid answered it, told her to bring his hat and his overcoat. He was no sooner in the street than he broke into a run, whistling a tune. So impatient was he that the journey seemed twice its normal length.

Madame Tellier's establishment had a holiday air. On the ground-floor, the men from the harbour were making a deafening din. Louise and Flora, confused by the spate of orders, did not know which way to turn, but drank first with one, then with another, and more than ever lived up to their joint nickname of the 'Two Pumps'. It was not possible for the pair of them to satisfy all demands, and it looked like being an exhausting night for them.

The circle in the upstairs room was at full strength by nine o'clock. Monsieur Vasse, the Judge of the Commercial Court, Madame's acknowledged but platonic suitor, was carrying on a low-voiced conversation with her in a corner. They were both smiling, and it looked as though some settlement was about to be reached. Monsieur Poulin, the former mayor, had got Rosa astride his knee, and she, nose to nose with him, was running her plump little hands through the old fellow's white whiskers. A scrap of bare thigh, under her tucked-up petticoat of yellow silk, showed white against his black trousers, and her red stockings were held in place by the blue garters given to her by the commercial traveller.

Tall Fernande was lying on the sofa with her two feet resting on the stomach of Monsieur Pimpesse, the Tax-Collector, and her body supported against the waistcoat of young Monsieur Philippe. Her right hand was round his neck, and in her left she held a cigarette.

Raphaële appeared to be talking business with Monsieur Dupuis, the Insurance Agent, and wound up the discussion by saying: 'To-

* Morue, *or cod, can also mean* prostitute. (*Translator.*)

night'll suit me fine, darling.' Then, executing a rapid waltz step across the floor: 'Anything you like, tonight,' she called back at him.

At that moment the door was flung open and Monsieur Tournevau appeared. An enthusiastic chorus greeted him: 'Long live Tournevau!' and Raphaële, still pirouetting, threw herself into his arms. He held her in a powerful embrace and, without speaking a word, lifted her off her feet as though she had been a feather, carried her across the room to the door at the far end, and disappeared with his burden up the stairs which led to the bedrooms, to an accompaniment of loud applause.

Rosa, who was fanning the lambent flames of the erstwhile mayor, kissing him repeatedly, and gripping both his whiskers at the same time so as to keep his head straight, took advantage of the example thus given to them. 'Why don't *you* do that?' she said, which had the effect of getting the old gentleman to his feet. He stood for a few moments adjusting his waistcoat, before following her out of the room, fumbling in the pocket which held his money.

Fernande and Madame were left alone with the other four men, and Monsieur Philippe suddenly exclaimed: 'Champagne on me! Be so good as to send for three bottles, Madame Tellier.'

Fernande gave him a hug, and whispered in his ear, 'Play us a dance, do!' He got up, sat down at the elderly spinet which stood dozing in a corner, and drew from the wheezing entrails of the instrument a husky, maudlin waltz. The tall girl put her arms round the Tax-Collector, Madame yielded herself to the embrace of Monsieur Vasse, and the two couples began to revolve, kissing the while. Monsieur Vasse, who, in the old days, had danced in smart society, performed with such elegance that Madame looked at him with an eye enthralled, an eye which said most clearly, 'Yes'—a more discreet and sweeter 'yes' than any word could have expressed.

Frédéric brought the champagne. The first cork popped, and Monsieur Philippe struck up the opening bars of a quadrille.

The four dancers trod it in the manner of high society, with restraint and dignity, bows and curtseys. When it was over, they drank. Then Monsieur Tournevau returned, satisfied, relieved, and radiant. 'I don't know what has happened to Raphaële,' he exclaimed. 'She is quite perfect tonight!' He was handed a glass, which he drained, muttering as he did so: 'All done regardless, I must say!'

At once Monsieur Philippe launched into a lively polka. Monsieur Tournevau made a dashing display with the beautiful Jewess, whom he lifted off the floor. Monsieur Pimpesse and Monsieur Vasse started off again with renewed vigour. Now and again one of the couples paused for a moment at the mantelpiece, to drink a long, narrow glass of sparkling wine. It was beginning to look as though the dancing would go on for ever, when Rosa opened the door with a candle in her hand. Her hair was loose, and she was wearing her nightgown and a pair of bedroom slippers. Her face was flushed and she was very lively. 'I want to dance!' she cried. 'How about the old boy?' asked Raphaële. 'Him? Oh, he's asleep already,' said Rosa, laughing loudly. 'He goes to sleep at once!'

She grabbed hold of Monsieur Dupuis, who was sitting on the sofa, doing nothing, and the polka was resumed.

But the bottles were empty. 'I'll stand another,' declared Monsieur Tournevau. 'Me, too!' said Monsieur Vasse. 'And so will I!' said Monsieur Dupuis, bringing up the rear. There was a general burst of applause.

The evening soon turned into a regular ball. From time to time even Louise and Flora dashed upstairs for a moment, waltzed rapidly once round the room, while their customers kicked their heels below, and then ran down again to the café, their hearts heavy with regret.

At midnight the dancing was still going on. Sometimes one of the girls disappeared and, when she was wanted as a partner, it was noticed suddenly that one of the men was also missing.

'And where have you been?' asked Monsieur Philippe quizzically, just as Monsieur Pimpesse came back with Fernande into the room. 'Watching Monsieur Poulin sleeping,' replied the Tax-Collector. The witticism had a great success, and all, in turn, went upstairs 'to look at Monsieur Poulin sleeping', accompanied by one or other of the girls who, on this night, seemed quite unbelievably willing. Madame shut her eyes to what was going on, and had a number of confidential asides with Monsieur Vasse, as though settling the final details of something already arranged between them.

At one o'clock, the two married men, Monsieur Tournevau and Monsieur Pimpesse, declared that they must really be getting home, and asked for their bills. Only the champagne was charged for, and even that at only six francs a bottle instead of the usual ten. When they expressed surprise at such generosity, Madame beamed at them, and said:

'It's not every day that we have an occasion like this to celebrate.'

(1881)

Marroca

You have asked me, my friend, to send you an account of my impressions, my adventures and, especially, of my love affairs in this land of Africa which, for so long, has held such a great fascination for me. You used to laugh in the old days about what you called my dusky beauties, and said you could imagine me returning home with an ebony-black woman in tow, with a yellow handkerchief wound round her head, striding along in all the colours of the rainbow.

No doubt the Moorish girls will have their turn, for I have already seen more than one who has tempted me to dip my pen in that especial ink: but let me begin differently. I have stumbled on something very much better and *most* unusual.

You said, in your last letter: 'When I know a country's habits in matters of love, that country is as familiar to me as the back of my hand, though I have never seen it.' Well, let me tell you at once that love out here is a sort of wild fever. From the moment of one's first stepping ashore, one is conscious of what I can describe only as a quivering ardour in the air. And with it comes a feeling that one's own desires have been raised to a higher power. There is a tension in the nerves, a tingling which runs through all one's body down to the very finger-tips, so that all one's potentialities of physical sensation are increased, from a simple handshake to those unmentionable cravings which lead us into so many follies.

Let me make myself clear. Whether what you are pleased to call sentimental love, spiritual affinities, idealism, or, in a word, Platonic Devotion, can exist in this part of the world, I very much doubt. But that other variant of love, the sensual, which certainly has something, indeed a great deal, to be said for it, assumes really terrible proportions in the atmospheric conditions of North Africa. The heat, the burning quality of the air, which breeds fever in the veins, the effect of the nearby desert, the stifling sirocco, more devastating and more desiccating than flame, the perpetual blaze of a whole continent scorched to the bone by an enormous and devouring sun—all these things combine to set a conflagration in the blood, to madden the senses, and to turn men into animals.

139

But to go on with my story. I won't bore you with a description of my first days in Algeria. It will be enough if I tell you that after visiting Bône, Constantine, Biskra, and Sétif, I came here to Bougie by way of the Chabet gorges. I know of nothing to compare with that road. It leads through the forests of Kabylia, and follows the coast-line at a height of some six hundred feet, hugging the indentations of a great mountain, and so reaches the Gulf of Bougie which is as beautiful as the Bays of Naples and Ajaccio, and even of Douarnenez, than which I know of nothing more wonderful. I omit from my comparisons that staggering Bay of Porto surrounded by cliffs of red granite on the west coast of Corsica, where stand those fantastic, bloodstained giants, known as the 'Calanche' of Piana.

From far, from very far away, before rounding the harbour of still water, one catches sight of Bougie. It is built on the steep side of a high mountain crowned with trees, and shows as a white patch on the green slope. It has the appearance almost of a foaming cataract falling to the sea.

I had no sooner entered this small, enchanting town, than I knew that I should stay there for a long time. Whichever way one looks, one sees a vast circle of toothed and rocky crests, notched, indented, and fantastically shaped, so closely set together that one can barely catch a glimpse of the open sea. In fact, the Gulf looks like an inland lake. Its water is a pale blue most wonderfully clear, and the azure of the sky, as thick and dense as though it had had two coats of paint, spreads over this scene of breath-taking beauty. Land and sky seem to be reflected in one another.

Bougie is a place of ruins. On the quay one finds oneself confronted by a pile of debris on so stupendous a scale that it might be part of a stage-set at the Opera. It is all that remains of the old Saracen port, now overgrown with ivy. In the woods on the high ground are scraps of Roman walls, Saracen monuments, and Arab buildings.

I have taken a lease of a small Moorish house in the upper town. I expect you know all about these dwellings, since they have so often been described. They have no windows in their outer walls, but draw all their light from an inner court. On the first floor there is a large, cool room in which one spends the days, and, higher up, a terrace where one passes the nights.

I have adopted the custom of the country—the custom, I mean, of taking a siesta after the midday meal. That is the hottest and most airless time of the day in Africa. One can scarcely breathe.

Marroca

The streets, the open country, and the long, blinding roads are empty of all life. Everyone is asleep, or trying to sleep, clad in the minimum of clothing.

In my living-room, with its colonnade of Arab design, I have installed a large and soft divan, covered with a carpet from Djebel-Amour. There, during those first weeks I lay down in the afternoon wearing little more than Adam, but found little rest, for I was tortured by continence.

There are two forms of torment on this earth, my dear friend, which I hope you will never experience: lack of water and lack of women. Which is the worse I am not prepared to say. In the desert a man will commit any crime for a glass of cold, clear water. What would he not do in some of the coast towns that I know, for a cool, clean woman? There is no shortage of the easy-virtued in Africa— the place swarms with them. But, to continue my comparison, they are as noxious and as putrid as the muddy liquid of Sahara wells.

Now it happened that one day, when my nerves were more on edge than usual, I was trying to get some sleep. But sleep would not come. My legs were twitching as though something inside was pricking them, and there I lay, tossing and turning uneasily upon my Djebel-Amour carpet. At last I could stand it no longer. I got up and went out.

It was a stifling afternoon in July. The pavement in the streets was so hot that you could have baked bread on it. My shirt was soaked through almost at once and stuck to my body, and there was a faint white mist on the horizon brought by the burning sirocco wind which is like heat made tangible.

I went down to the sea and, rounding the harbour, sauntered along the shore of the pretty bay where people go for bathing. Here the mountain falls sheer to the beech, covered with brushwood and tall aromatic plants which give off a heady fragrance. It forms the segment of a circle round a little creek where great brown rocks rise sharply from the water. No one was about. Nothing was stirring. Not a bird was visible, and there was no sound of any animal. Nothing broke the silence, not even the lapping of the wavelets, for the motionless sea lay torpid under the blazing sun. In the roasting air I seemed to catch the crackle of flames.

All of a sudden I noticed a slight movement coming from behind one of the rocks half submerged in the silent sea. I turned, and saw a woman bathing. She was tall and stark naked, standing with the water up to her breast. No doubt she thought that at this torrid moment of the day she would be undisturbed. As I watched, she turned to face the open sea, and started jumping gently up and down. She had not seen me.

No sight could have been stranger than this lovely creature in the glass-clear water under the blinding glare. For she *was* lovely, marvellously lovely, tall and statuesque.

She turned her head, uttered a cry, and, half swimming, half crawling, made for the shelter of the rock.

Since, sooner or later, she must come out, I sat down on the sand and waited. Very cautiously she raised her head with its great load of black and loosely knotted hair. She had a wide mouth and full lips which curled back from her teeth like two soft little pads. Her eyes were bold and very large, and her skin, faintly tanned, had the colour of old ivory, smooth and hard. It was the skin of a white woman darkened by a negro sun.

She called out: 'Go away!' and her full voice, strong like the rest of her, had a guttural accent. I did not move, and she added: 'It is not nice of you, Monsieur, to stay,' and the 'r''s' sounded in her mouth like the rolling of chariot wheels. I did not move. Her head disappeared.

Ten minutes passed. Then, first her hair, then her forehead, then her eyes rose cautiously and slowly above the rock, like those of children playing hide-and-seek and peeping out to detect the seeker.

This time she looked furious. 'You will make me catch cold!' she cried. 'I shall not come out so long as you are there!' Then I got to my feet and moved away, not without frequently looking over my shoulder. When she decided that I was far enough off, she left the water, bent almost double, and with her back turned to me. Then she crept into a crevice in the rock and disappeared behind a skirt which was hanging over the entry.

I came back the next day. She was again bathing, but this time wearing a complete costume. She began to laugh, and showed her gleaming teeth.

A week later we were friends, and, in another week, much more than that.

She was called Marroca—no doubt a nickname—and she pronounced it as though it were filled full of 'r' 's. Her parents were Spanish settlers, and she had married a Frenchman named Pontabèze. He was a Civil Servant, though I never discovered the exact nature of his work. I found out that he was kept very busy, and that was enough for me.

She changed her time of bathing and came, every day, after

luncheon, to take her siesta at my house. What a siesta! Not what you would call very restful!

She was a wonderful creature, with a good deal of the animal in her, but superb. Her eyes seemed to be always ablaze with passion, and there was something savagely sensual about her half-open lips, her pointed teeth, and even her smile. Her curiously shaped, long, hard, and pointed breasts, like pears of flesh, so resilient that they seemed to be made of rubber, gave to her whole body an almost bestial quality, making of her a magnificent yet inferior being created only for unbridled passion. She reminded me of those obscene goddesses of antiquity, whose unrestrained endearments were lavished in leafy bowers and grassy glades.

Never did woman itch with such insatiable desire! Her desperate ardours, her shrieks and claspings, the way in which she ground her teeth and bit convulsively, were the expression of a passion so demanding that it was almost immediately followed by a sleep of satiety so deep that it seemed like death. But she would start awake again in my arms quite suddenly, ready for fresh embraces, her breast aching for kisses.

Her mind was simple as two-and-two-make-four, and laughter did duty in her for thought.

Proud, by instinct, of her beauty, she had a horror of even the lightest of coverings, and walked and ran and gambolled in my house with unselfconscious shamelessness. When, sated with love and exhausted by her cries and by movement, she slept beside me on the divan, the torrid heat would pearl her sun-tanned skin, and draw from the arms she clasped beneath her head and from all the secret places of her body, that animal smell which so delights the male.

At times, when her husband had been called away on duty (whereto I did not know), she would come back in the evening, and we would lie together on the terrace, wearing the lightest coverings of Eastern gauze.

When the great glaring moon of Africa swam up into the sky, lighting the town and the gulf in the rounded frame of mountains, we saw on all the other terraces what looked like an army of silent ghosts stretched at full length, sometimes getting to their feet, changing places, and lying down again in the languorous warmth.

In spite of the brightness of those nights, she always insisted on lying naked, taking little notice of those who might see us, and often, in spite of my fears and objurgations, uttering long vibrant cries which set the dogs howling in the distance.

One night, when I was fast asleep under the firmament of powdered stars, she came and knelt upon my carpet, put her curled lips close to my mouth, and said:

'I want you to come and sleep in my house.'

I did not understand:

'What do you mean in your house?'

'Some night, when my husband is away, you must take his place beside me.'

I could not keep from laughing.

'But why—since you come here?'

But on she went, talking into my mouth, sending her hot breath down my throat, her breath moistening my moustache.

'So that I may have the memory'—and the 'r' in memory was a long trill, like water running over stones.

I still did not grasp her meaning. She put her arm about my neck: 'So that, when you are gone, I can remember it and, when my husband makes love to me, think it is you I am embracing.'

And her 'rrr' 's were like the rolling of familiar drums.

I was touched, but also moved to mirth:

'You must be mad: I would rather stay like this with you, at home.'

I have, I must confess, no fondness for lovers' meetings under the domestic roof. That is the kind of trap in which fools are always caught. But she begged, implored, and even wept. 'You will see how I will love you there,' she said, and the 'r' rattled like a drum sounding the charge.

So strange was this wish of hers, that I could not explain it to my satisfaction. Thinking it over later, I thought that I could read into it some deep hatred of her husband, one of those forms of vengeance so dear to the hearts of women who delight in deceiving a detested partner, and love to betray him under his own roof, in his own room, in his own bed.

I said: 'Does your husband treat you badly?'

She looked vexed, and answered:

'No, he is very kind to me.'

'But you do not love him?'

'Oh yes, I love him very much, but not as much as I love you, dearr hearrrt.'

I still did not understand her meaning, but as I was trying to find it out, she gave me one of those kisses whose power she knew full well, and murmured:

'Say you will come! say you will come!'

But I was adamant and, putting on her clothes, she left me.

For a whole week I saw nothing of her. Then, on the ninth day, she came again and, standing in the doorway, said with a serious look upon her face:

'Will you come tonight and sleep with me? If you do not, then I will go away.'

A week is a long time, dear friend, and in Africa a week is as good as a month. 'Yes,' I exclaimed, and spread my arms. She flung herself into them.

She was waiting for me in a nearby street, and acted as my guide.

She and her husband lived in a small house close to the harbour. I passed first through a kitchen where they took their meals, and was shown into a clean, whitewashed bedroom, with photographs of relatives upon the walls and paper flowers under glass domes. Marocca seemed mad with joy, jumping up and down, and saying repeatedly: 'Here you are in our home, in *your* home!'

And I behaved as though I was.

I was not a little embarrassed, I admit, even uneasy. Seeing that I hesitated, in this strange abode, about taking off a certain article of clothing without which a man, when taken by surprise, is no less awkward than ridiculous, and incapable of action, she tore it from me by force and put it in the next room with all my other clothes.

Self-confidence returned to me at last, and I gave such proof of it that, after two hours, the thought of sleep was still far from our minds. But, just then, the sound of violent knocking at the door made us start, and a man's voice called: 'It's me, Marocca!'

She jumped out on to the floor:

'It is my husband! Quick! hide under the bed!'

I looked round wildly for my trousers, but she kept pushing me, and panted out: 'Quick! quick!'

I lay down on my stomach and, without a word, slipped under the bed on which I had been so happily installed.

Then, she went into the kitchen. I heard her open and shut a cupboard, after which she returned, carrying some object which I could not see. This she hurriedly put down—exactly where I could not make out—and, since her husband was growing impatient, called in a loud and perfectly collected voice: 'I can't find the matches!' Then, suddenly: 'Oh, here they are! I'll let you in.' And so she did.

A man came into the room. I could see no more of him than his feet, which were enormous. If the rest of him is in proportion, I thought, he must be a colossus!

I heard the sound of kisses, of a smack on bare flesh, of laughter. Then he, speaking in a strong Marseillais accent, said: 'I forgot my purse and had to come back for it. I expect you were fast asleep.' He went to the chest-of-drawers and spent some time looking for what he wanted. Then, Marocca having lain down upon the bed as though she were dead-tired, he tried, so far as I could hear, to make love to her, for she snapped at him irritably and gave him the benefit of a shower of angry 'r' 's.

His feet were so close to me, that I was seized with a mad, stupid, inexplicable desire to touch them. But I resisted the temptation.

Since his amorousness was obviously meeting with no success, he grew annoyed. 'Not very welcoming, are you?' he said: but, seemingly accepting the inevitable, added: 'Well, so long, darling.' I heard another kiss. The big feet turned about, and I could see the nails in the soles as he moved away and left the room. The house-door slammed.

I was saved!

I crept slowly from my hiding-place, a pitiful and dejected object, and, while Marocca, still naked, jumped round me in high glee, shrieking with laughter and clapping her hands, I flopped heavily into a chair. But I was on my feet in a trice. I had sat down on something cold, and, having no more clothes on than my companion, the contact had given me a shock. I turned round.

I had been sitting on a small wood-chopper with a blade as sharp as a knife. How on earth had it come there? I certainly had not noticed it when I came in.

Marocca, seeing me jump, laughed so loudly, holding both her sides, that she fell into a coughing-fit.

I thought her merriment inopportune and unseemly. We had taken a stupid risk. I could still feel a cold shiver down my back, and I found her uncontrolled laughter rather offensive.

'Suppose your husband had seen me?' I said.

'There was no danger of that,' she answered.

'How do you mean, no danger? You can't expect me to believe that! Why, he had only to bend down to be sure of finding me!'

She had stopped laughing, and was now merely smiling at me, with her great wide eyes in which I could see the smouldering gleam of newly aroused desire.

'He would not have bent down!'

But I refused to be silenced. 'How can you say that?' I said.

'Why, he might have dropped his hat, and he'd have had to bend down to pick it up! A fine condition I should have been in for defending myself!'

She put her strong and rounded arms about my neck and, lowering her voice as she did when she said, 'I adorre you!' murmured:

'If he had bent down, he wouldn't have got up again!'

I still did not understand.

'Why?'

There was a wicked flicker in her eyes. She stretched her hand to the chair in which I had been sitting, and the way in which she curved her fingers, the pucker of laughter which showed in her cheek, her parted lips, and the glint of her savage, pointed teeth, all served to draw my attention to the little chopper with its sharp and gleaming blade.

She made the gesture of picking it up, then, with her left arm round my waist, pressing my body to hers, with her right she mimicked the motion of someone cutting off the head of a kneeling man . . .

So now, my dear fellow, you know how people here interpret wifely duties, love and hospitality!

(2 March 1882)

A Country Tale

THE two cottages stood next door to one another, at the bottom of a hill, not far from a small health resort. The soil was unproductive, and the two peasants, no matter how hard they worked, only just managed to bring up their children. Each family had four, and the combined swarms spent all their time in front of the two doors. The two eldest were six years old, and the two youngest about fifteen months.

It was only with difficulty that the mothers could tell their young apart, and the fathers were completely at sea; the eight names played a jig in their heads and became hopelessly confused. When one had to be called, the men frequently made three shots before getting it right.

The first of the two cottages, for anyone coming from Rolleport, the station which served the needs of the health resort, was occupied by the Tuvaches, who had three girls and a boy: the other housed the Vallins, with one girl and three boys.

The families only just kept body and soul together on a diet of vegetable soup, potatoes, and fresh air. At feeding-time—seven each morning, noon, and six in the evenings—the two housewives herded their urchins together, much as a goose-girl shoos her charges to the trough. The children sat, in order of age, at a wooden table to which fifty years of service had imparted a brilliant shine. The mouth of the youngest nipper scarcely showed above it. A large dish was set before them filled with a mash of bread soaked in the water in which the potatoes had been boiled, half a cabbage, and three onions, and the whole higgledy-piggledy ate until they could eat no more, the mother stuffing food into the youngest of her brood with her own hands. The weekly treat was a scrap of meat added to the vegetable stew on Sundays. On these red-letter days, the father would dawdle over the meal, saying: 'Us could do wi' that every day o' t' week.'

One August afternoon a light trap pulled up sharply in front of the two cottages, and the young woman who was driving said to the man beside her:

'Oh! look at all those tinies, Henri! how sweet they look rolling about in the dust!'

The man did not answer. He was used to these outbursts, which were like a stab of pain to him, almost a reproach.

His companion went on:

'I must give them a hug! Oh! How I should love to have one of them for my very own—like that little tot over there!'

She jumped down and ran to where the children were playing. One of the two youngest she took in her arms—the one belonging to the Tuvaches—and began to rain passionate kisses on his grubby cheeks, his curly golden hair all daubed with mud, and his tiny little hands with which he was trying vainly to break free from these tiresome embraces.

Then she climbed back into the trap and drove off at a spanking pace. But she came back the following week, squatted on the ground, took the urchin in her arms, stuffed him with cakes, and gave sweets to the others. She played with him as though she had been a child herself, while her husband sat patiently for her in their spidery conveyance.

On her next visit, she got into conversation with the child's parents, and, after that, came every day, with her pockets full of ha'pence and goodies.

Her name was Madame Henri d'Hubières.

One morning, when they drew up, her husband got down with her. Without stopping to play with the brats, who, by this time, knew her well by sight, she went into the cottage.

The mother and father were busy chopping wood for the daily soup. They straightened up in great surprise, offered their visitors two chairs, and stood waiting. The young woman started to speak in a broken, trembling voice.

'I have come to see you, my good people, because I very much want . . . to . . . to take your little boy back with me . . .'

The country couple, struck dumb with amazement, and not in the least knowing what she was talking about, said nothing.

She paused for breath, and then continued:

'We have no children of our own; there are just the two of us, my husband and myself . . . and we should dearly like to keep him . . . Will you let us do that?'

Her meaning slowly dawned on the mother:

'You mean as you's a-wanting to take our little Charlot away? . . . Noa, noa, us couldn't do that!'

At this point, Monsieur d'Hubières broke in:

'My wife, I fear, has not explained herself very clearly. Our wish is to adopt him. We should, of course, let him come to see you from

time to time. If he turns out well, as we have every reason to
suppose he will, we shall make him our heir. Should we chance to
have children of our own, he would share equally with them. But,
in the event of his not requiting our care and affection, then, when
he comes of age, we will give him twenty thousand francs. This sum
will be put in trust for him with a notary. And, since we have you,
also, in mind, an allowance of one hundred francs a month will be
paid to you. Have I made my meaning plain?'

The farmer's wife got to her feet in a towering rage:

' 'Tis asking us to sell Charlot! . . . Us isn't doing naught like
that . . . To ask such of a mother! Why, 'tis an abomination!'

The man said nothing. But he was thinking, and there was a
serious look on his face. All the same, he kept nodding his head to
show his approval of what his wife was saying.

Madame d'Hubières burst into a flood of unhappy tears, and,
turning to her husband, said, in a voice shaken with sobs—the
voice of a spoiled child accustomed to having its every wish granted:

'They won't let us, Henri! . . . They won't let us!'

He made one last effort.

'But think, my friends, of your child's future, of his happiness,
of . . .'

The peasant woman, now quite beyond herself, interrupted him:

'Us've done all that . . . seeing and listening and thinking . . .
Best thing you can do is go away, and not come back, neither. Folk
can't come a-taking of other folks' children!'

As Madame d'Hubières left the cottage, she noticed that there
were two small boys, and with the obstinacy of a self-willed woman
unused to being crossed, asked through her tears:

'Is the other little fellow yours, too?'

Old Tuvache answered:

'Noa, him's our neighbour's kid: you may go'n talk to him, if
you want.'

Then he turned back into the cottage which was still ringing
with his wife's angry voice.

The Vallins were seated at table, slowly eating slices of bread
with a skimpy top-layer of butter taken on the points of their
knives from a dish between them.

Monsieur d'Hubières repeated his proposal, but this time in a
more roundabout manner, choosing his words with great care, and
conducting the conversation a great deal more shrewdly.

The two country-folk shook their heads to convey refusal. But
when they learned that they were to have a hundred francs a

month, they seemed to be pondering the matter, and kept exchanging glances. They were clearly much shaken.

For a long while they said nothing. There could be no doubt about it: they were in two minds about what to say, and wrestling with temptation. At length the wife opened her lips:

'What dost think, dad?'

The reply came in a tone of weighty solemnity:

'I ses, Mother, that 'tis not to be despised.'

Then, Madame d'Hubières, who was trembling with anxiety, spoke to them of the boy's future, of his happiness, of all the money he would be in a position to send them later.

The man asked:

'This 'lowance of twelve hunderd francs, will it be swore to in front of a lawyer chap?'

Monsieur d'Hubières replied immediately:

'Most certainly it will, tomorrow.'

The wife, who had been thinking things over, here broke in:

'Hunderd a month don't make up for loss o' t'lad, seeing as 'e'd be working in a few years: hunderd and twenty more like.'

Madame d'Hubières, by now almost dancing with impatience, agreed at once, and, since she wanted to take the child with her there and then, handed the woman a further hundred francs as a present, while her husband was writing out a statement. The mayor, and one of the neighbours were sent for, and were very ready to act as witnesses.

The young woman, radiant with happiness, carried off the squalling brat, as she might have done some much-coveted piece of bric-à-brac from a shop.

The Tuvaches from their doorstep watched him go. They said nothing and looked stern. Perhaps they were feeling sorry that they had refused.

Nothing more was heard of little Jean Vallin. His parents went regularly, every month, to collect their hundred and twenty francs from the lawyer, and quarrelled with their next-door neighbours because old mother Tuvache was for ever saying abusive things about them, and declaring that only an unnatural mother would sell her own child, which, she maintained, was a horrible, filthy, and vicious thing to do.

Sometimes she would ostentatiously take her Charlot in her arms, and say, as though he could understand the words:

'*I've* done no selling of 'ee: *I'm* not one as turns 'er chickabiddy into dirty money: us mayn't be rich, but us wouldn't do like that!'

Year after year it went on, a never-ending shouting from her doorstep, and so loud that it could be heard inside the other cottage. By dint of repetition she convinced herself that she was morally superior to everybody in the district, just because she hadn't done a deal with Charlot. When people talked of her, they said:

'Must've been proper tempting, but 'er acted like a real good mother!'

She was held up to all as a model parent, and Charlot, who was now close on eighteen, and had had his mother's virtue unceasingly dinned into his ears, came to think himself superior to his comrades, for no better reason than that he had not been sold.

The Vallins got along very comfortably, thanks to their allowance, and it was the knowledge of their relative prosperity that poured oil on the flames of the Tuvaches' anger, for they were still poor.

Their eldest son went off to do his military service: the second died, and only Charlot remained to slave away with his father in order to provide food for his mother and two young sisters.

He had just had his twenty-first birthday when, one morning, a smart carriage drew up in front of the two cottages. A young man with a gold watch-chain alighted from it, giving his arm to a white-haired old lady.

She said to him:

'That is it, my boy: the second cottage.'

He entered the Vallins' shanty as though it had been his own home.

His old mother was washing her aprons, and his father, now very feeble, was dozing by the hearth. Both looked up, and the young man said:

'Good morning, Papa: good morning, Mama.'

The shock brought them both to their feet. So disturbed was the old woman by his arrival, that she let the soap fall into the tub, and stammered out:

'Be it really thee, my boy? Be it really thee?'

He took her in his arms, and said again:

'Good morning, Mama.'

The old man was all of a tremble, but his voice was calm and steady:

'So thee's back again,' he said, as though his son had been away for only a few weeks.

A Country Tale

When the first greetings were over, the aged couple insisted on trotting their son round the village, and showing him off to everybody. He was introduced to the mayor, to the mayor's deputy, to the curé, and the schoolmaster.

Charlot watched the triumphal progress from the doorstep of his wretched home.

That evening, at supper, he said to his old father:

'Proper daft you must've been, to let 'em take the Vallin kid!'

With stubbornness his mother answered:

'Us wasn't the kind to sell our child.'

His father said nothing.

Their son continued:

'Nowt much to blubber about in that sort o' sacrifice!'

At that old Tuvache piped up angrily:

'Holding it against us that we stuck to 'ee?'

With brutal directness the young man said:

'What I'm holding against 'ee is being nowt but two old fools. 'Tis parents like 'ee as brings ruination on their children. If I cleared out, 'twould be no more'n you deserve.'

The poor woman was crying into her plate, moaning to herself as she sucked soup from her spoon, and spilling half of it:

'And us a'most a-killing of oursels to bring our youngsters up!'

'I'd rather not 'a bin born than be wot I am. When I seed that there chap just now, 't made my blood boil. An' 't might'a bin me, I thought!'

He got up.

'See here—there ain't no reason in me staying here, I'll only be holding this agin' you from morn to night, an' making your lives miserable 'cos I s'all never forgive you—never!'

The two old people sat silent, crushed and snivelling.

' 'Tis more'n I can stand: 'tis better I should earn a living somewheres else.'

He opened the door. The sound of voices drifted in. The Vallins were celebrating the return of their son.

Charlot stamped his foot, and, turning to his parents, cried:

'Coupla old turmut-heads!'

Then, he disappeared into the darkness.

(31 October 1882)

That Swine, Morin

'My dear fellow,' said I to Labarbe, 'there you go again! Always those same three words—that swine, Morin—why the devil can I never hear Morin mentioned without that pig-epithet?'

Labarbe—who is now a Deputy—gave me an owl-like stare:

'Are you going to tell me that you come from La Rochelle, and don't know about Morin?'

I had to confess that I didn't, on which Labarbe rubbed his hands, and began:

'I have an idea that you once knew Morin, and, if that is so, you will remember the big draper's shop he had on the La Rochelle water-front, eh?'

'Yes, of course I remember it.'

'Good. Well, the story begins with a fortnight's pleasure trip—or, shall we say, a trip in search of pleasures—which he made to Paris in 1862 or '63. The excuse he gave was that he wanted to do some buying for stock. Now, you don't need me to tell you what two weeks in Paris are likely to mean to a provincial shopkeeper, nor how it stokes up the fire in the blood: theatres every night, no end of women, and a perpetual state of excitement. It pretty well sends the poor devil off his rocker, so that he can see nothing but dancers in tights, actresses in low-necked dresses, well-rounded legs, and plump shoulders, all to be had for the asking, and he not being able, or not daring, to do so much as venture a touch. The most he can hope for is an occasional sampling of inferior dishes. By the time he goes home, his heart is still in a flutter, his senses roused, and he has a strong feeling that he wants to kiss somebody.

'That is the state Morin was in when he took his ticket back to La Rochelle on the 8.40 p.m. express. Obsessed by regrets and unsatisfied longings, he walked up and down the booking-hall of the Orléans terminus, and suddenly he came to a dead stop at the sight of a young woman saying good-bye to an old lady. She had lifted her veil, and Morin had an immediate rush of blood to the head: "Gosh!" he said to himself, "what a stunner!"

'As soon as the "stunner" had parted from the old lady, she went into the waiting-room, and Morin followed her. Then she moved

on to the platform, with Morin still in pursuit. Finally, she got into an empty carriage, with Morin hard on her heels.

'There weren't many people travelling that night. The engine whistled. The train started. They were alone. Morin devoured her with his eyes. She appeared to be about nineteen or twenty. She was tall, fair-haired, and had a free-and-easy look about her. She wrapped herself in a rug, stretched herself on one of the seats, and went to sleep.

'Morin wondered who she was. A thousand suppositions, a thousand schemes took form in his mind. To himself he said: "One's always hearing about adventures in railway trains. Perhaps I'm going to have one! Wasn't it Danton who said, '*de l'audace, de l'audace et toujours de l'audace*', or was it Mirabeau? Trouble is, I haven't got any. If only one *knew*, if only one could read people's thoughts! I don't mind betting one misses the most wonderful chances every day without realizing that they're there! The tiniest little movement would be enough to show me that she's more than willing . . ."

'Then he started imagining all sorts of manoeuvres which might bring him a quick victory—striking up an acquaintance with her in a perfectly gentlemanly way, doing her some small service, embarking on a sprightly and flirtatious conversation ending in a declaration which, in its turn, would end in you know what. But the night passed, and the charming creature still slept on, while Morin sat planning her downfall. Day broke, and soon the first ray of the rising sun touched the sleeper's entrancing face.

'She awoke at last, sat up, looked out of the window, glanced at Morin, and smiled. Her smile was the smile of a happy woman. It was gay and inviting. Morin's heart missed a beat. There could be no doubt about it, the smile had been meant for him. It was, in fact, a discreet invitation, just that little sign for which he had been hoping and waiting. If it meant anything, it must mean: "What a fool, what a booby, what a *mug* you must be, to sit there all night long like a stick, without so much as lifting a finger! Look at me; am I not charming? Yet, there you've been since yesterday evening, alone with a pretty woman, without the courage of a mouse, you great stupid!"

'She was still smiling, and still looking at him. She even started to laugh, and at that he lost his head. He tried to think of some compliment to pay her, of something—no matter what—to say to her: but his mind remained a blank. Then, with that impulsive daring which sometimes comes to cowards, he suddenly made up his mind to take the plunge, and, without a word of warning, with arms flung wide and greedy lips, he flung himself upon her.

'She was on her feet in an instant, crying, "Help! Help!" and screaming with terror. She wrenched the door open, mad with fear, waving her arms and trying to jump out, with Morin, in a terrible state, clinging to her skirt, convinced that she was going to fling herself on to the rails, and spluttering, "Madame! Oh! Madame!..."

'The train slowed down and stopped. Two railway officials hurried up in response to the distracted waving of the young woman, who fell into their arms, stammering: "This man was trying to ... trying to ..." and fainted.

'They were at Mauzé, and the station gendarme at once arrested Morin.

'When the victim of his brutal assault came round, she made a statement. The representative of the law drew up a report, and the poor draper did not reach home until that evening with a charge of public indecency hanging over his head.'

PART II

'In those days I was editor-in-chief of the *Fanal des Charentes*, and used to see Morin every evening at the Café du Commerce.

'On the day following this adventure, he came to see me. He was at his wits' end. I was perfectly blunt with him: "You behaved like a swine," I said. "You can't do things like that."

'He burst into tears. His wife had been laying about him. He saw his business ruined, his name dragged in the mud, his reputation gone, himself an outcast from the society of his friends. Finally, I took pity on him, and sent for one of my staff, a cynical but sensible little chap, and asked him what he thought we ought to do.

'He advised me to see the Public Prosecutor, who was a friend of mine. I sent Morin home, and proceeded to visit the high legal functionary. From him I learned that the young woman in question was a certain Mademoiselle Henriette Bonnel, who had just got her Diploma as a teacher, in Paris, and, having neither father nor mother, spent her holidays with an uncle and aunt, a respectable middle-class couple living at Mauzé.

'What made matters worse for Morin was that the uncle was bringing an action against him. The Public Prosecutor was prepared to let the matter drop, provided the action were withdrawn. This was what we had to try to arrange.

That Swine, Morin

'I went back to Morin, whom I found in bed, terrified out of his life, and in a state of considerable emotional disturbance. His wife, a great grenadier of a woman, bony and bearded, was giving him the rough side of her tongue without a single let-up. When she showed me into his room, she screamed in my face: "Come to see that swine, Morin, have you? Well, there he is, the brute!"

'She stuck herself at the bottom of the bed with arms akimbo. I explained the situation, and he begged me to go and see the family. Delicate though the mission was, I accepted it. The poor devil kept on saying: "I swear I didn't give her so much as a kiss, not one!"

'To this I replied: "That doesn't alter the fact that you behaved like a swine." I took the thousand francs he gave me to use as I thought best.

'I did not feel up to entering the house of the girl's relations unsupported, and asked Rivet to go with me. He agreed, on condition that we set off at once, for he had an important business engagement in La Rochelle, on the following afternoon.

'Two hours later we rang at the front-door of a charming country house. It was opened by a remarkably good-looking young woman. It was undoubtedly "She". I said in a low voice to Rivet: "Damn it! I'm beginning to have a certain amount of sympathy for Morin!"

'It turned out that the uncle, Monsieur Ronnelet, was a regular subscriber to the *Fanal*, and a fervent political co-religionist of ours. He received us with open arms, complimented and congratulated us, and shook us warmly by the hand, full of enthusiasm at the idea of having two members of the staff of his favourite paper under his roof.

'Rivet whispered in my ear: "I don't think we shall have much difficulty in settling that swine, Morin's business!"

'The niece had vanished, and I broached the delicate subject. I paraded the grisly spectre of scandal, and pointed out how harmful such an affair would be to the young lady's reputation, for no one would believe that the incident had not gone further than a harmless embrace.

'The decent old fellow seemed undecided. He couldn't, he said, make up his mind one way or the other until his wife got back, late that evening. Suddenly, he gave a little exclamation of triumph. "I've just had a brilliant idea!" he said. "I'll keep you here. You shall both of you dine and sleep with us, and, when my wife returns, I hope that we can reach some sort of an agreement."

'Rivet at first protested, but his wish to get the swine, Morin out

161

of his scrape was the deciding factor, and we ended by accepting the invitation.

'The uncle was delighted, and, getting to his feet, sent for his niece. He suggested that we should all take a walk round the property. Our business, he said, could wait until the evening.

'Rivet and he at once embarked on a political discussion, and I very soon found myself some way behind them, with the young woman. She was really very charming.

'I tried, as tactfully as I could, to bring up the subject of her adventure, in the hope that I might be able to enlist her on my side.

'She appeared to be not in the least confused, but listened to what I was saying with an air of considerable amusement.

' "Just think, Mademoiselle," I said, "how very awkward it is going to be for you. You will have to appear in court. You will be stared at. You will have to tell your story in public, and describe the whole painful incident of the railway carriage. Just between ourselves, wouldn't it have been much better if you had put the nasty creature in his place without summoning the guard, and simply got into another compartment?"

'She began to laugh. "You're perfectly right, of course; but, you see, I was frightened, and when one is frightened one doesn't think straight. When I fully understood the situation, I regretted having made such a fuss, but by that time it was too late. Don't forget that the silly fool attacked me like a madman, without saying a word. I didn't even know what he was after."

'She looked me full in the face. She seemed to be neither much upset, nor at all abashed. She's quite capable of looking after herself, I thought: but I can quite see how that swine, Morin got the wrong idea.

'I continued on a lighter note: "Come now, Mademoiselle; confess that there is something to be said for him! No one could sit opposite so charming a young woman for long without feeling the perfectly natural wish to kiss her."

'She laughed louder than ever, flashing her teeth. "Between the wish and the act, Monsieur, there was room for good manners!"

'It was an odd thing for her to say, and I didn't quite see what she meant. I asked her straight out: "If I tried to kiss you at this very moment, what would you do?"

'She stopped dead and coolly looked me up and down. Then she said: "That, Monsieur, would be a totally different matter."

'I knew that, without her having to tell me. After all, wasn't I known all over the district as "The Handsome Labarbe"? I was thirty years old. Nevertheless, "What precisely do you mean by that?" I asked.

'She answered with a shrug: "I mean that you're not so stupid as he is"—and then, with a sidelong look—"nor so ugly."

'Before she could make a movement to avoid me, I had given her a smacking great kiss on the cheek. She jumped to one side, but too late. Then she said: "You're not what I should call exactly shy, are you? All the same don't do that again, please."

'I assumed an apologetic air, and said in a low voice: "There is nothing I should like better, Mademoiselle, than to appear in the dock on the same charge as Morin."

'It was her turn to say: "And what, precisely, do you mean by that?" I looked her full in the eyes with a very serious expression.

' "I mean that you are one of the loveliest young women it has ever been my good fortune to meet, and that I should regard it as a privilege, an honour, and something to be proud of, to have made a violent attack upon you, because anyone who had seen you would say; 'Labarbe richly deserved what he got, but he's a lucky chap, all the same!' "

'There was nothing half-hearted about her laughter.

' "What a funny man you are!" The words were scarcely out of her mouth before I had her in my arms and was showering greedy kisses on her wherever I could find a place to put them—in her hair, on her forehead, on her eyes, now and again on her mouth, on her cheeks, and all over her face, some parts of which she had to leave exposed in order to protect the others.

'Finally, she broke free, scarlet in the face, and furiously angry.

' "You are ill-mannered, sir, and make me regret having listened to you!"

'Somewhat abashed, I took her hand and stammered out: "I beg you to forgive me, Mademoiselle. I have offended you. I acted like a cad. But don't be too angry with me . . . If only you knew . . ." I searched my mind in vain for an excuse.

'After a brief pause, she said:

' "There is nothing for me to know, sir."

'But, by that time, I had found the excuse I needed. "Yes, Mademoiselle," I said, "there is. Please listen to me. I know nothing of Morin, and care less. Whether or no he is locked up and has to stand his trial, is a matter of complete indifference to me. A year ago, I saw you here, at the gate. I was completely bowled over, and the thought of you has never since left me. It matters little whether you believe me or not. I thought you adorable, and the memory of that moment has become an obsession with me. I *had* to see you again. I used that fool Morin as a pretext, and here I am. Circumstances led me to overstep the mark, and I can only beg you to make allowances for me."

'She searched my eyes for the truth. She was almost on the brink of a smile, and "Blarney!" she murmured.

'I raised my hand, and, with the true ring of sincerity in my voice (at least I think I was sincere), declared:

' "I swear to you I am not lying!"

'But all the answer she would make was "Really?"

'We were alone, completely alone. Rivet and her uncle had disappeared down one of the winding paths. I took this opportunity to make her a declaration in form, a prolonged and sentimental outpouring, accompanied by a great deal of pressing and kissing of her hand. She listened as though to something pleasant which she was hearing for the first time but could not be quite sure how far to believe.

'Before I finished, I had got myself quite worked up. I actually believed what I was saying. I was pale, ill-at-ease, and trembling. Very gently I put an arm round her waist.

'I whispered sweet nothings into the curls about her ears. She seemed like one dead, so deeply was she musing.

'Then her hand met mine, and pressed it. Very slowly, and with an arm that was far from steady, I tightened my hold on her waist. She no longer attempted to escape. My mouth just brushed her cheek, then, suddenly, my lips, without having sought them, closed on hers. It was a long, long kiss, and would have been even longer, had I not heard "Ahem, ahem" close behind us.

'She made a dash for it, bang through a bush. I turned and saw Rivet walking towards me.

'He planted himself full in the middle of the path, and said, without the flicker of a smile:

' "So that's how you give a helping hand to that swine Morin, is it?"

'Complacently I answered: "One does what one can, my boy. How about the uncle? Have you got anything out of him? I'll answer for the niece." '

That Swine, Morin

PART III

'Dinner set my head in a whirl. I sat beside her, and my hand kept pressing hers under the table. My foot touched hers. Our eyes met and mingled.

'Later, we took a stroll in the moonlight, and I unburdened my heart to her in whispered confidences. I kept tight hold of her, stopping, now and again, to press my lips to hers. Away ahead of us, Rivet and her uncle were still deep in argument, their shadows solemnly pursuing them upon the sanded path.

'We went in, and, shortly afterwards, a messenger-boy delivered a telegram from her aunt, to say that she would be back next morning by the first train.

'Her uncle said: "Show these gentlemen to their rooms, Henriette." We said good-night to our host, and went upstairs. She led us first to Rivet's room, and he whispered, "Not much likelihood of her starting with yours!" Then she showed me to my bed. As soon as we were alone together, I took her again in my arms in an attempt to sweep her off her feet and overcome resistance. But just as she was about to topple over the edge, she took to her heels.

'I got into bed, feeling excited, frustrated, and a bit sheepish. I was just resigning myself to the prospect of a sleepless night, and cudgelling my brain to think where I had put a foot wrong, when there came a gentle tapping at the door.

' "Who's there?"

'A low voice said: "It's only me."

'I hurried into my clothes, opened the door, and in she came. "I forgot," she said, "to ask whether you like chocolate, tea or coffee for breakfast?"

'My arms were round her in a moment, and between my burning kisses, I managed to stammer out no more than, "I like . . . I like . . . I like . . ." But she wriggled free, blew out my light and vanished.

'There I was, alone and furious in the pitch darkness, hunting for matches but not finding any. I discovered some at last, and, pretty nearly beside myself, went out into the passage with a candlestick in my hand.

'What had I in mind to do? The answer to that question is— nothing. My mind had ceased to work. I wanted to find her. I wanted *her*. I took a few steps with a perfectly empty head. Then, a sudden thought came to me: "Suppose I tumble into her uncle's room . . . What on earth shall I say? . . ." I stood stock-still, my brain a void, my heart thumping. After a few seconds, I hit on the solution. "I'll say I was looking for Rivet, because I had something important to say to him."

'I had a good look at the various doors, trying to discover which was hers. I took hold of a handle at random. The door opened, and I went in . . . Henriette, who was sitting up in bed, gave me a frightened look.

'Very quietly, I shot the bolt, and, tip-toeing across to her, said: "I forgot to ask you, Mademoiselle, for something to read." She struggled, but I soon found the book I was looking for. I shall not tell you its name, but it was really the most wonderful of stories, the most divine of poems.

'Once I had turned the first page, she let me run through it to my heart's content. So many chapters did I sample, that our candles burned down to the sockets.

'Then, having thanked her, I stealthily made my way back to my room. But, just as I reached it, a hand seized me roughly by the shoulder, and a voice close to my ear, Rivet's voice, said: "So, you haven't finished with Morin's business yet?"

'At seven o'clock next morning she brought me, with her own hands, a cup of chocolate. I have never drunk anything to compare with it; chocolate to make one swoon with pleasure; a fully-flavoured chocolate, velvety to the palate, fragrant, heady. I could not tear my lips from her cup's delicious rim.

'Scarcely had she left me than Rivet entered. He seemed all strung up, and as edgy as a man who has slept very little. He said, in a disgruntled voice, "If you go on like this, you know, you'll end by ruining Morin's chances."

'At eight the aunt turned up. What we had to say was said very quickly. The good folk agreed to withdraw the charge, and I, to give them five hundred francs for the poor of the parish.

'They very much wanted to keep us with them for the day, and even went so far as to arrange an expedition to some ruins. When their backs were turned, Henriette made signs to me with her head: "Do stay." I accepted the invitation, but Rivet was anxious to be off.

'I took him aside, I begged and implored him. "Be a good chap, Rivet," I said, "and do it for my sake."

'But he was in a thoroughly bad temper. "Look here," he answered, "I've had about enough of that swine Morin's affair!"

'So, off I had to go, and it was one of the worst moments of my life. I could willingly have spent all my life there, settling that affair.

'When we were in the railway carriage, after much hearty hand-shaking and many mute farewells, I said to Rivet: "What a brute you are!" To which he replied, "You were beginning to get damn-ably on my nerves, old man."

'On reaching the office of *Le Fanal* I found a crowd waiting for us. Questions were shot at us from all sides: "Have you settled that swine Morin's business?" All La Rochelle was in a state of sup-pressed excitement, and Rivet, who had now got over his ill-temper, could hardly keep from laughing. "Yes, thanks to Labarbe!"

'We went along to see Morin.

'He was sitting in an arm-chair with mustard poultices on his legs, and a cold compress on his head, half dead with anxiety. He kept on coughing like a man at his last gasp, though nobody seemed to know how he had caught his cold. His wife looked at him with the eyes of a tigress ready to pounce.

'As soon as he saw us, he started to tremble so violently, that his wrists and knees shook.

' "Everything's all right, you old ruffian," I said. "But you'd better behave yourself in future."

'He struggled to his feet, gasping for breath: he grasped my hands, and even kissed them as though I were a ruling prince: he burst into tears, very nearly fainted, embraced Rivet and embraced Madame Morin, who pushed him back into his chair.

'But he never got over the shock. It had been too much for him. From then on, he was never referred to as anything but "that swine, Morin", and every time he heard those words, it was like a sword-thrust to him. Whenever a pert young street urchin called out "Pig!" he instinctively turned his head. His friends made the most horrible jokes at his expense, saying, for instance, if they happened to be eating ham: "Is this a bit of you?"

'Two years later, he died.'

'When I was standing as a parliamentary candidate in 1875, I paid a call on the newly-appointed notary of Tousserre, Maître Belloncle, to solicit his vote. A tall woman of ample proportions opened the door:

' "Don't you recognize me?" she asked.

The question was decidedly embarrassing, and I floundered a bit before saying:

' "N . . . no, Madame, I am very much afraid I do not."

' "Henriette Bonnel!"

' "Ah!"

'I felt myself going pale.

'She, however, seemed to be perfectly at her ease and smiled at me.

'As soon as she had left me alone with her husband, he clasped my hands which he pretty nearly crushed, so warm was his welcome.

' "My dear sir," he said, "I have been looking forward to meeting you for a very long time. My wife has spoken a great deal about you . . . I know in what painful circumstances you first made her acquaintance, and with what perfect tact, understanding, and devotion you behaved in the unfortunate business . . ." He hesitated, and then, in a low voice, as if about to say something distressingly coarse . . . "of that swine, Morin." '

(1882)

Two Friends

PARIS was invested, starving, at its last gasp. There were fewer and fewer sparrows on the roofs. The sewers had been emptied of their population. People were eating anything they could find.

One bright January morning, as Monsieur Morissot, a watch-maker by profession, and a man who loved to take his ease when occasion offered, was strolling in a melancholy mood along the outer boulevard, with his hands in the pockets of his army trousers and a void in his stomach, he ran into a man whom he immediately recognized. It was Monsieur Sauvage, a riverside acquaintance.

Every Sunday morning before the war, Monsieur Morissot had been in the habit of setting off early, with a bamboo rod in his hand and a tin box slung on his back. He took the Argenteuil train, got out at Colombes, and walked to the small island which goes by the name of Marante. As soon as he reached this place of his dreams, he settled down to fish, and he fished till nightfall.

A tubby, jovial little man was always there before him, a draper from the Rue Notre-Dame-de-Lorette, as fanatical an angler as himself. They frequently spent half the day sitting side by side, rod in hand, and their feet dangling over the stream. They had become fast friends.

Sometimes they did not talk at all. Sometimes they chatted, but so alike were their tastes and their reactions, and so perfect their understanding of each other, that words were unnecessary.

Sometimes, on spring mornings, about ten o'clock, when the early sun had laid on the still surface of the river a faint mist, which flowed with the current, and beat down on the backs of the two enthusiasts with the welcome warmth of the waxing season, Morissot would say to his neighbour, 'Lovely, isn't it?' And Monsieur Sauvage would reply, 'I don't know anything lovelier.' That simple exchange was enough to bring complete understanding be-tween them, and make them like one another the more.

On autumn afternoons, when the day was nearing its end and the setting sun reddened the sky, when the water reflected crimson clouds and the far horizon seemed all ablaze, when the figures of the two friends seemed lit by fire, and the trees, already turning red, glowed and shivered with a foretaste of winter, Monsieur Sauvage would smile at Morissot and say: 'That's a sight for sore eyes.' And Morissot, struck with the wonder of it all, but keeping his eyes firmly fixed on his float, would answer: 'Better than the boulevard, eh?'

No sooner had the two friends recognized each other, than they shook hands warmly, caught up in a little eddy of emotion at meeting thus again in such different circumstances. Monsieur Sauvage sighed and said: 'What times we live in!' And Morissot, all gloom, lamented: 'And what a lovely day! The first really good weather of the year!'

That was undeniable, for the sky was an unclouded, brilliant blue.

They walked together, side by side, thoughtful and sad.

'Remember our fishing?' said Morissot. 'Those were the days.'

'Will they ever come again, I wonder?' said Monsieur Sauvage.

They went into a little café and had an absinthe each. Then they resumed their walk along the pavement.

Suddenly Morissot pulled up short: 'What about another?' 'I'm with you,' said Monsieur Sauvage, and they turned in at a second bar. By the time they left it they were slightly fuddled, as men are apt to be after drinking spirits on an empty stomach. The day was mild, and a pleasant breeze fanned their faces.

Monsieur Sauvage had been made more than a little drunk by the air. He stopped and put a question:

'Why shouldn't we have a shot?'

'What at?'

'Fishing.'

'Where?'

'At our island, of course. The French outposts are close to Colombes. I know the colonel in command—a chap called Dumoulin. He won't make any difficulties.'

Quivering with anticipation Morissot acquiesced: 'Done. I'm with you.' And the two friends separated to get their equipment.

An hour later they were striding together down the main road. They reached the villa in which the colonel had established his headquarters. He smiled at their odd request, but readily gave his consent. They started off again, armed with the necessary permit.

In next to no time they had crossed the outpost line, passed

Two Friends

through Colombes which had been evacuated, and found themselves on the edge of a small vineyard which sloped down to the Seine. It was about eleven o'clock.

Opposite them the village of Argenteuil seemed dead. The heights of Orgemont and Sannois dominated the countryside. The great plain which stretches as far as Nanterre was empty, completely empty, with its leafless cherry-trees and grey soil.

Monsieur Sauvage pointed with his finger at the high ground. 'The Prussians are up there,' he said. A sort of paralysis seized upon the two friends as they gazed at the desert before them.

The Prussians! They had never set eyes on them, but for months and months they had been conscious of their presence on every side, bringing ruin on France, looting, murdering, spreading starvation, invisible, irresistible. A sort of superstitious dread was added to the hate they felt for that unknown and victorious race.

Hesitant and fearful, Morissot said: 'Suppose we met some of them?'

In spite of everything, the mocking note of the Paris streets sounded in his friend's reply: 'We would offer them a fish-fry!'

But they still hesitated before venturing into the open country, for they were intimidated by the vast spread of silence round them.

It was Monsieur Sauvage who finally took the plunge.

'We'd better get going,' he said, 'but keep your weather-eye open!'

They clambered down through the vines, bent double, crawling on hands and knees, taking advantage of the cover offered by the bushes, their ears pricked.

They still had a strip of open ground to cross before they could get to the river bank. They broke into a run, and, when they reached it, went to earth in a thicket of dry reeds.

Morissot put his ear to the ground to catch the sound of footsteps. He heard nothing. They were alone.

Plucking up their courage, they began to fish.

Immediately in front, the deserted island of Marante hid them from the other bank. The little restaurant was closed, and looked as though it had been abandoned for years.

Monsieur Sauvage caught the first gudgeon, Morissot the second, and then, with scarcely a pause, they kept jerking up their rods with little silver creatures flickering at the end of their lines. A miraculous draught of fish, indeed!

Carefully, they put their haul into a fine-meshed net dangling in

171

the water at their feet, and a delicious joy took hold of them, the joy that comes when a favourite pleasure is resumed after long months of deprivation.

The kindly sun sent a ripple of warmth between their shoulder-blades. There was not a sound to be heard, nor was there a thought in their heads. The world was all forgotten. They were fishing.

But, suddenly, a dull, a seemingly subterranean sound made the earth tremble. The big guns were at it again.

Morissot turned his head, and above the bank, away to the left, he saw the great bulk of Mont-Valérien with, on its head, a white plume, a drift of smoke which it had just spewed out.

Almost immediately a second jet of smoke leapt from the summit of the fort, and a few moments later the noise of a second detonation reached their ears.

Others followed, and at brief intervals the mount puffed out its death-dealing breath, spreading clouds of milky vapour which slowly rose into the peaceful sky, covering it with a pall.

Monsieur Sauvage shrugged. 'There they go!' he said.

Morissot, who was anxiously watching the little feather on his float bobbing up and down, was suddenly filled with the anger of a man of peace at the maniacs with no thought for anything but fighting. 'Only fools,' he grunted, 'would go on killing each other like that!'

'They're worse than fools,' said Monsieur Sauvage.

Morissot, who had just landed a fish, burst out with: 'Nothing'll ever change so long as there are governments!'

Monsieur Sauvage corrected him: 'A republic would never have declared war . . .'

But Morissot cut him short: 'With kings there are foreign wars: with republics, civil strife.'

Without heat they started arguing the great political issues, showing all the sweet reasonableness of peace-loving men who cannot see beyond their noses. On one thing only they agreed: that mankind would never be free. And all the while Mont-Valérien kept thundering, bringing destruction on French homes, grinding flesh and blood to dust, crushing human bodies, and bringing to the hearts of women, girls, and mothers in other lands, an endless suffering.

'Such is life,' said Monsieur Sauvage.

'Say, rather, such is death,' laughed Morissot.

They both gave a frightened start. They had a feeling that somebody was moving behind them. Turning their heads they saw, standing at their backs, four great hulking brutes, armed and bearded, dressed like liveried footmen, with flat caps on their heads, and rifles levelled.

The rods dropped from their hands and went floating down the river.

In a matter of seconds they were seized, carried off, flung into a boat, and ferried across to the island.

Behind the building they had thought deserted, they saw about twenty German soldiers.

A sort of hairy giant astride upon a chair and smoking a long porcelain pipe, asked them in excellent French: 'Did you have good fishing, gentlemen?'

One of the soldiers laid the net filled with fish at the officer's feet. The Prussian smiled: 'Not too bad, I see. But we have other things to think about. Just listen to me and don't worry.

'So far as I am concerned you are two spies sent to keep a watch on me. I have taken you and I shall shoot you. You have been pretending to fish, the better to conceal your real intentions. You have fallen into my hands. So much the worse for you: but war is war.

'Since, however, you came through your own lines, I take it that you have been given the countersign which will enable you to return the same way. Give that countersign to me and I will spare your lives.'

The two friends standing side by side with ashen faces. Their hands were twitching nervously, but they said nothing.

The officer went on: 'No one will be the wiser. You will return undisturbed. The secret will go with you. If you refuse, you die— instantly. Which will you choose?'

They still stood motionless. Not a word came from them.

Quite calmly, the Prussian pointed to the river, and continued: 'In five minutes you will be at the bottom of that. Five minutes. I suppose you have relatives?'

Mont-Valérien was still thundering.

The two fishermen stood perfectly still and silent. The German gave an order in his own language. Then he moved his chair so as not to be too close to the prisoners, and twelve men marched up and halted at a distance of twenty paces, their rifles at the order.

'I give you one minute now, not a second more.'

Then he got quickly to his feet, approached the two Frenchmen, took Morissot by the arm, and led him to one side. In a low voice, he said: 'Give me the countersign. Your friend need know nothing. I will make it look as though I have relented.'

Morissot said nothing.

The Prussian repeated the manoeuvre with Monsieur Sauvage, and made the same suggestion to him.

Monsieur Sauvage said nothing.

They were back as they had been, side by side.

The officer gave an order. The soldiers raised their rifles.

Morissot's eyes happened to fall on the netful of gudgeon lying in the grass quite close to him.

A ray of sunshine fell on the pile of still-squirming fish, and made them glitter. He was guilty of a moment's weakness. In spite of his effort to hold them back, two tears came into his eyes.

'Good-bye, Monsieur Sauvage,' he said unsteadily.

'Good-bye, Monsieur Morissot,' Monsieur Sauvage said.

They shook hands, trembling uncontrollably from head to foot.

'Fire!' shouted the officer.

The twelve shots rang out like one.

Monsieur Sauvage fell forward like a log. Morissot, who was taller, swayed, spun round, and collapsed across his friend. He lay with his face to the sky, a few drops of blood bubbling from holes in the front of his coat.

The German issued some further orders. His men scattered and came back with some lengths of rope and a few stones which they fastened to the feet of the dead men. Then they carried them to the bank.

Mont-Valérien was still thundering. By this time there was a great mountain of smoke above it.

Two soldiers lifted Morissot by the head and feet. Two others did the same with Monsieur Sauvage. The bodies were swung violently backwards and forwards for a few moments, then pitched into the river, where they fell feet foremost, the stones weighting them down.

The water splashed, seethed, quivered, then grew calm again. A few small ripples broke against the bank.

A little blood floated on the surface.

The officer, still entirely unperturbed, said, in a low voice: 'It is the fishes' turn now.'

He noticed the net of gudgeon on the grass. He picked it up, looked it over, smiled and called: 'Wilhelm!'

A soldier in a white apron hurried up.

Two Friends

The officer threw him the haul of the two shot fishermen, and said:

'Fry these little creatures, quickly, while they are still alive. They will be delicious.'

Then, he returned to his pipe.

(24 March 1883)

A Vendetta

PAOLO SAVERINI'S widow lived with her son in a small, mean house on the ramparts of Bonifacio. The town, built on a forward spur of the mountains, and, in places, hanging sheer above the sea, faces the low-lying Sardinian coast across a strait which bristles with reefs. Below it, and on the inner side, a fissure in the cliff, which almost completely encircles it, has the appearance of a gigantic corridor, and serves as a harbour. The small Sardinian and Italian smacks, and the ancient, wheezy steam-packet which every fortnight makes the trip to Ajaccio, can moor immediately beneath the houses on the water-front, after making a long circuitous passage between two steep walls of rock.

On the white mountain, the clustered houses make a patch still whiter. They look like the nests of wild birds clinging to the rock above the terrible narrow stretch of water into which the bigger ships scarce ever venture. The unresting wind lashes the sea and all the barren coast, which it has already so deeply eroded that nothing grows there but sparse and windswept grass. It roars and whistles through the strait, both sides of which it devastates. Fragments of pale foam, clinging, here and there, to the innumerable rocks which show above the surface, look like tattered linen floating and fluttering upon the sea.

The widow Saverini's house stood firmly welded to the cliff-edge, and looked through its three windows on the wild and desolate scene.

There she lived with her son Antoine and their bitch, 'Semillante', a large raw-boned animal with a coat of long, coarse hair. It belonged to the sheep-dog breed, and the young man took it with him when he went out shooting.

One evening, in the course of a quarrel, Antoine Saverini was killed by a treacherous knife-blow from a man called Nicolas Ravolati, who got away that same night to Sardinia.

Some passers-by carried the body to his mother's house. She shed no tears but stood for a long while, motionless, looking at it. Then, laying her wrinkled hand upon the corpse, she swore that she would wage vendetta. She would let no one stay with her that night, but shut herself in with the body and the bitch. The animal began to howl, and went on howling without pause, standing at the foot of the bed, its tail between its legs, its head stretched out towards its master. And there it stayed, as motionless as the mother who, leaning above the corpse, stared fixedly at it, while now, at last, the great tears ran silently down her cheeks.

The young man lying on his back in his heavy serge jacket with the knife-gash in his breast, looked as though he were asleep. But there was blood everywhere: blood on his shirt which someone had torn open in an attempt to give first-aid; blood on his waistcoat and his breeches, on his face and on his hands. There were clots of dried blood on his hair and beard.

The old woman began to speak, and, at the sound of her voice, the bitch stopped howling.

'You shall be avenged, my little one, my son, my poor, poor child. You can sleep in peace, for you shall be avenged. Can you hear me? It is I who make that promise, I, your mother, and, as you know full well, your mother keeps her word.'

Slowly she bent down and pressed her cold lips to the dead lips of her son.

Then, Semillante once more began to whimper, and the whimper became a long-drawn-out keening on a single note, harrowing and horrible.

The two of them, the woman and the bitch, stayed there till the morning.

Antoine Saverini was buried the next day, and soon no one spoke of him in Bonifacio.

He had left neither brother nor close cousins. There was no man to pursue the vendetta. Only his mother, the old woman, brooded over it.

She could see, across the strait, from morning until evening, a small white patch upon the coast. It was a little village, called Longosardo, in which the Corsican bandits sought refuge when their enemies were close upon their heels. They were almost its only inhabitants, and lived there within sight of home, waiting for the day when they could go back and lie hidden in the *maquis*. She knew that Nicholas Ravolati had gone there for his safety.

Quite alone, and all day long, she sat by her window, staring towards Longosardo and thinking of revenge. How could she, crippled and so near to death, manage unaided? But she had promised; she had sworn upon the body of her son. She could not forget and she could not wait. But what should she do? She no longer slept at night. She knew neither rest nor peace. Stubbornly she brooded. The bitch lay sleeping at her feet, and, at intervals, raising her head, howled into the void. Now that her master was no longer there, she frequently howled in that way, as though, calling to him, as though, disconsolate, she, too, had kept a memory which nothing could efface.

One night, when Semillante began to whimper, the mother had a sudden thought, a savage thought, vindictive and ferocious. She turned it over in her mind till morning. Then, in the first light of the dawn, she rose and went to church. She knelt and prayed, abasing herself before God, begging Him for help and support, to give to her poor worn-out old body the strength she needed to avenge her son.

Then she went home. In the yard there was a stove-in cask which she used to catch the water from the gutters on the roof. She turned it upside down and emptied it, then fixed it firmly to the ground with stones and stakes. She chained Semillante to this improvised kennel, and went indoors. Up and down her room she paced endlessly, looking at the coast-line of Sardinia, where the murderer lived.

All day long, and all that night, the bitch kept up her howling. In the morning the old woman took her some water in a basin, but nothing more—neither broth nor bread. Another day passed. Semillante slept the sleep of exhaustion. Next morning her eyes were bright, her coat all staring, and she was dragging desperately at her chain.

Once more the old woman kept her without food. The animal, driven half insane, barked hoarsely. Another night came and went.

Early next morning, the widow Saverini went to see a neighbour, and asked him for two bundles of straw. Then, at home, she found some old clothes which her husband had once worn, and stuffed them with the straw to give them the appearance of a human body.

She fixed a post in the ground by Semillante's kennel and tied the dummy to it, so that it looked as though it were standing. Then she made a head for it out of some old linen.

The bitch, surprised by what she saw, looked at the scarecrow, but made no sound, though she was devoured with hunger.

Then the old woman went to the pork-butcher, and bought a piece of black-pudding. When she got home, she lit a wood-fire in the yard, close to the kennel, and broiled the pudding. Semillante jumped up and down in a frenzy, foaming at the mouth, her eyes fixed upon the cooking meat, the smell of which tortured her stomach.

Next, the old woman made of the smoking morsel a collar for the man of straw. She took a long time fixing it about its neck, pushing it inside as far as possible. This done, she unleashed the bitch. With a tremendous leap the animal managed to reach the dummy's throat, and, with her paws on its shoulders, tore at it with her teeth. Then she dropped to the ground, with part of her prey between her jaws. She leapt again, drove her fangs into the rope, wrenched away another portion of the food, dropped back again, and yet again sprang up, ferociously. She tore the face away with her teeth, and bit the collar all to pieces.

The old woman, silent and motionless, looked on with glittering eyes. Then she chained the bitch and kept her without food for two days more, after which she repeated the strange proceeding.

For three months she trained the animal in this mimic battle, teaching her to get her food with her teeth. She no longer chained her up, but set her on the dummy simply by pointing at it.

She accustomed the animal to tearing and devouring the man of straw, even when no meat was hidden in its throat. Then, as a reward, she gave her the black-pudding she had cooked for her.

As soon as she saw the dummy, Semillante trembled all over, then looked at her mistress, who, in a wheezy voice, said 'Go, get him!'—and pointed with her finger.

When she thought the time was ripe, old widow Saverini went one Sunday morning to confession. In a state of ecstatic fervour she took Communion. Then she dressed herself in man's clothes like a ragged old beggar, and bargained with a Sardinian fisherman to give her and her bitch a passage across the strait. In a canvas bag she took with her a large piece of black-pudding. Semillante had been starving for two days. Her mistress kept on letting her smell the savoury food, thereby working her up to a high state of excitement.

Together they entered Longosardo. The Corsican woman walked with a limp. She went to the baker and asked where Nicolas Ravolati lived. He had resumed his former trade of carpenter. He worked alone behind his shop.

The old woman pushed open the door and called:

'Hey! Nicolas!'

He turned his head, and, loosing the bitch, she screamed:

'Go! get him! . . . Get him!'

The animal, mad with hunger, sprang and seized him by the throat. The man, wrestling with it, rolled on the ground. For some seconds he writhed and twisted, drumming the ground with his heels. Then, he lay motionless, while Semillante nuzzled at his throat, tearing it to pieces with her teeth.

Two neighbours, seated at their doors, well remembered having seen an old beggar-man pass by with a raw-boned black dog, chewing as it walked at something brown which its master gave it.

The old woman reached home in the evening, and that night she slept soundly.

(14 October 1883)

The Hand

A CIRCLE had formed round Monsieur Bermutier, the Examining
Magistrate, who was giving his opinion about the mysterious
Saint-Cloud affair. For the past month this unsolved crime had
been the talk of Paris. No one could explain it.

Monsieur Bermutier was standing with his back to the fireplace,
talking. He marshalled the evidence, discussed a variety of
theories, but could reach no conclusion.

Several ladies had left their chairs to get closer to him, and they
remained standing, with their eyes on the magistrate's clean-
shaven lips, from which fell words of the utmost gravity. They
shuddered and were thrilled. That strange fear had hold of them,
that avid and insatiable love of being frightened which haunts all
women and torments them like a physical hunger.

A brief silence had fallen, and one of these ladies, who looked
paler than the others, broke it.

'It is positively horrifying,' she said. 'There is something almost
supernatural about it. I don't suppose we shall ever know what
really happened.'

The magistrate turned to her:

'That is extremely probable, Madame. But this I can tell you,
that the word *supernatural*, which you have just used, is entirely
out of place in this connexion. We are dealing with a crime which
was skilfully planned, most adroitly carried out, and so wrapped
in mystery that we have completely failed to free it from the
impenetrable circumstances which surround it. But I once had to
inquire into an affair about which there really was an element of
the fantastic. There, too, the investigation had to be abandoned,
for lack of evidence.'

Several of the ladies exclaimed, with such unanimity that their
voices sounded as one:

'Oh, do tell us about it!'

Monsieur Bermutier's smile was sober and serious, as the smile
of an Examining Magistrate should be. He continued:

'Please do not think for a single moment that I suppose there to
have been anything supernatural about the case in question. I

believe only in natural causes. It would be a great deal better if we used the word "inexplicable" rather than "supernatural" to describe matters we know nothing of. Be that as it may, what really interested me in the occurrence I am about to describe, were the attendant, the preparatory circumstances. Here are the facts.

'At the time of which I am speaking I was Examining Magistrate at Ajaccio, a small white town standing on the shore of a lovely bay surrounded on all sides by high mountains.

'I was chiefly concerned with matters having to do with *vendetta*. This tradition of private warfare is rich in superb, infinitely dramatic, fierce and heroic incidents. It provides us with the most wonderful stories of vengeance imaginable—hatred kept alive from generation to generation, momentarily appeased but never allowed to die, stratagems of the most horrible description, murders on such a scale as to deserve the name of massacres, and almost epic deeds. For two years I heard of nothing but bloodfeuds, of that terrible Corsican obsession which insists that a man must take vengeance not only on an enemy, but on his descendants and his relatives. I have known of old men, children, cousins having their throats cut in the name of that bloodstained doctrine. I have heard more stories of *vendetta* than I care to remember.

'I learned one day that an Englishman had taken the lease of a house, at the far end of the bay, for several years. He had brought with him a French servant whom he had engaged when passing through Marseilles.

'It was not long before the whole neighbourhood was buzzing with gossip about this strange character, who lived all alone in his house and never left it except to shoot and fish. He talked to nobody, never went into the town, and spent an hour or two every morning practising with a revolver and a carbine.

'He became the subject of many legends. Some said that he was a man of high rank who had fled from his country for political reasons; others, that he was hiding in order to escape the consequences of a detestable crime. People went so far as to give details of a more than usually blood-curdling nature.

'It was natural that, as an Examining Magistrate, I should wish to find out all I could about the fellow. But to learn much turned out to be impossible. He went by the name of Sir John Rowell.

'I had to be content with keeping such watch as I could upon him, but, even so, I could discover nothing in any way suspicious in his activities.

The Hand

'Since, however, rumours continued to circulate, to grow and to become widespread, I thought it my duty to make personal contact with this foreigner, and, with this end in view, I took to shooting regularly near his property. I had to wait some time for the chance I needed. But it came at last, in the form of a partridge at which I took a pot shot and happened to bring down under the very nose of the Englishman. My dog recovered it, and I went at once, with the bird in my hand, to apologize for my bad manners and to ask Sir John to accept the victim of my gun.

'He was a big man, with red hair and beard, very tall, very broad, in fact, a sort of urbane and quiet-mannered Hercules. There was nothing of the traditional British stiffness about him, and he thanked me warmly for my civility. He spoke French with an accent which undoubtedly hailed from across the Channel. By the end of a month, we had chattered together on five or six occasions.

'Then, one evening, when I happened to be passing his door, I saw him sitting astride a chair in his garden, smoking his pipe. I raised my hat, and he asked me in for a glass of beer. Needless to say, I did not wait to be asked twice. He received me with scrupulous English courtesy, was loud in his praise of France and of Corsica, and declared that he had developed a great fondness for "this country" and "this stretch of coast".

'With the utmost care, and pretending a lively interest, I questioned him about his life and his plans. He showed no embarrassment, and told me that he had travelled a great deal in Africa, India, and America, adding with a laugh:

' "I have had my full share of adventures."

'Then I started to talk shooting with him, and he told me many curious details about his experiences when hunting hippopotamuses, tigers, elephants, and even gorillas.

' "Those are all very dangerous animals," I said.

'He smiled: "But there is none more dangerous than man."

'All of a sudden, he laughed outright, and his laugh was that of a solid, satisfied Englishman.

' "I have hunted a good many men, too, in my time."

'Then he switched the talk to firearms, and asked me into the house to look at his collection of guns and rifles.

'The hangings in his drawing-room were black—black silk embroidered in gold. Great yellow flowers sprawled all over the dark material, glittering like flame.

' "It is a Japanese fabric," he said.

'But, in the middle of the largest panel, a strange object caught my eye. On a square of red velvet something black stood out in strong relief. I went closer. It was a hand, a human hand, not the hand of a skeleton, white and clean, but a shrivelled black hand with yellow nails. The sinews had been laid bare, and there were traces of dried blood, like a scab, on the bones, which had been cleanly severed about half way up the forearm.

'Round the wrist was an enormous iron chain, riveted and soldered to the unsavoury limb, and attached to the wall. It looked strong enough to tether an elephant.

' "What is that?" I asked.

'With complete composure the Englishman replied: "That belonged to my best enemy. Comes from America—cut off with a sabre, and the skin scraped away with a sharp stone. Left to dry in the sun for eight days. It was a bit of luck for me, I can tell you."

'I touched the grisly relic, which must have belonged to a man of tremendous size. The abnormally long fingers were attached to enormous sinews to which, in places, strips of skin were still adhering. Flayed like that, the hand was a disgusting sight, and seemingly bore witness to some act of savage vengeance.

'I said: "He must have been very strong."

Very quietly, my host replied: "He was: but I was stronger. I put that chain on to hold him down."

'I thought he was joking, and said: "But there is no reason for the chain now. That hand isn't going to run away!"

'In a perfectly serious voice, Sir John Rowell said: "It was always trying to get free: I had to chain it."

'I shot a quick, inquiring look at him. Was he, I wondered, a madman or just a practical joker?

'But his face remained inscrutable, calm, and benignant. I changed the subject, and much admired his collection of guns.

'I noticed, however, that there were three loaded revolvers lying about on various pieces of furniture, as though the man were living in constant fear of attack.

'I revisited him on several occasions. Then I stopped going. The locals had grown used to him, and nobody now gave him a thought.'

'A year went by, and then, one morning towards the end of November, my servant woke me with the news that Sir John Rowell had been murdered during the night.

'I went to the Englishman's house with the Chief Constable

The Hand

and the Captain of Gendarmes. The dazed and distracted valet was blubbering in front of the door. I immediately suspected him, but he was, as it turned out, innocent.

'The identity of the murderer was never established.

'On going into the drawing-room, the first thing I saw was the body of Sir John lying in the middle of the floor.

'His waistcoat was torn open, and one sleeve of the coat was hanging by a thread. There had obviously been a fierce struggle.

'The Englishman had been strangled. His black and swollen face was horrible to see and, in his eyes, there was a look of the most appalling terror. There was something between his clenched teeth, and his neck, pierced in five places by some sharp instrument, was covered in blood.

'A doctor joined us. He made a prolonged examination of the finger-marks on the dead man's neck, and then uttered these strange words:

' "Looks to me as though he'd been strangled by a skeleton!"

'A shiver went down my back, and I looked at the wall where I had once seen that dreadful flayed hand. It was no longer there. The chain had been broken and was hanging loose.

'Then I bent over the corpse. The object between its teeth was one of the fingers of the vanished hand, but cut, or rather bitten through at the second joint.

'A search was made but without producing any new evidence. Not a door, nor a window, had been forced. None of the furniture showed signs of violence. The two watch-dogs seemed to have slept through whatever had happened.

'Here, in brief, is the gist of the servant's deposition.

'For the last month, he said, his master had seemed to be uneasy and on edge. He had received a number of letters which he had thrown on the fire as soon as they arrived.

'He frequently took a hunting-crop, and, in a fit more of madness than of rage, had lashed blindly at the withered hand which, at the moment of the crime, had been spirited away from its place on the wall, no one could say how.

'He went to bed very late, and was careful to lock all the doors and windows. He always had some weapon within easy reach. He would frequently speak in a loud voice during the night. He seemed to be quarrelling with somebody.

'On the night in question, however, he made no noise, and it was only when his servant went into his room to open the shutters, that he found Sir John murdered. He could think of no possible suspect.

'I communicated all I knew about the dead man to the civil authorities and the police. The whole island was combed, but without result.

'About three months after the crime, I had a most terrifying nightmare. I dreamed that I saw that horrible hand scuttling like a scorpion or a spider along my walls and curtains. Three times I woke up: three times I fell asleep again, and three times I saw that hideous relic galloping round the room, moving its fingers like legs.

'Next morning it was brought to me. It had been found in the churchyard on Sir John Rowell's grave—for in the absence of any discoverable relative, he had been buried on the spot. The index finger was missing.

'And that, ladies, is my story. I know nothing more.'

The ladies were horror-stricken, pale, and trembling. One of them exclaimed:

'But you have suggested no solution, no explanation of the mystery! I am sure none of us will sleep unless you tell us at least what you *think* happened!'

The Magistrate smiled, but his eyes remained severe.

'I fear that, so far as dreams are concerned, I shall be a wet blanket. My theory, such as it is, is very simple, namely that the owner of the hand was not dead at all, but came to look for it. What he did, I have no idea, but I am inclined to think that the whole affair had something to do with a *vendetta*.'

'No,' murmured one of the ladies: 'that *can't* be the explanation!'

The Magistrate, still smiling, concluded:

'I told you that you would not like my theory.'

(23 December 1883)

The Drunkard

THE northerly wind at gale force was blowing across the sky a mass of black, heavy winter clouds which, in their passage, released a storm of rain upon the earth.

The unbridled sea bellowed and roared, shaking the shore with a bombardment of huge breakers, slow-moving and slobbering, exploding with a din of guns, moving in quietly to the attack in ranked succession, mountain-high, and scattering the spume which the screaming squalls of wind snatched from their crests like sweat blown from some monster's head.

The storm swept down the little valley of Yport, tearing tiles from the roofs, battering shutters, bringing chimneys crashing to the ground, swirling with such force along the streets that only by clinging to the walls was human movement possible. Any children out in such a gale would have been caught up like leaves and sent spinning across the house-tops into the open country.

The fishing smacks had been dragged high out of harm's way, for fear that the high tide might make a clean sweep of the shore, and, under cover of the pot-bellied hulls, lying on their sides, a few fishermen crouched, watching the maniac fury of sea and sky.

One by one, they moved away, for night was coming on, shrouding in darkness the maddened ocean and the torment of the unleashed elements.

Two men still remained, their hands thrust deep into their pockets, their shoulders hunched against the driving squalls, their woollen caps pulled down to their eyes—two tall Normandy fishermen with fringes of stubbly beard and skin tanned by the salty blasts of the open sea. Their eyes, blue with a black speck at the centre, were those of mariners who search the far horizons like birds of prey.

One of them said:

'Come, Jeremy, us'll pass the time at dominoes, an' I'll pay for drinks.'

The other hesitated, tempted by the prospect of play and brandy, but knowing that once in Paumelle's bar he wouldn't come out sober, and deterred, too, by the thought of his wife left all alone in the shack.

' 'Tis as though you'd made a bet to get I proper sozzled,' he said. 'What be 'ee a-getting at, so free with thy money and all?'

All the same, he laughed happily at the thought of so much liquor waiting to be drunk at somebody else's expense. His laugh was the satisfied laugh of your true man of Normandy getting something for nothing.

His friend, Mathurin, still had him by the arm:

'Ah, come along, man: 'tis no night to be going wome wi' a cold belly! What be 'ee afeard on? T'old woman'll keep t' bed warm, won't 'er?'

'T'other night,' said Jeremy, 'oi couldn't find door no 'ow—'ad to be fished out o' gutter front of our place . . .'

He was still chortling over this old soak's misadventure, and made no further difficulties about going along to Paumelle's bar, half dragged by Mathurin, half pushed by the wind, and incapable of resisting the combination.

The low-ceilinged room was chock-full of fishermen, smoke, and noise. The men, in woollen jerseys, with their elbows on the tables, had to shout to make themselves heard, and the more the place filled up with drinkers, the louder did they have to shout, so deafening was the din of voices and the rattle of dominoes on the marble table-tops.

Jeremy and Mathurin sat down in a corner, and started to play, and, as they played, the contents of the little glasses, one after the other, went chasing down their throats.

Game followed game and glass followed glass. It was Mathurin who did the filling, with a knowing wink at the proprietor, a fat man, with a face like a hot coal-fire, who seemed never to stop chuckling, as at some unending joke. Jeremy gulped down the brandy, wagged his head, and guffawed with a noise like a bull's bellow, looking at his friend the while with a dazed expression of contentment.

The other customers were now on the move, and each time one of them opened the street-door, he let in a blast of wind which made the heavy, smoke-laden air eddy, and set the hanging lamps swinging on their chains and the flames flickering. When that happened the room was suddenly filled with the crashing of waves and the moaning of the storm.

Jeremy, with his collar undone, was looking more and more like a sot, one leg stretched out, one arm dangling, holding his dominoes in the other hand.

The two of them were alone now, except for the proprietor, who came across to their table, in a mood of obvious curiosity.

'Feeling warm and comfy inside, Jeremy?' he asked: 'Taken enough liquor aboard to freshen you up?'

Jeremy spluttered over his words:

'More t'splashes down, more drier does oi get.'

The other shot a sly look at Mathurin:

'What 'bout that brother o' yourn, Mathurin?'

The fisherman exploded with silent laughter:

'Warm 'nough! Doan'ee worrit 'bout 'e.'

Both of them looked at Jeremy, who slammed down the double-six with a triumphant shout:

'Got 'ee oi 'ave!'

When they had finished their game, the boss declared:

'Well, boys, I'm packing it in. I'll leave lamp and bottle wi' you. There's still a dose or two left. See's you lock up proper when you go, and slip key under the shutter, like you did t'other night.'

Mathurin replied:

'I get 'ee: no need t' worry.'

Paumelle shook hands with the two laggards and lumbered up the wooden staircase. For a while his heavy footsteps sounded through the little house, then a loud creaking announced that he had got into bed.

The pair went on with their dominoes. Now and again a more than usually violent blast shook the door and set the walls trembling, so that they looked up as though expecting somebody to come in. Then Mathurin picked up the bottle and refilled Jeremy's glass. But all of a sudden, the clock over the bar struck midnight. Its hoarse chime sounded like the clatter of saucepans, and the strokes hung in the air with a jangle of old iron.

At last, Mathurin, too, got up, like a sailor whose watch is over.

'Us better get going, Jeremy.'

The other, finding it more difficult to move, staggered to his feet and managed to keep his balance by leaning against the table. At last he reached the door and opened it, while his companion blew out the lamp.

When they were in the street, Mathurin locked up. That done, he said:

'S'long, be seein' yer tomorrow.'

And he vanished into the darkness.

Jeremy took three steps, then swayed on his feet, put out a hand, bumped into a wall which kept him upright, then set off again, staggering. An occasional squall, caught in the narrow funnel of the street, drove him forward for a few steps. When it subsided, he stopped dead, at a loss without its support, then, after a bit, managed to continue on his zig-zag course, his drunkard's legs completely out of control.

He made instinctively for home, as birds fly back to their nests. At last he recognized his door, and started on a fumbling search for the lock. But he could not find the hole, and mumbled out a string of curses. Then he began thumping on the panel with his fists, shouting for his wife to come and help him.

'M'lina! Hey! M'lina!'

As he was leaning against the door to keep himself from falling, it yielded suddenly, and flew open. Jeremy, left without anything to lean on, crashed into the room beyond, and fell flat on his face in the middle of the floor. He had a feeling that something heavy had moved over him and run out into the darkness.

He lay there, motionless, paralysed with terror, frightened out of his life at the thought of devils, ghosts, and all the things that go bump in the night. And there he stayed without daring to move. But when it was gradually borne in on him that nothing was stirring, his muddied brain began to work, though sluggishly.

He sat down quietly, and waited for a long time, till, taking his courage in both hands, he shouted again:

'M'lina!'

No answer came from his wife. All of a sudden a doubt dawned in his befuddled brain, a formless doubt, a vague suspicion. He stayed where he was, sitting on the ground in the dark, trying to get his mind to work, grasping at the fragmentary thoughts, as swaying and unsteady as his legs.

Again he shouted:

'Who was't, M'lina? Tell oi who 'twas, and I won't do nothing to yer.'

Again he waited, but no voice broke the silence.

Then he started to think aloud.

' 'Ve had a drop . . . knows that . . . a drop. 'Twas him as got me boozed, t'barstard—so's I shouldn't be able get 'ome. I knows I 'ad a drop.'

Then he went on:

'Tell oi who 'twas, M'lina, or 'll do summat!'

After a further wait he continued, with the slow, bull-headed logic of the drunkard:

' 'Twas 'im as kept me at that dam' joint—and not first time, neither, so's wouldn't come 'ome. 'Twas plot of hisn, the swine!'

The Drunkard

Slowly, he got to his knees. A lumpish rage was rising in him, mingled with the fumes of drink.

'Tell oi who 'twas, M'lina, or 'll give 'ee a proper bashing! . . .'

He was on his feet now, trembling all over in a blaze of fury, as though the brandy in his belly had turned his blood to fire. He took a step forward, bumped into a chair, snatched it up, went on, knocked against the bed, fumbled at it, and felt under the blankets the warm body of his wife.

Mad with rage, he bellowed at her: 'There all time, eh, y' bitch? . . . Woun't answer woun't yer? . . .'

Raising the chair in his great fisherman's fist he brought it down in front of him in a blind fury. A shriek came from the bed, a frantic, rendering shriek. Then he set to beating at her like a thresher threshing grain. Soon, all movement stopped. The chair was broken in pieces, but he still had one leg in his hand, and he brought it down, again and again, gasping for breath.

Then, suddenly, he stopped, and said: 'Will 'ee say who 'twas now?'

Melina made no answer.

Then, utterly worn out, besotted with his own violence, he sat down again on the floor, stretched himself out, and went to sleep.

When day broke, a neighbour, seeing his door open, went in. He saw Jeremy snoring on the ground with the remains of a chair in his hand, and, in the bed, a shapeless mess of blood and flesh.

(20 April 1884)

The Necklace

SHE was one of those pretty, charming young women who have had the ill fortune to be born into a wage-earning family. She had no dowry, no prospects, no opportunities of getting to know some rich and distinguished man who might have understood her, loved her, and made her his wife. Consequently, she let herself drift into marriage with a junior clerk in the Ministry of Public Instruction.

Though her tastes were simple, anything else having been out of the question, she felt as unhappy as though she had come down in the world. Among women, caste and birth are meaningless. Beauty, sweetness, and charm take the place for them of blue blood and family connexions. Quick wits, instinctive elegance, and adaptability are the only degrees in their hierarchy, and can make of working girls the equals of the greatest of great ladies.

She was in a perpetual state of dissatisfaction, because she felt that luxuries and soft living were her natural birthright. The furnished flat in which she had to live, its squalid wall-papers, its shabby chairs, its hideous curtains and upholstery, were a constant source of torment to her. These things, which another woman with a background similar to her own might not even have noticed, she found unendurable and degrading. The sight of the Breton girl who did the humble domestic chores filled her with hopeless longings and idle dreams. She conjured up a vision of hushed entrance halls, hung with oriental fabrics and lit by bronze sconces, of tall footmen in knee-breeches dozing in deep armchairs in the drowsy warmth of a great stove. She dwelt in imagination on vast salons adorned with antique silks, on elegant tables littered with priceless knick-knacks, on perfumed boudoirs where she would sit in the late afternoons chatting with intimate friends—men well known and sought after, such as every woman wants to have dancing attendance on her.

When she sat down to dinner with her husband at the round table covered with a three-day-old cloth, and heard him say, with a delighted expression on his face, as he lifted the top from the soup-tureen, 'Ah! vegetable soup; what could be better than that!' she let her mind run on delicious dishes served in exquisite porcelain, on whispered gallantries, and the sphinx-like smile with which she would listen to them while eating the pink flesh of a trout or the wing of a chicken.

She had no evening dresses, no jewels, nothing. And those were the only things she cared about. She felt made for the life they represented. She longed to be envied, popular, seductive, and courted.

She had one rich friend, a woman she had known in their convent days. But she no longer went to see her, only too well aware, from experience, that everything seemed so much worse at home when she got back from one of those expeditions. For days on end she would cry and cry, shedding tears of misery, regret, despair, and anguish.

One evening, her husband came home looking unusually pleased, with a large envelope in his hand.

'This is something for you,' he said.

She quickly tore open the envelope and took from it a card on which were engraved the following words:

The Minister of Public Instruction and
Mme Georges Ramponneau
request the pleasure
of the company of

M. AND MME. LOISEL

on Monday evening, the 18th of January
at the Ministry

Instead of being overjoyed, as her husband had expected, she threw the card on the table in a pet, saying in a complaining voice:

'What use is this to me?'

'But, darling, I thought you would be pleased. You never go out, and this is a chance not to be missed. I had the greatest difficulty in getting an invitation. Everyone is longing to be asked. It is a very smart occasion, and not many of the staff have been invited. You will meet all the official world there!'

An angry look came into her eyes as she impatiently replied:

'And how do you expect me to dress for this smart occasion?'

This problem had not occurred to him.

'Why,' he muttered, 'that little frock, I suppose, which you put on when we go to the theatre: I must say, it always looks very nice to me . . .'

He stopped speaking, for his wife was crying. Two large tears were slowly moving down her cheeks, from the corners of her eyes to the corners of her mouth. At the sight of them he felt dumb-founded and bewildered.

'W . . . what's the matter?' he stammered.

By a violent effort she recovered her self-control, and answered in a calm voice while she dabbed at her tear-stained face:

'Nothing . . . except that I haven't a thing to wear. I can't possibly go to this party. You had better give the card to one of your colleagues whose wife has a more extensive wardrobe than mine.'

He was miserable.

'Look here, Mathilde,' he said: 'How much would the right kind of dress cost, something simple, I mean, which you could wear on other occasions?'

She thought for a while, totting up figures in her head, and wondering how much she could ask for without meeting with an immediate refusal and an exclamation of horror from her cheese-paring clerk of a husband.

At last, with some hesitation, she replied:

'I can't tell to a penny, but I think I could manage with four hundred francs.'

His face went slightly pale, for he had been keeping in reserve precisely that sum with the object of buying a gun, so as to be able to treat himself to a few outings next summer in the plain of Nanterre, with a few friends who went there for the lark-shooting.

Nevertheless, he said:

'Right: you shall have your four hundred francs. But try to make it a really nice dress.'

The day of the party was approaching, but there was something depressed, uneasy, and anxious about Madame Loisel, though her dress was ready. One evening her husband said:

'What's wrong? You have been acting very strangely for the last few days.'

'It vexes me,' she answered, 'to think that I have no jewellery, not a single thing to wear with my dress. I shall look like a poor relation. I would rather stay away from the party than go like that.'

'You can wear flowers,' he said. 'It's very much the thing this

194

season. For ten francs you can get two or three really magnificent roses.'

But she was not to be convinced. 'No . . . There is nothing more humiliating than to be the one poor little guest among a lot of rich women.'

'Why!' he exclaimed, 'what a silly you are! How about that friend of yours, Madame Forestier? Why not ask her to lend you something? You know her quite well enough for that.'

She uttered a joyful cry.

'Of course! Why did I never think of it?'

Next day she went to see her friend and told her of her trouble.

Madame Forestier went to her wardrobe with a looking-glass front, took from it a large locked box, opened it, and said:

'Take what you like, my dear.'

First of all she saw several bracelets, then a string of pearls, then a Venetian cross in gold and gems, of beautiful workmanship. She tried them on before the glass, unable to make up her mind, reluctant to take them off, to give them back. And all the time she kept on asking:

'Have you nothing else?'

'Why, of course. Look and see what you can find. You must know what you would like best.'

Suddenly, Mathilde came upon a black satin case with, in it, a superb diamond *rivière*. Her heart began to beat faster, and she was filled with a mad longing. With trembling fingers she fastened it round her throat against her high-necked dress, and looked at her reflection in a kind of ecstasy.

Then, with considerable hesitation, as though fearing a refusal, she said:

'Would you really lend me this? I don't want anything else.'

'Why, certainly.'

She flung her arms round her friend's neck, kissed her in a transport of affection, and fled away with her treasure.

The great day came. Madame Loisel was a tremendous success. She was the prettiest woman there, elegant, graceful, smiling, and wildly happy. The men all looked at her, asked who she was and tried hard to be introduced to her. All the Secretaries wanted to waltz with her. The Minister noticed her.

She danced madly. Pleasure had gone to her head like wine. She had no thought for anything but the triumph of her beauty, the splendour of her success. She moved in a happy mist made up of homage, admiration, awakened desires, and that sense of undisputed victory which is so dear to the female heart.

She stayed until four in the morning. Ever since midnight her husband had been fast asleep in a small, deserted *salon*, in the company of three other gentlemen whose wives were thoroughly enjoying themselves.

He put round her shoulders the wrap he had brought for this purpose, a shabby reminder of their day-to-day existence, the poverty of which was at odds with the beauty of her ball-dress. She was conscious of the contrast, and would have liked to slip away unnoticed by the other women wrapped in rich furs.

Loisel held her back.

'You'll catch cold outside. Wait here while I go and look for a cab.'

But she would not listen, and hurried down the stairs. When they got into the street, there was no cab to be found. They looked everywhere, calling to the drivers of those they saw at a distance.

In this way they walked on in the direction of the Seine, hopeless and with chattering teeth. At last, on the Quai, they came upon one of those ancient nocturnal prowlers which are never to be seen in Paris except after dark, as though they are too much ashamed of their poverty-stricken appearance to venture out in the daylight.

It took them to their door in the Rue des Martyrs, and gloomily they climbed up to their home. It was all over now, she was thinking, and he, that he must be at the Ministry by ten.

She took off her wrap in front of the glass, that she might once more see herself in all her glory. But, suddenly, she uttered a cry. The *rivière* was no longer round her neck.

Her husband, half undressed, asked her what the matter was.

She turned to him in a panic: 'I've . . . I've . . . not got Madame Forestier's necklace!' Distractedly, he jumped to his feet.

'But . . . that's not possible!' he exclaimed.

They hunted in the folds of her dress, of her cloak, in every available pocket. They could find it nowhere.

'You're sure you still had it when we started home?' he asked.

'Quite sure; I touched it in the hall at the Ministry.'

'But if you'd lost it in the street we should have heard it fall! It must be in the cab!'

'Yes, that's probably where it is. Did you take the number?'

'No. You didn't happen to notice it, I suppose?'

'No.'

They looked at one another in consternation. At last, Loisel began to put on his clothes again.

'I'll go over the part of the way we came on foot, just to see . . .'

He went out. She remained slumped in an armchair, still in her ball-dress, without the strength to go to bed, without a fire to warm her, without the power to think.

Her husband came back about seven. He had found nothing. They went to the Police Station, to a number of newspaper offices with an offer of a reward, to the hackney-coach companies, to any and every place that might offer them a gleam of hope.

She spent all that day in an unrelieved state of terror at the thought of the frightful disaster which had come upon them.

Loisel returned that evening, pale-faced and hollow-eyed. He had failed to discover anything.

'You must write to your friend,' he said, 'saying that you have broken the catch of her necklace, and that you are having it mended. That will give us time to have a further look round.'

She wrote to his dictation.

By the end of the week they had given up all hope.

Loisel, who looked five years older, said:

'We shall have to see whether we can't replace it.'

Next day they took the case to the jeweller whose name was inside it. He went through his books.

'It was not I, Madame, who sold this *rivière*; I only supplied the case.'

They went from shop to shop, trying to find a necklace like the lost one, trying to remember it in detail, both of them sick with misery and distress.

In a small shop in the Palais-Royal, they found a string of diamonds which looked like the exact double of the necklace they had lost. Its price was forty thousand francs, but they could have it for thirty-six.

They begged the jeweller not to sell it for six days. They further made it a condition of purchase that he would buy it back for thirty-four thousand should the original be found before the end of February.

Loisel had inherited eighteen thousand francs from his father. The rest he would have to borrow.

And borrow he did, getting a thousand here, five hundred there, five louis from one man, three from another, backing bills, pledging objects at a ruinous rate of interest, dealing with professional money-lenders or with anyone who would advance him cash. He loaded himself with debts for the rest of his life, rashly affixed his signature to promissory notes without being sure that he could meet them. Terrified by the prospect of his future and the black penury which was to be his lot, by a future of physical privations and moral torment, he took delivery of the new necklace, and put down thirty-six thousand francs on the jeweller's counter.

When Madame Loisel carried the *rivière* to Madame Forestier, all the latter said, in a rather injured tone, was:

'You really ought to have let me have it sooner. I might have needed it.'

She did not open the case, which was what her friend had feared she might do. What would she have thought if she had noticed the substitution? Might she not have taken her for a thief?

Madame Loisel's life, from then on, was one of miserable poverty. But she played her part, from the very first, heroically. The terrible debt had got to be settled, and settle it she would. The maid-servant was given notice. They moved to a cheaper flat, in the attics.

She undertook all the heavy work of the household, all the odious cooking. She did all the washing up, spoiling her pretty pink finger-nails on greasy crockery and dirty saucepans. She scrubbed the dirty linen, shirts, and dish-clouts, and hung them on a line to dry. She carried the refuse down every morning to the street, and brought up the water, stopping on each landing to get her breath. Dressed like a woman of the people, she made the round of the greengrocer, the grocer, and the butcher with a basket on her arm, haggling over prices, putting up with abuse, doling out her miserable pittance penny by penny.

Each month there were bills to be paid, others to be renewed, and a constant begging for time.

Her husband spent his evenings auditing the accounts of various shopkeepers, and often worked far into the night, doing copying at five sous a page.

This life lasted for ten years. At the end of that time they had paid back every penny with interest, plus accumulated compound interest.

Madame Loisel now looked like an old woman. She had the typical appearance of the working-class housewife, strong, hard, and coarse. Her hair was all anyhow, her skirt awry, her hands red. She spoke in a loud voice, and splashed water all over the place when she scrubbed the floors. But sometimes, when her husband was at the office, she would sit down at the window and dream of the long-distant evening when she had been the Belle of the Ball.

What would have happened if she had not lost the necklace? Who could say? How strange life is, how changeable! What small things make the difference between safety and disaster!

One Sunday, when she had gone to the Champs-Elysées for a little relaxation from the labours of the week, she suddenly caught sight of a woman walking with a child. It was Madame Forestier, still young, still beautiful, still seductive.

Madame Loisel felt strangely excited. Should she speak to her? Of course! And now that every debt was settled, she would tell her the whole story. Why not?

She went up to her.

'Good morning, Jeanne.'

The other did not recognize her and seemed surprised at being addressed so familiarly by such a low-class creature.

'I don't think I know you, Madame . . . I fear you must have made a mistake.'

'Oh no, I have not . . . I am Mathilde Loisel . . .'

Her friend uttered a cry:

'But, my poor Mathilde, how you have changed!'

'Yes, I have been through very hard times since I saw you last, and much unhappiness . . . all because of you!'

'Because of me? . . . How do you mean?'

'Do you remember the diamond necklace which you lent me for a party at the Ministry?'

'Certainly I do. What of it?'

'Only that I lost it.'

'But you gave it me back . . .'

'What I gave you back was another like it. For the last ten years we have been paying for it. You must realize that it was not easy for us to do that, for we had no money of our own . . . But it is all over now, and I am very happy to think that it is.'

'Do you mean that you bought a diamond *rivière* to replace mine?'

'Yes. You didn't notice any difference, did you? They were exactly alike.'

There was something at once simple and proud in her smile.

Madame Forestier, deeply moved, took both her friend's hands in hers.

'Oh, you poor, poor thing! Mine was imitation and worth, at most, five hundred francs! . . .'

(1884)

The Sign

THE young Marquise de Rennedon was still asleep in her snug and scented room. The low bed was wide, the sheets of the finest lawn, as delicate as lace, as caressing as a lover's arms. She was alone and at peace with the world. She was wrapped in the deep and tranquil slumber of divorce.

She was awakened by the sound of voices in the little blue drawing-room. She recognized the tones of her dear friend, the young Baronne de Grangerie. She was having words with the maid who was guarding her mistress's door.

The marquise got up, drew the bolt, turned the key, raised the curtain, and poked her head through, just her head, half-hidden in a cloud of curls.

'What on earth has brought you at so unearthly an hour? Why, it's not yet nine!'

The young baronne was looking very pale. She was clearly in a highly nervous state.

'I *must* talk to you,' she said. 'The most awful thing has happened!'

'Come in, darling.'

The baronne did as she was told, and they exchanged kisses. The marquise went back to her bed, while the maid opened the windows, letting in light and air. When she had left the room Madame de Rennedon said:

'Now, tell me all about it.'

Madame de Grangerie burst into tears, those charming, limpid tears which add to a woman's looks. She made no attempt to wipe her eyes, not wishing to make them red, but stammeringly embarked upon her story.

'Really, my dear, it's all perfectly horrible. I didn't have a wink of sleep last night, not a wink. Feel how my heart is beating!'

Taking her friend's hand, she laid it to her breast, to that round, firm envelope which contains a woman's heart, and is so satisfying to the male that he often does not try to find what lies within. Her heart was really and truly beating very hard.

'It happened yesterday . . . about four o'clock . . . or perhaps half-past, I can't be quite sure. You are familiar with my flat, and know that it is on the first floor, and that the small drawing-room, where I always sit, looks out on the Rue Saint-Lazare. You also know that I have a perfect mania for sitting in the window and watching people passing in the street. That station district is so gay, so full of movement, so very much alive . . . I just love it. Well, yesterday I was sitting on the low chair which I have had placed in the embrasure of the window. It was open, and there was I, thinking of nothing in particular, but happily breathing the fresh air. You remember how lovely it was yesterday?

'All of a sudden, I noticed, on the other side of the street, a woman also sitting in her window, a woman in a red dress—I had on that pretty mauve one, you know the thing I mean. I knew nothing about her, except that she's a new tenant who moved in only a month ago and, since it rained for most of last month, I hadn't so much as set eyes on her. But I could tell at once that she was a bad lot! At first I was rather put out and shocked to think she should be sitting in her window, like me, but I gradually began to find it amusing to study her. She was leaning on her elbows, keeping a watchful eye on the men, and all, or almost all of them, were looking up at her. It was just as though they had received some sort of a hint when they were getting near the house, as though they could smell her out as a gun-dog scents game. Anyhow, as I said, they most of them looked up, but in a peculiar way, like when Masons meet, you know. Her look said as plain as plain, "Like to come in?" And theirs, "No time!" or "Some other day!" or "Stoney", or sometimes in the cases of respectable husbands and fathers, "You'd better keep out of decent folks' sight!"

'You can't imagine what fun it was seeing her practising her little tricks, or perhaps I should say, carrying on her trade.

'Sometimes she shut the window with a bang, and a man slipped in at the street-door. That meant she had landed a fish. I looked at my watch. They stayed there between twelve and twenty minutes, never longer. It really was thrilling to watch that spider at work. As a matter of fact she wasn't at all bad-looking.

'I began to wonder how she managed to make her meaning clear so quickly. Was there more in it than just a special kind of look? Something I mean in the nature of a movement of the head, or a gesture of the hand?

'So I got my opera-glasses and tried to see how she worked it. The answer to my question was quite simple—at first a look, then

a smile, and finally, a little jerk of the head, meaning "Coming up?" But it was all done so quietly, so discreetly, that one scarcely noticed it. Obviously, one would have to have the knack to bring it off as she did.

'Could I learn how to do it—that little lift of the head, combining boldness and grace—because, you see, it really was very graceful?

'So I tried it in front of the glass. My dear, would you believe it, I did it even better! Much better! I went back to the window, feeling awfully thrilled.

'She wasn't getting any more bites now, poor girl, not a single one. She seemed to have struck a bad patch. It must be terrible having to make one's living that way, but rather amusing too, at times, because not all the men one sees in the street are awful.

'They were all on my side of the street now: not a soul on hers. The sun had shifted, and along they came, one behind the other, young and old, dark and fair, some with grey hair, some with white.

'A few of them were charming—but charming, my dear! Much nicer than my husband, or yours—your *former* husband I should say, for, of course, you're divorced now and can take your choice.

'So, I said to myself: if a respectable woman like me made that sign, would they take any notice? And, all of a sudden, I felt a mad longing to try. It was a positive *craving*—like that which women get when they are pregnant—a really frightful craving, quite irresistible. Honestly, darling, I do think we women are like monkeys! As a matter of fact a doctor once told me we have the same sort of brain. We've always got to be imitating *someone*— our husbands when we love 'em, our lovers, our women friends, or our confessors when they're nice. We adopt their ways of thinking, their words, their gestures, the whole bag of tricks. What fools we are!

'And then, you see, when I'm very much tempted to do something, I always do it.

'So, I made up my mind to try, just once. Nothing much could happen. We'd exchange a smile and that'd be that. I should never see him again. If I did, he wouldn't recognize me, or, supposing he did, I'd just pretend not to know him.

'I began to pick and choose among the passers-by. I wanted it to be someone really nice. Suddenly I saw a tall, fair, very good-looking young man. You know how I can never resist fair men!

'I looked at him. He looked at me. I smiled. He smiled back. Then, I made the sign—oh, very, very faintly—he nodded and, in a flash, had slipped into the front door.

'Can you imagine what I felt like, my dear! I really thought I should go out of my mind! I was absolutely terrified. He might say something to the servants—to Joseph, for instance, who's devoted to my husband, darling, absolutely devoted, and Joseph might think it was an old friend. What on earth was I to do? Any moment now he'd be ringing at the bell. I thought the best thing would be to go and meet him. I could say he'd made a mistake, and ask him to go away. Surely, he'd take pity on a woman, a poor, weak woman? So I rushed to the door, just as he'd got his hand on the bell.

'I stammered and stuttered. I behaved like a lunatic! "Please go away! Oh, *do* go away. You're making a mistake! I'm an honest woman! I'm married! It's all a horrid blunder: I took you for one of my friends—you're very like him!"

'But all he did was laugh in my face! "Good afternoon, lovely," he said. "Now I know all about you. You're married. That'll mean two louis instead of one. Well, I won't boggle at that. Show me the way."

'He pushed past me, shut the door and, as I stood there looking at him and absolutely *shaking*, my dear, he *kissed* me. Then he put his arm round my waist and led me back into the drawing-room, the door of which I had left open.

'Then, he began looking round, sort of taking stock, if you know what I mean, like an auctioneer. "Pretty slap-up place you've got: must be in pretty low water to play the window game!"

'I begged him again to leave me. "*Please* go!" I said. "My husband will be back any moment now: he always comes home at this time in the afternoon. I swear you've made a mistake!"

'He wasn't in the least flurried or put out. "That'll be quite enough from you, my girl!" he said. "If your old man turns up, I'll just slip him something, and he can go and have a drink across the way."

'Then, catching sight of Raoul's photograph on the mantel-piece, he asked whether it was my husband.

' "Yes," I said: "it is."

' "Looks a pretty poor fish! Who's that, one of your girl-friends?"

'He was looking at that photograph of you, my dear, the one in a ball-dress. I didn't really know what I was saying, and I stammered out:

' "Yes, a friend."

' "A nice little eyeful: hope you'll introduce us."

The Sign

'Just then the clock struck five. Raoul always gets back at half-past. Suppose he turned up before the other had gone! . . . I completely lost my head! . . . I thought . . . I thought . . . The best thing will be to get rid of him as quickly as possible . . . The sooner it's over and done with, the better . . . I *had* to let him, my dear, because, you see, he wouldn't have gone otherwise . . . so, I . . . I . . . shot the bolt on the drawing-room door.'

The young Marquise de Rennedon buried her head in the pillow and laughed and laughed till the whole bed shook.

When she had calmed down a bit, she asked:

'You say he was a good-looking young man?'

'Yes, very.'

'Then what are you complaining about?'

'But . . . But . . . You haven't heard the worst, darling. He said he'd come back today . . . at the same time. I'm absolutely at my wits' end! You've no idea how obstinate he is! Oh, what am I to do? . . . What am I to do?''

The marquise sat up in bed, thinking. Then she said:

'Have him arrested.'

The baronne was dumbfounded:

'Have him arrested, whatever for?'

'Easy. All you need do is go to the police and say some man has been following you about for the past three months, that he had the effrontery to go to your flat yesterday, that he has threatened to come again, and that you want police protection. They'll send two constables along and arrest him.'

'But, darling, suppose he tells . . .'

'Don't be a little fool. Once you've given your story to the police they won't believe a word he says. But they'll believe you, because you're a woman of fashion and above suspicion.'

'Oh! I'd never *dare*!'

'You've got to—if you don't, it's all up with you.'

'But just think! He'll say the most awful things when he's arrested!'

'What's that matter? You'll have witnesses, and you'll be sure of getting him a heavy sentence.'

'What sort of a sentence?'

'He'll have to pay damages . . . You've got to be ruthless.'

'Talking of damages . . . There's something else worrying me . . . worrying me a lot. You see, he left two louis . . . on the mantel-piece!'

'Two louis?'

'Yes.'

'Is that all?'

'Yes.'

'It isn't much: I should have felt horribly insulted if it had been me. Well?'

'What am I to do with the money?'

The marquise hesitated for a few seconds. Then, in a perfectly serious voice, she said:

'I really think, my dear, you ought to buy your husband a little present . . . It's the least you can do.'

(27 April 1886)

The Inn

LIKE all the wooden guest-houses of the High Alps, which stand at the foot of the glaciers in the gullies of bare rock between the tall, white peaks, the Schwarenbach Inn was a refuge for those making for the passes—in this case, the Gemmi.

For six months of the year it remained open, lived in by Jean Hauser and his family. Then, when the snow began to pile up, filling the valley, and making the road down to Loëche impracticable, the women, the father, and his two sons departed, leaving the old guide, Gaspard Hari, to look after the house, and with him, the young guide, Ulrich Kunsi, and Sam, the great mountain dog.

The three of them would be held captive till the spring in a prison of snow, with nothing to look at but the immense white slopes of the Balmhorn, shut in by palely glittering peaks, blockaded by, buried under, the snow which mounted higher and higher round them, enveloping, embracing, crushing the little house, piling up on the roof, reaching the windows, and walling up the door.

It was the day on which the Hauser family was going down to Loëche, for winter was approaching and the descent would soon be dangerous.

Three mules set off in front, laden with clothes and baggage, and led by the two sons. Behind them came the mother, Jeanne Hauser, and her daughter, mounted on a fourth mule. Thus arranged, the cavalcade began its journey.

The father followed with the two guides who would go with them as far as the point where the descent began.

First, they rounded the little lake, now frozen, at the bottom of a great rocky depression in front of the inn, after which they followed the valley—as smooth and empty as a sheet, and dominated on all sides by snow-covered crests.

The sun poured down on this white, glittering, and frozen desert, with a cold and blinding glare. There was no sign of life in all this vast ocean of the mountain ranges, no movement to be seen in the boundless solitude. No sound broke the profound silence.

Little by little, young Ulrich Kunsi, a tall and long-legged Swiss, left the other two behind, and hurried on ahead in an attempt to overtake the mule on which the women were riding.

The younger of the two watched him coming, and seemed to be calling to him with her melancholy eyes. She was a small, fair, peasant-girl, whose milky complexion and colourless hair looked as though they had faded as the result of long periods of living in a world of ice.

When he came up with the animal, the guide laid his hand upon its crupper and slowed it down. But at once, old mother Hauser began to talk, rehearsing with an infinity of detail all the tasks to which he would have to attend while she was away. This was to be his first experience of winter in the High Alps, whereas old Hari already had to his credit fourteen winters of being snowed up in the Schwarenbach Inn.

Ulrich Kunsi listened, though apparently not taking much in of what he was being told. He kept staring at the young girl. Now and again, he said 'Yes, Madame Hauser,' but his thoughts seemed to be elsewhere, though the calm expression of his face gave no indication of what they were.

In due course they reached the Lake of Daube, the smooth, frozen surface of which lay at the bottom of a narrow valley. To their right they could see the black rocks of the Daubenhorn rising sheer into the sky, while closer to them were the enormous slopes of scree brought down by the Loemmerm glacier which dominates the Wildstrubel.

As they approached the Gemmi Pass, where the descent to Loëche starts, the whole vast panorama of the Valais Alps lay spread beneath them, with beyond, the deep, wide valley of the Rhône.

In the far distance stood a crowded host of white peaks, some of them curiously squat, others pointed, and all of them glittering in the sun: the Mischabel with its twin projections, the tremendous bulk of the Wissenhorn, the heavy load of the Brunnegghorn, the high and formidable pyramid of the Cervin—that killer of men— and the monstrously coquettish shape of the Dent-Blanche.

Far below them, in a huge hole at the bottom of a terrifying abyss, stood Loëche with its houses looking like grains of sand flung into this vast crevasse, backed and shut in by the Gemmi, and opening further down into the Rhône Valley.

The mule stopped on the edge of the track which, twisting and turning endlessly upon itself in marvellous and fantastic loops, led down the mountain-side to the small and almost invisible village at its foot.

The women jumped down on to the snow. The two old men had now come up with them.

'Well, good-bye and good luck to you, my friends, until we meet again next year,' said Hauser, to which Hari replied, 'Until next year.'

They embraced. Then Madame Hauser offered her cheek and the young girl did the same.

When she came to Ulrich Kunsi, he whispered in her ear: 'Don't forget those who are left up here,' and she said 'No' in so small a voice that he guessed rather than heard what she was saying.

'Good-bye,' said Hauser once again, 'and take care of yourselves.'

Moving ahead of the women the four men started to go down. All four soon disappeared round the first bend in the track.

The two guides turned back in the direction of the Schwarenbach Inn.

They walked slowly, side by side, without speaking. It was all over now, and they would spend the next four or five months with no company but their own.

Then, Gaspard Hari began to talk about the previous winter. Michel Canol had been his companion, but he was now too old for such a life, since accidents may well happen during that long period of solitude. But they had not been bored. It was all a question of settling down at once into a routine. One could always, in the long run, invent distractions for oneself, games and other ways of passing the time.

Ulrich listened to him with downcast eyes. His thoughts were still with those others now moving downwards to the village, along the twists and turns of the Gemmi.

They soon came in sight of the inn. It was so small as to be scarcely visible, a black speck at the foot of the enormous snow-field.

When they opened the door, Sam, the great shaggy dog, rushed out and gambolled round them.

'To work, my boy,' said old Gaspard. 'We've no women now to get our dinner for us. Do you start peeling the potatoes.'

Seated on two stools, they began dipping their bread in the soup.

The next morning seemed long to Ulrich Kunsi. Old Hari sat by the fire smoking and spitting, while the young man looked through the window at the glittering mountain opposite.

In the afternoon he went out and retraced the journey of the previous day, trying to pick out the marks made by the mule which had carried the two women. When he reached the top of the Gemmi Pass he lay down on his stomach at the edge of the great precipice, and stared at Loëche.

The snow had not yet silted up around the village in its rock-sided well. Though it was now within a short distance, its drift had been stopped by the pine-wood screening the houses, which looked, from where he was, like flat stones in a meadow.

The Hauser girl was in one of them—but which? Ulrich Kunsi was too far away to see any of them clearly. How he wished he could go down while the road was still open!

But by this time the sun had disappeared behind the high peak of the Wildstrubel, and he turned homewards. Hari was still smoking. When he saw his companion come in, he suggested a game of cards, and they sat down, facing one another, at the table.

They played, for a long time, the simple game called *brisque*. Then, after the evening meal, they went to bed.

The following days were all precisely like the first, clear and cold but with no fresh fall of snow. Gaspard spent his afternoons watching the eagles, and such rare birds as ventured among the frozen summits, while Ulrich returned regularly to the pass, from which he could gaze down at the village. Then, they played at cards, dice, or dominoes for trivial sums, just to give an interest to the game.

One morning, Hari, the first up, called to his companion. A swirling cloud, deep, light, and looking like white foam, was close on top of them and all around. Little by little it was silently burying them under a thick, heavy coverlet of froth. This went on for four days and four nights. The door and the windows had to be dug out, a path made and steps cut to enable them to reach the surface of the powdered ice, which twelve hours of frost had made harder than the mountain rocks.

From now on they lived as prisoners, scarcely ever venturing beyond the house. They had divided the various tasks between them, and regularly did their stint of work. Ulrich Kunsi was in charge of the cleaning, the laundry work, and general tidying. It was he, too, who chopped the wood, while Gaspard did the cooking and saw to the fire. These recurring and monotonous occupations were varied with long games of cards or dice. They never quarrelled, being both of a placid temperament. They never even showed signs of irritation, nor spoke angry words, since they had accumulated a fund of patience for these winter months among the mountains.

The Inn

Sometimes Gaspard took his gun and went after chamois. Occasionally he killed one, and then there was rejoicing at the Schwarenbach Inn, and a great feast of fresh meat.

One morning he set off as usual for a day's shooting. The outside thermometer showed well below zero. He had started before the sun was up, hoping, in that way, to take the animals by surprise close to the Wildstrubel.

Ulrich, left alone, stayed in bed until ten o'clock. He was by nature a heavy sleeper, but dared not indulge this weakness in the presence of the old guide, who was always in a fever of activity and an early riser.

He ate his midday meal slowly, with Sam, who spent his days and nights sleeping in front of the fire. Then he began to feel oppressed by melancholy, almost by a fear of the loneliness, and a sudden craving came upon him for the daily game of cards, as a man may long for some habit which has become too familiar to be broken.

He went out, with the intention of meeting his companion, who should be home by four.

The snow had levelled out the whole of the deep valley, filling in the crevasses, blotting out the two lakes, flattening the rocks, so that now, between the towering summits there was but one immense white depression, smooth, frozen, and blinding.

For three weeks now Ulrich had not been back to the spot on the edge of the great abyss from which he had been in the habit of looking at the village. He would have liked to go back there before climbing the slopes which would take him to the Wildstrubel. He did so, only to find that Loëche, too, was under the snow. The houses in their pale winding-sheet were barely discernible.

Then, turning to the right, he reached the Loemmern glacier. He moved with the long, loping stride of a mountaineer, striking the iron point of his stick on the snow, which was now as hard as stone. He kept his sharp eyes on the alert for some tiny black spot in the distance against the limitless white table-cloth.

When he reached the edge of the glacier, he stopped, uncertain whether the old man had really come this way. Then he set off again, skirting the scree with a quicker and more uneasy step.

The light was fading; the snow was turning pink; a dry and freezing wind was blowing in little gusts across the glassy surface. He sent out a long, quavering yodel, but it was swallowed up in the deathlike silence of the sleeping mountains, rippling over the waves of icy spume now frozen into immobility, like the cry of a bird

P   *213*

above the sea. Then it died away entirely. There was no answering call.

He started off again. By this time the sun had sunk behind the crests. The afterglow in the sky still reddened the surrounding snow, but the deep valley was now in shadow, and suddenly the young man felt afraid. It was as though the silence, the cold, the solitude, and the winter death up here in the mountains, had entered into him, would freeze the current of his blood, stiffen his limbs, and turn him into a motionless pillar of ice. He broke into a run, fleeing for refuge to the inn. The old man, he thought, had probably returned during his absence. He must have taken another route, and would be sitting in front of the fire with a dead chamois at his feet.

Soon the inn came in sight. No smoke was rising from it. He ran more quickly still. He reached the house and opened the door. Sam flung himself upon him in an ecstasy of welcome. But Gaspard Hari had not come back.

The frightened Kunsi looked round the room as though expecting to find his companion hidden in a corner. Then he blew the fire into a blaze and prepared the soup, still hoping to see the other reappear.

From time to time he went outside to see whether there was any sign of him. Darkness had fallen, the pallid darkness of these mountain regions, thin and livid under the yellow sliver of a crescent moon dropping behind the crests.

Then he went back into the room, and sat warming his feet and hands, rehearsing in his mind every possible accident which might have happened.

Perhaps Gaspard had broken a leg, fallen into a crevasse, missed his footing, and twisted an ankle. He might be lying somewhere in the snow, stiff and frostbitten, lost, in an agony of mind, shouting perhaps for help, shouting with the full force of his lungs in the silence of the night.

But where? The mountains covered so vast an expanse, and were so harsh and cruel: the lower slopes, in particular, at this time of the year, were so treacherous that it would have needed ten or twenty experienced guides, working over the ground for a week on end, to find one lost man in this immensity.

If there was still no sign of Gaspard Hari, he decided he would set out with Sam between midnight and one o'clock in the morning.

He set about making his preparations. He packed a rucksack with enough food for two days, took his crampons, wound a long

The Inn

rope, thin and strong, about his waist, checked over his iron-shod alpenstock and the axe he used to cut steps in the ice, and then sat down to wait. The fire was blazing in the hearth; the great dog was snoring in the light of the flames; the clock was ticking like a heart in its resonant wooden case.

He waited with ears stretched to catch any distant sound, shivering when the light breeze ruffled the roof and walls.

Midnight struck. He gave a start, then, feeling cold and frightened, put some water to boil, so as to have some piping-hot coffee before setting out.

When the clock showed one o'clock, he got up, wakened Sam, opened the door, and set off in the direction of the Wildstrubel. For five hours he climbed, scaling the rock-faces with the help of his crampons, cutting steps in the ice, never stopping except when it was necessary to use his rope to pull the dog up an escarpment too sheer for it to climb unaided. It was round about six by the time he reached one of the crests where Gaspard often went in search of chamois.

He waited for the dawn to break.

The sky turned pale above his head, and suddenly a strange light, coming from he knew not where, sharply illuminated the immense ocean of pale peaks which stretched for hundreds of miles in all directions. It was as though this insubstantial radiance was born of the snow itself, and spread through the vast world of space. Very gradually, the highest of the distant crests took on a rosy tint as delicate as that of human flesh. A red sun appeared from behind the massive giants of the Bernese Alps.

Then he started again, walking like a hunter, with his body bent, looking for tracks, saying to the dog: 'Find him, boy, find him!'

He was now coming down the mountain, searching the hollows with his eyes, and, every so often, sending a long-drawn cry into the mute immensities where it quickly died away. Then he laid his ear to the ground to listen, thought he could catch the sound of a voice, broke into a run, called again, heard nothing more, and sat down, exhausted and despairing. At noon he ate, and made Sam, who was as tired as he was, eat too.

The meal over, he resumed his search.

When evening came, he was still walking, having covered some thirty miles, all in the mountains. Since he was too far from the inn to go back to it, and too worn-out to drag himself further, he scooped a hole in the snow into which he snuggled down with the dog under a blanket which he had brought with him. And there

215

they lay, man and animal together, giving such warmth as they could to one another, but, nevertheless, frozen to the marrow of their bones.

Ulrich slept scarcely at all: he was haunted by visions, and shivered continually.

Day was just breaking when he got up. His legs were as stiff as iron bars, his spirits so low that he was near to crying with misery. His heart was beating so hard that he felt quite dizzy with emotion each time he thought he heard a sound.

He realized that he, too, might die of cold in this high solitude, and terror at the thought of such a death gave him renewed energy and vigour.

He turned down towards the inn, falling, scrambling up again, followed by Sam, who was limping on three paws.

They did not reach Schwarenbach until four that afternoon. The house was empty. The young man made up the fire, had something to eat, and fell asleep, so overwhelmed with fatigue that he could think of nothing.

He slept for a long, a very long time, unable to fight against unconsciousness. But he was jerked into wakefulness by the sound of a voice, of a cry: 'Ulrich!' He sat up. Had he been dreaming? Was what he had heard one of those strange sounds which penetrate the dreams of troubled minds? No, he heard it again, a loud cry forcing an entry through his ears and taking possession of his body to the very tips of his tingling fingers. There could be no doubt about it: someone had cried out, someone had called: 'Ulrich!' Someone was there, close to the house. He opened the door and shouted, 'That you, Gaspard?' at the full pitch of his voice.

No answer came, no sound, no murmur, no moan: nothing at all. It was dark now and the snow was pale with the pallor of death.

A wind had risen; one of those winds which can split the rocks and leave nothing alive on the abandoned heights. It blew in sudden gusts, more parching, more death-dealing than the scorching winds of the desert. He shouted again: 'Gaspard! Gaspard! Gaspard!'

He waited. Unbroken silence lay upon the mountain. Terror gripped him, a terror that shook him to the very roots. With one bound he was back inside the house. He slammed the door and shot the bolts. Then, trembling all over, he collapsed on to a chair, convinced that he had just been called by his companion at the very moment when he was drawing his last breath.

He was as sure of that as one is sure of being alive or of eating bread. Old Gaspard had been lying at the point of death for two nights and three days, somewhere in a crevasse, in one of the deep, unspotted ravines where the whiteness is more sinister than a dungeon's gloom. For two nights and three days he had been lying at the point of death, and, but a moment ago, had died thinking of his companion. No sooner had his spirit been freed from the body than it had flown towards the inn where Ulrich lay sleeping, and had called to him by virtue of that terrible and mysterious power which makes it possible for the dead to haunt the living. The voiceless spirit had cried aloud in the exhausted spirit of the sleeper; had cried its last farewell, or perhaps called down a curse upon the man who had not searched long enough.

Ulrich felt its presence there, close to him, behind the wall, on the other side of the door which he had just shut and locked. It was wandering like a night-bird brushing a lighted window with its wing-tips. The young man almost screamed aloud in horror. He wanted to run away, yet dared not leave the house. He dared not now, nor would he dare, for day and night the ghost would wander round it until the body of the old guide had been found and buried in consecrated ground.

Day dawned, and with the coming of bright sunlight a little confidence returned to Kunsi. He prepared his meal and set out food for the dog. Then he sat motionless on a chair, his heart tormented by the thought of the old man lying in the snow.

As soon as night fell upon the mountain, fresh terrors came upon him. He walked about the dark kitchen which a single candle barely lit. From end to end he strode, listening, always listening, lest the horrible cry should once again cut through the gloomy silence of the outside world. The poor fellow felt most horribly alone, more alone than any man had ever been, alone in a vast world of snow, alone at six thousand feet above the world of men, above all human habitations, above the buzz and stir of life, alone beneath a frozen sky. A wild desire came to him to escape, no matter where, no matter how, to fling himself into the abyss and go down to Loëche. But he dared not so much as open the door, so sure he was that the other, the dead man, would bar the way, lest he be left unfriended on these heights.

About midnight, tired of walking up and down, overcome by terror and agony of mind, he dropped at last on to a chair, for he dreaded the thought of his bed as a man will dread a haunted place.

And suddenly the same strident cry battered at his ear-drums. It was so shrill that he thrust out his arms to push away from him

the visitant from another world, and fell on his back with the chair
on top of him.

Sam, awakened by the noise, started to howl in the manner of all
frightened dogs. He began to wander all over the house, trying to
find where the danger lurked. When he reached the door, he sniffed
beneath it, panting, snuffling, and growling, with staring coat and
tail erect.

Kunsi, half mad with terror, jumped to his feet, and, grasping
the chair by one leg, began to shout: 'Don't come in! If you come
in, I shall kill you!' And the dog, excited by this threat, barked
furiously at the unseen enemy who would not heed his master's
voice.

Slowly, the dog calmed down and went back to his place by the
fire. But though he lay down, he remained uneasy, with his head
raised, his eyes gleaming—and snarling between clenched teeth.

Ulrich, too, recovered some degree of self-control, but, feeling
weak with terror, fetched a bottle of brandy from the dresser and
swallowed several glasses in quick succession. His mind became
fuddled, but his courage grew. A burning fever was coursing
through his veins.

Next morning he ate scarcely at all, but continued with his
drinking. He lived in this way for several days, in a state of brutish
drunkenness. No sooner did the thought of Gaspard Hari come
back to him, than he started to drink, and went on drinking until
he fell unconscious to the floor. There he lay, face downwards and
snoring, his legs looking all disjointed. Then, when the effects of
the fiery liquor grew less, the same cry of 'Ulrich!' struck him like
a bullet crashing through his skull, and he tottered to his feet with
arms outstretched to keep himself from falling as he shouted to
Sam for help. At that, the dog, who seemed to be growing as mad
as his master, would fling himself against the door, scrabbling at
it with his claws, tearing at it with his long white teeth, while the
young man sat with his head thrown back, gulping down brandy
as though it were water after a gruelling race, until his power of
thinking, of remembering, and his overwhelming terror were
numbed.

In three weeks he got through the whole stock of brandy in the
house and, since his prolonged bouts of drinking had had the effect
merely of deadening his panic, it returned again as soon as the
means of drowning it was gone. His obsession, exacerbated by
liquor and increased by solitude, now bored like a gimlet into his
brain. He took to walking up and down the room like a wild animal

The Inn

in a cage, listening at the door for fear the other was outside, and
shouting abuse through the wall.

And then, when at last he fell asleep from sheer exhaustion, the
voice would come again and he would start awake.

One night he rushed to the door like a coward driven to ex-
tremities, and wrenched it open, thinking that he might see its
owner and force him to keep silent.

A gust of cold air caught him full in the face, freezing him to the
bone, and he slammed-to the door and shot the bolts, without
noticing that Sam had rushed out. Then, shivering, he threw more
wood upon the fire and sat down to warm himself. But, all of a
sudden, he started up: something was scratching at the door and
whimpering.

Beside himself, he shouted 'Go away!'

Prolonged and melancholy whining was the only answer.

Then his last remaining scraps of sanity were swept away, and he
looked round wildly for some corner in which to hide. But whatever
it was outside moved off along the wall still whining and rubbing
itself against the house. Ulrich flung himself upon the oak dresser
loaded with plates, dishes, and provisions, and with a show of
superhuman strength, dragged it to the door to serve him as a
barricade. Then piling on top of each other all the remaining pieces
of furniture, mattresses, and chairs, he blocked the window as
besieged soldiers do.

But the thing outside was uttering drawn-out and lugubrious
howls at which the young man howled in answer.

Days and nights went by, and still they never stopped howling
at each other. The one moved unceasingly about the house, scratching at the walls so violently that it seemed to be intent on pulling
them down: the other shut within, bent double, his ears pressed to
the stones, following every movement made by his enemy, and
answering its appeals for help with those same blood-curdling
howls.

At last a night came when Ulrich could no longer hear anything.
He sat down, but so exhausted was he that he fell asleep at once.

When he awoke he remembered nothing and had lost all power
of thought. It was as though his head had been completely emptied
while he lay asleep. He felt hungry, and he ate.

The winter was over. The Gemmi Pass was once more practicable,
and the Hauser family returned to the inn.

When the topmost point of the ascent was reached, the women

219

mounted their mule, and began to talk of the two men whom they were expecting very soon to see again.

They had been surprised that neither had come down with news as soon as the road was open.

At last they saw, far off, the inn still wrapped and cowled in snow. The window and the door were shut, but a little smoke rising from the roof assuaged old Hauser's fears. As they drew nearer, they saw upon the threshold the skeleton of an animal, its bones picked white by eagles. It was large, and it was lying on its side.

They all stared at it. 'Must be Sam,' said the mother, and called, 'Hey! Gaspard!' A cry came from within, a high-pitched cry like the howl of an animal. Hauser echoed his wife's 'Hey! Gaspard!'

Again that animal cry came back in answer.

The three men, the father and his two sons, tried to get the door open, but it resisted all their efforts. They took from the empty cowshed a long beam to use as a battering-ram. They drove it with all their strength against the door. The wood creaked and gave. The planks broke in pieces. The house shook with the violence of the crash. Behind the overturned dresser they saw a man with hair to his shoulders. His chest was covered by a beard; there were a few rags of clothing on his body, and his eyes glittered.

At first they did not recognize him, until Louise exclaimed suddenly, 'Oh! mamma, it is Ulrich!' And then her mother saw that this was so, though his hair was white.

He let them come in: he let them touch him, but to their questions he made no answer. He was taken to Loëche, where the doctors said that he was mad.

No one ever found out what happened to old Gaspard Hari.

Louise Hauser nearly died that summer of a wasting sickness, brought on, so it was said, by the mountain cold.

(1 September 1886)

Old Amable

THE wet, grey sky seemed to lie like a weight on the vast expanses of the dun-coloured plain. The melancholy smells of autumn—bare and sodden earth, fallen leaves and dead weeds—made the sluggish evening air seem heavier and more dense. A sprinkling of peasants was still at work in the fields, waiting for the Angelus bell to ring them back to the farmsteads, the thatched roofs of which showed, here and there, through the bare branches of the trees screening the orchards.

By the side of the road, a very small child was sitting on a pile of clothes, with its legs apart, playing with a potato which it kept on dropping into its frock, while five women, bent double, with their rumps in the air, were busy picking out colza seedlings in the hedgeless field nearby. With a quick, continuous movement, they worked their way along the great furrow which the plough had just turned up. First, making a hole with a pointed stick, they inserted an already withered and slightly drooping plant, covered the roots, and then moved on.

A man with heavy clogs on his feet and a whip in his hand, stopped beside the child, took it in his arms and kissed it. One of the women straightened up and went to him. She was tall and red-faced, with broad hips, a thick waist, and square shoulders, a great florid, yellow-haired Normandy female.

In a determined voice, she said:

'Well, Césaire, wot 'bout it?'

The man, a skinny, sad-faced youth, muttered:

'Nowt, 'tis as 'twas.'

' 'Ee won't?'

' 'E won't.'

'Wot's to do, then?'

'How s'ld I know?'

'Best talk to curé.'

'Aye.'

'Now.'

'Aye.'

They looked at one another. He still had the child in his arms.

He kissed it again, and set it down upon the pile of women's clothes.

On the distant sky-line, between two farms could be seen a horse pulling a plough and a man pushing it. Beast, implement, and labourer moved slowly against the leaden evening sky.

The woman went on:

'What's t'old man say?'

'As 'e won't hear nowt of it.'

'Why?'

The man jerked a finger at the child he had just set down, and nodded towards the labourer with his plough.

' 'Long of the kid being his.'

The woman shrugged. 'T'old fool!' she said angrily. ' 'Tis known the child is Victor's. Wot of 't? Wot if I did slip up? I baint t'only one. My mum went same away afore me, and yourn, afore she hooked up with thy dad. All's been in trouble here 'bouts. I did go wrong wi' Victor, but 'twas along of his catching I asleep in barn. To be sure, there was second time too, when I warn't asleep. 'E'd a married me too, if 'e warn't but a poor labouring man. Be I any worse for 't?'

The man said simply:

'I'm ready to have 'ee, wi' or wi'out brat. 'Tis only my dad as is agin it. But us'll settle it all right.'

She said again:

'Best talk to curé. Go now.'

'Aye.'

He moved on again with his heavy countryman's tread, while she, hands on hips, went back to her colza pricking.

Césaire Houlbrèque, the man now tramping along the road, was the son of deaf old Amable Houlbrèque. In spite of his father he wanted to marry Céleste Lévesque, although she had had a child by Victor Lecoq. Victor had been a farm-hand on her parents' land, and had been turned loose because of what had happened.

In farming circles there are no class distinctions. If the farm-hand can save enough to buy a farm of his own, he can become the equal of the man who was once his master.

Césaire Houlbrèque went on his way, his whip under his arm, chewing the cud of his thoughts, picking up his heavy mud-caked clogs one after the other. He wanted to marry Céleste Lévesque, child and all, because she was the woman he needed. Why, he could not have said, but there it was. He had only to look at her to be sure of that. She made him come over all funny, stirred up, and sort of dazed with happiness. It even gave him pleasure to kiss the child, Victor's child, because she was its mother.

There was no hatred in his heart as he looked at the distant figure of the man pushing his plough on the sky-line.

But old Amable would not hear of such a marriage. He had set himself against it with a deaf and furious obstinacy.

It was no manner of use Césaire shouting in his ear—the one that could still hear a bit:

'I'll look after 'ee, Dad: her's a good girl, sound in wind and limb, an' a proper manager.'

The old man merely said again what he had said before:

'Not whiles I be alive.'

Nothing could persuade him; nothing could shake his determination. Césaire had only one hope left. Amable was afraid of the curé, because he was afraid of dying and felt that his time was short. He did not much fear God, the Devil, Hell, or Purgatory—having but a very hazy idea of all four—but he did fear the priest, because he stood for burial, much as a man may fear a doctor because he has a horror of being ill. For a week now, Céleste, who knew all about the old man's weak spot, had been urging Césaire to go and see the curé. But Césaire had hesitated, having no particular liking for cassocks, which stood in his mind for hands always stretched out, either for alms or else with consecrated bread.

But he had made up his mind at last, and, as he went on his way to the presbytery, was thinking how best to explain matters.

The Abbé Raffin, a small, thin, bustling priest, who was never properly shaved, sat warming his toes at the kitchen fire while waiting for his dinner to be ready.

When the peasant came in, he merely turned his head.

'Well, Césaire, and what may you want?' he said.

'I'd like a bit of a talk wi' you, m'sieu le curé.'

The visitor stood shyly before the priest, his cap in one hand, his whip in the other.

'Talk away.'

Césaire looked at the old servant who was shuffling about, laying a place for her master on a corner of the table in the window.

' 'Tis summat almost like confession.'

The abbé studied him with close attention. He noticed his confused look, his embarrassed air, his wandering eye, and said:

'Maria, go to your room for five minutes while I have a little talk with Césaire.'

The old woman darted an angry look at the intruder, and grumbled her way out of the kitchen.

'Now that we're alone,' said the priest, 'out with it!'

The young man still hesitated, looked at his feet, played with his cap, then, all of a sudden, took the plunge.

' 'Tis this way; I wants to marry Céleste Lévesque.'

'And what is there to stop you?'

'My dad won't have it, not nohow.'

'Your father?'

'Yes, my father.'

'Why not?'

'Says as how she's had a child.'

'She's not the first to whom that has happened since the days of our mother Eve.'

'But it's one as Victor got on her, Victor Lecoq, Anthime Loisel's farm-hand.'

'Ah, so that's the trouble is it? Won't hear of it, you say.'

'That 'e won't.'

'Not at any price?'

' 'E be like a moke as won't budge—saving your presence.'

'What did you say to persuade him?'

'I said as she's a good girl, strong as a horse, and a fine hand at managing.'

'And that didn't make any difference? I suppose you want me to talk to him, eh?'

'That's right.'

'And what am I to say to this father of yours?'

'The sort of things as you says in your sermons when you wants to get our pennies.'

To the peasant mind, the sole purpose of religion is to loosen purse-strings and empty men's pockets in order to fill the coffers of Heaven, a sort of business concern on a large scale, in which priests act as salesmen, cunning, tricky salesmen, sharp as a needle, who carry on God's business at the expense of poor country-folk.

He knew perfectly well that priests rendered many and great services to the poor, the sick, and the dying, that they were always ready to help, console, and give good advice—but in return for money, for silver pieces, for shining coin which went to pay for Masses, Sacraments, remission of sins and indulgences, for purgatory and paradise, depending on the income and generosity of the sinner.

Old Amable

The Abbé Raffin, who knew his man and never lost his temper, began to laugh.

'All right, I'll spin my little yarn to your father, but you must promise, in return, to come and listen to my sermons!'

Houlbrèque held out his hand to clinch the bargain:

'Seeing as how you'll do that, I promise, on the word of a poor man.'

'Good: when do you want me to see your father?'

'Soon as maybe, this very night, if you can.'

'In half an hour then, when I've had my supper?'

'In half an hour.'

'Agreed. I'll be seeing you later, my lad.'

Césaire Houlbrèque went home. He felt as though a great load had been lifted from his back.

He was leaseholder of a small farm, a very small farm, for neither he nor his father had much money. They lived there together, with a little maidservant, a girl of fifteen, who did the cooking, looked after the chickens, milked the cows, and made the butter. They had a great struggle to make ends meet, good farmer though Césaire was. But they had not enough land, nor enough livestock to do more than keep them in the bare necessities of life.

The old man was beyond working. Gloomy, as all deaf persons are, racked with aches and pains, bent and twisted, he hobbled about the farm on a stick, looking at beasts and men alike with a hard, suspicious eye. Sometimes he would sit down on the edge of a ditch and stay there for hours without moving, thinking vaguely of the things that had been his only interest in life, the price of eggs and crops, and the weather that could make or ruin a harvest. Twisted with rheumatism, his old limbs still sucked up the moisture from the soil between the oozing walls of his low-built cottage with its thatch of soggy straw, as they had done for the last seventy years.

He returned home at nightfall, sat down at one end of the kitchen table, and, when the earthenware tureen of soup was put before him, clutched it in his crooked fingers, which looked as though they had grown into the rounded shape of the bowl, and, winter and summer alike, warmed his hands in this way, before eating, so as to lose nothing, not a scrap, of the heat of the fire, which cost so much, not a drop of the soup with its fat and its salt, nor a fragment of the bread which good corn had gone to make.

Then he climbed a ladder to the attic where he had his mattress, while his son slept below in a kind of recess by the hearth. The little servant shut herself away in a species of cellar, a black hole of a place, which had once been used for storing potatoes.

Césaire and his father seldom exchanged a word. Occasionally, when it was a question of selling a crop or buying a calf, the young man would ask his senior's advice, cupping his hands round his mouth, and shouting his views into the old man's ear at point-blank range: and old Amable would approve or dissent in a slow, hollow voice which seemed to come from his stomach.

In just such a way had Césaire moved close to him one evening, as though to discuss the purchase of a horse or a heifer, and had conveyed into his father's ear, at the top of his voice, his intention of marrying Céleste Lévesque.

The old man had flared up. Why? On moral grounds? Not a bit of it. A woman's virtue has little importance on the land. But his avarice, his deepest instincts, his passion of saving, rebelled at the thought of his son bringing up a child he had not begotten. In a sudden flash of clear-sightedness he had envisaged all the soup the little creature would consume before it was old enough to be of any use on the farm. He had silently calculated all the pounds of bread, all the litres of cider, the brat would get through up to the age of fourteen, and a mad fit of anger had set him against his son whose mind was far from such things.

In a voice much louder and stronger than usual, he had replied: 'Must be proper daft!'

Then, Césaire had tried to give his reasons, detailing Céleste's admirable qualities, in an effort to prove that she would bring in a hundred times more than the child would cost in keep. But his father was suspicious of these hypothetical advantages, whereas the child's existence was a fact. Without even trying to explain further his bull-headed opposition to the whole thing, he just went on saying the same words over and over again:

'I won't have't; not so long as I'm alive, I won't. There'll be no marrying atween you two!'

For three months things had stayed like that, neither man yielding an inch, and, once a week, at least, the same old wrangle had started again, with the same arguments, the same words, the same gestures and the same futility.

It was then that Céleste had advised Césaire to see what the curé could do.

When he got home that night, he found his father already seated at the table, for his visit to the presbytery had made him late. They sat facing one another in silence, eating a little butter with their

bread, after the soup, and drinking a glass of cider each. Then
they had sat motionless in their chairs by the dim light of a candle
which the little servant had brought in when she came to wash up
the spoons, wipe the glasses, and cut the bread for next morning's
early breakfast.

There was a knock at the door, followed at once by the appearance of the priest. The old man looked at him uneasily. There was
a suspicious gleam in his eyes, and, foreseeing danger, he started
up the ladder. But the Abbé Raffin laid a hand on his shoulder,
and shouted in his ear:

'I want to have a little talk with you.'

Césaire, taking advantage of the open door, had vanished. He
was frightened, and did not want to listen. He did not want to see
his hopes dwindle with every iteration of his father's obstinate
refusal. He would far rather learn what had happened, whether
good or bad, later on, and all at once. He went out into the darkness. There was neither moon nor stars. It was one of those misty
nights when the air seems heavy with moisture. A faint smell of
apples hung about the yard, for it was the time of year when the
early ripeners are gathered, the *euribles* as they are called in the
cider country. Through the narrow windows of the cowsheds, as he
passed them, came the warm smell of living animals asleep upon
the straw, and, as he neared the stable, he could hear the stamping
of standing horses, and the sound of their jaws as they pulled hay
from the racks and munched it.

He walked on, thinking of Céleste. In his simple mind, ideas
were little more than images aroused by solid objects, and thoughts
of love nothing but the evocation of a tall, red young woman
standing in a sunken road, with arms akimbo, laughing.

It was thus that he had seen her when, for the first time, desire
had stirred in him. He had known her since she was a child, but
never, till that morning, had he taken much notice of her. They had
chatted together for a few moments, and then he had left her and
gone on his way. And as he walked, he had kept on saying to himself: 'Christ! 'tis a fine girl, and more's the pity as she slipped up
with Victor.' He thought about her till evening, and again in the
morning.

When he saw her next, he felt a sort of pricking in his throat, as
though a cock's feather had been pushed into his mouth and down
into his chest. Ever since then, whenever he was near her, the
pricking sensation had begun all over again.

At the end of three weeks he had made up his mind to marry

227

her, so taken with her was he. He could not have said whence came her power over him, but expressed it by saying: 'There she be right and tight in me guts!' It was as though the longing for her were working in him like one of the mighty powers of hell. He gave scarcely a thought to her 'mistake'. It was too bad that it had happened, but it made no real difference, and he bore no grudge against Victor Lecoq.

But, should the curé fail, what could he do? He dared not think of that, so tortured was he by anxiety.

When he reached the presbytery, he sat down by the little wooden fence to wait for the priest's return.

He had been there for maybe an hour, when he heard the sound of footsteps on the road, and soon, dark though the night was, he could make out the darker patch of the curé's cassock.

He got to his feet. His legs were trembling, and he dared not speak for fear of what the news might be.

The priest saw him, and said, in a cheerful voice:

'Well, my lad, it's all settled.'

'B . . . b . . . but it can't be!' Césaire stammered.

'Yes it is. But I had a job. That father of yours is as stubborn as a donkey!'

'It can't be!' the other said again.

'It is, though. You had better come and see me about putting up the banns.'

The young man had gripped his curé's hand, crushing it and shaking it in his own . . . 'Oh! m'sieu le curé,' he babbled, 'on the word of an honest man you'll see I Sunday . . . for the sermon!'

PART II

The wedding took place half-way through December. It was simple, for the couple had no money to spare. Césaire, in a new suit, was up and ready by eight o'clock to fetch his bride and take her to the *mairie*. But, since it was too early, he sat down at the kitchen table to wait for the friends and relations who were to come for him.

It had been snowing for the last week, and the brown earth, already fertilized by the autumn sowing, had now turned white and lay sleeping under a great sheet of ice.

It was cold in the cottages with their bonnets of snow, and the round-headed apple-trees in the orchards looked as though they were in flower, all powdered over as in the lovely month of blossoms.

Old Amable

The great clouds from the north, the grey clouds with the weight of their glittering burden, had disappeared, and a blue sky spread over the white earth which the rising sun was touching to silver.

Césaire looked through the window, completely happy and with not a thought in his head. The door opened, and two women came in, two countrywomen in their Sunday best, the aunt and cousin of the groom. They were followed by three men, cousins, too, and by a female relation of the same degree. They sat motionless and silent on their chairs, the women on one side of the kitchen, the men on the other, in a sudden access of shyness, of that embarrassed melancholy which takes hold of people gathered for a ceremony. One of the cousins said:

'B'ain't it be toime?'

And Césaire answered:

'Aye, that it be.'

'Let's be on our way,' said one of the others.

They all got up. Then Césaire, in sudden uneasiness, climbed the ladder to see whether his father was ready. The old man, usually an early riser, had not so far appeared. His son found him rolled in a blanket on his mattress. His eyes were open and there was an ugly look on his face.

The bridegroom shouted in his ear:

'Get you up, dad: 'tis toime for t' wedding.'

The deaf old man muttered in a doleful voice:

'Can't, and that's the truth. Such a plaguey chill I got, that me back is fruzz. Can't move, not a inch!'

His son looked at him in consternation, suspecting a trick.

'Come, dad, y'maun try.'

' 'Tis no good.'

'I'll help 'ee.'

He bent down, loosened the blanket, took the old man under the arms, and lifted him. But old Amable began to groan.

'Hou! hou! hou! 'Tis turrible bad, with my back like it's tied in a knot! 'Tis all 'long of the wind as blewed through that dratted roof!'

Césaire realized that he would not succeed, and furious with his father for the first time in his life, shouted:

'Then there won't be no dinner for 'ee, seeing as we're eating at Polyte's Inn. That'll learn 'ee to be stubborn!'

He scrambled down the ladder and set off, followed by his relatives and guests.

The men had turned up the bottoms of their trousers so as not to get the snow on them, and the women were holding up their skirts, revealing their thin ankles, their grey wool stockings, and their bony legs as meagre as broomsticks. All the company teetered along, one behind the other, not exchanging a word, and moving quietly and carefully so as not to get off the road, now hidden under the flat, monotonous, unbroken expanse of snow.

Each time they drew near a farm, they saw one or two people waiting there to join them, and the procession grew progressively longer, twisting and turning, following the invisible windings of the road, and looking like a living rosary of black beads undulating over the white countryside.

In front of the bride's door several people stood, stamping their feet and waiting for the groom. His appearance was greeted with applause, and very soon Céleste came from her room, wearing a blue dress with a little red shawl round her shoulders, and a wreath of orange-blossom on her head.

All kept asking Césaire:

'Where be thy dad?'

And he, embarrassed, answered:

'Too stiff with that there rheumatiz to move.'

The farmers shook their heads with looks of sly incredulity.

Then the party started for the *mairie*. Behind the future husband and wife walked a peasant girl carrying Victor's child, as though for a christening, and, behind her, country youths, two by two and arm in arm, walked across the snow with the movements of a ship at sea.

When the mayor had united the bridal couple in the diminutive civic-house, the curé did the same for them in the modest house of God. He blessed their union and promised it a fruitful future. Then, he preached to them about the virtues of matrimony, the sane and simple manners of the countryside, work, concord, and fidelity, while the child, feeling the cold, whimpered behind the bride's back.

When husband and wife appeared again at the church door, shots rang out from the ditch surrounding the churchyard. Nothing could be seen but little spurts of smoke from the barrels of the guns. Then a face appeared, looking at the wedding group. It belonged to Victor Lecoq, celebrating the marriage of his dear sweetheart, and expressing his good wishes with a series of detonations. He had recruited five or six of his farm-hand friends to supply the fusillade, and the general opinion was that he had behaved very well.

Old Amable

The breakfast was held at the inn of Polyte Cacheprune. Twenty places had been laid in the big room used for the farmers' ordinary on market days. A great joint turning on the spit, fowls browning in their own juice, and a vast sausage frying over a clear, hot fire filled the house with a smell of burning charcoal spattered with fat, and the strong, heavy scent of country food.

The company sat down at noon, and the soup was at once poured into the plates. Faces grew animated, mouths were opened to a flood of jokes, eyes were creased in knowing laughter. Heavens! what a good time they were going to have!

Suddenly, the door opened, and there, on the threshold, stood old Amable. There was a wicked glint in his eye and a furious expression on his face. He dragged himself along with the aid of his sticks, groaning at every step he took, just to let everybody know how terribly he was suffering.

The sight of him had killed all talk. But suddenly, old Malivoire his neighbour, a jolly, fat man who knew everyone's little ways, began to shout, cupping his hands, as Césaire did: 'Hey, thee old rascal, what a nose 'ee's got, to be sure, to get a whiff of Polyte's cooking, up at thee's place!'

There was a roar of laughter at this. Malivoire, encouraged by his success, went on: 'There be nothing like sausage for the rheumatiz, keeps belly warm when took with a glass of spirits! . . .'

All the men shouted, banging the table with their fists, bending their bodies this way and that like pump-handles. The women clucked like hens, and the servants, standing against the walls, tied themselves into knots with laughing. Only old Amable did not laugh, but stood waiting, without uttering, until room had been made for him.

He was given a chair half-way down the table, opposite his daughter-in-law, and no sooner was he settled into it than he began to eat. After all, it was his son who was standing treat, so why shouldn't he have his share? With each spoonful of soup that splashed into his stomach, with each mouthful of bread and meat that he mumbled between his gums, he felt that he was getting a bit of his own back—pouching some of the money these greedy-guts were making so free with, and saving something out of what was his. He ate in silence, with the determination of a miser hoarding his pennies, and the same gloomy tenacity with which he had once tackled his daily work.

But, all of a sudden, he caught sight of Céleste's child perched on the knees of one of the women at the far end of the table, and

231

kept his eyes firmly fixed on it. All the time he was guzzling he
stared at the little creature. Its temporary guardian was giving it
scraps of stew to nibble, and the old man suffered greater torments
over those tiny mouthfuls than over all the eating and drinking of
the others.

The feast lasted until evening, when everyone went home.

Césaire got old Amable to his feet. 'Toime to go 'ome, dad,' he
said, and put the two sticks into his hands. Céleste took the child
in her arms, and they all walked slowly back through the pallid
darkness lit by the snow. The deaf old man, by this time more than
half-seas over, and made the more unmanageable by the effects of
liquor, obstinately refused to walk. Once or twice he even sat down,
hoping that in this way he would make his daughter-in-law catch
cold, and muttering complainingly in a long-drawn-out and doleful
monologue.

As soon as they reached home, he at once climbed up the ladder
to his attic, while Césaire arranged a bed for the child close to the
deep recess in which he and his wife were going to sleep. But the
bride and groom did not drop off at once, and they could hear the
old man tossing about on his mattress, and sometimes talking out
loud, whether it was that he was dreaming or just putting his
thoughts into words, in spite of himself, as though unable to hold
them back under the pressure of his own particular obsession.

When he came down next morning, his daughter-in-law was
already busy with the house-work:

'Don't 'ee hang around, dad,' she said. 'There be some good soup
a-waiting for 'ee.'

She put the black earthenware bowl, full of steaming liquid, on
the end of the table. He sat down without a word, picked up the
scalding receptacle, and warmed his hands on it as usual. Then,
since the morning cold was intense, he pressed the bowl to his chest
in an attempt to get some of the heat from the boiling water into
his old body, which a long succession of winters had stiffened.

Then he routed out his sticks and went into the frozen fields until
midday when dinner would be ready, for he had caught sight of
Céleste's brat sleeping in a large box which had once contained soap.

He could not resign himself to the new state of affairs. To be
sure, he went on living in the cottage, as formerly, but with the
look, now, of somebody who did not belong to it. He seemed to
take no interest in anything, seemed almost to look at his son, his
son's wife, and the wife's child, as though they were strangers.
He never spoke a word to them.

Old Amable

Winter dragged on. It was long and hard. Then, with the early spring, the seeds began to sprout. The peasants, like laborious ants, once more spent all their days in the fields, working from dawn to dusk, in wind and rain, along the brown furrows from which the bread of man would, later on, emerge.

The year started well for the newly-married pair. The crops came up strong and healthy. There were no late frosts, and the apple-trees shed their pink-and-white snow upon the grass, promising a fine fruit-harvest for the autumn.

Césaire worked hard. He got up early and came home late, thereby saving the cost of an extra pair of hands.

Sometimes his wife said to him:

'You be a-wearing of yourself out.'

'No fear,' he answered, 'I be used to it.'

But one night he was so tired when he came in that he went to bed without waiting for supper. Next morning he got up at his ordinary time. But he could not eat a thing, in spite of having fasted on the previous evening, and returned to the house half-way through the afternoon, and took to his bed. In the night, he started coughing, and turned and tossed in a high fever, with a burning forehead, a dry tongue, and a terrible, consuming thirst.

Nevertheless, he was off to the fields at daybreak. But next day the doctor had to be sent for. Césaire, he said, was very ill with inflammation of the lungs.

He never again left the dark recess which served him as a bed-room. He could be heard coughing, fighting for breath, and tossing in his little black hole. When anybody wanted to see him, when medicine had to be given or leeches applied, it was necessary to bring a candle to the entrance. It revealed a sunken face with a dirty growth of beard, lying under a canopy of spiders' webs hanging from the roof and waving in the draught. The sick man lay, as though lifeless, on the grubby sheet.

Céleste was tireless in her nursing, dosing him regularly, seeing that he was properly blistered, bustling here, there, and every-where. But her heart was heavy. Old Amable sat perched aloft in the attic room from which he could see the gloomy hole where his son lay fighting for life. But he never went near him. Hatred of the woman kept him away, and he sulked like a jealous dog.

Six days went by, and then, one morning, when Céleste, who now slept on two bundles of hay laid loosely on the floor, went to see how her husband was, the sound of his raucous breathing was no longer audible. In a sudden access of terror, she called out:

'Césaire, did thee have a easier night, lad?'

There was no answer. She stretched a hand to touch him. His face was icy cold. A scream broke from her, the prolonged screaming of a frightened woman. He was dead.

The noise she made was so loud that it brought the deaf old man to the top of his ladder, and when he saw Céleste rush from the house to get help, he quickly scrambled down and, in his turn, felt the dead man's face. The truth came to him in a flash, and he hastily locked the house-door on the inside, so as to prevent the woman from coming back and taking possession, now that his son was no longer alive.

Then he sat down on a chair beside the body.

Neighbours arrived. They shouted and knocked, but he did not hear them. One broke a window and climbed into the room. Others followed suit. The door was thrown open, and Céleste reappeared in a flood of tears. Her face was swollen and her eyes were red. Then old Amable climbed back, defeated, to his attic, without a word.

The funeral took place next day. When it was over, father-in-law and daughter-in-law were left alone at the farm, with the child.

Dinner-time came round. She lit the fire, made the soup, and set the plates upon the table, while the old man sat waiting. He seemed not to notice her.

When the meal was ready, she shouted in his ear:

'Come, Dad, mortals must eat.'

He took his place at the end of the table, emptied his bowl, chewed his bread with its scraping of butter, drank his two glasses of cider, and went out.

He walked along a narrow pathway through the fields, and, as he looked at the young wheat and oats, his thoughts were with that poor lad of his, now laid in earth. He moved with an old man's shuffle, dragging one leg and limping. There, in the empty fields, under the blue sky, alone with the growing crops and the larks over his head, whose song he could not hear, he began to cry as he walked.

He sat down by a pond and stayed there till the evening, looking at the little birds who came to drink. Then, when darkness fell, he went back to the farm, ate his supper in silence, and climbed up to his attic.

Life went on for him as usual. Nothing was changed, except that his son, Césaire, lay sleeping in the churchyard.

What was there now for him to do? He could not work. He was

good for nothing but to swallow the soup which his daughter-in-law made for him. Silently he sucked it down, night and morning, watching, with fury in his eyes, the child facing him across the table. Then, he went out to wander like an aimless vagabond, hiding behind barns to snatch an hour or two of sleep, as though fearing to be seen, and going home again when darkness fell.

But Céleste's mind was full of weighty matters. The farm needed a man's eye and a man's work, someone who would always be around, not just a paid hand, but a real farmer, a master who knew his job and had an interest in his fields. A lone woman could not look after these things, keep an eye upon the price of corn, and superintend the buying and selling of livestock. She began to make plans, simple plans, practical plans, on which she brooded all night long. There could be no question of her marrying again before a year was out, and meanwhile there were pressing matters to be attended to.

Only one man could help her in these difficult times, Victor Lecoq, the father of her child. He was strong, and versed in the mysteries of the soil. With a little money he would have made an excellent farmer. That she knew, having watched him working with her parents.

So, one morning, when she saw him on the road with a cartful of manure, she set off to have a word with him. When he saw her coming, he stopped his horses, and she, as though she had been with him no longer ago than yesterday, called out:

'Marning to 'ee, Victor: how be things with 'ee?'

'None too bad: an' how be'n wi' thee?'

'Right 'nough but for being alone-like up at t' farm. It be proper worriting what wi' keeping an eye on everything.'

So they talked together for a long while with their backs against the wheel of the laden cart. Now and then the man scratched his head under his cap, thinking, while she, with flushed cheeks, spoke eagerly of what was in her mind, telling him of her plans for the future. At last he grunted:

'Could be.'

She held out her hand, like a peasant clinching a bargain on market-day.

'Agreed?'

He took the hand she offered:

'Agreed.'

'Sunday, then?'

'Sunday 'tis.'

'So long, then, Victor.'
'So long, Madame Houlbrèque.'

PART III

That Sunday was a feast-day in the village, the yearly feast-day
of its patron saint, what in Normandy is called *l'Assemblée.*

For the past week the roads had been alive with shaggy ponies,
roan and grey, with slow-moving vehicles behind them in which
the gypsy-folk live who make the round of the fairs, with their
lottery-wheel, their shooting-galleries, their side-shows, their
freaks and oddities of all sorts, which the peasants call—'getting a
h'eyeful'.

The dirty caravans, with fluttering curtains at their windows,
and depressed-looking dogs with hanging heads between the
wheels, drew to a halt, one after the other, in the open space before
the *mairie.* A tent was set up in front of each, and in it could be
seen, through holes in the canvas, all kinds of glittering things
which worked the village urchins to a high pitch of longing and
curiosity.

On the morning of the Saint's-Day, all the booths were thrown
open to display their splendours of glass and china, and the
country people, on their way to Mass, looked with artless and
delighted eyes at the modest stalls which visited them regularly
every year.

From early afternoon, the Fair-Ground was crowded. From all
the nearby villages came farmers with their wives and children,
jolting along in two-wheeled traps which made a jingle like old
iron, and pitched and tossed like rocking-horses. They put up at
the homes of friends, and all the farmyards round were filled with
unfamiliar rattle-traps, painted grey, high off the ground, narrow
in the beam, warped, crooked, and looking like long-legged, deep-
sea monsters.

The various families, children in front, grown-ups behind,
walked through the show-ground, with slow and easy steps, grins
on their faces, and large red, spread, and knuckly hands accustomed to hard work, seeming curiously awkward and out of place
with nothing particular to do.

A showman was tootling on his trumpet. The mechanical organ,
belonging to a roundabout of wooden horses, was spraying the air
with a tinkle of sentimental tunes. The lottery wheel ground round
with a noise of tearing linen, and, every few seconds, shots rang

238

out from the shooting-gallery. The crowd moved slowly, flabbily past the booths, like rolled-out dough, swaying backwards and forwards with the aimless movement of a herd of sheep or lumbering animals let loose by accident.

Girls in linked rows of six or eight sang in shrill voices as they walked, followed by boisterous young oafs with caps pulled down to their ears, looking like blue balloons with their starched smocks standing stiffly away from their bodies.

Everyone was there, masters, hired-men, and servants.

Even old Amable, in an old-fashioned frock-coat, green with age, had come along to have a look at the Fair—for he never missed it.

He had a good stare at the lottery wheel, stopped at the shooting-gallery with a critical eye on the local marksmen, and seemed particularly interested in a very simple game which consisted in throwing a heavy wooden ball into the gaping mouth of a man painted on a board.

Somebody tapped him on the shoulder. It was old Malivoire, who shouted:

'Come 'long an' have a drop!'

So down they sat at one of the tables of a refreshment tent set up in the open air. They had a glass of brandy each, then a second, then a third, after which old Amable continued with his ramble. His brain was getting a bit fuddled. He grinned without knowing why, at the lottery, at the wooden horses, and especially at the Aunt Sally. He spent a long time there, delighted when some player knocked over the gendarme or the curé, both of them the representatives of an authority which he instinctively mistrusted. Then he went back to the refreshment tent, where he took a glass of cider to quench his thirst. It was late; the light was beginning to go. A neighbour shouted a word of warning:

'Thee'll be late for zupper, Dad!'

He started back to the farm. The warm and gentle darkness of the spring evening was slowly enveloping the earth.

When he reached his door, he thought that he could see, through the lighted window, two figures in the house. Surprise stopped him dead in his tracks for a moment or two. Then, he went in, and saw Victor Lecoq at the table, just where his son had used to sit, with a plate of potatoes in front of him.

He swung round, as though to go out again. It was now full night. Céleste had got to her feet, and was shouting to him:

'Don'ee dawdle, Dad, don'ee dawdle: stew be summat extra special for the 'casion.'

239

Apathetically, he obeyed her, and sat down. His eyes wandered in turn to the man, the woman, and the child. Then, very quietly as always, he began to eat.

Victor Lecoq seemed to be very much at home, exchanging an occasional word with Céleste, taking the child on his knee and kissing it. Céleste kept on replenishing his plate and filling his glass. She appeared to find satisfaction in having him to talk to. Old Amable looked at them both with a fixed stare, not hearing what they were saying. When he had finished his supper (he had eaten scarcely anything, so sick at heart did he feel) he got up from his chair, and, instead of going straight to his attic, as usual, opened the door of the yard and went out into the fields.

When he had gone, Céleste showed signs of uneasiness.

'Wot be 'im up to?' she asked.

'Now, don' 'ee fuss: 'll come back when's tired.'

Then she cleared away, washed the plates, and wiped the table, while the man quite calmly started to undress. Then he slipped into the bed in the deep, dark corner where she had slept with Césaire.

The door of the yard opened. Old Amable came back into the house, and began all at once to peer into all the corners of the room, like an old dog picking up a scent. He was looking for Victor Lecoq and, not seeing him, took the candle from the table, and went across to the dark recess in which his son had died. At the far back of it he saw the man stretched in the bed, and already asleep. He turned away quietly, put back the candle on the table, and went out again into the yard.

Céleste, by this time, had finished her work. She had put the child to bed, set the room to rights, and was waiting for her father-in-law to come back before joining Victor.

She sat on a chair, her hands idle, and a vague look in her eyes.

Still he did not come, and she grew irritated and annoyed:

'Making us burn a penn'orth of candle, th' old lazybones,' she muttered.

Victor answered from the depths of his bed:

'Bin away now more'n a hour: better see as 'e bain't fallen asleep on t' bench 'side the door.'

'I'll go,' she said, and got to her feet. She took the light and went out, shielding the flame with her hand, so as to see in the darkness.

There was nobody by the door, no one on the bench, no one on the manure-heap where the old man sometimes used to sit for the warmth.

Old Amable

But, just as she was about to go in again, she looked up at the big apple-tree which shaded the entrance to the farm, and, all of a sudden, saw two feet, a man's feet, hanging at the level of her eyes.

She gave a terrified scream:

'Victor! . . . Victor! . . . Victor!'

He ran out in his shirt. She could not speak, but, averting her face so as not to see, pointed to the tree.

Not understanding what she meant, he took the candle, and made out, in the foliage thus lit from below, old Amable hanging very high up, with a halter from the stable round his neck.

A ladder was leaning against the trunk.

Victor ran to get a bill-hook, and cut the rope.

But the old man was already cold. His tongue was protruding horribly in a hideous grimace.

(1886)

The Mask

IT was Mid-Lent, and there was a Fancy-Dress Ball at the Elysée-Montmartre to mark the occasion. A crowd was surging into the brightly lit passage leading to the dance-floor, like water into a lock. The orchestra was pounding away and walls and ceiling were shaking under the impact. The din spread through the neighbouring streets, penetrating even into remote bedrooms, arousing that irresistible longing to hop, to jump, to get warmed up, to have a good time, which lies deep in the heart of every human animal.

The regular frequenters of the place came from every part of Paris and from all classes of society, drawn together by a common liking for amusement in one of its cruder manifestations, slightly squalid and faintly depraved. There were city clerks, pimps, and tarts: tarts of every variety, from common cotton to finest cambric, rich tarts, old and bejewelled, poor tarts of sixteen, longing for a bit of fun, to go with men, to have money to spend. There were men of fashion, too, in well-cut evening clothes, on the prowl for tempting morsels with the bloom brushed off but still tasty, moving through the sweating crowd with watchful eyes, and noses to the scent. There were masked dancers all agog for a good time. Gaping groups had already gathered round the famous quadrilles to watch the caperings, a swaying hedge, a shifting dough of both sexes, twisting and turning like a snake, now forward and now back, in response to the movements of the four dancers at the centre. Two women, whose legs appeared to be attached to their bodies with india-rubber, were going through the most amazing acrobatics, performing such tremendous high-kicks that their limbs seemed about to fly away altogether, and then doing the splits so violently that they looked as though they were going to part up the middle, one leg in front, the other behind, like a pair of scissors, at once comic and repulsive.

Their partners were leaping and pirouetting, flapping their arms as though they were the stumps of featherless wings, and only too obviously sweating and panting behind their stuffy masks.

One of them, who was substituting, in the most popular of these troupes, for the celebrated and handsome 'Songe-au-Gosse', and making valiant efforts not to be outdone by the indefatigable 'Arête-de-Veau', was executing a number of eccentric solo steps, much to the delight of the onlookers, who were greeting his efforts with ironic laughter.

He was lean and dandified, and wore a handsome varnished mask with a fair twisted moustache and a wig of clustering curls.

He had the appearance of a wax dummy, of an odd, fantastic caricature of a charming young man in a fashion-plate, and he was dancing with so earnest, yet so clumsy a concentration, that the general effect was extremely ludicrous. As he joined in the friskings of his companions, his joints seemed to be stiff, rusty, and awkward. He looked, for all the world, like a mongrel gambolling with greyhounds. Mocking applause greeted his performance. Drunk with enthusiasm, he spun round with such energy that he ran head-on into the wall of spectators, which opened to let him through, then closed around him as he collapsed and lay at full length on his stomach, motionless, unconscious.

Some men picked him up and carried him away. There were cries of 'Is there a doctor here?' A gentleman stepped forward. He was young and very elegant, in evening dress with large pearls in his shirtfront. 'I am a member of the Faculty,' he said, with a pleasing show of modesty. Way was made for him, and he went into a small room crowded with box-files, like a business-man's office. There he saw the dancer, still unconscious and lying across two chairs. The first thing he did was to remove the mask, only to find that it was attached in so complicated a manner, with such a quantity of thin metal wires holding it in place beneath the wig, that it formed a sort of rigid framework round the head, and could be removed only by those familiar with the secret of its adjustment. Even the man's neck was encased, from the chin down, in a sheath of false skin made of kid, painted to resemble human flesh, and reaching as far as his shirt-collar.

All this had to be cut through with a pair of strong scissors. When the doctor had made an opening, from shoulder to temple, in this extraordinary contraption, he saw within it the withered face of an old man, pale, worn, and wrinkled. So great was the shock experienced by those who had been carrying the mask of a curly-headed youth, that no one laughed, and no one said a word.

They stood there, looking down at the sad old face with its closed eyes, at the old body lying extended on two straw-bottomed chairs. A few long white hairs hung over the forehead, and the cheeks and chin showed a growth of white stubble. Beside this

243

face lay the other, the shiny, smiling mask of a man in the full bloom of youth.

Consciousness slowly returned, but the old man seemed still so weak and ill, that the doctor feared some dangerous complication.

'Where do you live?' he asked.

The old dancer seemed to be cudgelling his brains. Then, suddenly, memory returned, and he mentioned the name of a street which none of those present recognized. He had to be asked for further details, and these he gave, though with the greatest difficulty. He spoke so slowly and so vaguely that it was easy to see how disturbed the balance of his mind must be.

'I will take you back,' said the doctor.

He was curious to know more about this fantastic old image, to see where this ancient Jack-in-the-Box lived.

In next to no time a cab was driving the two of them down the further side of the Buttes Montmartre.

The house at which they drew up was very tall, with a decrepit look and a greasy staircase. It was riddled with windows, looked unfinished, and stood between two patches of waste-land, a swarming hive of the ragged and the penniless.

The doctor, clinging to the handrail, a sticky piece of wood that turned and turned up the spiral ascent, supported the dazed old creature, whose strength was gradually coming back, to the fourth floor.

He knocked at a door. It was opened by a woman, also old, but clean, wearing a white nightcap which framed a bony face with strongly-marked features; one of those solid, decent, rough-hewn faces so often to be seen among honest and reliable women of the working-class.

'Dear God! what has happened to him!' she exclaimed.

As soon as everything had been explained in a few words, she seemed to be less uneasy, and managed to reassure the doctor, too, telling him that this was not the first time something of the same kind had happened.

'There's only one thing to do, sir, and that is to get him into bed as quick as may be. He'll sleep like a log, and by tomorrow morning it'll be all wore off.'

'But he can barely speak.'

'Oh, that's nothing worse than a drop too much! He didn't eat his dinner, so's to be light on his feet and nimble. What's more, he had a couple of absinthes to liven him up. The stuff helps his old legs, but it plays the devil with his wits. He didn't ought to go about at his age doing that there jigging and jogging. But there, I've long given up any idea of getting a bit of sense into him!'

The doctor seemed not a little surprised.

'But why should an old fellow want to go on dancing like that?'

'Why indeed! Well, if you want to know, it's so as folks shall think him young under that mask, so as women'll take him for a bumpkin up for a spree, and whisper sweet—and dirty—nothings in his ear, so's he can cuddle up against 'em—the poxy bitches with their scents and powders and stuff . . . Makes you want to bring up, that it does . . . Forty years it's been going on, and no fun for me, *I* can tell you! . . . But we'd better get him to bed in case he catches cold . . . Would it be asking too much for you to give me a hand, sir? When he's like this, I can't manage him alone.'

The old man was sitting up on the bed with a drunken look, and his long white hair hanging over his face.

His companion looked at him, with anger and pity in her eyes.

'Fine-looking chap for his age, too. But that isn't enough for him—oh no! Got to get himself up all la-di-da, so's people'll think as he's young. A real shame I call it, because it's a face worth looking at, you know, really it is. Just wait a mo' before we gets him into bed, and I'll show you what I mean.'

She went to a table which had a basin, a jug, soap, a brush, and a comb on it. She picked up the brush, went over to the bed, and lifted the drunkard's matted hair away from his forehead. The change was immediate and startling. In the twinkling of an eye she had him looking like a painter's model, with white curls clustering on his neck. Then she stood back to take stock of her work.

'Good-looking for an old 'un, isn't he?'

'He is, indeed,' said the doctor, who was beginning to enjoy himself.

'I wish you could've seen him when he was twenty-five!' she went on. 'But, there now, we must get him to bed, or the drink'll go bad on him. Would you mind pulling up his shirt, sir? . . . A bit higher . . . That's the ticket . . . Now his trousers . . . I'll take his shoes off . . . That's right . . . Now hold him up while I turn the sheet down . . . Into bed with him . . . And if you think he'll shift over to make room for me, then you'd better think again . . . Anywhere's good enough for me . . . *He* don't care! . . . There now, you old fly-by-night!'

As soon as the old chap felt himself stretched between the sheets, he shut his eyes, opened them, shut them again. He looked happy, contented, and all set for sleep.

The doctor was studying him with ever-increasing interest.

'So he plays the young gad-about at fancy-dress balls, does he?'

'At as many as he can find, sir, and the state he's in when he gets back next morning, well, no one wouldn't believe! It's regret as drives him to it, sir, with a cardboard face over his own—regret at not being what he was and not having no more successes with the girls!'

He was sleeping now, and beginning to snore. There was compassion in the look she gave him.

'He had 'em once, all right! You can take that from me—a great many more'n you'd credit, sir—more'n the toffs and the opera singers and the generals . . .'

'Did he, really? . . . What was his profession?'

'That'll be a bit of a surprise for you when you hear, seeing as you didn't know him when he was a-top of the world! It was at a ball as I first met him, if it comes to that, for he was always a one for the dancing. Got me, he did, as soon as I set eyes on him; got me good and proper, like a fish on a hook. A lovely young feller he was, sir, just to look at him made a body want to cry, if you take my meaning: dark as a crow, he was, with curly hair and black eyes as big as winders. Oh! he had looks all right! Swept me off my feet that night, and I've never left him since, not for a single day, in spite of everything—and, take my word for it, he gave me some bad times!'

'Are you married?'

She answered with complete simplicity:

'Yes, sir, otherwise he'd have given me the chuck, as he did the others. I was wife and servant to him, and everything he wanted, he had . . . Oh! the times I've cried my eyes out. Not that I ever let him see! . . . He used to tell me all about his adventures! . . . Me! . . . With never a thought for the pain it caused . . .'

'But you haven't told me what he was . . .'

'So I haven't . . . Slipped my mind . . . He was Martel's chief assistant, sir . . . But such an assistant as you never did see . . . A real artist . . . Ten francs an hour, on the average, he got.'

'Martel? . . . Who was he?'

'The hairdresser, sir, the famous hairdresser of the Opera: all the actresses went to him. Yes, all the smart actresses had their hair done by Ambroise, and what with the tips they give him, why, he made a fortune! But that's women all over, sir. When

they like a man, they give him all he wants . . . It's so easy . . .
But it was terrible hard for me to know about . . . You see, he
told me everything . . . Couldn't keep it to himself, just couldn't
. . . Those things do so please a man! . . . And talking about them
more perhaps than doing them!'

'When he come home at night, looking rather pale and so pleased
with himself, I'd say to myself: "Here we go again!" I'd say: "I
bet he's landed another!" Then I longed to question him, longed so
hard it made me feel sick, but with another part of myself I wanted
not to know, wanted to stop him when he started talking. An'
there we sat just looking at each other . . .

'I knew he'd never keep quiet, that he'd spill the beans, all of
'em! I knew it by the way he looked, by the way he laughed, just
so's to let me know it was coming. "I've had a good day, Madeleine," he'd say. Then I'd pretend I didn't see nothing, didn't guess
nothing—just laid the table, brought the soup, and sat down
facing him.

'At those times, sir, it was like someone had crushed my feeling
for him with a stone: and that hurts, hurts terrible. But he never
knew about that, hadn't a clue, not him! He just had to talk about
it all to somebody, to boast, to show how much loved he was . . .
And he hadn't nobody to tell it to but me . . . Just me . . . So I
had to listen and drink it in like it was poison.

'He'd start on his soup, and then he'd say:

' "Another of 'em, Madeleine," he'd say.

'And I'd think to myself: "There he goes! God! What a man! . . .
Why did I ever have to meet him!"

'Then off he'd go: "Another of 'em, and my! What a peach . . ."
It'd be a little chit of a thing from the Vaudeville or the Variétés
. . Or sometimes one of the top-notchers, a real star . . . He'd tell
me their names, what their houses were like, everything about
them, everything—details as tore me to pieces, sir. And he'd never
let it alone, told me the whole story, over and over, from the
beginning . . . And so pleased with himself that I had to pretend
to laugh, so's he shouldn't be angry.

'Maybe it wasn't all true. He did so love boasting of his con-
quests, that he was quite capable of making it all up! On the
other hand, maybe it was true. On those evenings he always
put on a great show of being tired; said he wanted to go to
bed straight after supper. We didn't have supper till eleven, you
see, sir, because he never got back earlier, along of the evening
hairdressing.

'When he'd finished telling me about his adventures, he'd walk up and down the bedroom, smoking cigarettes. So handsome he'd look with his moustache and his curly hair, that I'd think: "Oh, it's true all right! Seeing as I'm mad about him, why shouldn't others be, too?" Then, I wanted to cry, to scream, to run away, to throw myself out of the winder, and all the time I'd just go on clearing the table, while he smoked and smoked. Then he'd yawn, opening his mouth wide to show how tired he was, and he'd say once or twice before going to bed: "Bet I sleep well tonight!"

'I didn't hold it against him, because he never had no idea how much he was hurting me. He couldn't know! Boasted about his women, he did, like a peacock strutting with its tail spread. He'd got to believe that every woman he met just looked at him and wanted him.

'It was a bad time for him when he began to show his age.

'Oh! sir, when I saw his first white hair, I got such a shock it fair took my breath away! And then I felt a little stab of joy—a horrible, ugly joy—but tremendous, all the same. I said to myself: "There'll be an end to all that now!" And I felt as though I'd been let out of prison. I'd have him to myself, at last, now that those others wouldn't want him any more.

'It was one morning, in our bed. He was still asleep, and I had leaned over to kiss him awake. It was then as I saw it, in the curls on his temple, a tiny thread, shining like silver. What a surprise! I'd never have thought it possible! At first I made up my mind to pull it out, so's he shouldn't see it, but when I looked closer, I saw others, higher up. White hairs! He was really going white! My heart was beating fit to burst, and my skin was all damp, but, deep down, I felt ever so happy!

'It's not nice to feel like that, but I did the household chores that morning with a light heart, before he woke up. And when he opened his eyes, all by himself, I said:

' "D'you know what I found when you was asleep?"

' "No, what?"

' "I found you've got some white hairs!"

'He was so upset that he sat up with a start, as though I'd tickled him. He gave me an ugly look, and said:

' "That's not true!"

' "Oh yes it is, four of them, on your left temple!"

'He jumped up and ran to the glass.

'He couldn't find them, so I showed him the first one I'd noticed, the one growing low down, the little curly one, and I said: "It's not surprising, seeing the life you lead. In two years you'll be finished."

'And I spoke truer than I knew, sir. Two years later, you wouldn't have recognized him. How quickly that changes a man! He was still good-looking, but the freshness had gone, and the women no longer went after him. It was a hard time for me, though: proper took it out of me, he did; couldn't do nothing to please him. He left the hairdressing for the hat trade, and lost a lot of money over that. Then, he tried being an actor, but didn't have no success with that. It was then that he started going to public dance-halls. He'd had the good sense to put a bit of money aside; that's what we live off. It's just enough but no more, and to think that at one time he had something like a fortune!

'You've seen for yourself how he's going on now. It's a sort of a madness as gets hold of him. He's just got to be young, got to go dancing with women stinking of scent and stuff, the poor old pet!'

Deeply moved, and with tears in her eyes she looked at her snoring husband. Then tip-toeing across to the bed, she planted a kiss on his hair.

The doctor had got up and was preparing to leave. He had nothing further to say to the fantastic couple.

Just as he was going out of the room, the woman said:

'Would you mind giving me your address, sir? If he gets worse, I'll come for you.'

(10 May 1889)

One Evening

THE *Kleber* had stopped. We were lying at the entrance to the Gulf of Bougie, and I gazed, spellbound, at the beauty of the scene. The high mountains were covered in dense forest; the distant sands lay like powdered gold at the sea's edge, and the white houses of the little town stood drenched in a fiery flood of sunlight.

The hot wind of Africa brought to my charmed senses the smell of the desert which is the over-riding smell of that whole vast continent of mystery into which we of the North have so far barely penetrated. For the past three months I had been wandering on the outer edge of an immeasurable and unknown world, home of the ostrich and the camel, of the elephant, the gorilla, the hippopotamus, and the black-man. I had seen the Arab pass me at the gallop, speeding like a bird upon the wind, like a flung and flying banner. I had slept in the brown tents which are the wandering homes of those winged and restless nomads. I was drunk with light and fantasy and space.

This was the last of all my fond excursions, for soon I must return to France, to Paris, that city of aimless prattling, of trivial cares and innumerable handshakes. I must say good-bye to all that I had learned to love, to new things barely glimpsed and much regretted.

A flotilla of boats was crowding round our vessel. Into one of these, rowed by a young negro, I jumped, and was soon deposited on the quay close to that Saracenic gateway which stands like a noble blazon of antiquity at the entrance to the ancient Kabyle town.

While I stood there with my bag beside me, looking back at the big ship anchored in the roadstead, and overwhelmed with wonder at the sight of this unequalled coastline, this great arena of mountains with the blue sea at their feet, far lovelier than the Bay of Naples, no less lovely than those of Porto and Ajaccio in Corsica, I felt the sudden weight of a hand upon my shoulder. I turned and saw a tall man with a long beard, dressed in white flannel, with a straw hat on his head. His blue eyes were fixed upon me.

One Evening

'Weren't we at school together?' he asked.
'Quite possibly. What is your name?'
'Trémoulin.'
'Good heavens! We were in the same form!'
'I recognized you at once.'
His long beard brushed my cheek.

He seemed so pleased to see me, so gay, so happy that, moved by a sudden uprush of self-regarding pleasure, I warmly grasped the two hands of my former friend, no less charmed than he was by the sudden resurrection of a time long past.

For four years Trémoulin had been for me one of the best and closest of those friends whom we soon forget when school is over. In those days he had been a tall, thin boy with long legs and a great bullet head which had seemed to crush his narrow chest under its weight, and drag his neck now this way and now that.

He was extremely intelligent, and had a wonderful facility, a rare sensitiveness, and a sure instinct in all that had to do with literature. He was the great prize-winner of the school.

We had all been sure that he would make a name for himself, probably as a poet, for he wrote verses in those days and had a head chockful of romantic conceits. His father was a chemist who kept a shop somewhere near the Panthéon and was generally thought to be far from thriving.

After taking my *baccalauréat* I had completely lost sight of him.
'What on earth are you doing here?' I asked.
With a smile he answered:
'I have turned settler.'
'You mean you plant things?'
'Yes, and gather in the crop.'
'What of?'
'Grapes—and make them into wine.'
'Do you find it a paying business?'
'Extremely so.'
'Good for you, old man.'
'Were you planning to go to the hotel?'
'Of course.'
'Then stay with me instead.'
'But . . .'
'Not another word!'
A negro boy was standing by, watching our every movement.
'Home, Ali,' said Trémoulin.
'Foui, Moussi!'

Hoisting my bag on to his shoulder, Ali set off at a run, his black feet raising a cloud of dust.

Trémoulin linked his arm in mine and led me off. He questioned me about my journey, about my store of impressions. The enthusiasm with which I answered seemed to increase his liking for me.

He lived in an old Moorish house built round an inner courtyard. There were no windows in its outside walls, and the flat roof formed a terrace which dominated the nearby houses, and commanded a view of the gulf, the forests, the mountains and the sea.

'What a marvellous place!' I exclaimed: 'It speaks to me of all the East. You're a lucky devil! How marvellous the nights must be up here! Do you sleep on this terrace?'

'In summer, yes. We'll sleep up here tonight. By the way, are you fond of fishing?'

'What sort of fishing?'

'Fishing with flares.'

'I adore it.'

'Then, we'll go out after dinner, and, when we come back, drink sherbert on my roof.'

When I had had a bath he took me on conducted tour of the enchanting Kabyle town, a cascade of white houses tumbling to the sea. A delicious meal followed, after which we went down to the harbour.

By this time nothing was visible but the street-lights and the stars, those great gleaming stars that twinkle in the skies of Africa.

A boat was waiting in a corner of the quay and, as soon as we had stepped aboard, a man whose face I could not clearly see began to row, while my friend made the brazier ready for lighting.

'I do the harpooning,' he said. 'No one can hold a candle to me at that.'

'Good!'

By this time we had rounded a sort of a mole, and were in a small bay thickly sown with tall rocks which, in the darkness, showed like towers built in the water. I noticed suddenly that the sea was phosphorescent. Our boat was moving with a slow, regular rhythm, and each time the oar-blades struck the water they produced, deep down, a strange trail of light which followed for some distance in our wake before vanishing. I leaned over the side and watched this track of faint illumination, this scattering of light kindled by the oarsman's strokes, this indescribable fire of the sea, a cold fire, born of an impact and dying away as soon as the ripples had subsided. The three of us moved smoothly forward in the darkness on a faintly gleaming path.

Whither were we going? My companions were barely visible. I could see nothing but the little swirls of light, the sparkling drops of water from the blades. It was hot, very hot. It was as though the night had been baked in an oven, and I felt vaguely thrilled by this mysterious journey in the silent boat.

Dogs, the skinny Arab dogs with russet coats and gleaming eyes, were barking in the distance, as they bark always when darkness falls in this land of unmeasured distances, from the seashore to the remote corners of the desert where wandering tribesmen plant their tents. Foxes, jackals, and hyenas answered them, and doubtless in some defile of the Atlas not far away a solitary lion was roaring.

Suddenly, our oarsman stopped rowing. Whereabouts we were I did not know. I was conscious of a faint scratching sound close to me. A match flickered, and I saw a hand, just a hand and nothing more, applying the tiny flame to the iron cage which hung above the bows, stacked with wood, like a floating pyre.

The sound startled me, and, as though what I had seen were something new and disquieting, I watched, with an undefined emotion, the flame ignite a handful of dry twigs at the edge of the fire-box in which, immediately, a crackling became audible.

Then, in the sleeping night, in the hot and heavy darkness, a great blaze leaped into the air. Under the sky's high canopy which lay upon us like a weight it suddenly revealed the boat and its other two occupants, one of them an old sailor, all skin and bone, with a pale, wrinkled face and a handkerchief tied round his head, the other, Trémoulin, his beard gleaming in the glow.

'Go ahead!' he ordered.

The old man bent to his oars again, and on we glided, at the very heart of a meteor, under a moving dome of night which seemed to follow us in our slow course. Trémoulin kept feeding wood into the brazier, which flared red and dazzling.

Once more I leaned over the side, and there, beneath me, I could see the bottom. A few feet underneath the keel, as we slowly passed upon the surface, a strange seascape of the depths unfolded, where the water, no less than the air of our upper world, breeds growing things and living creatures. The brazier showed the submerged rocks, with the clarity of daylight, and on we moved above a wonderland forest of weeds, red and pink, green and yellow. Between us and it there lay a wonderfully transparent sheet of glass, of liquid glass. Of its presence I was scarcely conscious, so intent was I upon the fairy scene below. The clear and limpid water, not so much seen as guessed, set between the watching eye and all that riot of vegetation, a something that disturbed the mind as might a doubt in the existence of reality, giving to all that underwater scene the mysterious quality of dreams.

Sometimes the weeds reached to the surface and lay upon it like long strands of hair scarcely at all disturbed by the movement of the boat. Between them flickered silver fish, seen for a brief moment and then gone again. Others, drowsing, hung suspended in the dense watery undergrowth, shining, slender, and elusive. Frequent crabs hastened to find a hiding-place in some deep hole, and, now and then, a bluish jelly-fish, so transparent as to be scarcely visible, a flower of palest azure, a sea-flower, surrendered its liquid body to the faint eddy of our passage. Sometimes, on a sudden, the bed would vanish altogether, plunging down, far down, into a misted profundity of thickened glass. When that happened, all that could be seen was a shadowy blur of great rocks and dark weed, almost beyond the reach of the brazier's glow.

Trémoulin, leaning above the bows, with, in his hand, a sharppointed trident, was gazing fixedly at the rocks, the weeds, and the changing levels of the seabed with the eager eye of a beast of prey.

With a quick and sudden gesture he silently lowered his weapon to the surface, and then discharged it, as one might an arrow, so swiftly that it struck a great fish at the very moment of its plunge to safety.

I had seen only the movement of his thrust, but I could hear his grunt of satisfaction, and, when he brought the harpoon up into the brazier's light, could see a creature twisting and wriggling on the iron prongs. It was a conger. After taking a good look at his catch, and holding it in the flicker of the flames for me to see, my friend threw it into the bottom of the boat. There the serpent of the sea, with five wounds in its body, slithered and squirmed against my feet, seeking a hole in which to hide, and, having found at last a pool of brackish water between the ribs, took refuge there, floundering and well-nigh dead.

Then, in quick succession, he struck and struck with a skill so great, with lightning speed and such amazing accuracy, that he soon amassed a rich harvest from among the strange denizens of the salt sea. I saw him hold above the brazier's flames, wriggling in their death-agony, silver perch and dark-skinned, red-spotted eels, spiky hog-fish and cuttlefish, fantastic creatures which spat out ink and, for a few moments, turned the water round the boat to pitchy black.

And all this time I seemed to hear, around us in the darkness, the twittering of birds. I looked up, trying to make out from where the shrill sound came, now near, now far, now brief and now prolonged, but seemingly without a pause. It was as though a myriad wings were there invisible above our heads, creatures of the air, no doubt, drawn hither by the blaze. Sometimes they tricked my hearing into thinking that they came from the sea.

'What is this hissing sound?' I asked him.

'Red-hot wood falling into the water.'

That explained it. The brazier was showering down upon the surface of the sea a constant rain of burning ash. The fragments, glowing red or flaming, fell on the water, there to expire with a muted wailing, a strange and penetrating sound, sometimes a continuous chirping, sometimes a brief cry like that of a migrant bird in passage. Great drops of melted resin boomed like cannon-balls or hornets, extinguished quickly as they plunged. The effect was that of voices, the thin, indescribable sound of living things about us in the night.

Suddenly, Trémoulin gave a shout:

'Ah! . . . the slut!'

He flung his weapon, and, when he drew it up, I saw wrapped round the prongs, and clinging to the wood of the haft, what looked like a great, quivering, squirming lump of red flesh, curling and uncurling long strip-like appendages, flabby-looking but very powerful, and covered with suckers. It was an octopus.

He held it out to me, and I could see the monster's two bulbous eyes fixed upon me, prominent eyes, bleared and terrible, set in a sort of sack like a tumour. Thinking itself still free, the creature slowly extended one of its tentacles in my direction. I could see the white suckers creeping towards me. The member ended in a point as fine as a thread, and no sooner had it got a firm hold on one of the thwarts, than another rose into the air and followed it. I had a feeling that in this pulpy but muscular body, in the reddish, flaccid, living tentacle, there was tremendous strength. But Trémoulin had drawn his knife and plunged it straight between the creature's eyes.

There was a sound like a sigh, a noise of escaping air, and the forward movement ceased.

Not that the octopus was dead, for these creatures are tenacious of life and hard to kill, but its vitality had been destroyed, its pump-like body holed. It could do no further harm, suck no more blood, nor draw the flesh of crabs from out their armoured carapace.

Trémoulin now set about detaching the suckers from the wood-work, though they had now been rendered harmless. It was as though he were about to play a game with this dying creature. A spasm of fury seemed to seize him.

'Wait till I start warming up your feet!' he shouted.

He lifted it up again on the points of the trident, and passed it backwards and forwards over the blaze, deliberately bringing the delicately pointed tentacles in contact with the now red-hot bars of the cage.

They twisted and squirmed with a crackling sound, shrinking and reddening in the heat of the fire. I could almost feel in my finger-tips something of the torment which the hideous creature must be enduring.

'Oh! don't do that!' I cried.

But he was quite unmoved.

'Nonsense!' he said: 'it'll do her good!'

Then he flung the pierced and mutilated object into the bottom of the boat, where it squirmed between my feet until it reached the brackish puddle. And there it lay, waiting for death, among the fish already dead.

Our sport continued for a long time, until the supply of wood gave out.

When there was no longer enough to keep the blaze going, he pitched the brazier bodily into the sea, and darkness, until then held high above our heads by the pillar of fire, descended, and we were wrapped in night.

The old man resumed the slow and regular rhythm of his rowing. Where the harbour was, where the land, where the entrance to the Port, and where the open sea, I had no idea. The octopus was still moving at my feet, and the nails of my fingers were hurting as though burned by fire. On a sudden I saw lights. We were drawing in to land.

'Feeling sleepy?' asked my friend.

'Not in the least.'

'Then, let us sit and talk upon my roof.'

'Nothing would please me more.'

Just as we reached the terrace, a crescent moon was rising from behind the mountains. The hot wind came and went in lazy puffs, charged with a faint, a barely perceptible fragrance, as though it had gathered in its passage the scents of towns and gardens in all those countries where a blazing sun strikes down upon the earth.

Around us white and terraced houses dropped downwards to the sea, and on their roofs human forms were visible, lying and standing, dreaming under the stars, whole families of men and women swathed in long robes, resting in the quiet darkness from the heat of the day.

I felt on a sudden that the soul of the Orient had entered into me, the poetic, legendary soul of simple folk whose thoughts are fragrant with the scent of flowers. My mind was filled with memories of the Bible and of the Arabian Nights. I could hear the Prophets thundering of miracles, could see princesses in silken trousers walking on the palace terraces where, in silver pans, burned aromatic essences, the smoke from which took on the shapes of genii.

'You are a lucky man to live here,' I said to Trémoulin.

'Chance brought me here.'

'Chance?'

'Yes, chance and unhappiness.'

'You have known unhappiness?'

'Much unhappiness.'

He stood before me wrapped in his burnous. Such sadness sounded in his voice that I shivered slightly.

After a moment's silence he continued:

'If you want to hear my story, I will tell it you. To talk to someone of my grief may do me good.'

'Talk away.'

'You really want me to?'

'Yes.'

'Here goes, then. You probably remember what I was like at school: a sort of a poet brought up in a chemist's shop. I dreamed of writing books, and after I had got my baccalauréat I tried, but without success. I published a volume of poetry, and then a novel. Neither sold. Then I tried my hand at a play, but it never reached the stage.

'I fell in love, I won't bore you more than I need with that. Next door to my father's shop there lived a tailor who had a daughter. She was the object of my passion: an extremely intelligent young

257

woman with a teacher's diploma. She had a quick and lively mind well suited to one whose person was so pleasing. She was twenty-two but looked no more than fifteen. She was very small. Everything about her was delicate—her features, the lines of her body, her colouring. She was like an exquisite water-colour. Her nose, her mouth, her blue eyes and fair hair, her smile, her figure, and her hands, every part of her and every attribute seemed as though made to be kept behind glass where the winds of life would never touch her. Yet, for all her fragile appearance, she was vivid, versatile, and active to a quite extraordinary degree. I was deeply in love. Certain walks we took in the Luxembourg Gardens, near the Medicis Fountain, live in my memory as the happiest moments of my life. You, yourself, must be familiar with that sweet lunacy of love which makes it impossible for the sufferer to think of anything but acts of adoration? At such times one becomes, in very truth, a man possessed and haunted by a woman. To the lover nothing matters but the beloved, since she alone exists for him.

'We soon became engaged. I confided to her all my plans for the future, but she had no confidence in them. She did not believe that I had any true talent for poetry, fiction, or the theatre. Trade alone, she thought, when successfully carried on, could make for perfect happiness.

'So I gave up all idea of writing books, and turned to selling them instead. The owner of the *Librairie Universelle* in Marseille had lately died, and I bought the business.

'The next three years were full of happiness. We had turned the shop into a sort of cultural centre where the local intellectuals met regularly for talk and discussion. They used it as a club where views were freely exchanged about writers, books, and especially politics. My wife, who looked after the shop, had made quite a reputation for herself in the city, and while the downstairs premises buzzed with conversation, I sat working in my study on the floor above which communicated with the shop by way of a spiral staircase. The sound of voices, laughter, and argument used to reach me from below, and I would sometimes pause in my writing to listen. I was secretly engaged on a novel—which still remains unfinished.

'The most regular attendants at our "circle" were, Monsieur Montina, a man of independent means, tall, handsome, and black-haired, a typical southern lady-killer with the sentimental eyes of a faithful dog; Monsieur Barbet, a magistrate; two business-men, called Faucille and Labarrègue, and a general, the Marquis de

Flèche, local leader of the Royalist Party, an old fellow of sixty-six, and the most important person of the Province.

'The business was doing well, and I was happy, very, very happy.

'Then, one afternoon, when I had been out on some errand or other, I found myself walking home, about three o'clock, along the rue Saint Ferréol. All of a sudden, I saw, emerging from a doorway, a woman who bore so strong a resemblance to my wife, that I should have been completely taken in had I not left her at home, an hour earlier, with a sick-headache. She was just in front of me, walking very quickly, and did not turn her head. Feeling surprised and uneasy, I proceeded to follow her, almost in spite of myself.

'It cannot possibly be she, I told myself, for I left her indisposed at home. Besides, what should have taken her to that house?

'But so anxious was I to get to the bottom of the mystery, that I increased my pace with the object of overtaking her. Perhaps she felt, or guessed, that she was being followed; perhaps she recognized my step. Whatever the reason, she suddenly turned about. I had been right after all; it *was* my wife! Seeing me beside her, she blushed and stopped.

' "So, it's you!" she said.

'My heart was heavy.

' "Then, you did go out after all? What about the headache?"

' "I felt better, and I had a delivery to make: an order for pencils."

' "From whom?"

' "Lacaussade—rue Casinelli."

'She looked me straight in the eyes. Her face was no longer red, in fact, she looked rather paler than usual. Her clear and limpid eyes—what deceit there can be in a woman's eyes!—seemed eloquent of truth, but I had a vague and painful feeling that they concealed a lie. I stood there, facing her, more ill at ease, more embarrassed, more shaken than she was, not daring to suspect, but sure that she was lying. Why should I think so? I could have made no answer to that question.

'All I said was:

' "You did well to come out if your headache is better."

' "Oh, but it is; much better."

' "Are you on your way home?"

' "Of course."

'At that I left her and went on my way alone.

'What was going on? When speaking with her I had had a feeling that she was not telling me the truth. But now I doubted my instinct, and by dinner-time was blaming myself for having suspected her sincerity even for a moment.

'Have you ever been jealous? Not that it matters whether you have or not. The first drop of jealousy had fallen on my heart, and such drops are like a rain of fire. I could put nothing into words, had no real reason for suspecting her. All I knew for certain was that she had been lying. Every evening when we were alone, when the last customers had left and the assistants had gone home, it had been our habit to walk to the harbour when the weather was fine, or to sit chatting in my study when it was bad. At such times I opened my heart to her without reserve, because I loved her. She was part of my life, the most important part. In her was all my happiness, and in her little hands she held my faithful heart imprisoned.

'In those first days of doubt and misery, before I had given form and substance to suspicion, that heart was like a weight of ice within me. It was as though I were sickening for some illness. I was perpetually cold, really cold. I had no longer any appetite for food, and I could not sleep.

'Why had she lied to me? What had taken her to that house? I went there to see whether I could discover anything, but without success. The first-floor tenant, an upholsterer by trade, told me all he knew about his neighbours, but there was nothing in what he said to give me a clue. A midwife lived on the second floor, a dressmaker and a manicurist on the third. Two cab-drivers with their families occupied the attics.

'Why had she lied? It would have been so easy for her to say that she had been to see the dressmaker or the manicurist. I longed to question them as well, but feared she might be warned of my suspicions.

'The fact remained that she had been to that house without telling me. Mystery there was, but of what kind? I told myself that there was probably some perfectly innocent explanation, some visit of charity, perhaps, which she wished to keep secret, some piece of information she wanted. I blamed myself for being suspicious. Have we not, all of us, a perfect right to certain privacies? To enjoy the freedom of a personal life which need be shared with nobody? Just because a man has a young woman for companion,

does that entitle him to insist on her harbouring no thought, performing no action, without telling him? Does marriage mean the
renunciation of all independence, all freedom? Might she not have
been to see the dressmaker without saying anything about it, or
perhaps to give a little help to the family of one of the cab-drivers?
Perhaps her visit to that house, though no blame could attach to
it, was of a nature which she thought I might criticize adversely.
She knew everything about me, was familiar with my every fad
and prejudice, and might well be afraid, not perhaps that I should
reproach her but that I might start a tiresome argument. She had
been bred up in habits of thrift and orderliness, was mistress of all
those little arts familiar to every woman who runs her home
economically and understands the needs of a business. Probably
she felt that some small expenditure on personal vanity might
lessen my respect for her. Small tricks and wiles are part and
parcel of a woman's nature.

'But no amount of reasoning could bring me comfort. I was
jealous. Suspicion had become with me a nagging torment: not
any specific suspicion, but suspicion in general. Wherever I went,
whatever I did, I suffered a perpetual agony. I was haunted by a
thought. So far I had kept it veiled, and did not dare to draw the
veil aside, for I dreaded what might be revealed . . . Perhaps she
had a lover! . . . Incredible! . . . Impossible! . . . And yet . . . And
yet . . .

'Montina's face was ever before my eyes . . . I saw him clearly,
the handsome fop with the glossy hair, smiling at her . . . And to
myself I said: "That's who it is!"

'I invented every detail of an affair between them. They had
spoken of some book they both had read; had discussed the love
interest; had found something of themselves in the two persons
involved, so that, in a while, fiction had become reality. I watched
them: so hideous was my suffering that I could even do that! I
bought a pair of rubber-soled shoes so as to be able to move about
without being heard. I was continually going up and down the
spiral staircase hoping to take them by surprise. Sometimes I
crept head forwards, sliding on my hands down the rail, and then,
seeing an assistant in the shop with them, had to beat a difficult
retreat, edging backwards to my lair.

'There was nothing now in my life but torture. I could think of
nothing, do nothing. I no longer tried to write, I neglected my
business. Whenever I left the house and had walked a few steps,
the certainty was born in me that he was there, and I hastened

back, only to find no sign of him. Then off I went again, but the same thought halted me: "By this time he'll have come," and back I went.

'The obsession never left me. All day long and every day, it was there.

'At night it was even worse, for I could feel her beside me in the bed. She lay there, fast asleep, or pretending to sleep. I felt a terrible, an almost irresistible longing, to get up, to take a candle in one hand, a hammer in the other, and, with a single blow, split her head wide open, just to see what was in it. I knew, of course, that I should find nothing but a mess of brains and blood: her thoughts I could not see. By no possible means could I obtain the knowledge for which I longed. And then, those eyes of hers! Each time she looked at me, a frenzy seized me. I stared at her . . . She stared at me. Her eyes were frank, clear, and transparent—and false! false! false! What was going on behind them I could not even guess. I longed to drive a needle into them, to splinter those two distorting mirrors!

'How well I understood the Inquisition! I could so willingly have crushed her wrists in iron bracelets . . . "Speak! Confess! . . . You won't? . . . Then let us see what this will do!" Then, very, very slowly, I would strangle her . . . "Speak! . . . Confess!" . . . Gradually I would increase the pressure until I saw her twist in the final agony, suffocate and die . . . Or, I would burn her fingers over a fire . . . Oh! With what pleasure . . . "Speak! . . . Speak! . . . You still won't?" Then I should have pressed them to the red-hot coals till the tips sizzled . . . She would have spoken then, no doubt about it . . . That would have forced confession from her . . .'

Standing before me, Trémoulin raised his voice to a shout. All round us, on the nearby roofs, shadowy forms sat up, awoke and listened, disturbed in their sleep.

So moved was I, so enthralled by what he was telling me, that I could see that little wife of his, that tiny, fair-haired creature, so quick-witted and so sly, as clearly in the darkness as though I had known her. I conjured up a picture of her selling books and talking with the men whose senses had been stirred by her childlike airs. Behind the exquisite doll's face I could see the shifty little brain at work ringing the changes on mad and flaunting fantasies, the dream-images of scented milliners in which the heroes of popular fiction live and love. I, too, suspected her, as he had done, hated

her, and loathed her. Gladly would I have burned her finger-tips to
make her talk.

He resumed, but in a quieter mood.

'I don't know why I am telling you all this. I have never breathed
a word of it to any other living soul. Maybe that is because I have
seen nobody for two years to whom I could tell it. I have talked
with nobody, nobody at all. And all that time what I have voided
on poor you, has been festering in my heart.

'Well, I was wrong. What actually had happened was worse, far
worse, than anything I had imagined. In a final attempt to get to
the bottom of the mystery, I fell back upon that hoary old device
of jealous husbands: I pretended that business would take me
frequently away from home. I knew that in my absence she would
eat her meals in town, and I bribed a restaurant waiter—I won't
bore you with the details—so to manage things that I might catch
her in the act.

'The door of the private room was to be left unlocked and, at
the time arranged, I turned up, resolved to kill them both. For the
past twenty-four hours the inevitable scene had been as clear to
me as though it had already taken place. I should go into the room
where they were sitting with a table, laden with glasses, bottles, and
dishes, between them. Appalled by my sudden appearance they
would neither of them move. Without a word, I should bring my
loaded stick down on Montina's head, and he would fall forward
like a felled ox, with his face on the cloth. I should leave her just
enough time—a few seconds only—to realize what was happening,
to stretch appealing arms, mad with terror, before dying in her
turn. I was ready, strong, determined, and drunk with joy. The
thought of the terror in her eyes at sight of my raised stick, of the
sound of her strangled cry, of the spectacle of her outstretched
arms, her livid and contorted face, gave me a sweet foretaste of
revenge. I should be careful not to stun her with the first blow.
You think me no better than a savage, don't you? That is because
you do not know what suffering like mine can be. The thought that
the woman you have loved—whether wife or mistress—has given
herself to another, has taken his kisses as she once took yours, is
something so horrible, so appalling, that after but one day of such
torment, you will stop at nothing. I am astonished that there is not
more killing done, for all men who have been betrayed long to kill,
revel in the prospect of killing, to such an extent that when they walk
upon a lonely road, when they are shut away in the solitude of a

room, they go through the gestures of strangling or striking, obsessed by the fantasy of vengeance satisfied.

'But enough of that. I was punctual at the restaurant. I asked the waiter whether they were there. I had bought the fellow and he made no bones about saying that they were. He took me up the stairs and pointed to a door. I gripped my stick as though my fingers were of iron. Then I went into the room.

'I had chosen my moment well. They were in each other's arms. But the man was not Montina. It was General de Flèche, the aging warrior of sixty-six.

'So certain had I been that I should find the other, that I stood rooted to the spot, incapable of movement.

'And then . . . Well, even now I do not know what change took place in me . . . Faced by the man I had expected to find, I should have been mad and blind with fury. But at the sight of that old, paunchy creature with the sagging cheeks I felt only disgust . . . A sense of nausea rose in me at the knowledge that my dainty, delicate wife who looked little more than a girl had given herself to that gross, half-senile reprobate, for no better reason than that he was a marquis, a general, the friend and champion of kings dethroned. How my mind worked I do not know. I could not raise my hand to strike the dotard! The shame of what I saw had paralysed me. It was not my wife I wanted to kill at that moment, but the whole race of women who could do such things! I was no longer jealous but appalled as though the horror of hell lay open to my view.

'Say what you will of men, they are incapable of such baseness. When one of *us* behaves like that he becomes an outcast from his sex. A man who marries or makes love to an old woman is held in greater contempt by his fellows than a thief. But *they*, the women with fouled and filthy hearts, are any man's for the asking, whether young or old, for reasons that may differ though all are vile. They do as they do because it is their vocation, their profession, their function. They are the eternal, amoral, natural prostitutes, giving their bodies—without the slightest feeling of disgust because the body is the tawdry merchandize of love whether sold or freely offered—to any old man who hangs about street corners with money in his pocket, or, from vanity, to some ancient, randy monarch, some old repulsive creature whom fame has touched! . . .'

Under the starry sky he stood like some Prophet of the Old Testament declaiming with a wild despair, damning the gilded shame of

all the mistresses of dotard kings, the respectable shame of virgins who have taken old men to be their husbands, the tolerated shame of all young women who, with smiling lips, accept decrepit kisses.

I could see them there before me, as he had conjured them from all the past since the beginning of the world, crowding round us in that Eastern night, the beautiful women with vile hearts who, like animals caring not what age the male may be, had pandered to the lusts of ancient lechers. They moved before me, those servants of the Patriarchs renowned in Bible story: Agar and Ruth, the daughters of Lot, the dark-skinned Abigail, the Shunamite virgin whose kisses had brought warmth to David on his deathbed, and all those other unscrupulous females, young, plump, and fair, patrician and plebeian alike, who had served as slaves the hideous longings of old age, whether bought or dazzled.

'What did you do?' I asked.

'I went away—and here I am,' was all he said.

And there we stayed for a long while, silent and lost in thought.

I shall never forget the impression made upon me by the happenings of that night. All that I had seen, heard, felt, and guessed—the fishing expedition, the octopus, too, perhaps, the terrible story he had told me, and the ghostly figures on the nearby roofs—all seemed to converge in one single emotion. For there are meetings, inexplicable concatenations of events which, though they may not seem to be exceptional, hold more of life's secret essence than is spread thin over the ordinary routine of daily living.

(1889?)

Mouche

THIS is what he told us:

'I saw a lot of odd things, and odd women, too, in the days when I used to go boating regularly. Many's the time I've thought of writing a little book, to be called "On the Seine", just so as to describe that life of hard physical exercise, freedom, gaiety, poverty, and noisy racketing, which I lived when I was between twenty and thirty.

'I was a penniless clerk at that time. Now I am a successful man who can pay the earth to gratify a moment's whim. I had a thousand modest wants which I knew that I could never satisfy. But they filled me with an endless succession of fantastic hopes, all of which glittered with gold, all of which, I knew, would come to nothing. Today, I must confess, I cannot think of anything, no matter how far-fetched, which would induce me to leave my chair or interrupt a nap. How simple, enjoyable, and difficult was that life of ours, divided between an office-stool in Paris and the river at Argenteuil! My great, my only, my absorbing passion, for all of ten years, was the Seine, that lovely, smooth, variegated, and stinking river filled with visions and with filth! I think I loved it as I did because it gave me, or so, at least, I believed, the feeling that I was really alive. Ah! those saunters along the bank when the year was gay with green grass and wild flowers; when my friends, the frogs, dreamed the time away as they sat cooling their bellies on a water-lily leaf; when the lilies themselves were so dainty and so frail; when, seated in the long grass behind a willow, I would see a real Japanese print each time a kingfisher flashed by like a blue flame! I loved it all with an instinctive passion of the eye, which spread a deep and natural happiness through all my body!

'As some remember nights of passionate love, what I remember is the sun rising in an early morning mist, with drifting, aimless patches of vapour, white as ghosts before the dawn, and then, as it climbed, the first rays touching the dew-drenched fields, so that the heart swooned with ecstasy. And I remember, too, the moon turning the rippling surface of the stream to silver, and bringing dreams to life.

Mouche

'And all that, symbol of an illusion beyond the power of time to damage, was the gift to me of a stretch of evil-smelling water carrying to the sea the refuse and the filth of Paris.

'What fun we had! There were five of us, all now prosperous and solid citizens. In those days we were poor, and had established a kind of nondescript club in a terrible Argenteuil pot-house, the landlord of which supplied us with a dormitory where I, certainly, spent some of the maddest nights of my life. We thought about nothing but rowing and enjoying ourselves, for rowing was for all of us, save one, almost a religion. I recall the adventures we had, and the jokes we thought up, all of them so wildly fantastic that nobody, nowadays, could bring himself to believe them. That sort of life, even on the Seine, is a thing of the past, and the escapades which were the breath of life to us, exist no longer.

'The five of us had, with the greatest difficulty, scraped together enough money between us to buy a boat which we owned in common. It was the setting for laughter such as we shall never know again—a somewhat heavy yawl, broad-in-the-beam, solidly built, roomy, and comfortable. I won't describe my friends to you in detail. They consisted of a little chap, known as Petit-Bleu, as mischievous as a monkey; a tall fellow with a ferocious expression, grey eyes, and black hair, whom we called Tomahawk; La Tôque, bone-lazy and humorous—he was the one who never touched an oar, on the grounds that he would be sure to capsize the boat—a slim youth, very elegant and spick-and-span, nicknamed "N'a-qu'un-Oeil" after a recently published novel by Cladel, and also because he sported a monocle; lastly, myself, newly baptized as Joseph Prunier. We lived in perfect harmony. Our only regret was that we had no girl with us to take the tiller. A woman is an indispensable member of a boat's crew such as ours: indispensable, because she keeps minds and hearts up to the mark, because she provides laughter and distraction, which give a spice to life, and, also, because she strikes a decorative note with her red sunshade gliding past the lush, green banks. But what we needed was no ordinary cox, because none of us five was in any way ordinary. She would have to be unexpected and odd, and ready for anything; in fact someone hard, probably impossible, to find. We tried several, but without success—not honest-to-God helmswomen at all, but girls, most of them, who thought it fun to take an occasional turn at the tiller, and were really a great deal more interested in the wine that went to their heads than in the water that kept them afloat. We used to try them one after the other, on Sundays, and then turn them adrift disgustedly.

'But one Saturday evening, "N'a-qu'un-Oeil" brought along with him a thin, lively little creature, always hopping about like a sparrow, a bit of a wag, and brimful of that sort of humour which passes for wit among the street arabs—of both sexes—who have grown up in the highways and by-ways of Paris. She was pleasing rather than pretty, the rough draft of a woman, with a little of everything in her, and the sort of shape an artist will jot down in three strokes on the table-cloth of a café after dinner, between a glass of brandy and a cigarette. Nature does produce that type occasionally.

'On that first evening she astonished and amused us, but was so entirely unexpected that we could none of us make up our minds about her. Dropped out of a clear sky into a nest of men who would stop at nothing, she was very soon in complete control of the situation, and, by next morning, had won all our hearts.

'She was as crazy as a coot. She maintained that she had been born with the glass of absinthe inside her, which her mother had drunk just before having her, and had never been completely sober since, because, she said, her nurse used to keep up her strength with tots of rum. She always called the bottles on the shelves of bar parlours "My Holy Family".

'I have no idea which of us it was who first gave her the name "Mouche", nor why. But it fitted her like a glove and we stuck to it. Every week, our yawl—which we had named *Feuille-à-l'Envers* —used to float along the Seine, between Asnières and Maisons-Laffitte, with a load of five high-spirited hearties, steered by a vivacious and scatter-brained young creature under a parasol of painted paper, who treated us as slaves charged with the duty of taking her for a row, and to whom we were devoted.

'We were all tremendously fond of her, at first for all sorts of reasons, but later for one in particular. She sat in the stern of our boat like a little word-mill, chattering away to the breeze which played upon the surface of the stream. She babbled incessantly with the continuous whirring sound made by the sails of a mill turning in the wind, saying the most unexpected, droll, and staggering things. Her talk was a patchwork of incongruous bits and pieces, rags of all shapes and colours, not sewn together but lightly tacked—fairy-tale fantasy, bawdy, immodesty, impudence, improvisation, farce, fresh-air, and a feeling for scenery—so that listening to her was like travelling in a balloon.

Mouche

'We used to ask her questions, just to see what she would say. The most frequent one was:

' "Why are you called Mouche?"

'She found so many improbable answers that we had to stop rowing because we were laughing so hard.

'We had strong feelings for her, also, as a woman, and La Tôque, who never took an oar, but spent all his days lolling beside her in the stern, once said, in answer to the question, "Why are you called Mouche?"

' "Because she's a Spanish Fly, of course."

'Yes, that is what she was, a little buzzing, exciting Spanish Fly, not of the classic type, poison-bearing, glittering, and hooded, but a Spanish Fly with red wings who was beginning to have an uncomfortably disturbing effect upon the crew of *Feuille-à-l'Envers*.

'What stupid jokes there were on the Leaf where this Fly had alighted!

'Ever since Mouche had signed on with the crew, "N'a-qu'un-Oeil" had arrogated to himself the preponderant rôle, the superior rôle of a man with a woman, as opposed to four others with none. He abused his privilege to the point of sometimes getting on our nerves, what with kissing Mouche in front of us, perching her on his knee after meals, and assuming all sorts of humiliating and irritating prerogatives.

'We had rigged up a curtain in the dormitory to isolate them from the rest of the room.

'But I very soon noticed that the others were thinking very much along the same lines as myself: "Why, in obedience to what exception-proves-the-rule law, in virtue of what inadmissible principle, should Mouche, who seems so uninhibited, show to her lover a degree of fidelity which women of a higher social class most certainly do not show to their husbands?"

'In our summing up of her we were fully justified, as very soon became apparent. Our only regret was that we had not taken action sooner, and so lost much precious time. Mouche deceived "N'a-qu'un-Oeil" with every other member of the crew.

'This she did without raising the slightest difficulty, or putting up any show of resistance. We had only to ask.

'I am afraid that prudes will be deeply shocked at all this. But why should they? Has there ever been a fashionable courtesan who had not had a dozen lovers? And which of them was ever such a fool as not to know it? Is it not *modish* to have one's "evening" with some celebrated and much-sought-after woman, in the same way as one has one's "evening" at the Opéra, the Français, or the Odéon, on those nights when they are not playing the more sacrosanct of the classics? Ten men may club together to keep a *cocotte*, even though she may find it difficult to make a fair distribution of her time, as ten men will club together to buy a race-horse which will be ridden by only one jockey—true image of the fancy-man.

'From motives of delicacy, we let "N'a-qu'un-Oeil" have "the use of" Mouche from Saturday evenings until Monday mornings. The period of navigation was his. We deceived him only on week-days, in Paris, far from the Seine, which, for such enthusiastic boating men as we were, was almost tantamount to not deceiving him at all.

'There was this peculiarity about the situation, that the four sneak-thieves of Mouche's favours knew all about the sharing business, talked about it among themselves, and even made veiled allusions to it in her presence, which made her laugh a lot. Only "N'a-qu'un-Oeil" seemed to be completely oblivious to what was going on, and this lack of awareness on his part created something of an awkwardness between him and us. It set him apart, isolated him, as it were, and made our former frankness and old intimacy difficult. We looked upon him as a man playing the somewhat complicated and ridiculous part of a deceived lover, almost of a husband.

'But, since he was highly intelligent, and a past master in sly humour, we sometimes wondered, uneasily I must admit, whether, perhaps, he knew more than he showed.

'He took care to enlighten us in a manner which was more than a little painful for us. We were on our way to lunch at Bougival, and were putting our backs into it, when La Tôque who, on that particular morning, had the triumphant air of a fully satisfied man, and, seated beside our helmswoman, seemed to be pressing against her rather too freely for our liking, suddenly called "Easy All!"

'The eight oars rose from the water.

'Then, turning to his neighbour, he asked:

' "Why are you called Mouche?"

'Before she could answer, "N'a-qu'un-Oeil" who was seated well forward, said with an unusual note of dryness in his voice:

' "Because she settles on every sort of garbage."

'At first there was a dead silence, a general feeling of embarrass-

272

ment, followed by a strong inclination in the rest of us to laugh. Even Mouche was shocked into silence.

'Then La Tôque gave the order:

' "Come Forward!"

'The boat set off again.

'The incident was closed, the mystery cleared up.

'It had changed nothing in our habits. Its only result was to re-establish cordial relations between "N'a-qu'un-Oeil" and ourselves. He became once more the privileged possessor of Mouche from Saturday evening until Monday morning, his position of seniority having been once and for all established by this clearing of the air, which, incidentally, put an end to all questions on the subject of the word Mouche. From then on, we were content to occupy the secondary position of grateful and considerate friends, who took discreet advantage of week-days, without there being the slightest trace of any ill-feeling between us.

'Things went very well for about three months. Then, suddenly, Mouche's attitude towards us changed in the oddest way. She became much less high-spirited, showed signs of nerves, anxiety, and, almost, of irritability. We kept on asking:

' "What's the matter with you?"

'She answered:

' "Nothing at all: leave me alone, do!"

'We learned the truth one Saturday evening, and it came from "N'a-qu'un-Oeil". We had just drawn up our chairs to the table in the little dining-room which landlord Barbichon always reserved for us in his river-side restaurant, and, having finished our soup, were waiting for the fried fish, when our friend, who also seemed to be a bit subdued, first took Mouche's hand, and then began to speak.

' "My dear comrades," he said, "I have an extremely serious communication to make to you, which may necessitate a good deal of discussion. We shall have time for that between courses. Mouche has just confided in me a disastrous piece of news, and has asked me to pass it on to you.

' "She is pregnant.

' "I have only one thing more to say. This is not the moment to desert her, and any attempt to settle the question of paternity is forbidden."

'This information at first produced a general sense of blank amazement. There was a feeling of catastrophe in the air. We looked at one another. We felt that we wanted to accuse someone.

But whom? Never before had I been so conscious of that cruel jest of Nature's which makes it impossible for any man to know with certainty whether he is the father of his child.

'Then some degree of comfort came to us, born of a confused sense of solidarity.

'Tomahawk, who never said much, expressed what we were beginning to feel in these words:

' "Well, hang it all, you know: it can't be helped, and union is strength."

'A kitchen-boy brought in the gudgeon. We did not fall upon it as we usually did, because, all said and done, we were worried.

' "N'a-qu'un-Oeil" continued:

' "She has been good enough, in these circumstances, to make a full confession to me. My friends, we are all of us equally responsible. Let us shake hands on it, and agree to adopt the child."

'The motion was carried unanimously. We raised our arms above the dish of fried gudgeon, and took a solemn oath.

' "We will adopt it!"

'Then, suddenly realizing that she was saved, that the horrible weight of anxiety which had been upon her for a month, was removed, poor Mouche, that sweet, nerve-ridden beggar-girl of love, exclaimed:

' "Oh! my dear friends . . . my very dear friends . . . How good you are . . . How good . . . How good . . . I thank you one and all."

'For the first time we saw her in tears.

'From then on, when we were in the boat, we talked about the child as though it were already born, and each of us studied, with the exaggerated solicitude of someone personally concerned, the slow but relentless increase in our helmswoman's girth.

'We would stop rowing, and ask:

' "Mouche?"

'And she would answer:

' "All present and correct!"

' "Boy or girl?"

' "Boy!"

' "And what's he going to be?"

'Then she would give full rein to her imagination in the most fantastic way—telling endless stories, amazing inventions covering the child's life from the moment of its birth till the day of final triumph. That kid was everything under the sun in the simple-minded, touching, passionate dreaming of that queer little waif, who was now living in a state of complete chastity among the five men whom she called her "five papas". She saw, she described, him as a sailor discovering a new world larger than America; as a General delivering Alsace and Lorraine back into the hands of France; as an Emperor, founding a dynasty of wise and generous sovereigns, who should give lasting happiness to our country; as a scientist revealing, first the secret of how to make gold, and then that of life everlasting; as an aeronaut inventing a method of reaching the stars, and turning the infinite spaces of the sky into a vast area through which men could travel as they willed—a realization of all the most unlikely and magnificent of dreams.

'How dear and funny the poor darling was until the summer's end!

'It was on the twentieth of September that *her* dream came crashing to the ground. We were rowing back after lunching at Maisons-Laffitte, and had just passed Saint-Germain, when she said that she was thirsty, and asked us to put in at Pecq.

'For some time she had been growing heavy. It was a cause of great annoyance to her. She could no longer go jumping about all over the place, or leap from the boat to the bank as she had been used to do. She tried to, now and again, in spite of everything we could say or do to stop her, and twenty times she would have fallen, had not our arms been waiting to support her.

'That day she was foolish enough to try to leave the boat before we had tied it up. She was guilty of one of those acts of bravado, which, before now, have killed trained athletes if they happened to be sick or tired. Just as we were about to lay the boat alongside the landing-stage, and before we could do anything to stop her, she tried to jump ashore.

'But she was too weak to do more than touch the edge of the stone wall with her feet. She struck her stomach against the sharp corner, and with a dreadful cry disappeared into the water.

'All five of us dived at the same moment. When we brought her to the surface she was in a state of collapse, deathly pale, and already suffering the most frightful pain.

'We got her as quickly as possible to the nearest inn, and sent for a doctor.

'For the ten hours during which her miscarriage lasted, she bore the atrocious agony with heroic courage. We stood beside her bed in a condition of utter misery, grief and fear.

'At last she was delivered of a dead child, and for some days we almost despaired of her life.

'But a day came when the doctor said, "I think she is through the worst: she must have a constitution of iron!" Then we all went into her room, our hearts bursting with happiness.

' "N'a-qu'un-Oeil" spoke for us all when he said:

' "Out of danger now, Mouche dear, and I can't tell you how delighted we are!"

'Then, for the second time, we saw her cry.

'With swimming eyes, she whispered:

' "Oh, if you knew . . . If you knew . . . How miserable I am . . . I shall never get over it!"

' "Over what, darling Mouche?"

' "Why, killing him—for I did kill him. Oh! without meaning to, I know, but that doesn't make the pain any less!"

'She was sobbing bitterly. We stood round her bed, deeply moved, not knowing what to say.

'Then, she asked:

' "Did you see him?"

'With one voice we replied:

' "Yes!"

' "It was a boy, wasn't it?"

' "Yes."

' "And handsome?"

'We hesitated. Petit-Bleu, less scrupulous than the rest of us, decided to say what she wanted to hear:

' "Very, very handsome."

'It was foolish of him, for she began to moan and groan, almost to scream, in her despair.

'Then, "N'a-qu'un-Oeil", who, perhaps, loved her better than any of us, thought of something funny to calm her. He leaned down, kissed her tear-dimmed eyes, and said:

' "Cheer up, dear Mouche, cheer up: we'll start making another!"

'The sense of humour which was part and parcel of her being, suddenly came alive, and, half convinced, half laughing, but with tears still flowing, and her heart contracted with pain, she said, looking at us all:

' "Really and truly?"

'And as one man we answered:

' "Really and truly!" '

(7 February 1890)

The Olive Grove

WHEN the longshoremen who hang about the little Provençal port of Garandou, at the far end of the Bay of Pisca between Marseille and Toulon, saw the Abbé Vilbois' boat coming back from fishing, they went down to the beach to help him pull it up.

There was no one in it but the abbé, and he was rowing like a sailor born and bred, with a vigour rare in men of fifty-eight. His rolled-up sleeves revealed a pair of muscular arms, and the skirt of his cassock was tucked between his knees. A few buttons on his chest were unfastened. His shovel hat lay beside him on the thwart, and he was wearing on his head a close-fitting affair made of cork and covered with white linen. He had the solidly-built and rather odd appearance of a missionary from the tropics, better suited to a life of adventure than to saying Mass.

Every now and again he looked over one shoulder to get his bearings, and then began to pull again with a regular, steady, powerful stroke, just to show the lazy boatmen of the south how a northerner could row.

The boat shot forward, scraped along the sand, and seemed as though it would continue under its own impetus right up the beach. Then it stopped dead, and the five men watching the curé bring it in, sauntered up, affable, easy-going, and full of friendliness.

'Thee had a good day, Feyther?' asked one of them with a strong Provençal accent.

The Abbé Vilbois shipped his oars, exchanged his headgear for the shovel hat, pulled down his shirt-sleeves, buttoned up his cassock, and then, having resumed the dignified appearance expected of a village incumbent, replied with considerable self-satisfaction:

'Very good: three bass, two eels, and a few flounders.'

The five men had gone up to the boat, and, leaning over the gunwale, were sizing up the dead creatures with expert eyes: the plump bass, the flat-headed eels—those hideous serpents of the sea—and the bluish flounders zig-zagged with golden stripes, the colour of orange peel.

'I'll carry they things up to that shack o' yourn, Feyther.'

T

'Thank you, my lad.'

Having shaken hands all round, the priest set off, followed by one of the men, while the others stayed behind to see to his boat.

He strode ahead with long, measured steps, a strong and dignified figure. Since he was still warm from his strenuous exercise, he took his hat off now and then when he came to a stretch of road sheltered by the thin shade cast by the olives, to let the air, still hot but faintly freshened by a slight sea-breeze, play about his square-shaped head with its thatch of white, cropped hair—the head of a soldier rather than a priest. The village came into view. It stood on a small hill in the middle of a wide valley sloping at an easy gradient to the sea.

It was a July evening. The blinding sun, now only just above the serrated crest-line of the distant hills, cast the seemingly endless shadow of the priest obliquely across the road which lay buried under a shroud of dust. The outsize hat paraded across the nearby field—a large, black patch. It seemed to be engaged in some sort of a game, which consisted in its climbing nimbly up all the olive-trunks it met, and then, at once, dropping to the ground again, where it crept between the trees.

Under the abbé's feet, fine powder of that impalpable floury consistency with which Provençal roads are thick in summer, rose in a cloud, eddying like smoke round his cassock, almost hiding it from view, and covering its lower edge with a greyish stain which grew progressively lighter in colour as he walked. He felt cooler now, and strode along with his hands in his pockets and that slow, powerful slouch which the mountaineer employs when climbing. His untroubled eyes took in the village, his village where he had occupied the post of curé for twenty-five years, the village he had chosen and been given as a great favour, the village where he hoped to stay until he died. The church, his church, crowned the wide-based pyramid of houses at its feet. Its two, square, unequal towers of brownish stone dominated this southern valley with their ancient walls which seemed more appropriate to a fortified castle than to the house of God.

The abbé was feeling pleased with himself, for he had caught three bass, two eels, and a few flounders.

They represented another little triumph in the eyes of his parishioners whose respect he had gained mostly because, in spite of his age, he was one of the strongest men for miles around. Such small and harmless vanities were among his greatest pleasures. He could hit a flower-stalk with a pistol-shot, sometimes fenced with

The Olive Grove

his neighbour, the tobacconist—who had been a regimental master-at-arms in his youth—and was a better swimmer than anyone along that stretch of coast.

Time was when he had been a man of fashion, the Baron de Vilbois, who had turned priest at thirty-two as the result of an unhappy love affair.

Born of an ancient Picardy family, royalist and religious by tradition, whose sons for centuries past had made their mark in the Army, the Law, and the Church, he had at first, under the influence of his mother, intended to take holy orders. Later, however, on the advice of his father, he had decided to go to Paris, read law, and eventually obtain some solid, serious employment in the Courts.

But just as he was finishing his studies, his father fell a victim to pneumonia contracted while on a shooting-party in the marshes. His mother was heartbroken and, shortly after, died. Finding himself suddenly heir to a great fortune, he gave up all thoughts of a career and was content to live the life of a rich man. Good-looking and intelligent, though with a mind somewhat limited by those traditions and beliefs which he had inherited along with the sturdy build of a Picard squire, he became a popular and successful figure in the more serious circles of Society, and led the pleasant existence of a conventional, opulent, and highly esteemed young man.

But, as things turned out, he fell in love, after several meetings at a friend's house, with a young actress. She was a student at the Conservatoire and had just made a brilliant début at the Odéon.

He loved her with all the violence, all the fire of a man trained to believe in fixed and absolute ideas. He saw her through the prism of the romantic role in which she had made a great success at her first appearance on the public stage.

She was pretty, temperamentally depraved, and had the ingenuous air of a child—what he called her 'angel look'. She made a complete conquest of him, so that he became one of those frantic lunatics, those ecstatic half-wits whom the mere glimpse of a woman's skirts can fire with a mortal passion. He made her his mistress, insisted on her leaving the stage, and loved her for four years with increasing intensity. In spite of the name he bore and the honourable traditions of his family, there can be little doubt that he would have married her, had he not suddenly discovered that she had been unfaithful to him for a long while with the very friend who had first brought them together.

The blow was the greater because she was already with child by him, and he was waiting only until the baby was born to take the fatal step of matrimony.

As soon as the necessary proofs were in his hands—letters found by accident in a drawer—he accused her of faithlessness, treachery, and vile behaviour, with all the brutality of his half-savage nature.

But she—an offscouring of the Paris streets, no less brazen than promiscuous, as sure of her power over the other man as over him, and with that passion for striking an attitude which has so often sent the women of the people to the barricades out of sheer bravado —outfaced and insulted him, and, when he threatened violence, played on the only too-obvious evidence of her condition.

When she did this, he stopped in his tirade and turned pale, appalled to think that a child of his was already growing in that tainted, that vile, that unclean body. He rushed at her, intent on crushing both mother and baby at a single blow, on annihilating his double shame. In sheer terror and despair, reeling under the blow he had already dealt her, and seeing his foot raised to kick her swollen belly and the living embryo within it, she stretched her hands to ward off the impending attack, and cried:

'Do not kill me! It is his, not yours!'

He staggered back, so dazed and stupefied, that his fury, like his foot, remained for a while suspended.

'What's that you say?'

Mad with fear, and seeing in his eyes and gestures the threat of imminent death, she said again:

'It is his, not yours!'

Half crazed by what he had heard, he muttered through clenched teeth:

'The child?'

'Yes.'

'That's a lie!'

Again he raised his foot, while his mistress, on her knees, trying to back away, kept babbling on:

'I tell you, it is his. If it were yours, should I not have had it long ago?'

This argument struck him as undoubted truth. In one of those flashes of revelation which, with blinding clarity, show evidence, formerly rejected, to be distinct, precise, irrefutable, conclusive, and irresistible, he stood convinced. He was certain now that he was indeed not the father of the wretched child this whore was carrying. Eased on a sudden, freed from his great burden and almost soothed, he felt the ebb of all desire to kill.

The Olive Grove

In a quieter voice, he said:

'Get up, and get out. I wish never to see you again.'

The victory was his, and she obeyed. She went away.

He never saw her again.

And he, too, went away, making for the south and for the sun, and stopped in a village standing in the middle of a valley dropping down to the Mediterranean. He took a fancy to the inn, which faced the sea. He settled down there. For eighteen months he stayed in agony of mind, despair, and utter isolation. His sole company was the memory of the woman who had betrayed him, of her charm, of all she had meant to him, of her unbelievable power to enchant his senses, of his longing for her presence and her ways of love.

He wandered through the valleys of Provence and, in that sun-lit air and in the cool shade of the grey olives, he still carried his monstrous obsession.

Gradually, the old pious faith which once was his, crept back into his lonely heart, though calmer now, less burning, less ecstatic. The religion which, in the old days, he had seen as a refuge from the yet unknown complexities of life, he saw now as an asylum from life's torments and disappointments. He had never lost the habit of prayer and to prayer he now clung in his pain. Often at dusk he knelt in the darkened church where the only light came from the distant flicker of the Sanctuary Lamp, that symbol of God's presence.

To that God, to his God, he confided all his misery. He sought counsel of Him, pity and help, protection, consolation. Into the prayers he said each day more fervently, he put an increasing weight of feeling.

His bruised heart, torn and tormented by the love of a woman, was still exposed and throbbing, still hungry for tenderness. Little by little, as the result of constant prayer, of living like a hermit subdued by a growing habit of devotion, of yielding himself to the secret communication which pious hearts can establish with that Saviour who can draw to Himself the unhappy, and bestow His comfort—the mystical love of God entered into him and overcame the other.

He turned back into the ways of his early manhood, and decided to make an offering to the Church of that now broken life which, in its virgin freshness, he had withheld.

He became a priest. Through family influence he succeeded in being made curé of that village in Provence where chance had cast him, and, having devoted to good works the major part of his fortune, keeping only just enough to enable him to live the rest of his life as a man who could be useful and helpful to the poor, he found a sanctuary in the quiet pursuit of pious practices, and in devoting all his days to the service of his neighbours.

His views might be narrow, but he was a good man, a religious guide with the temperament of a soldier, a guide in the service of the Church, driving by force into the strait and narrow way a blind and erring flock, lost in the forest of this world where all our instincts, all our tastes and our desires are so many false paths that lead astray.

But much of the former man still lived on in him. He still loved violent exercise, noble sports and the use of arms. Women he detested without exception, with the fear of a child threatened by some mysterious danger.

PART II

The fisherman who was following the priest was feeling the true southerner's itch to talk. But he dared not do so, for the abbé had great prestige with his flock. At last, however, he took the plunge.

'Getting along all right in your shack, Father?' he asked.

The shack in question was one of those tiny places in which the town-dwellers and villagers of Provence like to ensconce themselves during the summer months, so as to get a breath of fresh air. It stood in a field a bare five minutes from his presbytery, which was too stuffy for him and tucked away at the very centre of his parish, up against the wall of the church.

He did not regularly inhabit it, even in summer, but went there only for a few days at a time, now and then, to be among growing things, and to have a bit of pistol practice.

'Yes, my friend, it suits me very well,' said the priest.

They were now within sight of the low-built dwelling among the trees. It was painted pink, and was striped, speckled, and cut into small sections by the leaves and branches of the olive trees with which the unwalled field was planted. In that setting it looked like a Provençal mushroom.

A tall woman came in sight, moving about in front of the door, preparing a small table for dinner. She came and went with methodical slowness, laying a single place, and bringing out in turn a plate, a napkin, a piece of bread, a glass. She wore a little cap

The Olive Grove

of the kind favoured by the women of Arles, a small cone of black silk or velvet topped by a white mushroom of some material.

When the abbé was within earshot, he called to her:

'Hey, Marguerite!'

She stopped and stared, then, recognizing her master, answered: Oh, it's you, is it, Father.'

'Yes, indeed, and I've brought you a fine haul of fish. Hurry up and grill me this bass, bass in butter, nothing but butter, d'you hear?'

She had come to meet the couple, and was examining, with the eye of a connoisseur, the fish which the man was carrying.

'We've already got a chicken risotto,' she said.

'Never mind: fish kept overnight are not a patch on fish just out of the sea. I'm going to have a real blow-out this evening. That's something I don't often allow myself. Besides, it's a very small fish-sin.'

The woman picked out one of the bass, and, just as she was making off with it, turned her head to say:

'There's a man come looking for you, Father: been back three times.'

The abbé showed no interest in this piece of news.

'A man, you say? What sort of a man?'

'A man as I don't much like the look of.'

'A beggar?'

'May be, but I can't tell, looks more like a *maoufatan*!'

The Abbé Vilbois burst out laughing at this Provençal word, which means a no-good, a tramp, for he knew how timid Marguerite was, and that she could never stay for long in the shack without imagining, every day, and especially, every night, that they were bound to be murdered. He gave a few sous to the fisherman, who made off. Then, having retained some of the cleanly habits of a man of fashion: 'I'll just give my face and hands a sluice down,' he told her. But, just at that moment, Marguerite called from the kitchen, where she was scraping the bass with a knife, and removing the blood-speckled scales which looked like tiny pieces of silver:

'There he is!'

The abbé turned towards the road and saw a man who, from the distance, looked very badly dressed, walking slowly towards the house. He stood waiting, still smiling at his servant's fears, and thinking: I really do believe she was right: he certainly does look like a *maoufatan*.

The stranger showed no signs of being in a hurry, but was
sauntering along with his hands in his pockets. He was young, with
a full, curly, light-coloured beard. His hair hung down in ringlets
under his soft felt hat which was so dirty and battered that it was
impossible to say what its original shape and colour had been.
He was wearing a brown overcoat, trousers frayed at the ankles,
and rope-soled shoes. He moved in a quiet, stealthy manner, which
was rather disquieting, resembling, as it did, the secretive, slouching
walk of a tramp.

When he was a few steps from the priest, he removed the shapeless object from his head, uncovering with a slightly theatrical
gesture, and revealing a blotched and dirty, though well-shaped
skull, bald on top—the sign of a hard life or precocious debauchery,
for he could not have been more than twenty-five.

The abbé at once took off his own hat, for he had a feeling that
this was no ordinary vagrant, no mere out-of-work, no hardened
jail-bird on the road between stretches in prison, and incapable of
speaking anything but prison jargon.

'Good-day to you, Father,' said the man. The priest replied with
an unadorned 'Good day', not feeling inclined to address this
doubtful ragged intruder as 'sir'. The two men stood staring at one
another, and, under the scrutiny of this tramp, the Abbé Vilbois
felt curiously uneasy. He was conscious of a slight shiver, as though
the man were an unknown enemy.

After a long pause, the visitor said:

'D'you recognize me?'

The priest, in some surprise, replied:

'Certainly not: I have never seen you before.'

'No idea who I am, eh? Take a good look.'

'No matter how hard I look, I still do not recognize you. I have
never seen you.'

'True enough,' said the other, and there was a note of mockery
in his voice: 'but I'll show you someone you know a deal better.'

He put on his hat again and unbuttoned his coat, displaying a
naked chest. A red sash wound round his flat stomach kept his
trousers up.

He took an envelope from his pocket, an envelope so worn and
dirty, so blotched with stains of every kind, as to be almost unbelievable: one of those envelopes which vagrants carry about
with them in the lining of their clothes, containing such papers as
they have, genuine or faked, stolen or legitimate, and which form
their only protection against the curiosity of chance-met constables.

The Olive Grove

From the envelope he took a photograph. It was about the size of a piece of writing-paper, and of a kind once popular. It was yellow with age, stained and faded, as a result of having been carried for years inside the man's clothing with its face to his sweating body.

He held it up on a level with his face. 'Doesn't that do anything to stir your memory?'

The abbé took two steps forward, the better to examine the picture, and remained rooted to the spot, pale and shaken, for it was a portrait of himself, taken for Her, in the far-off heyday of their love.

Not knowing what his visitor was after, he said nothing.

The tramp repeated his question: 'Doesn't that remind you of someone?'

'It does,' said the priest, deeply disturbed.

'Who's it of?'

'Me.'

'Quite sure of that?'

'Quite sure.'

'Now take a good look at the two of us, your picture and me—well?'

The unhappy priest had already noted the resemblance. The man portrayed in the photograph, and the grinning creature who held it in his hand, were as like as two brothers. But still he did not understand.

'What do you want of me?' he stammered.

There was a vicious ring in the other's voice:

'All in good time, all in good time. First, I want you to say you recognize me.'

'Who are you?'

'Who am I? Ask the first person you meet; ask that skivvy of yours, ask the mayor—and show 'em this picture. I don't mind betting they'll laugh in your face . . . Not too keen about recognizing your darling son, eh—dear Father-daddy?'

The older man, raising his arms in a gesture of biblical denial, groaned:

'That is not true!'

The young scallywag came close to him, and they stood with their faces almost touching.

'So it's not true, that's your line, is it? Lying'll do you no good, Father.'

His looks were threatening and his fists were clenched. He spoke with so violent a conviction that the priest, backing away from him, found himself wondering which of the two of them was wrong.

In a firm voice, he said:

'I have never had a child.'

'And no mistress, either, I suppose you'll say?'

In a tone that was resolute and almost proud, the priest replied:

'Certainly I had a mistress.'

'And I don't suppose she happened to be in the family way when you showed her the door?'

Suddenly, the fury of that long-dead day, which had lain stifled within him for twenty-five years, or not so much stifled as smouldering in the lover's heart, burst through the vaulted fabric of his faith, of the resignation, the devotion which he had raised on that foundation, of what he had thought of as his complete resignation, and, beside himself, he shouted:

'I showed her the door, as you call it, because she had deceived me, because she was carrying the child of another! But for that, I should have killed her, Monsieur, and you with her!'

The younger man hesitated, surprised, in his turn, by the sincerity of the curé's passion. When, at last, he spoke again, it was in a quieter voice:

'Who said it was someone else's kid?'

'She did . . . To save her life.'

The tramp, without so much as challenging this statement, clinched the matter in the disinterested fashion of a young tough delivering judgment in a street-brawl.

'Well, then, my dear mama got things wrong, that's all I can say.'

The priest had by this time pulled himself together after the first outburst of his anger. It was he now who did the questioning.

'And who told *you* that you were my son?'

'She did, when she kicked the bucket, Father: and there was this, don't forget . . .'

He held the photograph close in front of the priest's eyes.

The abbé took it from him, and looked at it long and silently, with an aching heart, comparing his casual visitor with his own portrait of long ago. He could no longer doubt that he was, indeed, his son.

Misery flooded in upon him, an emotion for which he could find no words, as searing as remorse for some long-buried crime. He understood a little, guessed the rest. That brutal scene of separation was still vivid to the eyes of memory. To save her life from the fury of an outraged lover, that lying, treacherous woman had flung a lie full in his teeth. It had succeeded, and unknown to him a son had been born, had grown up, had become this squalid haunter of hedges and ditches, with about him a stench of depravity as strong as the animal reek of a goat.

In a low voice he said:

'Suppose we take a little walk, and get this matter clear?'

The other burst out laughing:

'What d'you think I came here for?'

They moved off side by side through the olive-grove. The sun had gone down. The evening freshness of these southern lands had spread a chill, invisible cloak over the countryside. The abbé shivered, and raising his eyes in that manner of the celebrant which had become second nature with him, saw all about him, suddenly, trembling against the sky, the grey leaves of the sacred tree which had once witnessed the supreme agony, the unique moment of weakness, of the Christ.

A prayer welled up within him, a short and despairing prayer, spoken by that inner voice which never passes the barrier of the lips, and is the utterance of all believers when they call upon their God for help.

Then, turning to his son:

'So your mother is dead?'

A fresh wave of misery broke over him as he formed those words, and stormed upon his heart; a strange anguish of the flesh in the body of a man who had never forgotten, a cruel recrudescence of the torment he had once suffered, but something more, too, now that she was dead, a momentary starting into life of that short and heady happiness of which nothing now remained but the still aching scar of memory.

The young man answered:

'Yes, Father, my mother is dead.'

'Is it long since she died?'

'Three years.'

A new doubt swept over the priest.

'Why did you not try to find me sooner?'

The other had a moment's hesitation.

'I couldn't . . . There were difficulties. I'll tell you all about that later, if you want me to, but not now. You see, I haven't had a bite of food since yesterday morning.'

Pity caught at the older man, and he suddenly stretched out both his hands:

'Oh! my poor boy!' he said.

The wastrel took the great hands which closed round his thin, hot fingers. Then he answered with that sardonic note in his voice which scarcely ever left it:

'Somehow I think we shall come to an understanding!'

The curé resumed his walking.

'Let us have dinner,' he said, remembering suddenly, with a little confused thrill of pleasure, the fine fish he had caught. That, with the chicken risotto, would make a good meal for the wretched youth.

His servant, who was feeling anxious, and had already begun to grumble, stood waiting at the door.

'Marguerite!' cried the abbé: 'take the table indoors at once, and lay another place. Hurry!'

She was aghast at the thought that her master should eat with such an obvious bad lot.

Then, the Abbé Vilbois started, with his own hands, to strip the table and carry the preparations for his solitary dinner into the only room on the ground-floor of the shack.

Five minutes later, he was seated opposite the tramp with a great tureen of cabbage soup between them, from which rose a cloud of steam.

PART III

When the soup had been ladled into the two plates, the down-and-out began to gulp spoonful after spoonful with the voracious appetite of a starving man. The abbé no longer felt hungry, and merely sipped a little of the appetizing broth, leaving the bread untouched at the bottom of his plate.

Suddenly, he asked:

'What is your name?'

The man grinned, pleased to have food before him.

'Father unknown,' he said. 'No surname but my mother's, which I don't expect you've forgotten. On the other hand, I've two first-names, which, by the way, don't somehow suit me very well—"Philippe-Auguste" . . .'

The priest went very pale, and said, with a choking sensation in his throat:

'Why were they given to you?'

The other shrugged:

'Can't you guess? After you cleared off, my dear mother wanted to make the other chap think I was his. And it worked fine and dandy till I was fifteen. But then I began to look like you. Awkward that was! So the swine wouldn't have anything to do with me. Those two names were his, and if I'd been lucky enough to look like no one in particular, or just been the side-blow of a third chump as no one knew about, I'd be swaggering round today as the Vicomte Philippe-Auguste de Pravallon, acknowledged a bit late in the day by the count and senator of the same name, as his son. My own name for myself is "No-Luck." '

'How do you come to know all this?'

'Oh, there was quite a lot of having-things-out when I was listening—and pretty rough stuff it was, I give you my word! That way I learnt a lot about life!'

Something still more painful, something with an even sharper edge than anything he had as yet experienced, struck at the priest. He felt as though he were suffocating. It was beginning now, and would go on getting worse and worse until at last it killed him. It was caused not so much by the things he was learning, as by the way in which those things were said, and by the dissolute face of the young tough who would clearly spare him nothing. He was aware now, between himself and this man, between himself and his son, of a running sewer of moral filth such as, on some people, acts like a mortal poison. Was this really his son? Even now he could scarcely believe it. He wanted to be given every available scrap of proof. He wanted to be told everything, to hear everything, to be spared no suffering. His thoughts went again to the olive trees growing around his little house, and, for the second time, he murmured: 'Help me, O God! Help me!'

Philippe-Auguste had finished his soup:

'Is that all the grub there's going to be, abbé?'

The kitchen being outside in an adjacent shed from which Marguerite could not hear the curé's voice, he communicated his requirements by means of a Chinese gong hanging on the wall behind him.

He took up the leather-padded stick which he used for the purpose, and struck the round metal surface several times. The sound was low at first, then grew and spread, loud, vibrant, shrill, shriller, rending, horrible, the lamentation of beaten brass.

His servant appeared. Her face was twisted in a grimace, and she directed a furious look at the *maoufatan*, as though, like a faithful dog, she could smell the drama which had struck her master down. She was carrying the grilled bass in a dish, from which came a delicious smell of melted butter. The abbé took a spoon, divided the fish lengthways, and gave the top slice to the child of his youth.

'I caught this an hour or two ago,' said he, for a remnant of pride still floated on the surface of his misery.

Marguerite did not move.

The priest turned to her:

'Bring some wine, good wine, the white Cap Corse.'

She made a gesture expressive almost of revolt, and he had to repeat his instructions, this time with a stern look.

'Don't stand there! Go and fetch the wine, two bottles.'

Whenever he offered wine to a visitor—a not-too-frequent pleasure—he always treated himself to a bottle.

By this time, Philippe-Auguste was beaming:

'Damme, if that isn't a first-rate notion!' he said. 'It's a long time since I had a tuck-in like this!'

At the end of two minutes, Marguerite came back with the wine. They had seemed to the abbé two eternities. The craving to know, to know everything, was burning in him like hell-fire.

The bottles had already been uncorked, but the woman stood where she was, her eyes fixed on the stranger.

'Leave us,' said the curé.

She pretended not to have heard.

He said again, almost harshly:

'I told you to leave us!'

Then she went.

Philippe-Auguste got through the fish with startling speed, while his father looked at him, more and more surprised and harrowed by the signs of debasement and depravity which he could read in the face so like his own. Such small scraps of food as he carried to his mouth, remained there, for the constriction of his throat made swallowing impossible. He sat there, chewing, seeking, from all the questions which had come into his mind, the one to which he most desired an answer.

At last, he murmured:

'What did she die of?'

'Lungs.'

'Was she ill for long?'

'About eighteen months.'

'How did she get that sickness?'

'Can't say.'

They stopped talking. The abbé was deep in thought. So many

things lay heavy on his mind about which, for a long time, he had wanted to know. Since the day of that final break, the day when he had very nearly killed her, he had heard nothing. True, at that time, he had not wanted to know, for by a great effort of will he had thrust her, and everything to do with her, into a deep pit of forgetfulness, and all memory of his time of happiness. But now, suddenly, since she was dead, he felt the birth in himself of a fierce wish to know, of something like jealousy, of a lover's desire.

He went on:

'She was not alone, was she?'

'No, she was still sticking to him.'

The priest winced at the words.

'With Pravallon?'

'Of course.'

The man who had been betrayed was brooding, now, over the thought that this same woman who had been unfaithful to him, had lived for more than twenty years with his rival.

Almost in spite of himself, he said:

'Were they happy?'

The answer came with a sneering laugh:

'I suppose you could call it that, though, mark you, they had their ups and their downs. They'd have got along fine if it hadn't been for me. I spoilt everything.'

'How and why?'

'I've told you already: because he'd thought I was his kid, till I was about fifteen. But he's no fool, that old bastard: didn't need any prodding to see the likeness, and then—were there fun and games! Used to tell poor old mum that she'd done the dirty on him. But she wouldn't stand for that! "Don't you start putting it on me," she'd say. "You knew well enough when you took up with me that there'd been someone else," the someone else being you.'

'So they spoke about me sometimes?'

'Not in front of me, they didn't, except at the end—the very end, before she kicked it, when she knew she was dying. They were careful not to say too much, though!'

'And what about you? . . . You had found out fairly early on, I imagine, that she was leading an irregular life?'

'Hell! What d'you take me for, a softy? No one can say I wasn't always as sharp as a needle. Besides, things like that stick out a mile, to anyone, that is, who knows the world.'

Philippe-Auguste was emptying glass after glass. His eyes were shining. He had been under-nourished for so long that the wine went to his head at once.

The priest noticed this, and was about to restrain him when he remembered that drink makes men incautious and loosens their tongues. Taking the bottle, he refilled the other's glass.

Marguerite brought in the risotto. Having put it on the table, she gave the tramp a long look, and then said to her master indignantly:

'Can't you see he's drunk, Father?'

'Leave us alone, and go away,' said the priest.

She went out, slamming the door behind her.

'What did your mother say about me?' he asked.

'What women always say about the bloke they've chucked— that you weren't easy to get on with, that you were a bore, and had got all sorts of ideas which made life difficult.'

'Did she say that often?'

'Yes, but sometimes in a hidden sort of way, so's I shouldn't cotton on. But it didn't take me long to guess what she meant!'

'And how were you treated?'

'Me? Pretty well at first, but very bad later on. When mum realized that I was spoiling everything, she just dropped me overboard.'

'How do you mean?'

'Wasn't difficult: I was a bit wild at sixteen, and, damme, if that pair of you-know-what's didn't send me to a reformatory, just to get me out of the way!'

He propped his elbows on the table, with his face between his hands. By this time he was so completely drunk, that his wits were all over the place, and he was suddenly seized with one of those irresistible cravings to talk about himself, which set old soaks boasting and swaggering in the most extravagant manner. There was a curious charm about his smile, a feminine charm, a depraved charm which the priest recognized only too well. Not only did he recognize it, but felt again the hateful and cajoling attraction which had swept him off his feet long years ago, and been his ruin. It was his mother now that the man resembled, not in his features so much as in the expression of his face, at once utterly false yet strangely entrancing, and especially the beguiling quality of his lying smile which seemed to open the door to all the baseness concealed within him.

Philippe-Auguste launched out on the story of his life.

'I've seen a thing or two, and pretty odd things, too, since those old reformatory days. Some of those novel-writing chaps'd pay a pretty penny for what *I've* seen. I bet old Dumas never put anything funnier into *Monte-Cristo* than some of the things that have happened to me!'

He broke off, and sat with the solemn, philosophic look of the drunkard plunged in thought. Then, more slowly, he went on:

'Take my 'dvice and don't send any kid o' yours to a 'formatory, not if you want to see 'm go right, because of the pals he picks up there—never! no matter what he's done. I got a good idea once, but it went wrong. I was having a bit of a lark with three blokes, a bit lit up we were—all four of us—one night round about nine, on the road at the Folac Ferry, when what should come along but a carriage with every dam' soul in it doggo—the driver and his family, from Martinon they were, coming back from a bit of a spree in town. So I laid hold of the horse by the bridle, got the whole boiling on to the ferry-boat, and gave it a bit of a push into the middle of the river. Made a noise, it did, and the chap who was driving woke up. But he couldn't see anything, so he flogged away at the old nag, and bang it went over the side into the water. Drowned they were—the whole blooming lot. My pals split on me, though they'd fair laughed 'emselves sick over my little joke. We hadn't thought it'd turn out like that, we only meant to give 'em a ducking, just for fun.

'I've done worse things since then, just t' get me own back for being treated in a way I didn't deserve. But I won't tell you all 'bout them, 'cept only the last. You'll like that one, I bet. Paid off *your* little score, daddy, that I did!'

The abbé looked at his son with terror in his eyes. He had given up all attempt to eat.

Philippe-Auguste started off again:

'No,' said the priest: 'not now, later on.'

He turned round and hammered at the clanging Chinese gong. Marguerite came at once.

Her master spoke so roughly that she hung her head, frightened and docile.

'Bring the lamp and anything else you've got for the table, and then don't show your nose again until I sound the gong.'

She went away, and returned, carrying a white china lamp with a green shade, which she put on the table, together with a piece of cheese and some fruit. Then she made off.

In a determined voice, the abbé said:

'Now I'm listening.'

Philippe-Auguste leisurely piled some fruit on his plate, and filled his glass. The second bottle was almost empty, though the curé had barely touched a drop.

The young man, his mouth clogged with food and drink, spluttered once again into words.

'I warn you—it was a bit tough. I went back home . . . And I stayed there, 'spite of 'em . . . They were 'fraid o' me . . . *really* 'fraid, they were . . . Bad thing to get in wrong wi' me . . . When chap gets in wrong wi' me . . . no knowing wot'll do . . . They were livin' together and not together, if you take me. Had two homes, he did—senator's home an' lil love-nest—but was more with mum than at t'other place . . . Couldn't do without her . . . She was a one was mum! . . . Talk o' keeping tags on a man! She'd got him, body an' soul, and kep' him too, right to the end. Bloody fools men are! So back I went, and frightened 'em into doing what I wanted . . . Got me wits 'bout me, I have! . . . No one like me there isn't, for tricks and dodges an' bashing . . . Well, mum got ill, an' he put her in a lovely place he's got out Meulan way, in the middle of a park big as a forest . . . Lasted 'bout eighteen months as I told you . . . When we knew it couldn't be long now, he used to come from Paris ev'ry day. Proper cut up, he was, an' that's the truth.

'One morning they'd been jabbering away for 'bout a hour, and I was wondering what it were all headed for, when I was called in. Mum said to me:

' "I'm goin' to die," she said. "There's something I've got to tell you, though the count doesn't want me to," she said, "and that is, the name o' your pa, who's still living."

'I'd asked her over and over . . name o' my pa . . . but she woul'n't let on . . . I r'member once when I lammed into her good and proper just to make her, but it wasn't any good. Then she told me how you'd hopped it without a penny, but that that didn't matter anyway, because you were nothing but a mistake of her youth, a young girl's error . . . Did it so well too, that I swallowed the lot . . . So she ups and says:

' "It's your father's name I'm going to tell you."

'Then the other bloke who was sitting in a armchair, said three times:

' "You're wrong, Rosette, wrong, wrong."

' Mum was propped up in bed . . . I can see her now, red cheekbones and her eyes all bright. Y'see, she was fond o' me, and——

' "Do something for 'm, Philippe," she said.

'When she was a-talking to him, she always called him Philippe an' me Auguste. Then he started shouting like a loony:

' "Damned if I do anything for that piece o' dirt! . . . for that no-good, that gaol-bird . . . that . . . that . . ."

'The things he called me! . . . Might 'a been spending all's life thinking 'em up!

'I was getting a bit wild, but mum shut me up . . . an' got going with him again:

' "D'you want 'm to starve to death? You know I've got nothing."

'Then he answered, all calm and smooth-like:

' "Rosette, I've given you thirty-five thousand francs a year, for thirty years—more'n million all told. You've lived the life of a rich woman at my expense, of a dearly loved woman, and a happy one. I owe nothing to this young scamp who has ruined our last years together, and nothing's what he's going to get. It's no use your going on about it," he said. "Tell 'm the other fellow's name, if you want to, though I'd rather you didn't, but I've washed my hands of the whole business."

'Then ma turned to me, an' I thought to meself . . . good, I'm going to find out my real name . . . If dad's got any dough, I'm sitting pretty . . .

'Then she went on:

' "Your father, the Baron de Vilbois, now goes by the name of the Abbé Vilbois. He's curé of Garandou, near Toulon. He was my lover before I left 'm for this man."

'And then she told me everything, except the bit about her lying over the kid she was going to have. But women never tell the whole truth.'

He sniggered, quite unconcerned at pouring out all the filth that was in him. He took another drink, and, with a grin still on his face, continued:

'Mum died two days later . . . We went with 'er to the cemet'ry, him and me . . . Odd, isn't it, him and me and three servants . . . No one else . . . And he cried like an old cow . . . We were side by side . . . Anyone'd've said daddy and daddy's boy.

'Then we went back to the house, just the two of us. Said I to meself, "It's the pay-off for you, m' lad, and not a penny piece in your pocket." I'd got just fifty francs, and I was wondering what I could do t' get m' own back.

'He touched me on the arm:

' "There's something," said he, "I've got to say to you."

'So I followed him into 's study, and down he sits at his table, all muddled-like and snivelling, and said he didn't want to be as hard on me as he'd let on to mum. He said not to worry you . . . "It's just something 'tween you and me," he says . . . an' he offers me a thousand-franc note . . . What the hell use to me was a thousand? . . . I'd noticed there was a lot more in a drawer, a great pile of 'em . . . an' the sight of all that dough made me want to do 'm in. I put out a hand for the one'd offered me, but 'stead of taking that little bit o' charity, I jumps on top of 'm, throws 'im to the floor, and squeezes his windpipe till 's eyes begin to pop, and then, when I sees he's about to peg out, I gags 'm, ties 'm up, strips 'm starko, rolls 'm over, and then . . . Ha! Ha! Ha! . . . I gets your own back on 'm! . . .'

Philippe-Auguste spluttered, half choking with delight at the memory, and in the curl of that cruel and mocking lip, the Abbé Vilbois saw the smile of the woman who had once made him lose his head.

'And then?' he prompted.

'Then . . . Ha! Ha! Ha! . . . There was a great fire in the grate . . . It was December . . . cold weather . . . Mum had died of it . . . a great coal fire . . . So I gets the poker red-hot . . . an' I makes a lot of crosses on 's back . . . don't know how many, then I rolls 'm over and does the same on 's belly . . . Good joke, daddy, eh? . . . Same as they used to brand criminals . . . He squirmed like an eel, but I'd gagged 'm good and proper, an' he couldn't so much as squeak . . . Then I took the notes, twelve of 'em . . . with the one I had that made thirteen . . . but they didn't bring me no luck. Then I cleared out, see?—Told the skivvies not to 'sturb him till dinner-time, seeing his nibs was having a bit o' shut-eye. I thought how he wouldn't say anything 'cos of the scandal, him being a senator and all, but I was wrong. Four days later I was nabbed in a Paris restaurant, an' got three years. That's why I couldn't look you up sooner.'

He took another drink, and, when he spoke again could barely get the words out:

'So now . . . daddy . . . daddy-curé . . . Funny have curé as daddy . . . You better be nice . . . nice t' yours truly . . . 'Cos yours truly's no ornary bloke . . . An' played a nice trick on th' old genelman . . .'

The same fury which had once swept the Abbé Vilbois off his feet in that last scene with his lying mistress, surged up again at the sight of this loathsome creature.

He who, in the name of God, had pardoned so many infamies whispered to him in the privacy of the confessional, now felt himself to be without pity or mercy in his own. He could no longer call to his aid the all-merciful God, for he knew now that for those on whom such horrors have fallen, there is no protection in heaven or upon earth.

All the fervour of his passionate heart, all the violence in his blood, temporarily extinguished though it had been by his priestly office, rose in irresistible revolt against the wretch who was his son, who looked so like him and so like his mother, that miserable mother who had conceived him in her own image, and against the fatality which had fastened this ruffian to his father's feet like the weight round the ankle of a galley-slave.

In a sudden lucid flash of vision, brutally awakened from his twenty-five years of tranquillity and slumber, he saw what lay ahead.

Convinced, on a sudden, that he must speak in no uncertain tones if he was to awaken terror in the wretch before him, he said, through teeth clenched in fury, and quite forgetful of the other's drunkenness:

'You have told your story: now, listen to me. You will leave this house tomorrow morning. You will settle in some place of my choosing, and not leave it without permission from me. I will make you an allowance large enough to keep you alive, but only just, for I have no money. If you disobey me even once, this arrangement will come to an end, and you will have me to reckon with . . .'

Stupefied by wine though he was, Philippe-Auguste was still capable of taking in the threat. All the criminal in him came rushing to the surface. Between hiccups, he spat his answer in the other's face.

'You can't do that to me, daddy . . . You're a priest . . . I've got you where I want you . . . And you'll come quiet, like the others did!'

The abbé gave a start. The muscles of the old Hercules longed to take this monster by the throat, to bend him like a stick until he cried for mercy.

He drove the table against the other's chest, and shouted:

'Take care! Take care! I'm afraid of nobody!'

The drunkard lost his balance and swayed on his feet. Feeling that he was about to fall, that he was in the priest's power, he stretched out his hand, with murder in his eyes, with the intention of snatching up one of the knives from the table. But the Abbé Vilbois saw what he was up to, and gave the table such a shove that his son fell on his back, at full length on the floor. The lamp toppled to the ground and went out.

For a few seconds the noise of crashing glasses filled the darkness; then there was the sound of a body softly crawling, then nothing.

The breaking of the lamp had brought black night upon them so suddenly, so unexpectedly, that they were as dazed as they would have been in the presence of some catastrophic occurrence. The drunkard, wedged against the wall, made no movement. The priest, still in his chair, was plunged in an obscurity which pressed in upon, and muffled his anger. Darkness had checked the movement of his passion and stayed the fury in his heart. His mind was busy now with other thoughts as sad and sombre as the sharp descent of blackest night.

Silence, too, had come with darkness, that clogging silence of the grave in which nothing lives nor breathes. Not a sound came from beyond the house, no rumble of distant wheels, not the barking of a dog, not the rustling of branches, not the light whisper of the breeze.

And so it continued for a long, a very long while, perhaps for an hour. Then, with shattering suddenness the gong sounded, as though in response to a single powerful blow. It was followed by the odd, irrelevant noise of an overturned chair crashing to the ground.

Marguerite, already on the alert, came hurrying to see what had happened, but, having opened the door, hastily drew back, terrified by the impenetrable blackness of the room. Trembling in every limb, and with her heart pounding, she called in a low and breathless voice:

'M'sieu le curé, mon'sieu le curé, it is me, it is Marguerite!'

No one answered, nothing moved.

Dear God, she thought, what have they been doing, what has happened?

She dared not go in, she dared not fetch a light. A mad longing came over her to take to her heels, to shout, to run, though she felt her legs quaking beneath her. Then she called again:

'M'sieu le curé, m'sieu le curé, it is me, it is Marguerite!'

Then suddenly, in spite of her fear, she felt an instinctive need to help her master. She was supported and stiffened by that spirit of extreme recklessness which can so often turn perfectly ordinary

women into heroines. She ran to the kitchen and came back with a light.

She stopped on the threshold. The first thing she saw was the body of the tramp lying along the wall, asleep or apparently asleep. Then her attention was drawn to the smashed lamp under the table, and, a moment later, to the feet and black-stockinged legs of the Abbé Vilbois, who must have fallen on his back and struck the gong with his head.

Shaking with terror, she said aloud:

'Dear God! what has happened!'

Then, as she took a few slow steps into the room, she slipped on something sticky, and almost fell.

Bending down, she saw that over the surface of the red tiles, something, also red, was oozing, spreading round her feet and moving quickly in the direction of the door. She guessed that it was blood.

Mad with terror, she turned and ran, throwing away the light she held, so as to see no more. She rushed from the house and made for the village, bumping against the trees, her eyes fixed upon the distant lights, and screaming at the top of her voice.

Her shrill cries sped through the darkness like the sinister hootings of an owl, and, as she ran, she kept on shouting—'le *maoufatan* . . . le *maoufatan*! . . . le *maoufatan*! . . .'

As soon as she reached the first houses she was surrounded by a group of frightened men. But she struck out blindly, not answering their questions, not knowing what she was doing.

At last, they gathered that something terrible had happened at the curé's, and an armed party was hurriedly assembled to go to his aid.

The little pink-washed shack in the middle of the olive-grove, was almost invisible, a patch of deeper blackness in the black and silent night. Now that its one lit window had gone out like an eye shutting, it stood swamped in darkness, lost in obscurity, so that no one who was not a native of the place could have found his way to it.

Lights were moving now at ground level, coming towards it through the trees. They threw long yellow beams across the burned-up grass, and, in the wavering radiance of the advancing lanterns, the twisted trunks of the olives looked sinister and frightful, looked like a writhing tangle of snakes from hell. The rays penetrated forward to a considerable distance and suddenly revealed something whitish, something shadowy emerging from the darkness. In another moment the low wall of the squat building showed in its natural pink, caught in the beams of the lanterns carried by a few peasants acting as escort to two gendarmes, revolvers in hand, the mayor, and Marguerite, in a state of collapse and supported by some of the men.

In front of the open, terrifying door there was a moment's hesitation. Then, the police sergeant, snatched one of the lanterns and entered the house, followed by the others.

The old servant had not been lying. Blood, now congealed, lay like a carpet on the flags. It had reached the tramp, soaked into one of his trouser legs, and smeared one of his hands.

Father and son lay sleeping, the one, with his throat cut, in the sleep of death, the other, in a drunken stupor. The two constables flung themselves upon the latter, and, before he was full awake, had slipped the handcuffs on his wrists. He rubbed his eyes, his wits still thick with drink. When he saw the body of the priest, a terrified, uncomprehending look showed in his eyes.

'Why didn't he clear off?' said the mayor.

'Too drunk,' replied the sergeant.

The others agreed with him. It never occurred to any of them that the Abbé Vilbois might have taken his own life.

(14–23 February 1890)

Useless Beauty

A SMART victoria, drawn by two magnificent black horses, stood waiting at the front steps of a great town-house. It was half-past five o'clock of an afternoon in late June, and between the roofs that hedged the courtyard, the sky was drenched in light, warmth, and gaiety.

The Comtesse de Mascaret appeared at the front door, just as her husband, who was on his way home, came through the carriage entrance. He stopped for a moment to look at his wife, and turned slightly pale. She was very beautiful: slim, distinguished-looking, with a long, oval face which had the golden colour of old ivory, large grey eyes, and black hair. She got into the carriage without paying the least attention to him, without seeming even to have noticed him, and so eloquent of high breeding were her move ments, that the vile jealousy which had been gnawing at him for so long, brought, once again, a sharp pang to his heart.

He went straight up to her and bowed:

'You are going driving?'

Her face, as she answered briefly, showed disdain:

'That, surely, is obvious!'

'To the Bois?'

'Not improbably.'

'Have I permission to accompany you?'

'This is your carriage.'

He gave no sign of surprise at the tone of her voice, but got in and sat down beside her. Then he said to the coachman:

'The Bois.'

The groom clambered on to the box-seat, and the horses, as usual, pawed the ground and tossed their heads before turning in the required direction.

Husband and wife sat side by side without exchanging a word. He tried to think of something to say, but her expression was so hard and hostile that he did not dare to speak. After a while he made a cautious movement with his fingers towards the countess's gloved hand, and touched it, as though by accident. But her gesture of withdrawal was so quick and so expressive of disgust that

303

he was overcome with embarrassment, commanding and despotic though he was by nature.

'Gabrielle!' he murmured.

She did not turn her head.

'What is it that you want?'

'I find you quite adorable.'

She made no answer, but leaned back in the carriage with the air of an outraged queen.

They were driving up the Champs-Elysées towards the Arc de Triomphe. The towering monument at the far end of the long avenue was framed in a great blaze of reddened sky. The sun seemed to be setting full upon it, misting the horizon with a golden dust.

The flood of carriages, catching little dazzles of light on gilt and silver harness and the glass of lamps, moved in two parallel streams—one, outward to the Bois, the other, inward to the city.

The Comte de Mascaret tried again:

'My dear Gabrielle!'

Her patience was worn to a thread, and she answered irritably:

'Oh! do, I beg you, leave me alone! Have things come to such a pass between us that I may not even enjoy the privacy of my carriage undisturbed?'

He pretended not to have heard her, and continued:

'You have never looked more charming than you do today.'

She was, most certainly, at the end of her endurance, for she answered him now with an anger she made no attempt to conceal:

'It is unfortunate that you should think so, for I swear that I will never again let you come near me!'

He was so completely dumbfounded and amazed, that his natural violence got the better of him:

'What the devil do you mean!' he burst out, and the manner of his speech revealed more of the brutal master than the lover.

In a low voice, though the two men on the box could hear nothing through the deafening rumble of the wheels, she shot at him:

'What the devil! There speaks the man I have learned to know! Do you really wish me to tell you?'

'Yes.'

'Everything?'

'Yes.'

'All that has been in my mind since I became the victim of your savage egotism?'

Astonishment and annoyance had turned his face a fiery red. Through clenched teeth, he muttered:

'Go on!'

He was tall and broad-shouldered, with a great red beard, a fine-looking man, a man of good birth, a man of the world, who had the reputation of being a perfect husband and an excellent father.

For the first time since they had left the house, she turned her head and looked him straight in the eyes.

'You will not like what you are going to hear, but you may as well know that I do not care, that I am afraid of nothing now, least of all of you!'

He returned her look: he was already trembling with anger.

'You must be mad!' he muttered.

'No, I am not mad, but I refuse any longer to endure the odious torment of that perpetual breeding which for eleven years you have imposed upon me! I want to live the life I have a right to, the life that all women have a right to!'

His former pallor had returned.

'I don't understand you,' he stammered.

'Oh, yes, you do! It is three months now since my last child was born, and, since I am still beautiful and, in spite of your efforts, have not yet lost my figure—as you realized just now when you saw me standing on the steps—you think it high time that I should once again be pregnant!'

'You are out of your mind!'

'No: I am thirty. I have got seven children. We have been married for eleven years, and it is your intention that this state of affairs shall go on for a further ten years, by the end of which time you will have ceased to be jealous!'

He gripped her arm:

'I refuse to allow you to talk to me like that!'

'I shall talk like that for just as long as I wish, until I have said all I have to say. If you try to stop me, I shall raise my voice sufficiently to be heard by our two servants on the box. I let you come with me for that purpose only, for here I have witnesses whose presence will compel you to listen and to control your temper. I have never had any fondness for you, as I have always made perfectly clear, nor, whatever I may be, am I a liar. I never wanted to marry you, but you forced my parents' hands. They were poor, and you are very rich. They made me consent, though I cried my heart out.

'Not to put too fine a point upon it, you bought me, and, as soon as I was in your power, as soon as I began to show signs of being a dutiful wife, of forgetting your methods of intimidation and coercion, and remembering only that I ought to love you so far as it was possible for me to do so, you turned jealous, more jealous than any man has ever been. You spied upon me. Your behaviour was base, ignoble—degrading for you, insulting for me. We had not been married for eight months before you began suspecting me of every sort of treachery to you. And you let me know it! You could scarcely have sunk lower! And, since you could not prevent me from being beautiful and attractive, from being known in the world and in the newspapers as being one of the loveliest women in Paris, you did everything you could to keep me beyond the reach of compliments, and conceived the abominable plan of putting me out of harm's way by ensuring that I should be in a condition of almost perpetual pregnancy, until at last, no other man would want to look at me! It is useless for you to deny it. For a long time I did not understand what was happening: then, I guessed. You even boasted to your sister of what you were doing. She passed it on, for she is devoted to me and revolted by your boorish brutality.

'Cast your mind back to the fights we had, to the number of doors you broke down, of the locks you forced! For eleven years you have condemned me to live the life of a brood-mare on a studfarm! Then, as soon as you had got me with child, you, too, regarded me as an object of disgust, and, for months on end, I never saw you. I was sent to your family's house in the country, and put out to grass until the baby was born. After that blessed event, I was allowed to return. And I did return, fresh, beautiful, indestructible. Men once more found me attractive: I was surrounded by admirers. I hoped that, at last, I might be allowed to live as a rich young woman with an assured place in society expects to live. But then your jealousy flared up again and you pursued me with the same vile and hateful desire which you are feeling at this very moment, here, beside me! What you want is not to possess me— I would never have refused myself to you—but to make me ugly!

'There is another abominable thing of which you are guilty, a thing so mysterious that it took a long time for me to realize it, though I did, eventually, for I have developed a pretty sharp nose where your thoughts and actions are concerned. You began to cling to your children, not for their own sakes, but because they had made you feel safe all the while that I was carrying them. Your love for them has been born of your aversion to me, of the ignoble fears from which you suffer, which they had been able momentarily to subdue, of the satisfaction you felt whenever you saw my body become shapeless.

'Oh! how often have I been aware of that satisfaction in you! I could read it in your eyes, I could guess at it. You love your children as the symbols of victory, not as human beings in whose veins your own blood runs! They represent your triumphs over me, over my youth, my beauty, my charm; over the compliments I was paid, and those others, too, which were whispered among my friends, though they never reached my ears. And you are proud of all this! You make a point of being seen with your children. You take them for drives in the Bois, and for donkey rides at Montmorency. You go with them to matinées, so that people may say "What a good father!" and talk about the good father to everyone they meet! . . .'

His grasp upon her wrist was now so savagely brutal that she had to stop speaking in order to keep back a cry of pain.

In a very low voice, he said to her:

'I love my children, do you hear! What you have just been saying is a disgraceful confession for any mother to make. But you belong to me! . . . I am the master . . . Your master . . . I can insist on having from you what I want, and when I want it . . . I have the law on my side.'

He attempted to crush her fingers in his vice-like grip. Livid with pain, she tried, though unsuccessfully, to withdraw them from the intolerable pressure. She was panting for breath, and there were tears in her eyes.

'I hope you realize now that I am the master, the stronger.'

He had slightly loosened his grip.

'Do you think that I am a pious woman?'

Surprised by these words, he stammered:

'Why, yes.'

'That I believe in God?'

'Yes.'

'That I could lie to you if I swore upon the altar which holds the body of Christ?'

'No.'

'Will you go with me into a church?'

'What for?'

'That you shall see. Will you?'

'If you insist—yes.'

She raised her voice, and called:

'Philippe!'

The coachman, leaning his head to one side, without taking his eyes off the horses, seemed to be attending to his mistress with his ears alone.

'Drive to the church of Saint-Philippe-du-Roule,' she said.

The carriage, which had just reached the entrance to the Bois de Boulogne, turned back in the direction of Paris.

During the rest of the drive, neither husband nor wife spoke a word. Then, when the carriage drew up in front of the church, Madame de Mascaret jumped out and went into the building, followed, at a little distance, by the count.

She went straight to the Choir-Screen, and there, kneeling on a chair, buried her face in her hands, and prayed. She prayed for a long while, and he, standing behind her, saw that she was crying. She cried silently, as women do at moments of great grief. Her body was shaken by a shudder which ended in a little sob, though this she concealed and stifled in her hands.

But the Comte de Mascaret, thinking that the situation had gone on long enough, touched her on the shoulder.

The feel of his fingers roused her like the touch of a red-hot iron. Getting to her feet, she looked straight at him.

'Listen carefully to what I am going to say. I am not frightened. You can do as you will. If you wish to kill me, then kill me. One of my children is not yours. That I swear in the presence of God who can hear me in this place. It was the only vengeance I could take on you, on the intolerable tyranny of the male, on those enforced pregnancies to which you had condemned me. You will suspect everybody, but you will never discover the truth. I gave myself to him without love, without pleasure, for the sole purpose of deceiving you. He, too, got me with child. Which of all our children is his? That you will never know. I have borne seven: see if you can find out which it is. I always meant to tell you this, but later, much later. For this vengeance to be complete, it is necessary that the man deceived should know it. You have driven me to make my confession now. That is all I have to say.'

She ran down the church to where the door stood open, expecting to hear behind her the footsteps of an outraged husband, prepared to fall to the floor under a blow from his fist.

But she heard nothing. She reached the carriage, and jumped in, rigid with pain, breathless with fear, and called to the coachman:

'Home!'

The horses set off at a rapid trot.

Useless Beauty

PART II

The Comtesse de Mascaret, shut in her own room, waited for dinner-time as a condemned criminal awaits the hour of his execution. What would her husband do? Had he come back? A man so despotic and violent as he was would stop at nothing. What was he thinking? What had he made up his mind to do? The house was silent. She kept looking at the hands of the clock. Her maid had come to help her dress, but now had left her.

Eight o'clock struck, and, almost at once, there was a double knock at the door.

'Come in.'

It was the butler.

'Dinner is served, Madame,' he said.

'Has the count returned?'

'Yes, Madame: Monsieur le Comte is in the dining-room.'

For a few moments she played with the idea of taking with her the little revolver which she had recently bought with a view to the coming crisis. But she remembered that the children would be there, and armed herself with nothing but a bottle of smelling-salts.

When she entered the room, her husband was standing by his chair, waiting for her. They exchanged the slightest of bows and then sat down. The three boys, with their tutor, the Abbé Marin, were on their mother's right; the three girls, with their English governess, Miss Smith, were on her left. The baby, barely three months old, was upstairs with its nurse.

The girls, the eldest of whom was ten, fair-haired and dressed in blue frocks with lace trimmings, looked like a trio of exquisite dolls. All three were pretty, and promised to take after their mother.

Of the three boys, two had light-brown hair. The eldest, aged nine, was already a great deal darker. They would be tall and broad-shouldered when they grew up. The whole family seemed to come of the same strong and active stock.

The abbé said grace, as he always did when there were no guests. When strangers were present the children were not allowed down. The meal began.

The countess, in the grip of an emotion she had not foreseen, sat with downcast eyes. The count looked appraisingly first at his three sons, then at his three daughters. There was a worried expression in his eyes. Suddenly, in setting down his thin-stemmed glass, he broke it, and a reddish stain spread across the table-cloth. At the slight noise made by this accident, the countess gave a start. For the first time they exchanged glances, and from then on, in spite of themselves, in spite of the taut nerves and strangled hearts which every look produced, they continued to eye one another like two duellists.

The abbé, conscious of an awkwardness in the room about which he knew nothing, tried to make conversation. He touched on subject after subject, but his efforts produced no response.

The countess, who combined worldly tact and feminine instinct, tried once or twice to give him her support, but in vain. Her troubled mind made it impossible for her to keep any general conversation going, and the sound of her own voice in the great room where, otherwise, the silence was broken only by clatter of plates and the tinkle of cutlery, frightened her.

Suddenly, her husband leaned forward and said:

'Here, with your children round you, are you prepared to swear that what you told me recently is true?'

The hatred smouldering within her burst into sudden flame. The intensity with which she answered this question was no whit inferior to that which showed in her eyes when she looked at him. She raised her two arms and held them suspended over, on one side her sons, on the other her daughters, and in a firm, resolute voice, in which there was no hint of weakness, she said:

'On the heads of my children I swear that what I told you is the truth!'

The count jumped to his feet, and, with a furious gesture, flung his napkin on the table. Then he swung round, pushed his chair against the wall, and left the room without a word.

But she, drawing a deep breath, as though she had just won her first victory, said with perfect composure:

'Pay no attention to your father, darlings: he has been much upset and is still worried. In a few days he will be all right again.'

Then she conversed with the abbé and Miss Smith, and, whenever she addressed her children, spoke in soft and kindly tones, behaving in a way that always gladdens young hearts.

When dinner was over, she went into the drawing-room with all her brood. She made the elder children chatter, told stories to the younger, and, when the general hour for bed came round, gave each a long and lingering kiss. Then, having packed them off, she returned to the solitude of her own room.

She waited, fully expecting him to come. Being at a safe distance from her children, she was determined to defend her body as she had already defended her rights as a woman living in the community of her peers. She therefore hid the little revolver in the pocket of her wrap, having first taken care to load it.

Time passed, the hours struck. The various noises in the house were stilled. Only the rumble of the streets, with their unending stream of carriages, reached her ears, dulled by distance and the thickness of the curtains.

She was nervously strung-up, but determined. Her fear of him had gone, and she felt ready for anything. She was in a mood almost of gloating, for had she not found a way of punishing him which would never give him a moment's peace for the rest of his life?

But when the first light of the new day filtered between the window-curtains, he still had not come, and now she realized with amazement that he would not come. Locking her door, and shooting the safety-bolt which she had had fitted, she went to bed at last, and lay, open-eyed and brooding, powerless to understand, incapable of guessing what he had it in his mind to do.

When the maid brought her early tea, there was a letter from her husband lying beside it. He told her that he was going on a long journey, and added, in a postscript, that his lawyer would keep her supplied with all the money she might need.

PART III

At the Opéra, the curtain had just fallen on *Robert le Diable*, for the interval. Two men were standing in the stalls. They had their hats on their heads, and their low-cut waistcoats revealed gleaming expanses of white shirt-front, in which their jewelled studs caught the light. They were looking at the boxes, where women, in evening dresses, pearls, and diamonds, sat like rare flowers in a garish greenhouse, exhibiting their loveliness, in a setting of music and human voices, to catch admiring eyes.

The two friends, with their backs turned to the stage, were chatting, and, with their opera-glasses raking this great display of elegance—both real and simulated—of luxury and ostentation, set out, for all to see, in a half-circle which extended round the vast expanse of the auditorium.

One of them, Roger de Salins, remarked to his companion, Bernard Grandin:

'Look at the Comtesse de Mascaret, over there. She is as lovely as ever.'

The other stared through his glasses at a tall woman in one of the boxes immediately opposite to where they were standing. She looked remarkably young, and her dazzling beauty seemed to be drawing admiring glances from all over the house, like a magnet. Her pale, ivory-tinted complexion gave her the appearance of a statue, and, in her hair, as black as night, a slim, rainbow-shaped circlet, powdered with diamonds, shone like the milky-way.

After gazing at her for some time, Bernard Grandin, lightly, but with a note of sincere conviction in his voice, replied:

'Her beauty can never be in doubt!'

'How old should you say she is?'

'I think I can tell you her age exactly. I have known her since she was a child. I saw her make her debut as a young girl. She must be now, at least thirty . . . perhaps thirty-six.'

'Impossible!'

'I am quite sure of my facts.'

'She looks twenty-five!'

'And, to make it more extraordinary, she has had seven children.'

'No one'd think it.'

'All of them living, too. She is an excellent mother. I occasionally visit at the house—such a pleasant change after some I know —so peaceful, so thoroughly wholesome. She is that most rare of combinations—a fond mother and a leader of society.'

'How very strange! Never a breath of scandal?'

'Never!'

'What about her husband? A curious chap from what I hear.'

'Yes and no. I don't deny there may have been a little something, one of those small domestic dramas, perhaps, which one suspects but never knows about, the faintest feeling in the air, if you know what I mean!'

'Any idea what it was?'

'Not a flicker. Mascaret is a bit wild nowadays, after being the perfect husband. But, even then, he was never the easiest of men— more than a bit touchy and surly. The funny thing is that since he's gone off the rails, he gives the impression of not caring about anything. It's almost as though he were nursing a secret sorrow, as though he had something on his mind that won't let him alone. He, at any rate, has aged a lot.'

Then, the two friends indulged in a little philosophizing on the subject of those hidden miseries which differences of temperament, or, maybe, a physical antipathy, unrealized at first, can produce in a family circle.

Roger de Salins, who had still got his glasses focused on Madame de Mascaret, exclaimed:

'I just can't believe that woman has had seven children!'

'And all in the space of eleven years, since when she has rung the curtain down on her period of production, and raised it again on a very brilliant one of public display, which shows no sign of coming to an end, even now.'

'Poor women!'

'Why should you pity them?'

'Why? My dear fellow, just think! Eleven years of almost continuous child-bearing for a woman like that! What a hell on earth! All her youth, all her beauty, all her hopes of making a success in the great world, everything romantic and brilliant in her life, sacrificed to that abominable law of reproduction which turns a normal woman into a mechanical hen for ever laying eggs!'

'If you're looking for a scapegoat, blame Nature!'

'Oh, I don't deny that! All I am saying is that nature is our natural enemy, that we must never, for a single moment, slacken in our fight against her, because, if we do, she'll turn us all into animals before we know where we are. It is not God who is responsible for the sweet and lovely things of life, but man and man's brain. It is we who have introduced into the chaos of creation, grace, beauty, charm, and mystery. For it is we who have sung of these things, bodied them forth as poets, idealized them as artists, explained them as scientists. God merely provides the raw material, a diseased and germ-ridden horror which, after a few years of bestial well-being, sinks into an infirm old age, a prey to ugliness and all the impotence of human decay. He, it would seem, made men merely that they should reproduce themselves in filth and squalor, and then die, like the short-lived insects of a summer's day. I say "to reproduce themselves in filth and squalor" and I mean it. For what could be more debased, more repulsive, than the grubby act of animal reproduction, against which our sense of delicacy is in continual revolt? Since all the bodily organs invented by an economical and malignant Creator serve a double purpose, why should He not have provided others, less unsavoury, less fouled, to perform the sacred mission, the most noble and exalted of all human fashions? The mouth which conveys food into the body, is also the medium through which words and ideas are spread abroad. It nourishes the flesh, but also gives expression to the mind. The nose, by means of which the necessary air reaches the lungs, sweetens the brain with all the perfumes of the world. The ear, which makes it possible for us to communicate with our fellows, has also enabled us to invent music, and to draw from it dreams and happiness, a sense of the infinite, and even physical delight. But it looks as though our cunning and cynical Creator had done His best to deny nobility, beauty, and idealism to the relationship of the sexes. Nevertheless, it was man who found love —no bad answer, I think you will agree, to the laughter of a mocking God—and decked it out with so much poetry that women not infrequently forget to what traffic they have to submit. Those of us who are unable to delude ourselves with a flattering self-portrait, have invented vice and the refinements of debauchery, which, after all, is but another way of pulling God's leg, and paying homage, albeit a bawdy homage, to beauty.

'But the ordinary human being begets children like a beast of the field mated by law.

'Look at that woman! Is it not outrageous that such a jewel, such a pearl, whose function it is to be beautiful, admired, acclaimed, and adored, should have spent eleven years of her life in providing heirs for the Comte de Mascaret?'

Bernard Grandin laughed:

'There is a good deal of truth in what you say, but few would understand it.'

Salins was becoming excited.

'Do you know what I think God is like?' he said. 'I see Him in the form of a monstrous organ of generation concealed from us, sowing innumerable worlds in space, as a single fish lays innumerable eggs in the sea. He creates because creating is His *raison d'être*. But He has no idea what He is doing. He is just stupidly prolific, perfectly unaware of the combinations which His scattered seed will produce. Human thought is but one happy accident of His fecundity, a local, a casual accident, not intended, and fated to vanish with the disappearance of this earth, and to begin again, perhaps, here or elsewhere, similar or different, in the new combinations produced by new beginnings. To that little accident of intelligence we owe our unhappiness in conditions never made for us, never designed to accommodate, house, feed, and satisfy thinking beings. To it we owe, also, the fact that those of us who are really refined and civilized, are engaged in a constant struggle against what are called the designs of Providence.'

Grandin was listening attentively. He had long been familiar with the brilliant improvisations of his friend's fantastic mind.

'Do you believe, then, that human thought is a spontaneous

product of blind parturition on the part of the Divine?' he asked.

'Of course I do! It is a fortuitous functioning of the nervous centres of the brain, similar to unforeseen chemical activities due to fresh combinations of various elements, or to electrical phenomena caused by chance contacts and frictions, in fact, to all manifestations resulting from the infinite and fecund fermentations of living matter.

'Why, my dear chap, the proof of that is obvious to anyone who will use his eyes. If the human mind, willed by a conscious Creator, was intended to be what it has become—so different from the mental processes and basic resignation of mere animals, in that it is ceaselessly demanding, inquisitive, restless, and tormented do you really think that a world created to be the home of beings such as we are, would have been this small, uncomfortable rabbit-warren, this country kitchen garden, this cabbage bed, this stony sphere in which blind Providence has seen fit to condemn us to a life of naked savagery in caves or trees, living on the slaughtered flesh of the animals, our brothers, or on raw vegetables grown in earth and rain?

'You have only to think for a moment to realize that this world was never made for creatures such as we are. Thought, which has miraculously flowered and prospered as the result of some accidental activity of our brain-cells, powerless, ignorant, confused though it is and always will be, has turned all us intellectuals into eternal and miserable exiles on this earth.

'Look well at it. Study this earth as God has given it to those who live on it. Is it not obviously and uniquely designed, planted, and wooded for the accommodation of animals? What is there on it for us? Nothing. But for them it has everything they need: caves and trees, leafy shelters, rivers, lairs, food, and drink. And so it is that those who are difficult to please, as I am, never feel at home on it. Only people who have scarcely risen above the level of the brute creation, are content and satisfied. But the rest, the poets, the sensitive souls, the dreamers, the seekers, the restless—they, indeed, are to be pitied!

'I eat cabbages and carrots, Heaven help me! And onions, too, turnips and radishes, because we have been forced by circumstances to get used to them, actually to like them, and because the earth produces nothing else. But those things are food, really, for goats and rabbits, as grass and clover are for horses and cows. When I look at a ripe cornfield, I do not doubt for a moment that grain was sown in the ground for the beaks of larks and sparrows, but certainly not for me. When I munch bread I am stealing food from the birds, as I am stealing from foxes and weasels whenever I eat chicken. Are not quails and partridges and pigeons the natural prey of hawks? Sheep and goats and oxen, of the great carnivores, and not creatures to be fattened for our tables, and served up roasted, with truffles especially routed up for us by pigs?

'My dear fellow, animals have nothing to do upon this earth, but live. They are at home here, lodged and nourished. They have only to browse or hunt, to eat one another as instinct tells them, for God never intended gentleness and peaceful co-existence. All He has ever planned is the death of creatures made to destroy and to devour.

'How different is our case! We have been thrown on our own devices. We have had to work in the sweat of our brows, we have had to show patience, inventiveness, industry, talent, and genius, merely to make habitable this wilderness of roots and rocks. But think what we have achieved, in spite of nature, against nature, in making for ourselves a home, poor though it is, scarcely even clean, scarcely even comfortable, scarcely even elegant, and wholly unworthy of us.

'The more civilized, refined, and intelligent we become, the harder we have to struggle in our attempts to conquer and to tame that animal instinct which represents in us the Will of God.

'Just think how we have had to invent a civilization which comprises so many, so very many, things of all kinds, from socks to telephones. Think of all you see about you every day, of all the things that serve our needs in different ways.

'To soften the asperities of our animal existence, we have had to discover and to make everything: houses to begin with, then delicious foods, sweets and pastries, wines and spirits, fabrics and clothes, adornments, and beds, mattresses, carriages, railway trains, and machines innumerable. Furthermore, we have invented science and the arts, writing, and verse. Yes, those things are all of our own invention, poetry, music, painting. All that partakes of the ideal comes from us, and also all the little gaieties of life, women's clothes, and the talents of those men who have succeeded in making a little more pleasing to our eyes, a little less stark, less hard, and less monotonous, that simple life of reproductive animals which was what Providence intended for us.

'Look at this theatre. Does it not contain a human world which we have created, a world never intended by the eternal Fates, unknown to them, comprehensible only to *our* minds, a stylish distraction, sensual and intelligent, invented only for and by those restless and discontented creatures that we humans are? Look at that woman there, Madame de Mascaret. God made her to live in a cave, naked or wrapped in the skins of animals. Is she not better as she is? But now that we are speaking of her again, why and how is it that her brute of a husband, having ready and waiting a companion of such quality (especially after he has been sufficiently boorish to make her a mother seven times over), how and why, I ask, must he go chasing after prostitutes?'

'Dear boy,' said Grandin, 'that is probably the reason. He found that it cost him too much always to sleep at home. Domestic economy has led him to much the same conclusion as your philosophy.'

The three knocks sounded for the last act. The two friends returned to their places, took off their hats, and sat down.

PART IV

Driving home from the Opéra in their carriage, the Comte and Comtesse de Mascaret sat side by side, saying nothing. But, suddenly, the husband turned to his wife:

'Gabrielle.'

'Yes?'

'Do not you think that this has lasted long enough?'

'Of what are you speaking?'

'The abominable torture to which you have condemned me for the last six years.'

'What can I do about it?'

'Won't you, after all this time, tell me which one it is?'

'Never.'

'Just think what it means to me. I can never look at my children, nor see them round me, without having that doubt perpetually gnawing at my heart. Tell me which one it is, and I swear that I will forgive, that I will treat it just as I treat the others.'

'I have no right to do that.'

'Do you not see that I can no longer endure this life I am compelled to live; that this uncertainty is eating my heart out, this question which I never cease to ask myself, which tortures me each time I see them? It is driving me mad!'

'So, you have really suffered?'

'Atrociously! How could I have endured the horror of living in the same house with you, and not have suffered? How could I have endured the even greater horror of feeling, of knowing, that there is one of them, though which I do not know, who makes it impossible for me to love them?'

She said again:

'I may take it then, that you have really suffered?'

His voice, as he replied, was sad but controlled:

'Has a day passed without my telling myself that I can no longer bear this torment? If I did not love them should I have come back, should I have consented to live in the same house with you and them? Your behaviour to me has been abominable. The only affection of which my heart is capable is for my children, as well you know. For them I am the father of an older age, as I was for you a husband as husbands once were, for I am still a man of impulse, a natural man, a man lost in a world which is not his. You have, I confess, made me furiously jealous, because you are a woman of a different race to mine, of a different temperament, with different needs. I shall never forget what you told me. Ever since that day you have ceased to be a matter of concern to me. I did not kill you, for, if I had, I should have lost the only means of knowing which of our . . . of your . . . children is not mine. I have waited long, and I have suffered more than you will ever know, for I dare no longer love any of them, except, perhaps, the two eldest. I can no longer look at them, nor speak their names. I can no longer take one of them upon my knee without saying to myself, "Perhaps it is this one." For six years I have treated you well. I have been kind, I have borne with you. Tell me the truth, and I swear that I will do nothing harsh or wrong.'

In the darkness of the carriage he thought he could make out that she was moved, and felt she was about to speak again.

'I beg,' he said, 'I implore you . . .'

When she spoke at last, it was in a very low voice:

'I have, perhaps, been more to blame than you think. But I could not go on, I could not, with that odious life of continual pregnacies. There was only one way in which I could keep you from my bed. I lied before God, I lied with my hand upon my children's heads. You see, the truth is that I was never unfaithful to you.'

He seized her arm and gripped it as he had done on that terrible day when they had driven to the Bois.

'Is that true?' he stammered.

'It is the whole truth.'

But he was still a prey to strong emotion:

'There will never be an end to it,' he groaned. 'Never, for fresh doubts will ever be assailing me. Which is the lie—what you told me then or what you tell me now? How can I believe you? How could I believe any woman after what I have been through? Now I shall never know what to believe. I had rather you had said to me, "It is Jacques" or "It is Jeanne." '

They turned in at the gate of the count's courtyard. When the carriage stopped before the steps, he got out first, and, as always, gave his arm to his wife into the house and up the stairs.

When they reached the first floor, he said:

'Will you grant me the favour of a few more minutes?'

'Most certainly.'

They went into one of the smaller drawing-rooms, where a footman, not a little surprised, proceeded to light the candles.

As soon as they were alone, the count went on:

'How am I to know where the truth lies? I have begged you a thousand times to speak, but you have always maintained an attitude of impenetrable, inflexible, inexorable silence. And now, you suddenly tell me that you have been lying to me all this time! For six years you have let me believe the terrible thing you told me then. No! It is *now* that you are lying. Why you should do so I do not pretend to understand—perhaps from a feeling of pity, who knows?'

There was sincerity, conviction in her voice, as she replied:

'There was no choice for me six years ago. I had to act as I did, otherwise I should have had four more children by now!'

'How can you, a mother, talk like that!' he exclaimed.

'How can I be expected to have a mother's feelings towards my unborn children? It is enough for me that I am the mother of those I have, and them I love with all my heart. We women, Monsieur, live in a civilized society. We are no longer, we refuse to be, mere females whose only function is to increase the population!'

She got to her feet, but he took her hands in his:

'I want only one thing, Gabrielle: that you should tell me the truth!'

'I have already done so. I have never been unfaithful to you.'

He looked her steadily in the face. How beautiful she was with those grey eyes of hers, so cold and so remote! In the dusky depths of her black hair the circlet powdered with diamonds shone like the milky-way. It was borne in upon him on a sudden wave of intuition that she was more than a woman whose sole destiny it was to perpetuate his race. She was the strange, mysterious

319

product of a whole complex of desires built up in the thoughts and feelings of mankind through the long succession of the centuries, diverted from their primitive purpose in the Divine plan, and now bodying forth a strange new beauty, only half glimpsed, and even now not wholly grasped. In that moment he saw women, with new eyes, as creatures made to incarnate our dreams, adorned with all that civilization could supply of poetry and the ideal, of allurements and aesthetic charm, statues of flesh and blood which could arouse in men not only a fever of the senses, but also strange and insubstantial appetites.

Her husband stood before her, bewildered by this tardy and obscure discovery, uncertainly feeling his way back to the cause of all his former jealousy, and only partially understanding it.

At last he spoke:

'I believe you. Here, at this moment, I feel you are not lying. To be perfectly frank, in those old, unhappy days, it seemed to me you were!'

She held out her hand:

'So, we are friends now, are we not?'

He took her hand and kissed it:

'We are friends. Thank you, Gabrielle.'

Then, he left the room, with his eyes still upon her, marvelling that she was still so beautiful, and feeling rise within him a strange emotion, more to be feared, perhaps, than the old, uncomplicated passion he had known.

(2-7 April 1890)